RUINS
OF
CHAOS

AMELIA HUTCHINS

Authored By: Amelia Hutchins

Cover Art Design: Eerily Designs

Copy edited by: Melissa Burg

Edited by: Melissa Burg

Published by: Amelia Hutchins

Published in (United States of America)

10 9 8 7 6 5 4 3 2 1

Other Books by Amelia Hutchins

The Winter Court

A Demon's Plaything

More coming – To Be Announced

A GUARDIAN'S DIARY

Darkest Before Dawn

Death before Dawn

Midnight Rising – To Be Announced

PLAYING WITH MONSTERS

Playing with Monsters

Sleeping with Monsters

Becoming his Monster

Becoming her Monster Spring 2021

WICKED KNIGHTS

Oh, Holy Knight

If She's Wicked

If He's Wicked – To Be Announced

MIDNIGHT COVEN BOOKS

Forever Immortal

Immortal Hexes

Midnight Coven

If you're following the series for the Fae Chronicles, Elite Guards, and Monsters, reading order is as follows.

DISCLAIMER

This book is dark. It's sexy, hot, and intense. The author is human, as you are. Is the book perfect? It's as perfect as I could make it. Are there mistakes? Probably, then again, even New York Times top published books have minimal mistakes because, like me, they have human editors. There are words in this book that are not in the standard dictionary because they were created to set the stage for a paranormal-urban fantasy world. Words in this novel are common in paranormal books and give better descriptions to the action in the story than other words found in standard dictionaries. They are intentional and not mistakes.

About the hero: chances are you may **not** fall instantly in **love** with him, that's because **I don't write men you instantly love**; you grow to love them. I don't believe in **instant love**. I write flawed, raw, caveman-like **assholes** that eventually let you see their redeeming qualities. They are **aggressive assholes**, one step above a caveman when we meet them. You may *not* even like him by the time you finish this book, but I promise you will **love** him by the end of this **series**.

About the heroine: There is a chance you might think she's a bit naïve or weak, but then again, who starts out as a badass? Badass women are a product of growth, and I am going to put her through **hell**, and you get to watch **her** come up **swinging** every time I knock her on her ass. That's just how I do things. How she reacts to the set of circumstances she is put through may not be how you as the reader, or I, as the author would react to that same situation. Everyone reacts differently to circumstances and how she responds to her challenges, is how I see her as a character and as a person.

I don't write love stories: I write fast-paced, knock you on your ass, *make you sit on the edge of your seat wondering what is going to happen next* in the books. If you're looking for cookie-cutter romance, this isn't for you. If you can't handle the ride, ***unbuckle your seatbelt and get out of the roller-coaster car now.*** **If not, you've been warned.** If nothing outlined above bothers you, carry on and **enjoy the ride!**

FYI, this is not a romance novel. They're going to **kick** the shit out of each other, and **if** they end up together, well, that's **their** choice. If you are going into this blind, and you complain about abuse between two creatures that are **NOT** human, well, that's on you. I have done my job and given **warning**.

No babies that occur or are created because of this work of fiction are the author's responsibility. Blame the penis mojo that you rode like a bronco for it, not me.

Dedication

To the warriors out there fighting to get through this shit-show year, we're almost there. Keep your head up and know that it isn't a bad life; it's just a really bad year. We're going to get through it together, and we're going to be stronger for surviving 2020.

THE MAP OF VISITED REALMS

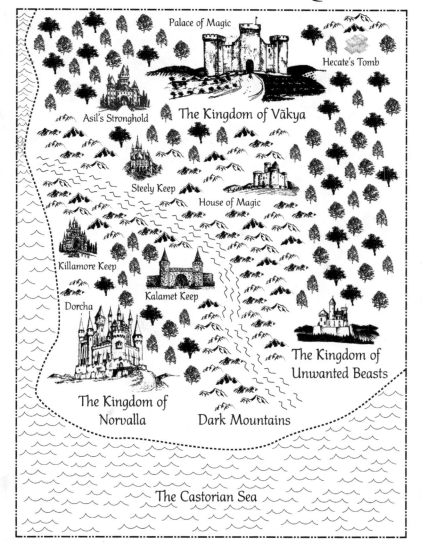

RUINS
OF
CHAOS

AMELIA HUTCHINS

Chapter One

Knox, Outside the Border of Norvalla in Steely Keep

My eyes slid over the dead warriors lying beside camp followers and witches alike. Outside of the keep, the putrid scent of death filled the air. Kneeling, I turned over a warrior, his sightless eyes covered in a milky-white film of death. Studying his body, I noted the lack of injury before standing and staring at the ravens feasting on the dead.

One raven sat fixated on me, an eyeball hanging from its beak, then dropping it loose. Opening its mouth, it forced out a loud gurgling croak before retrieving its find and taking to the sky. Hounds had moved in, growling while ripping parts and pieces from the deceased, unbothered by our presence as we walked through them, searching for any signs of injury that would explain the deaths.

"Well, they didn't just drop dead all on their own,

but I can't see a cause of death," Brander stated, holding his forearm against his nose.

I undid the sash from my waist, tying it over my mouth and nose before kneeling beside the next warrior who had fallen onto another body. I noted the marking on the woman's wrist below him, watching with unease as something moved beneath her lips, forcing them to part. A rat pushed from her mouth, squealing and scurrying across the field, away from those interrupting his supper.

"Nothing but fucking scavengers are alive within this keep and its village. I see no wounds and no trace of dark magic that would have brought them down without a full assault. They had magic protecting them," I stated, standing to nod at the six-foot towers of smoky quartz that marked each corner of the camp. "The land remains purified and protected, yet something powerful got through their wards and spells. This keep is one of the older, more powerful strongholds in which we trade, yet their lord and lady sit headless, with no other signs of injury, and all their guards lay dead but unwounded."

Someone massacred every village we passed through on the way here. Bodies were shredded and mutilated until they were unidentifiable as human or anything else. Either the dark witches had grown bolder, or they no longer fought alone. They hung people and enjoyed their victim's deaths as entertainment before removing their heads. "Whoever went through those villages before us, relished in the deaths of their inhabitants. My guess is the beasts that fled from the Kingdom of Unwanted Beasts joined forces with Ilsa. I can't explain this shit, though. It is morbid and just fucking wrong," I said, sliding my attention over the chaos.

They pillaged most of the annexed villages we've protected and used for trade, slaughtering all life, sparing no one. I agreed it didn't seem like something witches would do. Then rumors surfaced from those who had seen the unwanted beasts slaughtering and creating chaos in villages that had joined the trade agreement with Norvalla. Suddenly the thought of them joining the dark witches seemed plausible, but what were the unwanted beasts gaining in return?

The high queen was trying to stop Norvalla from receiving food or other goods that supplied my kingdom. It was a bloodbath, one meant to send a warning to any of the villages wishing to join the annex, and I'd failed to protect them.

I hadn't expected Garrett, the newly crowned King of Unwanted Beasts, to change sides in the war. After what Aria had done to her sister, Amara, his wife, I should have predicted it, but I was too focused on recapturing Aria, knowing that she held the keys to winning this war.

"I don't see any sign of the council among the bodies," Brander stated, drawing me from my thoughts and reminding me of the purpose of this journey since they had sent for me. Maybe it was a ruse, and the council was never here.

"What about the tents?" I peered at the camp that sat off to the side.

"Haven't made it that far," he admitted.

I moved toward a tent, withdrawing blades and using one to pull back the flap. Inside was a witch, straddling a warrior mid-fuck, both dead and bloated. Sightless eyes stared toward me, and I frowned. I moved deeper into the tent with Brander on my heels, both of us barely containing the need to gag as the heat made the scent of death overpowering without the wind and breeze to carry it away.

Staring at their eyes and the way they looked at the flap, my blood curdled. They'd seen their death coming. Their mouths were open, as were the others outside the tent. The witch's corpse slid to the side, and Brander withdrew his blade as rats emerged from the warrior's chest. Chew marks covered the witch's stomach as if the rodents had gnawed on her to escape his stomach. Brander swore, covering his mouth as their bodies released gasses, and the witch's mouth opened further, dispelling more rats from her corpse.

"This is so fucking wrong. They're rotten from the inside out." Brander continued to gag on the rancid taste of death filling the tent.

I moved outside to check the other shelters, finding each pair of eyes within, staring at the entrance. They'd looked upon whoever had delivered death to the inhabitants surrounding and within the stronghold. Standing in the middle of the camp, I swallowed down the urge to scream in frustration.

"Beasts didn't kill here. This is the work of dark witches, and they didn't fear someone overpowering them." I eyed the keep and pointed at the battlement wall. "I'm going up to get a better look at the carnage from above."

I moved through the dead, passing over the corpses while ignoring the carrion birds that continued to feast on the deceased. Green water filled the moat, and bloated bodies were half in and out of the water as if they'd drank from the cesspool upon death.

Unlucky bastards.

The gatehouse was open, which wasn't surprising with the full force of an army camped out front. The portcullis was raised, and bodies hung from the wrought-iron gates on each side of the opening. I looked to the ceiling and found the men guarding the entrance slumped in death, hanging from the murder holes from which they should have laid siege, but there was no evidence of battle. Beyond the gates, more bodies covered the inner courtyard and the grounds leading to the castle.

Within the keep was a grotesque display of well-orchestrated deaths. Men and women sat before a rotted meal, their severed heads placed before them. Food shoved in their mouths, which were wide open, frozen in horrified screams as if the stiffness of death had set in immediately.

The display was a warning meant for me. It also told me that the witches weren't alone since they didn't typically remove their victim's heads. The evil bitches didn't like to get their hands dirty, choosing to use their magic instead.

I forewent seeing it again and moved up the stairs of the battlement wall, cresting it to peer out over miles and miles of the camp, filled with thousands of *dead* warriors and witches, all of whom had seemingly died from sheer terror or fright.

"Fucking hell, that's a sight to behold," Brander whispered, his hands resting on the wall. "They didn't even spare the horses." My attention slid to the stables, noting the dead horses that littered the ground as if trying to flee when struck down. "That's fucked up."

"I've never had a problem determining the cause of death before. There's always been a way to sense if magic was used, but I can't find any residue. The fear that the victims felt was real. Was it something conjured or someone they had seen moving through the camp, holding them locked in fear unto death?"

"They look fucking terrified with their mouths wide open and eyes larger than the snow owls that should be feasting on the rodents," Brander stated. "Look at the trees, Knox."

My eyes swung to the trees, noting the large birds of prey perched on their branches. They didn't move even though easy meals ran about, eating the dead. My blood chilled, continuing to watch them stalk their prey but never making a move to strike.

Something dropped inside the tower beside us, and we both turned, eyeing it suspiciously. I nodded to Brander, creeping toward the darkened building, bathed in shadows. Brander went around the battlement, his speed effortless as he appeared on the other side, trapping whatever had fallen. I drew my swords, slowly holding Brander's stare before we slid into the small, protected tower that sat on the corner of the castle wall.

"Don't kill me!" a lad screamed.

"Who are you?" I demanded icily.

"I'm Kreyton, Lady Katherine and Lord Demetrius's son! I am the heir to this keep," he whimpered.

I exhaled slowly, pushing my blades back in their scabbards while Brander kept his ready to strike if the need arose. The boy was sickly looking, his face a mass of thin black lines that pulsed with the poison of dark magic.

"What happened here?" I asked. Kreyton's mouth opened and closed before his head shook from side to side, his eyes widening with horror.

"They came in and killed everyone," Kreyton whispered. "Lord Andres removed the wards, allowing the dark witches to breach our defenses." My blood chilled at his words. "Darkness filled his eyes as the witches tried to kill everyone while he watched, showing his true devotion to the High Queen of Witches. He betrayed us."

"How did you survive?" I demanded, hating the uneasiness that settled into my mind. Aria was within Lord Andres's grasp at the camp where I'd left her.

"I was in my room when they came," Kreyton stated thickly, his teeth chattering. "I hid but couldn't escape the mist that filled the castle. I can't get out of the wards, and you're the first to come that didn't leave upon seeing the bodies."

"The council was coming here," I growled. "Did they arrive?"

"They came but stopped outside the keep at the sight of the dead. The King of Wolves and the Queen of Nymphs were here. They entered the edge of the woods but didn't pass the wards to come any closer. I didn't see any other council members, but I've been unwell since the mist touched me."

"Tell me what you saw," I said, watching haunted eyes fill with the memories.

"Lord Andres came with a handful of witches in chains. He asked one of his men to remove the wards so he could take the prisoners to the keep. We lowered the wards, and all hell broke loose. I watched it all from my bedchamber but couldn't move to warn my parents because the mist unleashed by the witches paralyzed me. When it touched me, it froze me in sheer terror as it did to the others. They all succumbed to death or turned into something *else,* allowing the darkness inside them. I should have died or turned into a monster as Lord Andres had become, but I didn't."

I watched the black lines move up his face, lifting my gaze to Brander's as the poison moved through Kreyton. He hadn't survived; he just hadn't succumbed to death yet. Something within him had prevented the poison from killing him instantly, as it had the others. It explained why there were no wounds or injuries found among the dead, other than the keep's lord and lady.

"You did well, Kreyton," I assured. He nodded sluggishly, eyes bloodshot and filling with black magic.

Stepping back, Brander lifted his blade as Kreyton's face twisted with malice, the magic changing him into Ilsa's minion. Brander swung his sword, removing the lad's head adeptly so he wouldn't suffer. Blood painted my face as I stared down at the headless boy. He'd had something dark within him meant to turn him into a tool, unlike the others who had succumbed to the poison.

"Lord Andres wouldn't have done what Kreyton described," Brander stated, and I frowned before sliding my eyes back to the carnage.

"Not unless someone poisoned him with dark magic, controlling him as they did Kreyton. Aria is within

Andres's grasp. If what the kid said is true, Andres could be there to take or murder Aria for Ilsa. She has to know that Aria is the one who set siege to the stronghold Asil held. I don't like Aria being out of my sight. Not with the witches growing bolder and the King of Unwanted Beasts joining his forces to that evil bitch's army."

I glanced at the hawks, owls, and other birds of prey, watching the scavengers feasting upon the dead. My creature peered out and frowned, staring down at the barrier that prevented those wishing to do harm from entering the keep. Unlike the scavengers below, the birds sensed the poison within the dead. My eyes slid to the rodents, finding hundreds of beady eyes trained on our every move. Ilsa was using the familiars of lesser witches to watch us.

"Send for Aria. If Lord Andres is under the control of the high queen, she's in danger. We can meet them on the passes. Have Killian leave immediately with the army to follow. Instruct him to prevent Lord Andres from joining them."

"You're bringing Aria to a fucking slaughter," Brander snorted. "They'll travel through the annexed villages to reach the passes, and Aria's too soft to see the carnage those bastards left behind."

"Killian would take the quickest route through King's Crossing or King's Road to reach us. Knowing Killian, he'll go around the villages to avoid detection. Aria won't see the dead in those villages. She needs to see what her precious witches have done to innocent people. But I don't want her to see people split open and ripped apart. She hasn't seen the evilness of the witches yet, and she needs to. What happened here wasn't the same as what transpired within those other villages. That was the work of monsters; this was something else entirely."

Brander whistled down at one runner and watched as he tripped over the dead in his haste to get to us. I could have told them we had to move into the keep to secure ink and parchment, but I had no intention of going inside again.

I'd known the lord and lady of the keep, having blessed their union many years ago myself. They were good people and fed the poor who suffered at the hands of the witches. Lady Kathrine was gentle and a friend. Her marriage wasn't a love match, but she'd been a good wife to Demetrius. They'd deserved better than to die in pain or from poison at the hand of the witches.

I handed Brander my wax and seal and leaned over the battlement, staring at the rodents who continued to watch us. I sent a wave of power from me, spreading through the bodies of the dead and the creatures who fed upon their corpses.

Turning, I looked up at the setting sun before moving toward the tower, as the sky turned vibrant with shades of red, an ominous color considering the number of dead littering the ground.

I exited the battlement, moving through the courtyard and toward the rodents. I sent my drawn power into them, smiling as they exploded without warning, cutting off Ilsa's sight into the keep. The ravens cawed, ruffling their wings as they took to the air, circling us.

"Fly to Norvalla and ensure no one is marching upon it. Once you've confirmed their safety, spread out and find the unwanted beasts that are wreaking havoc on the annexed villages, and return with their location," I ordered. The ravens swooped low before twirling and sailing south toward my home.

A smile flittered over my mouth as I thought of Aria beside me, her tiny frame curled into mine as the nights grew colder the closer we traveled to my homeland.

I'd missed her, her warmth, her snarky comments, and the look in her eye that tinged her cheeks pink from wanting what we both craved. Still, she denied me her body. I hadn't pushed her, sensing the need to heal from her time in the Kingdom of Unwanted Beasts. Soon, she'd be unable to fight the need to mate, even if she didn't understand what was happening to her.

I hated that this world would make Aria colder, but there was no escaping the horror of what the Nine Realms had become. Once we reached my home, I'd have to present Aria to the council and figure out whom among them had asked to spare her life. Someone had wanted my Little Monster alive, and I needed to know who it was, soon.

First, I owed it to the warriors who had died to find and eliminate whoever had done this to them. I owed the Lord and Lady and Steely Keep peace in their deaths. I paused beside a group of warriors and frowned as they discussed how to handle the mass burials.

"There's too many to bury," I muttered.

"The Lord and the Lady?" Brander asked, coming to stand beside me with the parchment and pen.

"They will remain with the men who died protecting their land," I announced.

"They're the lord and lady," a warrior argued.

"And they're with their people in death. We are not above those who serve us. I am not a king who holds titles above honor and bravery. They served with those who held peace until something evil and sinister took them all together. They no longer house their bodies and are free of their shells."

The witches believed Hecate blessed them to move onto the realm where she dwelled. We believed death offered peace among the otherworld, where new life began. Not unless you went into the Void of Nothingness. There, eternal darkness and emptiness consumed everything within you, reducing your soul to shredded particles while forbidding rebirth, like Liliana.

Chapter Two

I stared out over the mountain pass that wound down into the valley where Killian's route would bring Aria to me. It had taken us days to reach the pass where I had instructed them to meet us. They should have beaten us to the spot, but they had yet to arrive.

Smiling, I imagined Aria curled up beside me, throwing one of her fits. Once sleep overtook her, she would curl her body against mine for warmth, and hell if I didn't enjoy the feel of her against me. Aria was the first woman to sleep in my bed, and I'd be lying if I said it didn't feel right.

I'd missed Aria since leaving her in camp. I hated I missed her and that my mind always wandered to what she was doing or if she missed me. Fucking pussy shit. I didn't miss women, nor crave them curled up beside me.

Her banter gave me life. Her snarky comments and quick wit promised to engage my mind. I didn't just miss sex with Aria; I missed her mind. I fucking hated it. I hated that I craved her intelligence that matched mine and her smirk that promised she imagined disemboweling me. I missed her fire that burned brighter than any sun or moon in the Nine Realms, even the desert lands that sweltered like a forge.

I fucking missed the companionship her presence offered me. When had it changed from sex to more with her? She was quirky and a little spitfire of energy. She fought me toe-to-toe on what she believed, and I fucking respected her for it. She challenged me, and people didn't fucking do that, but Aria did. She stood her ground and stood for those who couldn't stand up for themselves.

Shit. I'd gone to stop the separation of the mothers and children coming into the camp, and Aria had gone full battle queen on Bekkah. I'd no sooner told the lord to stop his men from assaulting the witches and their offspring to hearing the men shouting that the witches were fighting. It enraged me that I'd fucking caved to stop what had upset Aria, only to find her assaulting the fucking witches I ordered to remain unharmed.

I'd never noticed the damage inflicted upon her by the guard. The anger that filled me when she'd attacked Bekkah blinded me and forced me to punish her for assaulting someone under my order of protection. The penalty for that crime was death or fifty lashes. I would have had to stand in judgment for Aria's slight and either whip her smooth, supple flesh or sentence her to death. My word was law. My word as King was my bond to my people. Aria had broken it, and as a result, I had broken my vow to my people to protect her soft skin from the cattail whip. In no world could I whip Aria and be okay with it. That terrified me because she continued to fight me.

It hadn't gone unnoticed by my men either. They'd seen the favoritism after Bekkah had made damn sure that everyone knew Aria Hecate had broken the law of protection. Luckily, having the men stand as a witness to Aria's treatment by the guard and me, and relaying those details to Bekkah, provided her with the information to brag how badly Aria was beaten, sparing me from losing face amongst my people.

"You think something happened?" Brander asked, settling beside me as I leaned against the boulder, watching the sun setting over the furthest mountain range.

"I think they should have fucking been here by now," I growled, unwilling to allow the uneasiness to settle within me.

"Killian is never late." Brander ran his hand through his hair in worry. "I hope Lord Andres isn't the reason for their delay."

I considered his words, acknowledging that Killian had only been late once in the entire time I had known him. He was a warrior, a brother in arms that had been through hell with us. He was dependable and honest to a fault. My stomach flipped while I considered what could have forced the indomitable warrior to be late.

"Aria wouldn't give Killian trouble. Not with Greer and Lore present," Brander stated, troubleshooting and eliminating obstacles they may have faced.

My eyes followed the path to the bottom of the pass, and the crease in my brow deepened. "Killian wouldn't have waited for the army to prepare before leaving. That would slow down their arrival, and I instructed him to leave immediately. He'd have taken King's Crossing and moved deeper into the forest, but that wouldn't slow him down. That would have shortened their journey. Even if they'd taken another route to be safe, or because of some unseen issue arising, they'd have still beaten us here."

"And yet they didn't," Brander exhaled slowly, turning to look at me.

I shook my head, throwing the stone I'd been tossing up into the air over the edge. Turning on my heel, I headed for my warhorse. I wasn't waiting any longer as a foreboding feeling had entered my mind. Pausing at my horse, I whispered a command that sent a raven from my skin into the air. Telepathically, I gave the ravens an order to find Killian.

Mounting the horse, I waited for Brander and the men with us to catch up before starting down the long, winding trail through the pass that took us back to a branch of my army. It should have been entire army. It wasn't.

A thousand scenarios went through my head. Had Aria escaped? It would make sense why Killian hadn't shown up on time. I had ordered him to use all resources to capture her if she ran. Had the silver-haired men set a trap and lured them in, capturing Aria to take her to wherever the fuck they lived? Had Kreyton told the truth, and Lord Andres slaughtered his army to prove his loyalty to a witch?

Any of those scenarios were possible. I'd gone back to the cavern beneath the waterfall after leaving Aria to search for any signs of Eva and Aden and found nothing. The entire cavern had collapsed as if Eva held it together with her presence while she slumbered. It was likely a sanctuary spell used by witches, keeping ancient places intact with magic to ensure an undisturbed, eternal rest. Eva hadn't been in eternal slumber, though. I'd felt the spell outside the barrier that had placed her in stasis.

Whoever Eva and Aden was, they'd vanished with the rest of their men into a layer of the Nine Realms I couldn't trace, which was worrisome since we knew nothing about the pricks. It had floored us to learn there were more women like Aria out there, but Eva hadn't excited me. She lacked pretty much everything that drew me to Aria.

Fucking Aria.

She was my perfect ideal vision of what I'd craved as a mate. She was bare-bones, beauty, brains, and very brave, which floored me. She didn't even realize how stunning she really was. Her innocence was a flaw, but one I enjoyed. Her loyalty was unshakable. I respected her for the way she stuck to her principles and dug her heels into the ground when she believed in something.

Aria Hecate was born to be a queen of the Nine Realms, but the fact that she was born to be Queen of Vãkya made me ill. How was it possible that five hundred years to the day after losing my mate, a woman who was my perfect ideology of what I wanted in one, walked in and shook the shit out of me, rattling my world? Add that she was a Hecate witch and very powerful, making me crave her like opium after a bender in a den, and it made me question everything. Aria was too perfect. Her timing was too fucking convenient. If I had planned to turn the head of the rebellion with a pretty pair of turquoise eyes and rare silver hair, I'd send Aria in too.

She made me want to change shit that I'd never questioned before. Aria made me crave things I'd stopped wanting and thought gone forever. Shit, I got hard at the thought of her swollen with my babe in her belly, and then I hated her even more for betraying my wife with the idea of it. Aria was right. I lashed out hard and fast to protect myself.

Aria had made the image of Liliana fade to nothing. She lessened the pain of Sven's death with her sweet smiles and shy glances. I needed that pain to fight the war I'd started. The Nine Realms depended on me to keep my shit together to fight for them. As much as I wanted Aria, I wanted to protect the innocent lives lost every fucking minute in this place, besieged by evil and witches that claimed they were the superior race.

My people crowned me King when Aria's grandmother murdered my parents. Hecate had forced me into this role. She took everyone I loved from me and made me become King before I was ready, and now the one woman I wanted to keep was her granddaughter? No, that was a design in play, a well thought out plan to throw me off.

Brander and I paused as downed trees came into view. I noted the exposed roots pulled from the ground as if the wind or something else had knocked the trees over. Exhaling, I slid my attention around the forest before nodding to the other trail.

"That's strange," Brander stated, pointing to the trees behind the fallen ones that were still standing and undamaged.

"Be vigilant. Spread out into fighting formation and be silent." I looked back at the trail, frowning as it occurred to me that we might have been called away so Aria could escape.

Anger rushed to the forefront of my mind at the thought her family would be so evil as to murder thousands of people to free her. If anyone could have accomplished that spell to bring down an army of warriors, it would have been Hecate witches, an entire coven of them to be exact. Aurora had ulterior motives. That much I'd discovered in Haven Falls. She'd planned on bringing the girls back into the Nine Realms, but why?

She'd spoken about it openly to the alphas. Aurora had asked them to return with her, yet she hadn't mentioned it to Freya's daughters, who she'd raised as her own. What were her motives? It was unheard of for Hecate witches to sacrifice for their sisters or offspring. I didn't trust them, not one fucking bit. Aurora fed Aria's mind with knowledge, while Aria fed her mind folklore, legends, and fantasy books.

Aurora had hidden Aria's scent, knowing she wasn't meant to be among those in the mortal realm. Aria had been a ticking time bomb set to go off, but Aurora had allowed Aria to remain where she could have slaughtered an entire race of innocent people. That didn't speak *sweet mother figure* to me, and I didn't assume she wasn't aware of Aria's father's identity.

We moved back onto the road, and I stopped dead in my tracks, staring at the sight before my eyes. Blood turned to ice in my veins as Killian lifted his gaze, his hands covered in blood. He lowered his eyes and bowed his head where bodies lay ready for burial. I remained frozen in place, unwilling to see who we'd lost.

"Who fucking did this?" I demanded.

"Witches," he swallowed.

"I'll fucking kill Aria myself," I growled.

"I wouldn't be too quick to kill Aria. I don't think they intended her to live for long," Killian stated. "She was fighting with us against them, but we got overpowered, and something prevented us from calling our creatures to the surface. My guess is magic. They dragged Aria into the forest as I stayed to defend Lore and Greer. She didn't go willingly."

"Lore and Greer?" I asked, frozen in place.

"Alive. They're wounded but alive."

"How bad?" Brander asked, dismounting to walk toward the dead soldiers.

I dismounted to join him until a noise started, stopping me in my tracks. The hair on my neck rose as I turned in the sound's direction. My heart pounded against my ribs, painfully mirroring the need to rush blindly toward the noise.

"What the fuck is that?" Brander groaned, his teeth pushing through his gums as his claws did the same.

A quick glance toward Killian showed he'd fared no better. Everything within me demanded I go to it, that I follow the sorrowful howling coming from off in the distance. It was a broken wail, one that begged to be answered. My soul cried to go, and before I'd given the order, we all rushed toward our waiting mounts.

"You feel that?" Killian asked as he turned his horse, facing the forest that loomed endlessly before us.

"To my fucking soul," I whispered. "It's Aria. I know it is. I can feel her fear."

"It could be a trap," Brander pointed out, and we all turned toward him.

"It could be, but we're ready for whatever they try to use against us," I snarled, unable to fight the beast within me, demanding I rush to her.

"Then why the fuck are we on horses?" Killian asked, and we dismounted, pulling magic to us as we became one with the jetstream.

"Let's go witch hunting, brothers."

Chapter Three

Aria

Someone dragged me into the forest and tossed me onto something hard and unforgiving. The dark bag over my head prevented me from seeing what was happening around me. My body lay prone, unmoving as I pretended to be beneath the witch's spell. Grunting sounded, and the whinnying of horses filled the woods as the sound of steel meeting steel abated as if the fighting had ended.

Pain echoed through my head while blood pumped through my veins, causing my ears to fill with the roar of it coursing through me. The wagon lurched forward quietly, and the sound of the wheels and horse's hooves crunching over the forest floor filled the air. I assumed they were taking me north, to Ilsa, and the Kingdom of Vãkya instead of Norvalla.

I could hear hushed grunts and words that flowed around me. Men talked in a strange language I couldn't identify or understand. The witches within the caravan spoke the language taught to me since birth, uncaring that I would hear them if I woke, which meant they didn't intend to keep me alive.

Tears burned my eyes at the thought of Knox finding his brother and men slaughtered without a sign of me, and pain rocked through me. He'd assume I had helped murder them, and that would send him off the rails, hunting me down to end my existence. My heart lurched, tightening until a sob threatened to explode from me.

Greer, Lore, and Killian couldn't be dead. It wasn't right for them to die on some road because witches wanted me dead. I'd rushed through the kingdom, leaving havoc and ruins in my wake of chaos, and now they were all dead because of my body count while showing Knox I wasn't some child he could threaten and own.

"Lord Andres had better hope he is present when we arrive. I am not willing to allow her to live much longer. Her death should prevent the king from finding her, with her sickly sweet breeding stench oozing from her. Lord Andres should have told us what she was so we could have had something to counter her aroma. I'm not even her species, and I can smell her reek."

I sniffed myself, frowning. Was I the only one who couldn't smell my scent?

"The bodies we left on the road will slow down the king. One is his brother, which means we should go before he arrives. If he shows up with an army, they will outnumber us, and not even you can match the King of Norvalla in strength."

"We won't be here when he arrives. I only need to extract her scent and mirror her image. Once we have finished with that, I will appear like her, and the king won't be able to tell the difference between Aria Hecate and myself."

I rolled my eyes at the woman's reasoning and then frowned. Was it possible to duplicate someone and appear as them? Yes. Easily, but this was Knox. He'd figured out my replica within minutes of being close to me when I'd used it on him. Not that it would matter if I were dead.

"Ditch the wagon. It's slowing us down," a woman ordered.

Someone wrenched me up like a sack of potatoes and slammed me onto the back of a horse. I sucked in air, forcing no response to escape my lips or lungs. Beefy hands pushed into my spine, using me as a prop to get onto the horse's back. Even the horse grunted beneath the heavyweight.

We took off again, this time at a faster pace as if fear were rushing us away from the site where they'd murdered Knox's brother and friends. Like that would prevent him from reaching us? For once, I was glad for the tattoo on my inner thigh, relieved that he would track us, drawn to the general vicinity in which they intended to murder me. Hopefully, he'd show up before they ended my life.

Hours passed before we entered what sounded like a camp as metal clanged and voices spoke or argued. The moment we breached the hub of noise, silence reigned. The male that had ignored my existence, other than to grab my body when I started to fall, yanked me from the horse, and held me in his arms.

"Bring her to the tent," the witch ordered. "Is Lord

Andres here?"

"He is here, Mistress," someone answered.

"Good. Find the runner who failed to return and take her head."

The male took me into a tent and dropped me on the ground unceremoniously. I sucked in air, remaining limp as the sound of heavy breathing entered behind us.

"I see you found the bitch," Lord Andres snorted. "I trust you murdered Killian and Lore to stall the king from hunting her?"

"Easily. It's a pity that I couldn't play with the king's brother. He excited me. Had I more time, I'd have enjoyed cutting him into pieces to leave a trail back to Ilsa for King Karnavious to find," the witch stated, her tone high and nasally.

The witch ripped the hood from my head, and I lunged, slamming my face into hers before she could react. Lord Andres gripped my hair, pulling me upright as my muscles screamed in protest.

"Stupid bitch," he snarled, shaking me by my hair as my scalp screamed and rebelled.

Lord Andres turned me to face the witch, and she slapped her hand against my cheek. Bone crunched as I took in the haggard face of the witch. Her lips pulled back over blackened teeth as she sneered at me, striking me again before cradling her hand to her chest, her fingers broken from hitting me.

It was a bad sign she was so brittle, showing dark magic had tainted her for a prolonged time. Just like Asil, she was rotten from the inside out. I held her sightless black eyes, daring her to hit me again. Blood dripped from my broken nose as a smile broadened across my lips.

"Aria Hecate, the High Queen of Witches, has sentenced you to death," she crooned, reaching forward to run her fingers through my silver hair. "You downplayed her beauty, Andres. She's gorgeous. It makes perfect sense why the King of Norvalla used her nightly in his bed."

"Indeed," Andres chuckled, pulling me back to lick the side of my face with his putrid-scented mouth.

"Do not mess up her face. I need it to be perfect for replicating," she ordered.

"She's in heat," Andres grunted, running a hand over my breast, squeezing it painfully.

I whimpered at his touch, choking down memories of Garrett's hands on me. Lord Andres jerked me back, handling me like a rag doll as he shoved me toward a stench-covered bed that caused my eyes to water. Rolling over on the mattress, I stared at the couple who watched me.

"So, what's your brilliant plan, Kristal?" Andres asked, moving toward the simple table where amber liquid sat in a glass carafe.

"The same one I used when I created the king's last lover. I will take her face and use it to become her. After that, I will replicate the scent of her womb to make him think I am her. It worked with the last one well enough. He never even realized she was one of us," the witch chuckled coldly.

"You can't be that stupid, Kristal," Andres snorted, downing the contents of the goblet before setting it back down. "It isn't her face that draws him to her. It's the scent of her womb and her pussy. He's tasted her, which means you can't replicate Aria. He'd figure you out before you ever entered his camp. One taste of you and you would be dead, woman. She's rare, like the king's own bloodline. Aria Hecate isn't only a witch. She's also the same as the king, or she's close enough to it that he's drawn to her. You could take her face and wear it, but you'd never be able to duplicate her sounds or her scent."

"We cannot allow her to live. You understand that, don't you? She has left our witches in fear of her marching upon them with her undead army. They're hiding, and witches of dark magic do *not* hide."

I snickered, drawing her wrath to me.

"And when you find the one creature that can bring the king to his knees, you don't kill it. You turn it into a weapon and send it back to him like a bomb, Kristal. Have Aria become like us and send her back to him." Lord Andres turned, smiling coldly at me as his eyes glazed over to obsidian, but it wasn't the same as when Knox's eyes turned dark, allowing his creature to peek out at me.

Whatever Lord Andres held within him, it was ancient magic and powerful. It was also evil. Pure, horrifying, dark magic slithered over my flesh as his hand grabbed my face. Pain filled my chin where he held me, pinching tightly as he tilted my head, forcing my jaw open so he could peer inside.

When he released me, I backed up, but he grabbed my legs, yanking them apart before lowering his nose to my sex, inhaling it deeply. Andres's hands left my thighs, pushing my body backward, and I fell, unable to stop myself from toppling over with my hands bound tightly behind my back. My eyes slid to the rising sun outside the tent, detaching myself from the situation as he pushed his fingers against my core, entering my body with one, then withdrawing it, making grotesque noises as he tasted his finger.

"She's in heat, which means the king is coming for her. Everything within him demands he doesn't lose her during a cycle."

"King Karnavious can't tell the difference between an actual heat cycle and a tonic induced cycle. We stick to the plan. She dies, and I replace her long enough to take his head," Kristal snapped.

"You're not hearing me. The king has tasted her cunt, heard her noises, and knows her scent by heart. You cannot replicate Aria's scent with magic like your mistress did to his other lover. We gave the tonic to the last one before he'd ever known her carnally."

Andres pushed his finger back into my sex, forcing it further into my body as I cried out, struggling to get away from his touch as he reached for something within my body. His other hand slapped me, and darkness danced in my vision as he snorted.

"She isn't pregnant, and his scent is weak on her," Andres declared, pulling his finger up to his nose while smiling at me cruelly.

"Then what do you suggest we do? She's a bloodline Hecate witch with too much power to control, Andres. What the dark mistress did to us, I cannot do to Aria or her kind. She's entirely too powerful to manage while alive. The last one was much weaker and altered at birth to fit her role as his lover. The king was drawn to her from the first scent he caught. We created her to play a role, and once everything unfolded as we'd planned, we freed her from his unwanted affection and touch."

"That sounds like your issue. If you can't figure out a way to control Aria, I'll keep the bitch and use her to build an army of monsters to go against the king. That," Andres said, pointing at me, "is unheard of, and executing her is the last resort. No woman has rattled and purred in the last five hundred years. Not that history recorded, nor was it noted in the Library of Knowledge. Most can't even do one or the other these days, and if she can breed children who can, that makes her worth a fortune. Your mistress wants to use her, but she doesn't even realize what the little bitch is yet. So go converse with that evil bitch, Ilsa, because you're not killing Aria."

"You're not in charge here!" Kristal snarled. The magic she rushed through the tent sent bile pushing against the back of my throat.

My entire body tightened, preparing for the assault that Kristal intended to unleash. Lord Andres snapped, pointed at me, and growled low from deep in his chest. "We can breed that bitch to create monsters. Her womb is fertile and can be filled often. You think of power, but that girl is raw power who can breed an entire army of monsters for your High Queen. Smell her womb, Kristal. That scent oozing from her lures beasts to breed with her, and I intend to do just that. Why do you think the King of Norvalla claimed her? Because he's very aware of what she is and what she can do. Your queen would be foolish to waste this resource simply because she fears her. I refuse to allow that to happen!"

Magic shot toward Lord Andres, who jerked back the moment it slithered over him. His hand moved forward, slashing through the air with his blade as Kristal snarled. Blood splattered my face as she howled, shooting dark magic toward me. I rolled before it could slam into my body, groaning as pain burned in my bound wrists, secured behind my back.

The tent became smothered in magic as Kristal returned her focus on Andres, and he swung his blade wide, cutting deep into her throat. I shivered, gagging on the taste of copper that filled the air, mingling with dark, oily magic. Kristal's hands lifted, and she sent a powerful wave of magic rushing through the tent, sending us flying in separate directions.

I peered at the sky, whimpering as I slid onto my side, staring through the bedlam ensuing through the camp. The power in the air was stifling as witches' battled warriors. Slowly, I lifted onto my knees, searching the area for a direction in which to escape. Men were slaughtering witches while magic rushed through the air, creating plumes of pink mist that had once been warriors.

Once I'd got to my feet, magic shot toward me, sending my body careening down an embankment. I cried out, forcing myself to get back on my feet once more. I glanced around, listening to the fighting ongoing above me. Exhaling, I closed my eyes to hear what was near me, discovering rushing water.

Without waiting to see if they'd give chase, I moved toward the sound with my arms screaming in pain. Shouting sounded from the top of the ridge, and I spun in a tight circle, fighting past nausea that burned my throat. My eyes watered from the magic used, causing my mind to lose focus. I gasped as yet another wave of power rushed through the forest, forcing me to choose a path.

"Find her!" Lord Andres shouted, and I bolted, heading into the thickening forest toward the water to cover my scent.

My heart pounded, and fear spiked through me, causing the blood to move through my veins like thunder, echoing in my ears deafeningly. Sweat covered my brow, giving them a scent trail on which to follow me. I skated to a halt by the raging river, staring at the other side with despair.

Turning, I listened as boots crunched over debris, and my adrenaline spiked. Chewing my lip to ignore the morning's crisp breeze, I moved into the water with my hands still bound behind my back. They had secured them far enough up that I couldn't reach to sever the rope binding them. My foot slid over slick rock, and I gasped as I went down, shooting back to the surface, coughing icy water from my lungs.

I pushed through the current and finally made it to the other side of the river. I landed on the bank, gasping at the frosty chill that settled into my bones. My wet dress felt like lead as I struggled back onto my feet. Shouts sounded from the other side of the fast-moving water, and I hurried into the foliage.

"She's here! Find the little bitch!" Lord Andres yelled.

I trembled, fighting the chattering of my teeth as everything inside of me scrambled to control my body temperature. Hiding in the undergrowth, I watched the men follow my trail to the river's edge, turning to call out before they pushed into the water. I struggled to my feet as they shouted out my location. I dashed deeper into the woods on burning, aching legs that screamed in pain.

Chapter Four

I'd been running for what felt like hours with men shouting behind me. My entire body shook violently from the need to survive. I grew lethargic from the chill in the morning air and the wet dress that clung to me. The shouts were steadily getting closer as exhaustion filled my mind and my body. Pausing, I listened to the thundering sound of rushing water I could see in the distance, vanishing over the edge of what appeared to be a cliff.

Moving to the ledge, I looked over its side, unable to judge the distance to the falls' bottom. Shouting sounded behind me, and I turned, shuddering as men rushed forward. Tears pricked my eyes, burning them as I stepped back while gathering strength to leap into the rapids.

"You've nowhere to go," Lord Andres scoffed as he moved near me, his mouth curling into a cruel smile.

I sent a silent prayer to the Goddess of Mercy,

swallowing bile as his yellowing teeth appeared from his victorious smirk. Going over a cliff with Knox was one thing. Going over one with my hands bound behind my back was suicide. I wished for Knox to appear and end this nightmare. Even if he took my life, it would be better than what Andres had planned for me.

My foot neared the edge, and Andres dove toward me as I spun, leaping blindly into the air. A scream escaped my throat moments before I hit the water jarringly. Pain shot through my legs, and I slowly sank, pushing off the bottom and gasping for air when my head breached the surface.

Men shouted, and I watched as they ran to a trail that led to the river from the cliffside. Turning in the water, I screamed as the current slammed me into a giant boulder, smashing against my head, causing light to burst behind my eyes. I sank once more beneath the surface, fighting to reach the bottom of the quickly moving river that was turning into raging rapids.

Something brushed my leg as I shot back toward the surface, and I glanced down as blonde hair became visible through the frothing white water. Nails dug into my legs, pulling me under as I sucked in air, yanked beneath the surface by a nymph.

My heart echoed through my ears as she smiled coldly, revealing serrated teeth. Once she had me beneath the water, she lunged to tear into my throat, but I was faster. My teeth found her cheek, slicing through it before she pulled back. The rattle that exploded from my lungs sent bubbles moving to the surface, and a burst of energy shot through me as I pierced the nymph's throat with my fangs, ripping her vein open. Blood pooled around us, and I turned, sucking in water as yet another nymph attacked, using her claws to slice into my stomach.

I pushed from the bottom, kicking my legs to breach the surface. I gulped in air, noticing the nymph had followed me. I lunged, and we both gasped, crashing into a huge jagged rock that impaled the nymph, leaving her behind as the current slammed me against rock after rock until consciousness faded.

The sound of more rapids drew my attention, and I shuddered through the fear and chill that rushed through me. I saw movement beside me, and I groaned as I prepared for an attack, only to have something land close beside me in the water.

My eyes slid to the bank, finding a woman in the water with me. In her hand was a rope, but I couldn't get enough air through my chattering teeth to tell her my hands were bound. I went below the surface as a rapid caught me, sucking me in without warning. My feet slid over the slippery rocks as I tried to get enough energy to shoot back toward the surface.

Failing, I blinked past the dark dots that swam in my vision as my lungs released the last of my air. The river tossed my body around its bottom, crashing into rocks and other things before someone grabbed me and pulled me toward the surface.

The woman stared down at me, slapping my face as I sputtered, expelling water from my flooded lungs. She turned me over onto my side and then lifted her head toward the direction in which I'd come.

"Get up," she demanded. "They're coming."

She didn't wait to see if I did as she'd instructed,

leaving me to run from the men chasing me. I rolled onto my stomach, sucking in more air past the pain in my chest as I stood on shaking legs. I started forward, following her into the woods to find a place to hide from Lord Andres and his men.

The woman turned, staring over my shoulder as others moved in around me. I slowed down, leaning over to throw up water while they watched. Witches had found me and saved me. I stared at one who moved closer with a dagger in her hand, studying me.

"Thank you," I whispered through trembling lips.

"Who is chasing you?" she demanded, closing the distance between us.

"Witches. Dark witches and the men who captured me for them," I admitted, foregoing the murderous nymphs in the water that had tried to ensure I didn't escape a watery grave.

"They're coming, Adele!" one of the younger women cried, and the witch moving toward me paused, her eyes filling with regret before they rushed away from me.

"Don't leave me," I pleaded, running toward them until the reality of the situation slammed into me. If I followed these witches, I'd lead Lord Andres and his men right to them.

I turned, hating the angry tears of frustration that blinded me as I ran in the opposite direction with my hands still bound behind my back. Branches slapped me in the face, scratching my bare arms, and I gasped as something cut my leg. Staring down, I looked at the sliver of wood protruding from my thigh. I lifted my head just as something slammed into my temple, causing my vision to swim before me.

"Fucking little whore," Lord Andres snarled.

Someone grabbed me from behind and dragged me back toward the large boulders that littered the riverbank. They slammed me down over one, my stomach lurching with the need to throw up as I watched Lord Andres slowly removing his armor.

"You thought I would allow you to escape me?" he chuckled coldly. "I agreed to let that witch slaughter my entire army just to get my fucking hands on you."

I couldn't speak, couldn't move with the soldier holding me down as Lord Andres finished removing his armor, and I noted the burn marks and loose-fitting flesh covering his body. Tears swam in my vision as he reached into his trousers and stroked his flaccid cock. Fear burned through me, and I cried, knowing that no one was coming to save me.

Screaming ripped from the forest, and I sobbed when warriors brought the witches who had tried to save me into the clearing as they fought to escape. My heart sank in my chest, bottoming out against the boulder on which I was held. I shouted in denial as Lord Andres snorted, adjusting himself before he retrieved his blade.

"What do we have here?" he asked in mock curiosity.

"Witches within the woods, hiding," a warrior sneered, gripping a witch by the hair before he shoved her to her knees before him.

"The only good witch is a dead witch," Andres laughed coldly as his tongue slipped over his lips.

Fighting against the male holding me down, I watched in horror as another warrior brought more witches from the forest and shoved them to their knees. A scream ripped from my throat as a blade swung, ending the life of the woman who had pulled me from the water. My vision swam as they dispatched each witch until all their headless bodies lay twitching on the forest floor.

Lord Andres turned, smiling cruelly as he walked over to me. He yanked my head back, and I prepared for the assault that would surely unfold. My mind tried to slip away, to go where nothing could touch me, but teeth sank into my shoulder, and a loud wail escaped my throat, echoing through the forest.

The wrongness of his teeth against my flesh caused an inhuman noise to escape my lungs in a wailing rattle. I screeched loudly, and it echoed through me into the forest like a beacon sent for someone to find me. I screamed as tears burned my eyes, and the unnatural feeling of the bite caused bile to fill my throat, muting the sound I made, but unable to stop it from building in my throat, escaping through my lungs.

"Shut up, you stupid bitch!" Lord Andres snarled.

He ripped me from the boulder, burying my face against the forest floor, which only caused the sound to grow in force. His hands slammed against my ear, and I rattled louder until my body trembled from the strength of the sorrowful noise escaping me. His teeth sank deeper into my shoulder, marring Knox's bite as he fought to subdue me.

I felt fingers pushing against my opening as Lord Andres prepared to rape me, forcing them in roughly while he continued biting into my shoulder. I couldn't stop the noise I made as it grew until it became deafening. I couldn't fight him with my magic bound and my hands tied behind me. I was powerless to stop what was coming, and I knew it.

He lifted my head by my hair, abandoning my sex to slam my face into the ground while trying to end my rattles and shrieks. Light burst behind my eyelids before Andres's teeth returned to shred my shoulder, severing flesh from bone as he tried to subdue me.

He forced my body upright, moving my legs apart as he snarled against my shoulder. Power erupted around us, and Andres paused, standing as he shouted orders. I sat on my knees; my body propped there at an awkward angle as I tried to catch my breath. No one moved as the power grew thicker around us.

I blinked several times, trying to clear my vision while forcing air into my lungs. Shadows shifted around us as Lord Andres's men withdrew their weapons. Still, I wailed, unable to prevent the sound from escaping. Everything inside me ached. Pain wrapped around me as he sent his foot directly into my stomach, forcing me to gasp, which only made the sound more painful.

"Shut up, you stupid whore!" he shouted, turning toward me. "Kill her if she moves or doesn't stop that fucking noise!" Lord Andres stepped out from in front of me as someone else took his place.

"Shut up, woman!" the warrior snarled, and then Lord Andres yelled, causing everyone within the clearing to move into action.

"Kill her! The king and his men are here!" he demanded.

The world stopped moving as the warrior's blade sailed toward my throat. Someone deflected it just before it reached me, and the warrior fell to the ground in several bloodied pieces. I blinked slowly. My rattle grew in volume, unable to prevent it from escaping as dark shadows covered in armor encircled me protectively.

"I think you have my girl, asshole," Knox growled, peering over his shoulder through his visor to look at me. His eyes narrowed as the noise I made filled the area relentlessly.

"Your days as King are numbered!" Lord Andres snarled, taking a fighting stance. "You will die!"

"Not today, and not by you," Knox laughed soundlessly. "You touched my woman, which means you and your men's lives are forfeited."

Knox turned, deliberately dismissing the lord while his piercing blue eyes locked with mine. A warrior rushed toward him, and he lifted his blade, pushing it between his arm and body, impaling the man who had thought to stab him in the back. Knox turned, lowering his head, and swung so quickly that my eyes couldn't follow the movement. Body parts hit the forest floor, painting it crimson as a river of blood coated it.

More power entered the clearing as Knox's men drew their blades around me. Lord Andres's warriors closed in from the surrounding forest. Knox, Killian, and Brander chuckled, soundlessly watching them circle us. Dark witches with sightless eyes joined the warriors, building a barrier to prevent our escape.

Relief washed through me at the sight of Killian, hope flaring in my chest that the others may have also survived. Yet Lore was absent, which terrified and worried me. If he'd lived, wouldn't he have been here too?

A blade swung toward me without warning, but Brander intercepted it, slicing through a warrior that rushed forward with his sword lifted. The man's obsidian eyes marred his face as ugly spider webs covered his flesh. Brander leaped into the air, cutting through another male without stopping until he was on the ground. Brander used his arm to swing his blade wide as he severed the head, sending it bouncing across the forest floor.

Killian angled toward a group of warriors, his blades swinging precisely and adeptly. His swords met and crisscrossed against the other male's blades, unhanding them before he swung, severing the body at the waist. Killian moved to the next, blindly swinging, or what I assumed had been blind, only to remove heads and limbs from more warriors.

Knox stalked toward Lord Andres, who wielded dual blades. Andres snarled, cursing the king for being weak, goading him into anger, yet Knox didn't take the bait. Knox said nothing; his anger radiated from him silently as he held his swords at his side. He stared at Andres with death exuding through the skull visor he wore.

Andres lifted his blades and swung, and Knox countered, sending one of Andres's arms to the ground, still holding the sword. I hadn't even been able to follow the speed of Knox's blade as it moved.

Andres howled but still lunged, intending to catch Knox off-guard with his attack. Knox sent his blades into the air, coming down in an X before he lifted them, slicing both through Lord Andres's throat. His body cut into sections and slid to the ground. More warriors came from the forest as if they'd intended to be a second wave of attack, but Killian and Brander dispatched them as Knox moved to me, dropping to his knees in front of me.

He turned as more men escaped the woods and whispered a single word, which caused the men rushing forth to turn to ash, as the wind caught and carried it through the air. Slowly, he turned back, staring at me as the pained sounds continued escaping my throat.

Knox cupped my face between his thick gloves before shifting his attention to my mangled shoulder. I didn't stop the sounds. I couldn't. My entire body shuddered from the rattling wail escaping me.

"Aria, you're okay," Knox whispered, his eyes dipping down my body to the soaked dress covered in mine and everyone else's blood. "I got you," he swallowed, his throat bobbing as he studied me.

I could see Knox, but I couldn't process him. My mind refused to allow the fear to slide away. Everything within me was repelling against the feeling of Lord Andres's bite. His mark on my flesh was vile, detested, and offensive. The wrongness of it consumed me.

Something touched my hands, and I screamed over the rattling wail. My hands broke free, rushing toward the shoulder to rip the mark from my flesh. Knox noted their direction and grabbed them with one of his, shucking his glove and visor before securing it with his bare hand. He jerked me against his body, cradling me as I fought him.

Everything within me was going haywire. Something was wrong on a deeper level than I could process. Knox struggled with me in his arms as his men moved in around us. He purred, rattling loudly while the others echoed him. He released me, and my hands flew to my shoulder as my nails pushed free.

Knox removed my hands again and covered his mouth over my shoulder. My hands ran through his hair, jerking him closer as the wail continued. His teeth pushed through my skin, and his other hand cradled me against him. The bite was painful, but there was peace within his mark's pain, righting the wrong that was done.

Knox's men purred around us, their comforting noises adding to his as he held his bite there. I melted into him, sobbing loudly as he cradled my shuddering form, tightening his hold. Knox pulled away, and I lunged, wrapping my arms around him as I continued to cry, oblivious to those watching as everything crumbled around me.

"You're safe now, Little Monster. I got you. Lord Andres can't ever hurt you again. I promise. Aria, you're safe."

"She's wounded badly. She looks like she fought hard and lost," Brander stated.

"She was probably…" Killian paused at Knox's violent rattle.

Knox picked me up without waiting to see if I could walk. My arms held him against me as he kissed my cheek, holding me tightly. "Raped?" he snapped, and I tensed, which caused them all to purr loudly around me. "Set up a fucking camp. We'll move to the other in the morning. I don't smell his scent within her, but that doesn't mean he didn't do other things to her body."

Less than twenty minutes later, Knox had me in his shirt, wrapped in a blanket and cradled against him. I didn't speak, and he didn't ask questions. The men slept on the ground while Knox held me, pushing my hair away from my face to stroke it softly. His lips continually brushed over my forehead and ear while he purred. Brander eventually checked my wounds while keeping silent. No one asked the one question they were thinking, the one burning in their eyes. I didn't offer what had happened.

It didn't matter because Knox had come for me. He'd had enough trust to know I wouldn't have left his men to die if I'd been able to prevent it from happening. I couldn't bring myself to ask if Lore and Greer lived because I couldn't form the words. I bathed in Knox's heat, allowing him to comfort me through the tremors and fear that had yet to subside.

I closed my eyes, and he tucked me against him, holding my bloody, dirty body flush with his without care that I was filthy. Knox whispered soft words and used gentle touches to calm my broken edges, promising that everything would be okay.

It wouldn't.

I'd let his lies appease me for now. I'd allow him to comfort me through the darkest hour and keep away the icy chill that had soaked into my bones. Knox was weathering the storm with me, and I didn't care if it was a lie or if he hated me, so long as he held me through the tremors and kept the nightmares away for a little while longer.

Chapter Five

The next morning, someone lifted me to Knox on his horse before I'd even awoken. I screamed, hearing his purr the moment my eyes gained focus, echoed by the other men. Knox's body stiffened against mine, and I removed my claws from his arms as I stared into his soft gaze. He hadn't tried to touch me other than to hold me.

"You're okay, Aria," Knox stated like he couldn't find anything else to say beyond that. I nodded, slowly turning to face forward. His lips brushed against my throat, kissing the rapidly beating pulse to calm my fears.

Nodding, I settled in front of him, shivering against the heat his body created while we started toward the camp. I still hadn't spoken and was grateful he hadn't prodded me. I knew it was coming the moment we got back to camp. I could feel his tense body, the way his arms clenched me as if he feared I would shatter.

I was in shock and exhausted, but not broken by any means. My entire body ached, and I'd been through hell to escape Lord Andres. I couldn't get the faces of the witches who had helped me out of my mind. They'd died because the cuffs Knox placed on my wrists had weakened me. I'd been a sitting duck, defenseless and exposed as we'd moved through the forest to meet up with him.

Every time my eyes would start to close, I'd see Lord Andres touching me, tasting me, and I'd jerk upright. Knox would brush his nose against my ear, purring into it. I'd permit him to calm me before allowing my gaze to wander over the terrain, ever watchful of a trap.

Knox and his men offered me comfort the entire trip back to camp. The moment Knox started his soothing purr, they mirrored it absently, as if forced to do so by their King. Knox held me against him with one arm while the other grabbed the reins confidently, as if used to riding with women in his arms.

We reached camp at dusk, and Knox rode straight to a large tent, dismounting without missing a step with me in his arms. Inside, a large bath was poured, and he set me down beside it, holding me close. Women moved around, easing toward me when he stepped back. Their eyes filled with understanding, which told me that between falling asleep and waking up, Knox had sent a rider ahead of us with orders.

I watched him inhale, baring his teeth as if he couldn't help it while Brander slid a chair beneath him, then moved toward me. The women removed my clothes while Brander assessed the damage to my shoulder. Stepping back, he looked lower to my abused thighs.

"Were you sexually assaulted?" Brander asked.

"I'm fine," I whispered thickly.

"He didn't fucking ask if you were fine, Aria. He asked if Lord Andres got inside your body!" Knox snarled, and I recoiled as if he'd struck me. He exhaled anger and tried again in a calmer tone, "Lord Andres marked you, and his scent showed he intended to breed you. Did he succeed?"

"He didn't rape me, Knox." I trembled violently as Brander observed. Knox lifted his hands, and his purr filled the tent. He silently pushed the panic away from me with his touch. "He wanted to breed me. He did things, but he didn't get that far before you came for me."

Knox swore beneath his breath as he stood, sending the chair crashing to the ground with his abrupt abandonment of it. He lifted his nose as a deep rattle filled the tent, threatening to come down on us. Knox walked toward me, pulling me against him as his eyes shifted between black and blue as if he were fighting to remain in control. His body shook with anger, and I swallowed the urge to back up. His anger wasn't directed at me. It was because of what they had done to me, causing tears to swim in my eyes.

"What *things*?" Knox hissed.

"He used his fingers to check the status of my womb," I admitted, barely above a whispered breath. "He used them and then tasted me. He told the witch, Kristal, not to kill me because I could breed an army to oppose you. He said they could turn me into a bomb to send back to you, and to murder me would be a wasted opportunity."

He snorted, lifting my chin to peer into my eyes

while his arms moved around me. "What else did they say?"

"That the high queen wanted me dead. That my skipping across the Nine Realms leaving skulls for my current crush wasn't acceptable," I blabbed, holding his angry glare. "They were going to replicate my face and body onto another witch to get to you, but Lord Andres said you'd tasted me and would smell the difference."

"Get in the bath and wash his scent off of you before I lose control, woman," Knox stated, lifting his hand to tip my head, kissing my lips softly.

He silently retrieved his chair to set it close to the large tub. Killian entered, bringing in a dress and a blanket. His eyes slid over me before he moved to a large bed that sat beside a similar chest to Knox's.

I slipped into the tub, covering my breasts as the men offered me their backs. Knox grabbed the bottle of soap and began carefully washing me himself. It was an intimate action, which made me shiver as the others made busy around us.

It was as if they'd practiced this before, Knox being seductive, and Brander and Killian pretending it wasn't happening. I knew I was still in shock from running and what had almost happened, but I felt safe with Knox and his men, and so did my creature.

"Why would the dark witches think their plan would work, Aria?" Knox asked, watching as I lifted and dropped my shoulders in a shrug.

"Lord Andres and Kristal said they had done it to you before, using another woman to pose as your lover to get close to you," I muttered, noticing his hands had stopped moving.

Killian tensed, and Brander turned toward me slowly, narrowing his eyes to slits as he listened. I chewed my lip at the awkward silence in the tent, wondering if they knew who it was.

The mood in the tent had shifted to something bordering violence as Knox's hands moved back to my hair, pulling on it as he washed it. I tried to turn to look at him, but he forced me to stay where I was, facing Brander, who silently studied me. I continued shielding myself from their eyes while Knox's hands grew hard, his actions jerking and worrisome.

"Did they mention a name?" Knox asked softly. There was a steel edge to his words, sharp enough to double as a blade.

"No," I replied carefully.

"What else did they *tell* you?"

"They didn't *tell* me anything. Lord Andres and Kristal spoke to each other, and I don't think they cared if I listened since they intended to murder me. Kristal intended to murder you, assuming she could get close enough if she looked and smelled like me. Lord Andres argued it, stating that you knew me in a carnal way that she couldn't imitate with magic."

"And how had they managed to do it before with my other lover?" he countered before snorting loudly.

"They said you fell in love with her because of the tonic she drank. It induced her unique scent, which you couldn't decipher from an actual heat cycle. Kristal said they planted her in your life when the girl was young and kept up the ruse until her death." I felt my skin pebble as realization dawned on me as to who they'd meant.

How had I missed it? Knox had only ever loved one person in his entire life. In my trauma, I'd missed connecting the dots. I'd missed the clues of whom they'd spoken. I shivered, fighting the fear that wrapped around my stomach and throat with my mistake. I wanted to take the words back, return them to the tip of my tongue, and swallow them down. The tension in the tent was stifling, and my heart pounded deafeningly in my ears, the admission cutting Knox deeper than if I'd taken a knife and stabbed it into his chest.

"And you expect me to believe that?" he sneered.

"No. You asked me what else I had heard. That's what I heard. It doesn't mean it is right, or maybe I just misunderstood what Lord Andres and Kristal said because of what was happening when they spoke of it. I was in pain and exhausted. Maybe I misheard." I lied, praying he accepted my explanation.

"And did you inform them I only enjoyed using your body and had no affection for your heart? Or did you assure them you would help them get to me?"

I tensed as my chest tightened. "I didn't inform them of anything or how you felt about me. I was too busy having a finger shoved into my body so Lord Andres could taste the state of my womb and breeding cycle. It didn't seem the right time to speak, all things considered. Next time one of your men are molesting me, I'll be sure to stop fighting them to get the details for your next interrogation, King Karnavious."

"You think to sway me to you with your assault as you soil the memory of my wife with your fucking lies?"

"She's a lying bitch," Killian snarled, lunging toward me, but Brander moved to intercede, preventing him from reaching me. I shivered as tears slipped free. "Liliana was his mate, witch! She birthed his son. He ought to take your fucking tongue for your lies."

"Answer my fucking question, witch," Knox demanded coldly.

"No, I don't intend to do anything with you, Knox. Had I realized it was your wife who they spoke of, I would have held my tongue on what I'd heard. I do not wish to soil her memory, nor to inflict more pain onto you. I repeated what I had heard. I know nothing of you or who you have loved in your long life. I told you what Lord Andres and Kristal said, which doesn't make it a fact. You asked a question, and I answered it to the best of my ability."

"The only woman I have ever loved, or will *ever* love, was my wife. You use your assault to strike against her memory? Fuck you, Aria." Knox stood, pulling me up with him. He grabbed the towel, shoving me away from him as if he couldn't stand to touch me. "You're just like your fucking mother."

I felt the slap of his words as if he'd physically struck me. I held out my hand for the towel, and he shook his head, glaring at me as if I were some disgusting thing he wanted to remember before he destroyed it. My hands trembled, and tears swam in my eyes before he threw the towel at me, hitting me in the face. My hands shook so violently that I couldn't wrap it around me, so I held it in front of me instead.

"Did you arrange it all? Did you help the witches slaughter an entire army and capture Lord Andres, turning him against me and pretending to be kidnapped so I would rush in and rescue you? Was that your plan, to defile and make me second guess my entire life and my wife?" Knox snarled as his nails lengthened. "Pretty fucking convenient that you go missing, only to return and say things that would make me question my reason for war and my fucking life."

"No," I replied firmly. "I wouldn't do that!"

"You called me to you with your rattling cries, and we're not fucking mates."

"I called for help because Lord Andres was about to rape me! I cried out because he slaughtered the women who helped me out of the water, right in front of me! I called for you because his bite turned me inside out, ripping me apart until I wanted to *die!*" I screamed through angry tears. "It felt vile and awful. It felt like he was making me his, and I wanted it to stop by any possible means. I wanted to die before he claimed me. I didn't want to be saved, Knox. I wanted not to be his!" I held my stomach, uncaring that he watched me falling apart.

"You're an excellent actress, but so were your grandmother and mother. It must run in your bloodline, just like treachery."

"Sure, Knox," I whispered thickly, fighting for control. "Let's go with that. Put me in the cage, or show me where I may lie down. I'm exhausted from playing *'let's rape the witch and take off her head'* today. Maybe tomorrow you can do it and end this game of whom can fuck over whom the most because you're exhausting, and I don't want to play with you anymore. Every chance you get to think the worst of me, you jump on it. I have done nothing to you or your people. I have harmed no one who didn't deserve to die a horrible death. I kept my word and began cleaning my house, and I didn't ask to be here. I'm not five steps ahead right now. I'm tripping over my feet and just trying to stay alive."

Knox swallowed, nodding at Brander. "Take her to your tent tonight and chain her to your bed. Gag the bitch if you need to shut her lying mouth," he snapped coldly.

"She's in heat," Brander argued before running his hand down his face.

"And?" Knox countered, glaring at Brander. "I'll return tomorrow after I've cooled off. If you've taken her by then, keep her. I'm done playing with her too."

"Knox, that's not happening," Brander assured.

"Then lock her ass up, but do it now."

"It is fine, Brander. Just take me to the cage, and I'll sleep there."

"She can sleep with me," Killian announced, and we all turned toward him. "I don't want to fuck her, not after what she just said about my sister. Chances are, you'll return to her pretty throat slit during the night, and we can all quit playing her games." Hatred burned in Killian's eyes. I slid my attention to him, shivering at the coldness I saw.

"You will not kill her. No matter what her poisonous lips speak, her power would still aid us in the war." Knox stared at Killian before turning back to me. "If you try to lure him to you, you won't have to worry about my people raping you. My beast will handle that scent of yours to stop the problem. I promise you that, Aria Hecate."

"Understood, *Your Majesty*. You could just allow me to choose someone to deal with it, and we could end that issue. Anyone would be preferable to you at this point. Maybe Aden can come in and *handle* my needs."

Knox's lips turned up in the corners as he stepped closer. "You think anyone actually *wanted* you, Aria? The only reason you've interested anyone is because your body lured us in like a poisonous trap. No one wanted *you*. We just wanted your pussy." I slapped him hard, unable to stop my hand from moving as his words knifed through my heart.

Knox grabbed me by the throat, shoving me into the bathtub. He pushed me beneath the water, holding me there as he watched me struggle. My hands lifted to his, scratching him as my lungs burned. I screamed, sending bubbles to the surface, kicking my legs while he glared down at me beneath the watery grave in which he intended to leave me.

Stars filled my vision, removing his image as my body jerked, and everything ceased. My hands stopped moving, and my legs went limp over the edge of the tub. He yanked me up and dropped me to the ground, stepping back as I threw up water, coughing until I'd expelled it all from my lungs. My eyes lifted, and I smiled coldly.

"You weak-ass bastard," I taunted through the hoarseness of my throat. "Stop half-assing it and finish it already!"

"Aria, shut the fuck up," Brander urged.

Knox's nostrils flared, studying me through the cold detachment in his eyes. His entire body was tense, filled with the need to end my life because of my words, but he couldn't. I didn't back down, and neither did he.

"Don't promise me an ending you can't deliver, King Karnavious." He stepped closer as I got to my feet, uncaring that I was naked. "Come on. Do it. You can't, can you? I can't hurt you either, and I've had plenty of opportunities to do it. I've been behind you, so fucking close to your unguarded back, without you even realizing I was there. It pissed me off because I should have murdered you and spared myself from being your *bitch*. Yet here I am, at your fucking mercy, of which you have none to offer. For the record, you should have let Lord Andres's warrior take my head because, unlike you, he would have ended this shit show in which you brought me."

His eyes searched mine as if he were just realizing the truth that no matter how much we went to war, we didn't want the other harmed. Something stopped us, something more profound than either of us cared to look at or explore. I'd stood behind him with a chance to end his life. Instead, I'd watched him with a hunger that terrified me.

"Careful, Aria. It's treason to threaten the king's life."

"Only if he is your King," I laughed soundlessly. "You're not my King, Knox. Whoever I take as my husband, he will be *my* King, as is the Hecate witch line's law. No king has ever sat on *our* throne." His eyes narrowed with my words, and his smile took on a sinister look. A ripple of warning rushing down my spine, but my mouth refused to cease speaking with the anger coursing through me. "A queen is so much more powerful without a king, anyway. That is why the Hecate line never allows a man to sit upon our throne. You are nothing more than a nightmare from which I'll eventually wake."

Knox stepped closer, threading his fingers through my hair, tilting my head back. His mouth brushed against mine even though I fought to turn my head away from his seductive lips. "You're never escaping me and never waking up from this nightmare you're living. You should have left my wife out of your ploy, witch. You've reminded me of who you are. Apparently, I'd forgotten. You needed a reminder of who I am and what I've done to your people. I intend to make damn sure you don't forget it again. The king always takes the queen, and she is silent afterward, isn't she?" I shivered as he pressed his lips against my throat, kissing the pulse that raced there before his tongue slowly traced against it. "I was too quick to speak earlier. I haven't finished playing with you quite yet, Aria." Knox nipped his teeth against the delicate flesh of my throat, laughing ominously before running his tongue against the skin, tasting me. "Take my prisoner to my tent, Killian. Don't let the little bitch out of your sight for any reason. I'll be there shortly, and I'll get the truth out of her one way or another."

Chapter Six

Sitting on the bed, I wrapped the blanket tighter around my shuddering body while Killian stared daggers at me. He hadn't spoken a single word other than to demand I sit and keep my poisonous, lying mouth shut. His eyes radiated a murderous rage from their depths. The anger inside the tent refused to abate, and every minute that ticked by only made it increasingly worse.

I reminded myself that he was Liliana's brother and Knox's best friend, who assumed I was plotting against them all. Knox had been gone for over an hour, and every time I closed my eyes, Killian would slam something down on the table to keep me awake.

My body ached, and exhaustion was taking over without having slept enough to heal, which drained me rapidly. Not to mention, I'd run my body hard in the time since escaping Kristal and Lord Andres, only for Knox to add to the emotional overload. I was running on fumes and sitting in a tent with a male that literally hated me, and it sucked.

I leaned over, resting my head on the palms of my hands to apply pressure where my head pounded. Killian slammed something down again. I ignored it, unable to hold my head up any longer. My body became weighted down, and my eyes felt like they had glass in them from not enough sleep and crying.

"Sit up," Killian snapped harshly.

I lifted my head, and it rolled backward, jerking as my eyes closed. Knox's scent hit me before he even entered the tent, and my body came alive. It would be so much easier to control the urges and my response to him after I rested. He strolled in, turning toward me as he narrowed his eyes.

"Move to the table and sit, Aria."

I stood, swaying forward, causing my hold on the blanket to loosen, accidentally dropping it. I bent to retrieve the blanket as Knox watched me with a stony expression that spoke of disdain and indifference.

Fuck him. He'd told me exactly what I was worth, which meant I'd die before giving it to him now. I grabbed the blanket, wrapping it around my body tightly, and sat at the table, fighting to keep my eyes open while he studied me.

He set a small tincture bottle onto the table. Frowning, I watched the bubbles rising to the top of the blue liquid within the bottle. Lifting my attention to him, I grunted while holding his hate-filled stare with one of my own.

"Drink it now, Aria," Knox ordered. "All of it."

"Is it going to kill me?" I asked in a hopeful tone.

When he just watched me wordlessly, I reached for the bottle. Using one hand to clasp it while the other held the blanket closed, I sank my teeth into the small cork to remove it. Spitting it onto the floor, I smelled the potion and rolled my eyes. "No hemlock for me? Just so you know, that's what kills me but remember, remove the head afterward. Hemlock grows wild in these mountains in case you're too fucking stupid to be aware of it. If that's not a harsh enough death for me, you could raise my mother from her grave and ask her about the other ways she tried killing me. Speaking of my loving mother, you and she would have a lot in common these days. You'd have enjoyed her methods since she excelled at causing me the most pain imaginable." Snorting at the burning hatred in his gaze, I tipped the tonic back, drinking it as he watched.

Knox withdrew an hourglass from his pack and turned it over, causing my eyes to narrow on the sand falling into the bottom. His fingers drummed on the table, unnerving me, and apprehension slithered through me while heat filled my cheeks. I frowned, swallowing past the excessive saliva building in my mouth. My hands tightened on the blanket, and his gaze dropped to them, slowly lifting to lock with mine.

He slid his eyes to the hourglass before turning to Killian, who observed us silently. Brander entered the tent, looking at me before turning his attention to Knox, dismissing me.

"Lore has stabilized, and Greer is up but still in a great deal of pain," Brander announced, and the men exhaled. "They'll survive, but it will take a few days before they're ready to be moved."

"They lived?" I asked, feeling immense relief that they were alive. No one answered me, and I frowned before exhaling a shuddered breath of relief. Brander took a seat beside Killian, letting his sapphire stare slide over my mutilated shoulder.

"Is your name Aria Primrose Hecate?" Knox asked, and I slid my gaze to his.

"Yes," I answered, wondering if he thought I was Kristal after all.

"Did Freya Hecate give the name to you?"

"No," I said, frowning at the line of questions. "My mother left me on an altar to die. She didn't name me or even care if I had a name before I left the world."

His eyes held mine prisoner as if he wanted to say something about it but chose not to. "Do you enjoy riding my cock?"

I swallowed and tilted my head, opening my mouth to give him a solid hell no, but it wouldn't come out. "A truth serum, really? Interesting choice for torture, King Karnavious," I grunted, shaking my head. "I don't think you're going to like my answers, though."

"Do you enjoy riding my cock, Aria?"

"Yes, which is probably a good thing since I'm only worth the scent it makes, right?" I frowned, picking at the invisible lint on the blanket I tucked around me. I chewed my lip, ignoring Knox's condescending stare.

"Do you know what you are?" he asked carefully.

"No, nor do I even care anymore."

"How you can be so strong at some things while

weak at others?"

"I'm young, and I never allowed myself to use much magic in the human realm. I couldn't test my limits there, and here they work exceedingly well unless they don't. In those cases, I'm rather weak as fuck. Like when I'm wearing your jewelry, it leaves me weakened, yet I can feel the magic itching to get free. Care to take them off and have a real go at me, Knox?"

His eyes burned into me like he was considering it, or worse, craving the chance to kill me. I wasn't stupid. I knew Knox was more powerful than I was, but then he'd had much longer to learn how to control and harness the magic and power he held. Hand to hand, he'd probably take my head before I'd even moved to stand from the chair. His lips curled into a smirk as if he were imagining doing just that.

"The creature in the cave, Eva, you're like her. Aren't you?"

"No. I'm much stronger and more advanced than Eva. I felt her when she rattled, and she felt me. She tested me, and I prevailed. She was proud of me, which is a little unsettling if I'm honest, and since you're forcing that issue, I'd say it is."

"Was it Hecate?" he countered.

"No."

"Do you know who the men in the cavern were?" he asked, his eyes narrowing to angry slits while I swallowed hard.

"No, I don't. I know Aden wants me and that he and the other silver-haired men are like us. His rattle made me ache, and I think I should explore that option once I escape you."

Knox's eyes slid to black bottomless pits with fiery embers floating within them before he snorted and sat forward. His tongue slid over his lip, revealing elongated teeth. It created an ache in my shoulder that burned, and my hands itched to rip it to shreds.

"Did you order the death of Lord Andres's army and turn him dark to use against me?" I snorted until I realized he was serious.

"No."

"Did you set up the ambush against my brothers, Aria? Did you slaughter my men and arrange your kidnapping to make me buy your lies about my wife?"

"No."

"Did you plan for someone to kidnap you, knowing I would save you?" His fingers tapped against the table.

"No, I did not. In fact, I was certain you'd find some way to pin it all on me and that when you caught me, you'd kill me. I wasn't far off, now was I?"

"Did you overhear them speaking about a woman I loved? One who they controlled with magic," Knox asked as the tic in his jaw hammered.

"This is where you let me be your bad guy, Knox. You don't want to know this answer. You need to hate me, so just hate me. I'm okay with that, but you won't like it if you make me answer this question. You'll still probably blame me anyway, so take the easy way out of this and let me be your monster."

Knox's eyes studied my face before he spoke through

clenched teeth. "Answer the fucking question, witch."

"Yes. I heard Kristal state they gave a tonic to a woman at a young age to change her scent and that they controlled her to get to you. They magically enhanced her to be your perfect mate, which her scent would have confirmed. That was why they couldn't use me to create a double because you already knew my scent and taste. That saved my life. Go figure," I swallowed as his jaw clenched.

"Sven?"

I studied the hurt in his eyes, but worse, there was hatred burning in them as if he blamed me. "No one mentioned Sven, and they never spoke of the woman by name, only your love for her and what created her scent."

"Were you created to be the same as her? Were you created to appear as the perfect mate for me, Aria Hecate? Did they enhance you with magic to smell and appear as something you're not?"

I swallowed and shook my head slowly. "No, not to my knowledge, at least," I whispered, sucking my lip between my teeth before releasing it. "I don't think I'm your perfect mate, asshole."

Knox's eyes held mine prisoner, causing a wave of heat to wash through me. "Are you plotting against me?"

"Absolutely," I said without pause while holding his stare.

His eyes searched my face before he asked another question. "What are you plotting, Aria?"

"I'm planning to bring this world to its knees, and I will do it while you watch, unable to prevent it from happening. I will protect the innocent witches from you and slaughter the others while you stand outside a barrier as you did before. I will kill the High Queen of Witches, and I will send you her skull to ease your need for revenge. Aurora will take the throne, and I will stand behind her to enforce her rule for a time until we've achieved peace. Once accomplished, I will vanish into the shadows and go somewhere that you, my family, or anyone else who sees me as nothing more than a weapon to wield against their enemies can use me. Maybe I'll find a man who will treat me well, and fall in love with someone who will love me back. I won't ever think of you again, King Karnavious." I laughed at the look of anger in his eyes. "Keeping me here doesn't change what happens outside your reach. The dominos are falling, and the witches are on the run, gathering together, making it much easier to destroy those I've marked for death." I smiled as his mouth opened, then snapped closed.

"Do you know who you are?" he asked, turning the minute glass over in his fingers.

"I'm Aria Primrose Hecate, Princess to the Throne of Hecate witch line and the Kingdom of Vãkya, the youngest daughter of Freya Hecate," I supplied softly without looking up at him.

"What game are you playing, Aria?" he countered, his hands gripping the edge of the table.

"None, as I told you, I'm done playing games."

Knox growled, lunging over the table to grab my arms. "Who the fuck are you, really? You're not some twenty-five old year witch, woman. You're entirely too powerful to be so young, and you play me so fucking well, *Hecate*."

I laughed coldly, holding his stare. "I am twenty-five years old. I was born in Haven Falls but conceived in the Nine Realms after my mother entertained kings inside her bedchamber for days in a drunken state of debauchery. I am not Hecate, asshole. I do not know who my father is, nor do I give a fuck to play your twisted games. I came here to clean my house and any others I find dirty. I am a witch, but I am also something else. I am not your mate, nor do I ever care to be yours again, King Karnavious. You have more fucking mood swings than anyone I have ever met."

"Why are the witches digging up my past and using you to make me question my wife and son now?"

"How would I know that? It's not like they're friendly before I take their fucking heads. If I were to guess, I'd say they're a little pissed off that you're murdering witches and feeding their magic into Norvalla, which in turn, fuels you and your people along with the witches you deem savable."

"Do you want to be a queen?" Knox watched me closely, studying the way my eyes narrowed at his question.

"No."

"Do you want to become my mate?" he asked, releasing my hands while I fixed the blankets.

"Absolutely never would I wish to be yours again. I don't want to be your mate or even in the same space with you anymore. I want someone who isn't bipolar or haunted by ghosts. Being your mate would be the worst mistake *any* woman could *ever* make. You won't let anyone love you because you're too broken. You might as well have lain down and died with your wife and son, Knox, because you're buried in their tomb, beneath the same dirt. That's rather sad since it's a waste of good dick." He flinched at my words laid bare to him, filled with truth pushing them down his throat. "Luckily, there's more dick in the Nine Realms, and I'll find it, eventually." I leaned over, smiling while holding his stare. "I'd rather fuck Lord Andres's dead cock than ever touch you again. How's that for some truth for you?" My smile turned bitter as the deadness in my stare held his.

"Where's your family hiding, Aria?" Knox asked through clenched teeth, and I shook my head.

"Don't do that," I warned, feeling the burning on the inside of my thigh. "Knox, don't."

"Where are they hiding?" he asked again as pain shot through me, jolting my body.

I cried out, grabbing my thigh. I looked at Knox with fear burning in my eyes. My teeth slid free, and I clamped them down on my tongue. I bit into it, but he moved with inhuman speed, prying my jaw open. Brander jumped forward, staring at the blood dripping from my mouth to dribble down my chin.

"Bloody fucking hell, Knox," Killian snapped, staring at the blood rushing from my mouth down my chin. "Too fucking far!" He removed his shirt, pushing it against my mouth as Knox continued preventing me from entirely removing my tongue.

"Help me hold her mouth open before she bites her tongue off," Knox ordered, continuing to hold my jaw open by force. "I release you from answering my question, woman," he growled, staring into my eyes. I gagged on the blood pooling in my mouth, rushing down my throat while I glared at him, choking on it. "Gods damn it, Aria."

"You found her breaking point, and you knew it. You knew she hadn't lied, and you pushed her further, Knox. She's been kidnapped, assaulted, and molested by no fault of her own. You should have stopped once you had your truth. Even you knew Liliana's scent was wrong when your beast refused to acknowledge her presence," Brander growled.

"I needed to know she spoke the truth! She could have been immune to the tonic," Knox argued, running his thumbs over my cheeks. "Now, I know she believed what she said."

Pain consumed my mind while Knox held my mouth open. Blood pooled into my ears and soaked my hair as everything muted around me. My eyes slid closed, and my body jerked, fighting to succumb to the exhaustion that wrapped around me.

"She wasn't lying, obviously. She believed what she had heard. You can't keep doing this, Knox. Look at her! She was willing to remove her fucking tongue to protect her family, and you knew she'd do something stupid to stop the words from coming out! She told you what she heard, and although none of us liked what she said, you should have accepted it," Killian snarled, purring low in his throat while he watched my eyes roll back in my head.

"Explain Sven's existence then, assholes," Knox hissed angrily. "We can only breed with our mate, and Liliana bore me a child. Sven was mine. Tell me he wasn't, Brander." His eyes filled with regret as I gagged, and he pulled me up, holding me against his chest.

Blood dripped onto the white blanket, soaking it and Knox's clothes. I fought to stay awake through the pain in my mouth and jaw as he continued holding it open. I could feel my tongue swelling, feel the blood sliding down my throat as he turned, staring down at me with a pained expression. My lashes fluttered against my cheeks as Knox held me against his warmth, releasing his scent to soothe me.

"If what Aria says is true, my wife was a ruse, planted in my life, and yet she bore me a son? No. Someone is wrong here, and it isn't me. Sven existed, and he was mine. He was my son, and I loved him more than I cared for anything else. He was my world."

"It's what she heard, but it doesn't make it correct, Knox. She told you what she thought was the truth. Aria told you that. You keep hurting her because you're hurt. She's right. It isn't fair. You can't want her and hold her at arm's length to protect yourself from the pain you feel over the dead. There are four of you in this relationship; two want one another, but the shells that house them are fighting tooth and nail to escape what is happening. Who the fuck do you think is going to win that fight? *Your* beast, because he is absolute power in the purest form, and she's a fucking newborn who doesn't even realize what she is yet," Killian growled as Knox loosened his hold, and I felt him staring down at me, burning my face with his ocean gaze.

"If they planted my wife, then it means Hecate and her witches dictated my entire life. Who had the vendetta against me? Hecate. We know Hecate forced the witches to murder my son and my wife, which is why I intend to end her line as she has done to mine. Why plant my wife into my life, intending to take her away?"

"You wouldn't have loved Liliana if you didn't feel she was your mate. Providing her scent ensured it would draw you to her. As for taking her away, Liliana left on her own, seeking death after losing Sven. If I had to guess, I don't think the witches planned that part. We're not made to love normal women, brother. We mate for eternity, so they have to be our perfect match in every way possible. We follow our mates into death, and you didn't. Why? Was Liliana your perfect mate, Knox?" Brander asked, his tone carefully controlled as both Knox and Killian rattled in warning.

"You ask me that now?" My attention focused on my pain, dismissing them, and their self-discovery session. I'd be lying if I said I wasn't listening, but my brain was shutting down. Exhaustion and pain was one hell of a combination. "Liliana gave me Sven," Knox growled.

"I didn't ask about Sven, Knox. I'm not the right-hand man to the king right now. I'm your fucking brother who loves you. The same brother who would give his life to protect yours," Brander explained, emotion causing his tone to grow thicker. "Did Liliana ever seem like your perfect mate, other than her scent? Did she do everything you needed as your mate? Or did you pull back and put distance between you and Liliana to protect her from your beast?"

"You know the answer to that."

"I *do* know that answer, but do *you*? Your perfect mate would go toe-to-toe with your beast. She wouldn't back down, and she would savage the fuck out of him in bed. She'd give you bare-bones and rip the heads off anyone who tried to hurt you. She'd be able to handle you in any form and be more than willing to take your beast when his need arose. Did Liliana do that?" Brander asked. Something smashed against the table, then Killian's scent exited the tent, and Brander exhaled slowly.

"She was my mate, end of fucking discussion. This is exactly what the witches want. They want us to question everything, to disorientate us and throw us off our course. Sew her damn tongue back on and put her into my bed when you're finished. I need a drink and time to think. My guess is this, Brander. Someone created Aria, who just happened to check all my fucking boxes. Suddenly, Liliana's name is brought up, and her image tainted amid me finding someone so utterly *fucking* perfect that I want her with everything within me. That's not a coincidence. That's a premeditated plan played against us flawlessly. Aria even carries my battle ravens on her flesh and couldn't discern that mine had joined with hers. My tattoos adorned her skin, and neither beast nor host felt them. That's impossible, and you know it. We'd have to be perfectly matched for her not to have felt them. She's too fucking flawless and everything I've ever wanted, which means she isn't real. She can't be my mate because that would mean I got fucking played from the beginning."

"Or Aria's your mate, and that is why she's perfect to you because she's flawed, Knox. The need to be around her isn't primal to the rest of us, and you're fighting that urge to claim her even now. The scent of her blood, the call of her womb, we felt it and have resisted it. You? You're in a war to defy those impulses, which we all are feeling the closer she gets to her time. Only one of us is fighting our beast to remain in control, and that's you, brother. Don't make Aria into your enemy because she's not wrong. She is very powerful. Whatever she is, they made her to rule this world."

Knox snorted, pushing the hair away from my face. His mouth lowered, brushing against my forehead softly. "Whatever she is, she is mine. That isn't changing, Brander."

"I know you don't want my advice, but here it is anyway. Marry Aria. Claim her as your Queen and claim her throne before she rises because when she does, and she will, well, the king takes the queen, and that is one rule within the Nine Realms that no one can argue. She's an unwed Hecate witch, and we both know what that means better than she does. Claim her, marry her, and then do whatever the fuck you want with her, but do it soon, brother. She's about to come into her power, and when she does, only the laws will prevent her from ending the world in her fury. We caused that fury. So don't let her fucking rise without a king at her side to harness her rage and protect the Nine Realms. If nothing else, you'll be ahead of damage control before it's a fucking problem."

I couldn't even blink at what he'd just stated. Brander was on the asshole list. Hell, they all were. I was going to eat their fucking faces and laugh while doing it! Bastards! Did they really think I'd marry Knox and allow that to happen? I would have to claim the throne, and the only way to challenge the high queen was to place a crown on my head and announce my intention to take it by force, which wasn't happening!

Knox brushed his fingers over my cheek before

his lips touched against my forehead again. I groaned, wanting to push him away but unable to even lift my arm. He swept the hair away from my face, lifting my lips to take in the damage, and Brander snorted as if shocked at how far I would go to protect my family.

That answer was very simple.

All the way.

I'd sell my soul to the devil himself to protect my family. Considering who held me and what he intended to do with me, I was pretty sure Knox was the devil incarnate, and I was his current chew toy. That was a disaster given the present conversation and the fact that he hadn't disavowed or argued with Brander this time.

Chapter Seven

Knox

I watched as Aria slipped from the tent, scanning her surroundings before moving to a tree and folding her body beneath it to sit. I fisted my hands at my sides, needing to offer comfort but knowing she wouldn't take it from me. I'd tried soothing her the last few nights when she'd awoken amidst a nightmare. Her sorrow-filled screams ripped me apart, but the moment I touched her, they'd only grown louder.

She ached and probably hated me, and I didn't fucking blame her. I couldn't stand myself either. Her words about my family had cut deeper than anything else had since discovering my wife's corpse on our bed. I'd lashed out, hurting her badly, needing to make her words stop, yet needing to hear the horrid lies whispered from her pretty lips, meant to rip me apart inside and out.

If I admitted Liliana wasn't my perfect mate, it

meant this war and everything I'd done had been for nothing. It suggested my entire life had been a lie, and the family I'd loved and mourned hadn't been mine. I couldn't believe that they weren't real. Sven was mine. I felt his loss to this day. His death had ripped me apart. Each of his thousand deaths had torn me open anew, ripping me to shreds while disease ravaged his tiny body in my arms as I held him.

Aria felt right, but her timing was too perfect. I'd gone to find the strongest Hecate witch, needing her magic to feed my land power. Instead, I'd found a woman that suited me to the fucking letter. I'd discovered the other half of my soul, with the wrong blood rushing through her veins. That felt more like design than a twist of fate. The gods would have to be some fucked up assholes to hand me a mate with the Hecate symbol embedded in her skull.

I'd been in Haven Falls to push the final plan into action, and Aria came back to town hours before I'd started the dominos falling in motion and couldn't be stopped. She'd been a hurricane of attitude and beauty that sucked the air from my lungs, leaving me gasping for fucking breath. Aria had changed my plans, and that shit never happened. I'd never altered my plans or stopped what I'd already begun, yet she'd given me pause from the first moment I'd clapped eyes on her.

My heart had fucking beat for the first time since being ripped out so long ago, and raven wings had taken flight within me. I'd been struck stupid by Aria's beauty, and her gorgeous eyes that glowed with defiance had hit me in the gut, hard. Aria made me *feel* again, and it wasn't easily shut down. The pain I could handle.

She made me feel overwhelming pain and need, and a wealth of emotions that tiny slip of a woman forced me to experience. I'd never wanted anyone as much as I wanted and craved her. That felt like a betrayal to my wife and mate. Wanting Aria created a deep-seated pain that I didn't know how to feel or acknowledge.

Finding Aria on her knees, wailing in fear, had fucking damn near killed me. I'd been unable to ignore her call, and she'd continued it after the threat had passed. Her eyes had been sightless, panic tearing her apart from the inside. Worse, I'd smelled that traitor's scent on her, and I'd wanted to mark her everywhere, again. I'd wanted to sink my teeth into the soft column of her throat and mark her so fucking deep that she'd always be mine.

I'd hesitated at marking the mangled flesh on her shoulder, needing not to cause her any more pain, but her hands went right for it, and I knew. I knew what was wrong. Her screaming wail was because my mark was fighting for dominance. She'd had a battle waging within her, one she hadn't even known was happening amongst the trauma she'd endured.

Two alphas marking the same female made them spiral out of control, sending their creatures into chaos they couldn't contain. Andres was the weaker alpha, and my mark was proving its dominance. If Andres's mark had remained, Aria would have gone insane. Aria was too young to understand, but she'd still held my mouth to her mutilated shoulder for me to remove his claim. She was choosing me, even though she wasn't even aware of what was happening to her. Aria's eyes hadn't regained focus for several moments afterward, and then she'd flung herself into my arms as if she'd given up on me coming to her rescue.

Tears had burned my eyes, and they'd felt strange there. I hadn't felt shit since I'd exited the tomb that held my family's corpses, not until coming face-to-face with Aria. But her words had held barb. Her whispered truth of what she had overheard had ripped holes deep into my soul, releasing the poison I'd held there. She'd turned everything inside out, and the only emotion I'd felt was rage. A red, hot rage that the woman I wanted and craved would throw the one I'd loved to the wolves, making me second guess my wife and son.

My fucking son!

If I admitted that Liliana had been all wrong and that she hadn't been mine, how had we created Sven? It couldn't be true, because I'd felt him. I'd held him in my arms and watched him open his eyes for the first time. I could remember peering at the perfect little pink form, and I'd felt my chest cracking open as he cried angrily at being displaced from his mother's womb.

"I healed Aria," Brander stated, standing beside me where I watched her from the shadows. "It wasn't as bad as we'd first thought, but I'm not so certain it is her physical injuries holding her tongue. Lord Andres assaulted her, and you just added salt into that seeping wound."

"I know what I fucking did. Imagine having your mate questioned and feeling relief that you are some coldhearted prick who felt that twinge. Aria's words made me feel liberated from the guilt of not feeling enough for Liliana. I loved her with everything I had, Brander, which turned out to be not enough." I pushed my hand through my hair before swallowing audibly. "I never slept with my wife next to me in my bed, yet I can't stand being away from Aria at night. I never craved my wife beneath me, but I am fucking addicted to the taste of Aria's lips against mine and her body close enough to hold. I feel her, brother. I feel that *witch* in my soul. I've never felt anything like her. And when I thought of Lord Andres touching her, smelling him on her? I lost my fucking shit, and that never happens to me. I didn't lose my shit when I placed our Queen into her tomb. I was cold, detached, and I allowed myself to become unfeeling. I hated her for dying and leaving me to the pain of Sven's loss alone. I cursed Liliana to death, and she fucking died."

"This isn't about you or Liliana, Knox. Look at Aria, and tell me what you see," Brander growled.

"I get it, asshole."

"No, I don't think you do. Killian said she fought hard to help them from being overtaken on that road. Even after they'd dragged her off, she continued fighting to protect Lore from poisonous arrows, not knowing that it wouldn't kill him. She told you the truth, and you didn't like it. You pushed her because you wanted her to hurt so that you hurt."

I snorted, watching Killian move closer.

"That makes you the biggest asshole here," Killian stated, peering across the camp to where Aria stared sightlessly at the ground. "If you don't marry her, I will."

"Excuse me?" I snapped, hating the tightness that filled my chest.

"Someone has to claim her before she rises. I

watched a queen fighting to protect her people on that road, Knox. Aria isn't some weak being that will stay down. She will get back up, and she will rise. I may not like it, and I may not like her, but what and who she is cannot be ignored anymore. We lost Aria, and yeah, we got her back. That only happened because she fucking fought them hard to get free, which allowed us time to get to her. Had it been her people, she'd be on their side of this war, and we wouldn't be having this conversation right now."

"Aria doesn't want to be my Queen. I don't blame her either. I was a shitty husband and mate to your sister."

"Yes, you were. Not because you didn't love your family, because you did. You were a shitty husband because witches waged war and pushed their agenda to keep you occupied and away from the kingdom. This isn't about love, though. It's about marrying a Hecate witch before she rises to her throne. We all know what Aria will become, and only one of us can marry her," Killian explained.

"You really think marrying Aria Hecate is a good idea? She is from the same blood that murdered my son and wife. The people of Norvalla would revolt if I placed Aria on Liliana's throne."

"Stop looking at it like that," Killian grumbled, folding his arms over his chest. "It isn't about you or her or anyone else for that matter. It's about two kingdoms, and who will control them. Aria will rise to be Queen of Vãkya. You are the King of Norvalla. Brander is right, claim her and be the first king ever to claim a Hecate witch."

"You think she is going to agree to marry me?" I

snorted in anger. I was already beyond frustrated with myself for hurting her more when I knew she was already in pain.

Aria was strong, but I'd pushed her hard. She'd pegged me deep with her truth, telling me I should have lain down and died with my wife and son, and maybe she was right. Perhaps I'd left my heart and soul behind in that fucking tomb, but Aria was forcing it back into me, and it hurt viscerally. She'd also said she'd rather fuck the man who almost raped her than me, and that fucking burned because, at that moment, it had been the absolute truth.

"I think Aria's hurting, and if left alone to fester, those wounds you inflicted will get deeper. You both aim for one another's hearts when you're hurt or forced to feel something you don't want to feel. You lied to her when you said she was only worth her scent, and we all knew it. *She* didn't. She thinks she's only worth her power and her scent now. So fucking fix it because only you can undo the wounds you inflicted onto that little woman's soul," Killian said, his eyes slowly sliding over Aria. "As I said, you don't claim her, I fucking will. Lore isn't the only one who wants one, asshole."

They were right, which I had no intention of admitting. Aria was born to be the Queen of Vākya. Forcing her into marriage wasn't something I planned to do, though. She deserved more than that. She'd been manhandled and abused since arriving in the Nine Realms.

I'd only added to her pain, and I hated that we went at one another hard and dug in deep. Unlike Aria, I knew it was my need to rip her down to her barest form to see what made her. I knew my creature wanted her soul exposed and bared naked to him because he tested her for mating.

The mating ritual was simple between creatures, but it wasn't easy on the shells that housed them. My creature was ripping Aria down to her barest form. He wanted to see her rage, see the flames dancing within her pretty eyes as she bathed in his chaos. I'd forgotten it, figuring no female would do something so crazy since our women had long ago lost the ability to breed or even feel their beast within them. It was as if they'd just lost them, and their creatures had gone dormant.

Aria's creature hadn't. Hers was in a heat cycle, fighting it and me. She was an anomaly. Things like us didn't fight against what occurred naturally. My creature sensed hers, and he was shredding her flesh to expose her soul to him. She was doing the same without even realizing it. They were goading one another through us, forcing spikes of anger to ignite to see how much the other could take.

"Bloody hell," I grunted, scrubbing my hands over my face.

"I'd say he's figured it out, Brander," Killian snorted.

Brander studied me, a sly smirk playing on his mouth. "From the look of panic and horror in his eyes, I'd have to agree."

"You fucking assholes knew?" I demanded.

"That your beast was baiting hers and creating hell for both of you? Some of us aren't thinking with our dicks, Knox. It's been a thousand years since we've been privy to creatures testing one another. I'd forgive yourself that one. It's been a while since we've had to think beyond our shells to consider a female's motives." Brander laughed, patting Killian on the back.

"Two alpha creatures going at one another to rip the other to shreds? You're in for one hell of a fight. That woman is fierce, and there's not a weak bone in her entire body. I don't envy you the battle, but I do the prize," Killian chuckled.

"You're both assholes." I turned toward the tree, finding Aria gone.

My stomach sank to the ground as I lifted my nose to the air, following her scent into the tent. I didn't need to see inside to know she'd be cuddled on the floor in the corner, the furthest she could get from me.

Aria had every right to be pissed. I'd been a heartless prick, but at least I knew why I'd flown off the rails. I growled inwardly, listening to my beast snicker. Asshole. He hadn't cared that Aria had been through hell because her creature should have reacted, taking control to turn off her host's mind from the assault. She hadn't, though, because she was young and knew that Aria was stronger because of the horrors she'd survived as a child.

Aria was strong, but she was also delicately made. Aria still believed in fantasies, holding the illusion of love on her fucking sleeve. She was this wide-eyed, beautiful creature that looked at the Nine Realms with hope burning within her when there was none here to be found. This place would crush her dreams, stomp her fucking heart into the ground, and ruin the beauty that shined from within her soul before she'd ever make a dent in this hellhole.

I'd protected Aria during her tour around the Nine Realms. I hadn't fought her battles for her, but at night, I'd kept the evil away so she could rest. I'd slit the throats of the monsters that had wanted to hurt her. Men had been drawn to her scent, even the subtleness of it as she hid the temptation with her magic. I'd murdered them for tracking my girl down, and she'd never even known they were there drooling over her. I didn't want her to get hurt, but I had needed to see how she worked, her strategy, and her plan to clean house.

I hadn't expected this slip of a girl to walk into castles and set them on fire from the inside. I hadn't anticipated her to be a fucking Trojan horse, using human tactics that this world hadn't seen before. I hadn't thought her pretty little ass would beat mine to castles and bring them to their knees without me. I assumed I'd arrive, save the day, and show Aria what it would be like to work together. Instead, Aria had waged battle alone, laughing and dancing while she decimated an entire keep like they were children, all while wearing a unicorn raincoat.

"If I were you, I'd get to fixing her before you lose her," Brander offered.

Killian smirked, his eyes sparkling with mirth. "Or don't, because some of us want her for ourselves. You were right. Up close, she's intoxicatingly delicious. I went into battle with the worst case of blue balls. Watching that battle queen fighting beside me only made it worse."

"Maybe next time, focus on the fucking road and avoid the trap, asshole," I snarled.

"Easy enough for you to say," Killian laughed soundlessly. "I had a woman against me who couldn't sit still. Her need for you enhanced her sweet scent, and fuck if I didn't want to divert with her and make her scream as you do. The thing is, she wanted you, asshole. She issued an alpha challenge before we ever left camp," he snorted, and I swallowed hard, knowing it had to have played hell on them.

"Bloody hell," I snorted, Brander echoing my statement.

"She issued the challenge to Lord Andres, but it was wide open for any male close enough to hear. Aria didn't understand the rattle that escaped or why she'd made it, other than to assume she was backing us up. She's lucky we got there in time. Andres would have hurt her to assert dominance. Aria is an alpha, and whatever the fuck is slumbering within that girl is a fucking killer. It's too young, though, which is dangerous."

Killian was right. Once a challenge was issued, it couldn't be taken back. Aria wouldn't have known that. Killian had to have gone through hell to ignore that call. I patted him on the back as he chuckled, shaking his head.

"Go fix the damage, Knox. Aria gets enough hate from me, and maybe Greer is right. Maybe you don't deserve her, and she's better than all of us. She didn't deserve last night, though. That's on us for being so fucking twisted and jaded that we can't see past the hate we breathe."

Chapter Eight

Soraya

I had watched Aria all day, noting the pale color of her face while her eyes remained on the ground. Ilsa had failed to end her life, but whatever had happened, it hadn't been good. She looked lost, broken, and worse, hopeless. My stomach had tightened seeing the men leave the tent covered in her blood after screaming had erupted from inside.

Ilsa was going to be pissed that she'd failed in her plan to eradicate Aria Hecate from the Nine Realms. Siobhan had crafted a truth potion for the King of Norvalla, but she'd placed something else into it as well. I'd watched her in the tent with the king aimlessly pacing around, his anger palpable. I'd felt worried for Aria, noting that his hands had balled into fists.

The king's fingers pushed through his tawny-colored hair, eyes sharp and focused as they scanned over me like I wasn't a threat. His brand now marred my wrist, marking me as a slave and owned by him. I hated him for it, but was also impressed that no one had mistreated me since arriving. I'd witnessed others of our kind as slaves before, using us for whatever they could imagine. To them, we weren't even living beings anymore, just a commodity.

One owner had lined the witches up, taking a turn with each one to breed the evil out of us. Another had cut off fingers for slights, and when he ran out of those, he took other parts of them. Some claimed witches, slaughtering them for fun. One had found me on an errand run, tying me to the tree, using knives to hold my body still while he shoved into me brutally. I'd slit his throat on my way out, cutting off his flaccid cock, shoving the thing into his mouth as a warning to anyone who thought to use me again.

"What are you doing, Soraya?" Siobhan asked, and I straightened, hiking a thumb to where Aria sat in the same spot she had for the last couple of days.

"That's a legendary witch who looks pretty pathetic if you ask me." I wished Esme could see her savior now, broken, mentally detached from the living, and pathetic as fuck.

"I'd hold your tongue and not let anyone else hear you speak of her," Siobhan warned.

I snorted, watching as the men moved around Aria. They monitored her closely. Even the king himself seemed opposed to letting her out of his sight. He was always someplace where he could visually see her and know what she was doing. It was pitiful in the grand scheme of things since he was renowned for sleeping with a witch once and leaving her bed afterward. Frowning, I watched the children gravitating toward Aria as if drawn to her.

Her silver hair was unique and pretty, even though it was an odd color for a witch to have. Wide, turquoise eyes framed with thick black lashes dusted her cheeks. She was petite, and while lithe and small, she had a look in her eyes that spoke of fire, or had. Now it actually hurt to look at the pain in her eyes.

It was a pain I knew intimately. I had learned to turn it off, to put Julia and her needs before my own. I'd spent the last couple of years forcing my emotions to a deadened state. I didn't allow fear to slip from me, knowing exactly how to respond to Ilsa on cue. I'd trained for battle, learned to creep up on a powerful enemy, striking hard and fast.

Learning to survive hadn't been a simple thing, but it was the only option left to me. I shivered at the memories, dismissing the dismal state of the witch. Siobhan opened her mouth to speak but straightened at something behind me. Turning to see what had drawn her attention, my mouth opened at the dark-haired male with sapphire eyes that slid over me before moving back to Siobhan.

"I need a favor, Siobhan," the male stated, his voice sliding over me like honey melting on warmed bread.

His voice was a sexy, deep, rich baritone that slithered through every nerve ending, firing them up. I stepped back, trying to break whatever spell had entered my system with his nearness. The male's eyes moved to me again, noting the way I'd tensed. My body heated beneath the stare, forcing my legs to clench with anticipation.

What the hell was happening? I didn't like men. They wanted one thing, and they took it brutally, uncaring what happened to us afterward. How many bastard babes had these assholes left in their wake while marching across the Nine Realms? It numbered in the hundreds of thousands like it was their right to breed us out of existence now that Hecate was gone.

"How can I assist you, Brander?" Siobhan asked, her tone sultry and filled with lust.

His chuckle sent gooseflesh rushing over my skin, and I swallowed at the sound of it. "Aria hasn't bounced back," he stated, and I perked up at his interest. "I wanted to see if maybe you could reach her."

"Why would I try to reach a Hecate bloodline witch? I am beneath her," Siobhan returned, pushing her dark hair behind her ear.

"You're a woman who knows the pain of being assaulted. It isn't about her heritage. She's not from the Nine Realms and doesn't care about shit like stature or bloodlines. She's hurting, and I fear our part in it won't allow us to change that for her."

I swallowed at the words Brander said. A witch who didn't judge someone based on bloodlines? *Right.* I could see it if Aria didn't have the royal blood pumping through her veins to her heartless chest.

Her name made her royalty, with or without the magic to back it up. I'd seen her fight and take the element from the Keeper of Lightning. She was one of the promised witches, the one that should have been here to protect the witches from turning dark.

"You think she'll talk to me?" Siobhan scoffed,

crossing her slender arms over her ample breasts. "I am a camp follower, which is one step up from being a whore. I make tonics and serve her enemy. She's very aware of my stature here, Brander."

"Aria differs from what you assume. Could you try?" he pleaded, his eyes filling with hope.

"Fine, but when she spits in my face or kicks my ass like she did Bekkah's, you will be the one doing the suturing."

"I'll use butterfly fingers to fix your beautiful face." I watched him, narrowing my eyes at his smooth play on words. Siobhan blushed, and I barely contained the snort that threatened to leave my lips.

"Come, Soraya. You've been through hell, correct?" Siobhan asked, and I turned from the mesmerizing sapphire eyes to look at her. "You're entirely too gorgeous to have made it this long without being forced into sex."

My throat bobbed, and I dropped my eyes beneath Brander's curious gaze. I nodded, and Siobhan unfolded her arms. Shame burned in my eyes as I lifted them to hers before glancing at Brander to find him studying me, pain tightening in my chest.

"Do you want the fucking details?" I snapped, watching Siobhan's eyes narrow. At her nod, I recanted my time on my back, servicing beasts that had brutalized me. I'd barely survived, and by the time I finished my tale, both of them looked at me with pitying eyes that I wanted to scratch from their sockets. "Is that enough abuse to fit in, Siobhan? Or do you want more details about the time they raped and mutilated me beside the road because I wasn't fast enough to escape my attackers?"

Siobhan swallowed with tears swimming in her eyes before shaking her head, peering up at the cerulean blue sky. Her throat bobbed before she lowered her gaze, locking with mine once more. I shoved the emotion away while she watched, uncaring that the king's brother noted my reaction.

"Then you can assist me in trying to bring back Princess Hecate." Siobhan shoved her trauma down as we both glanced at Aria, who had risen from the ground and was staring at the people brought into camp. "Come, she's flighty as shit right now."

I didn't speak as we moved toward her, watching as Aria's wide, turquoise eyes swung to us before we'd even gotten close to her. Even with the trauma fresh, she was sharp and defensive, alert of threats. Her gaze narrowed, moving between us as if she expected an attack. Her hands balled into tight fists at her sides, and I swallowed, pausing at a safe distance from her.

"It is my understanding that you could use some female companionship," Siobhan offered lamely.

Aria didn't speak, sliding her stare between us. She turned to where Brander stood with the king and another man. Her throat moved, but she stayed silent. Her attention focused on me, and I paused, frozen in place at the golden flecks that seemed to float in her eyes.

"It's okay to feel angry or even ashamed that it happened at all," Siobhan continued. "It isn't your fault or anything like that."

"It's okay to want the mother-fucking slime-ball dead," I stated, watching the full force of her attention swing to me again. There was power in her stare, and it gave me pause. It was like standing in front of raw, unchecked power that leaked from her eyes to hold mine, locking me in place. Something within her was studying me, and it caused my heart to jackhammer against my chest. "Anger is good; rage is healthy. I screamed when I escaped. I screamed until my voice was raw, and the pain was gone."

"Yes, that's good. Let's scream," Siobhan offered.

Siobhan screamed, but it was weak. Aria's eyes swung from her to me, and I opened my mouth as a squeak escaped. Aria snorted, opening her mouth, releasing a horrifying scream that ripped from her throat. Flames erupted, forcing us to jerk back as everything around her caught fire. Her agony-filled scream changed to rage, and then raw, unchecked anger that had me gasping as I stepped further away, opening and closing my mouth as she fucking *burned*.

Aria didn't stop, not even when the entire camp stood staring at her in open shock. She tightened her hands at her side and bent over. Her scream grew in force until it changed to the rattle for which the King of Norvalla was known. My body trembled along with Aria's, watching as the flames licked her flesh, and I waited for her skin to melt from her bones.

It didn't happen. Instead, the moment Aria righted her body, the flames sucked back into her mouth and nose, and she tilted her head, staring at our horrified faces.

"It didn't help," Aria admitted, her eyes deadening before she turned away from us. She walked back to her tent with her blackened clothes flaking off, uncaring as she slipped inside.

"What the fuck just happened?" I asked.

"She houses flames? Witches don't carry flames," Siobhan whispered through trembling lips. "What the fuck is she?"

"What the fuck did you two say to her?" The king demanded, moving angrily toward us.

His tone brokered death, and I hit my knees, bowing my head while my entire body shuddered from what I had just seen. Siobhan didn't bend, standing there to face the king. A hand brushed my shoulder, sending sparks jumping into my soul as I turned, peering up into Brander's eyes.

"Up, witch," he stated softly.

He helped me to my feet, ignoring the way my body shivered with fear. Witches feared flames and burning alive since it was the method the lords used to torture us. Aria had literally burst into flames, and yet she hadn't had a single mark on her skin.

"We suggested she scream to release the anger she felt," Siobhan offered, crossing her arms over her fringed shirt, scorched from Aria's fire.

They didn't seem worried about the fact that a Hecate witch had just burst into flames and remained untouched by them. In fact, they looked more perturbed that we'd upset her. My eyes swung to the tent, watching Aria exit in a silver dress that left her arms bared. The entire camp watched her uneasily while she moved to the table that had drinks placed upon it.

"Witches do not wield fire, ever," I stated, fighting my ragged breathing that I couldn't seem to turn off.

The king's eyes slid to me slowly, roaming over my face with disinterest. His attention swung to Aria, watching as she lifted a cask of amber liquid and held it to her nose, tipping it up and downing it in one drink. Her eyes closed as she ingested it all, smiling as she got the last drop.

The king walked toward Aria, but her eyes slid to the ground, and a frown tugged at her mouth as she walked past him. She shrunk away from his touch when he reached out for her, ignoring him as he called her name.

She may have been wounded, but she wasn't broken. She was filled with rage and pain that had finally exploded. I looked down at the sear marks on my arms and shirt. I lifted my arm to touch the burn, but Brander grabbed it, avoiding the damaged area.

"Come, I have cream the witches made to treat burns. I will take care of you. I didn't catch your name."

"Soraya. And you're the Prince. You need not tend to me. The witches will," I swallowed, lowering my eyes from the intensity of his stare.

"I insist, Soraya. You can also explain to me how you ended up here. You are from the city outside of Vākya, and there have been no reports of witches surviving Ilsa's service from that area. In fact, there's been no word of anyone or anything escaping the queen's territory in months."

"I said I escaped, but not when. I escaped years ago," I swallowed, noting the way Brander searched my face. "My family wasn't so lucky. I've not looked for others, wanting to hide the shame of what I endured." I lowered my eyes, swallowing tightly. It wasn't a lie.

I didn't look for people because the only other life that mattered to me was still in service to the queen. "I wasn't proud that they captured me and allowed monsters to use me. I have not told many my story, as it brings no honor to have been raped by creatures that weren't compatible with my anatomy." Tears swam in my eyes as I lifted them to his. I turned, staring at where Aria stood directly behind me, glaring at Brander.

She didn't speak or move, but the look in Aria's eyes condemned Brander for forcing me to tell my story. She smiled, placing her hand on my shoulder as she exhaled slowly. Siobhan stepped closer, her eyes taking in Aria with curiosity while I stood frozen to the spot.

Brander cleared his throat, and Aria stepped closer to me, slipping her hand into mine while she pulled me with her toward the largest tent in the middle of the camp. I followed her with unease rushing through me; as if she felt it, her eyes found mine. She turned, smirking before she shook her head. I felt nervous and something else, something strange from her touch that caused my stomach to somersault.

At the front of the tent, Aria turned, blocking Brander's entrance as Siobhan paused as Aria stood her ground. Brander stepped back, bumping into the king, who observed what was unfolding.

Aria rattled, and I swallowed hard as the men nodded, stepping back. No one else was inside the medical tent, and from the look of it, Aria didn't intend to let them in either. She let the flaps close and turned, slowly looking around the area until she spotted the tonics, and I followed her.

"You're a phoenix, aren't you?" I asked, unable to

keep the awe out of my tone. She turned, smirking at me as she shook her head. "Can you speak?" Aria lifted her finger to her lips, her eyes sparkling as she pointed to the front of the tent, then her ear.

I smiled awkwardly, watching her grab for the tonic to open it, tending to my arm while Siobhan stood in shock. I tried to stop Aria, but her eyes lifted, and I saw the pain in them if only a glimmer. Her fingers slid over my burns, and I gasped as pain shot through my charred flesh.

"I'm sorry. I didn't mean to hurt you," Aria whispered, barely above a breath.

"You're the Princess, and I am a peasant," I announced.

"And?" she shocked both Siobhan and me into silence. "I am Aria, and no matter what blood runs through my veins, we're all in the same boat, just trying to survive. There are better chances in greater numbers, are there not?" Aria laughed, and I swallowed hard. "Wish I were the peasant, and you the princess." She tended my wounds as if I wasn't at the bottom of the food chain and her atop it.

Aria had meant what she'd said, which shocked me. She was royalty, one of only a few who carried Hecate's magic within her veins. Aria held immense power, and yet there was a humility within her that floored me. She wasn't what I'd thought she would be. She was... humble.

"Did I burn you too?" Aria asked, sliding her attention to Siobhan.

"No, My Princess," Siobhan uttered, her eyes wide

with confusion. "I thought all Hecate witches were vain, hostile bitches who didn't bother themselves with peasants or those beneath them?"

"You were told what to think and how to act in our presence. I was taught to be above you and rule with coldness. I choose not to be that cold-hearted, uncaring bitch they told me to become. Life is entirely too short to be an asshole, is it not?"

Siobhan laughed, her hands moving to touch Aria's face. She jerked back, and Siobhan's hands dropped. Aria exhaled slowly, holding her hand out to accept Siobhan's, but they trembled. It scared Aria to touch her or to be touched. I watched in silence as she allowed Siobhan to place her hand into hers before covering it with her other.

"Blessed be," Aria whispered, yanking her hands back.

"Blessed be, Princess Aria." Siobhan shook. Her eyes were wide with shock from Aria's touch. Had she felt what I had when I touched her?

"Just Aria," she insisted. "I don't want to be a princess. It sounds entitled, and I'm just a girl trying to survive, like you."

"But you're a Hecate witch," I pointed out.

"I am. But I am one held by her enemy, and nothing more than his slave. I am powerless and trapped, just like you. The only difference is I don't plan to stay trapped or remain his prisoner."

"He can hear you," I whispered.

"I'm aware, and I honestly can't be bothered to give

a fuck. He broke the last one I had to offer him. Is your arm better?" Aria's eyes held mine, which sent hope shooting through me; deadly, dangerous hope that Aria was everything Esme had said she would be.

"Yes, thank you," I said, noting the tears swimming in her eyes. "I am sorry that you were hurt and assaulted."

"Others have endured a lot more than I have. I will survive because it's not within me to accept defeat. It was very nice meeting you, but in the future, I think I'll stick to my silence instead of my screams," Aria said with a wicked smile lifting her mouth. "My silence is entirely more dangerous. I am a witch, but I am also a monster." Aria backed up, turning as she left the tent, leaving us both dumbfounded by her words.

"She's not right, is she? I mean, Aria Hecate just tended your wounds. Hecate witches are notoriously snobbish and aloof to our kind. She seemed…"

I nodded slowly. "Aria seemed unreal and calm. She isn't broken, meek, or wounded. She's calm and collected, terrifyingly so. Did you see her eyes when she stopped screaming? They were almost lifeless, and then flames danced within them. If she is a phoenix, she could set the Nine Realms on fire and force the darkness into the shadows. She could kill Ilsa. Aria Hecate is powerful enough to kill the High Queen of Witches and take her throne."

"She could kill everyone," Siobhan whispered, threading her fingers through mine, forcing my eyes to where she held my hand.

Esme was right. Aria was different. She was a lot scarier than Ilsa because Aria held something within her, and I felt the need to stand beside her. I'd felt a peace in her presence that had left me uncertain how to respond to her. It was like standing next to a storm you knew could let loose turbulence and chaos, yet you still *needed* to stand beside it.

"Aria's the High Queen of Witches. That girl is our Queen, and she doesn't even fucking know it," I whispered low enough that the sound hardly registered.

"Neither do they because they cannot feel what we do. Hold your tongue and don't repeat it because we place our rightful queen in danger if we do. I felt peace for the first time in my life when she touched me."

I nodded, fighting the thickening in my throat. "I felt it too when she tended me. I've felt nothing like it before. I don't know if I want to scream or cry that she is in the hands of our enemies and so calm about it. Aria literally screamed and burst into flames, and they didn't bat an eye when she was on fire. Then, because that wasn't crazy enough, she sucked the flames back into her body."

"Her soul. If she's a phoenix, it went back into her soul."

I blinked, turning to look at Siobhan as we stood in silence. The tent flaps moved, and we slowly stepped away from one another, turning to place the salves and things back where they went. Turning, we saw Brander coming toward us with Killian at his side.

"What you saw tonight doesn't leave camp. If either of you tries to leave, you die. Nod and tell me you understand," Killian stated, his eyes on me.

"I understand, My Lord," I swallowed, nodding.

"Good, now go," he growled, turning to look at Brander while we slipped out of the tent.

I rushed beside Siobhan back to the herb tent, sliding inside as the warning echoed through me. They knew what she was, and they intended to unleash her upon the witches, which meant my baby sister was directly in their path. Julia was ten times more powerful than I was, and she was Ilsa's current slave, continually supplying her power. Their target was Ilsa, which meant I had to get my sister out of that palace before they reached it.

Chapter Nine

Aria

For days I'd avoided speaking with Knox. I needed the space from him to clear my head because my psyche's pain had been debilitating. I'd spent hours going over facts and working through reasoning, such as Knox knowing how to ferret out my family but hadn't used it until I'd forced him to question everything about his life with Liliana.

At any time, he could have forced me to tell him where my aunt and sisters were hiding, but he hadn't. He could have hurt me, and even though he'd held me underneath the water, he'd refrained from causing me pain. Yes, we went at one another hard and fast, and we tore into each other deeply. I was starting to believe it was more to do with what we were and what we carried within us that made us battle one another.

Over the few days that I'd avoided him, I'd felt my anger spike without reason. I'd wanted to rip into Knox's skin, digging into his heart to sink my claws, and there'd been nothing to set me off to induce such a feeling. It had been instinctive, the need to force myself beneath his skin, flesh him out, and see what made him tick.

Instead, I'd spent the day in the tent in pain. I'd slipped into my head, speaking with my creature. She was keen on talking about how we could torture Knox, slowly peeling the skin from his body to eviscerate him from our system through painful techniques.

Knox was trying to get me out of my head, initiating conversations that ended one-sided. He'd brought me fruit and whiskey, spending several hours silently waiting for me to speak, but I refused. I was exhausted, mentally and physically, and Knox continued to add to it. Any chance he got to strike out at me, he took it.

Knox entered the tent, and I paused, turning my downcast eyes away from where he stood. My body tensed as he moved to the table, sitting in front of me. His fingers drummed on the wood top while he sat back, relaxing as I glanced at him from beneath my lashes.

"How long do you intend to pretend you can't speak, Aria?" He sat forward, clasping his hands in front of him on the table. "Brander said the damage to your tongue wasn't extensive. He also said that it didn't interfere with your ability to speak."

I turned, staring at the front of the tent, wondering if I could escape him or if he'd try to prevent me from leaving. Knox had given me space, which I'd appreciated. Today, however, he'd apparently decided I'd had enough time to heal in silence. Swallowing past the tightening in my throat, I ignored him and the rapidly increasing beat of my heart.

At night, when I'd chosen the floor over the bed, he'd allowed it until I'd fallen asleep, then he'd pick me up and tuck my body against his. The first couple of days, I'd fought against his hold until I'd realized it was futile to try escaping him. His arms would wrap around me, trapping me against his steel-like grip. I hated he offered comfort, and my body craved it from him.

Knox swore under his breath, slamming his hands on the table, causing me to jump. My eyes swung to his, watching his lips tugging down into a frown at my reaction. Standing, he paced in the small tent, exhaling as he set his hands on his narrow hips.

"I shouldn't have mistreated you. I know that now. I reacted poorly when you brought up Liliana and acted worse when you forced her memory into question." His eyes slid over my face, trying to read my expression, but there was nothing for him to read. I'd mastered schooling my features around Knox since he'd hurt me deeply, visualizing mortar around my skin to save it since I was still soft when I needed to be hard.

Knox strode closer, kneeling in front of me, forcing me to back up in the chair, away from him. He slowly released the breath he'd held and scrubbed his hand down his face. Knox radiated regret, but I didn't care. He'd told me my worth and had cut me deeply.

"Killian was bringing you to me when the witches captured you. I'd passed villages filled with mangled, mutilated corpses on my way to Steely Keep. I found Lord Andres's entire army dead, without a single wound upon their bodies. Witches and warriors alike had appeared to drop dead without cause. Good men died without being given a chance to die in battle, Aria. I found Killian on the road. He was still sending wounded men back to camp. Finding you gone made me question if you were a part of what had happened. Then we heard your rattled cries, and everything within me snapped. I lost control to get to you, woman," Knox grunted, looking away as he stood, slowly moving back to his seat.

Silently, he poured two glasses of whiskey and pushed one toward me. I ignored it, looking anywhere but at him. My breasts rose and fell with my breathing while he studied me. His heated gaze scorched the side of my face while I refused to speak.

"You assumed this world was black and white, but it's not. You thought I would take your word when I have no reason to do so? You spoke of my wife, trying to make me question everything that had happened over the past five hundred years, Aria. What you heard was what they wanted you to hear because the other option wasn't possible. Liliana was my mate and my only love. She gave me my son, Sven. So whatever the witches were trying to do through you, it won't work." He lifted his cup, sipping the whiskey before leaning closer.

His hand moved to touch mine, and I yanked them away. I forced my chair back until the chill of the morning, covering the side of the tent, touched my skin. Knox chuckled, shaking his head, and released a shuddered breath before he pulled his hand back, studying me.

"I'm sorry, Aria."

Tears swam in my vision, but I refused to allow them to fall. He was *sorry?* Sorry for what? For telling me he only wanted to *use* my body? For trying to *drown* me in the bathtub filled with dirty water? Or accusing me of being such a *monstrous* bitch that I'd use his dead wife against him like some blackmailing whore?

"You should drink the whiskey to stay warm. It's cold out today, and we're going to be moving camp again. It will warm you against the chill in the air," he stated, pushing it closer.

My eyes continued to stare at the tent flap, wishing I could escape through it. I knew if I so much as inched toward it, Knox would stop me. I almost craved the cage that only held enough room for one prisoner to fit. Knox lunged, grabbing my hand, staring at me while I pulled on it.

"Let me go," I whispered so softly that it was barely audible.

"Never," he swallowed, searching my face.

"Let me go now!" I screamed vehemently, and he did, releasing me as tears rolled from my eyes. "Do not touch me again," I warned with venom and barbs coating the words.

"So you can speak," he snorted, sitting back down. "You've just chosen not to speak to me?"

"I have one use, King Karnavious. You don't need my words to use my body," I hissed, sitting back down as his mouth fell open and then snapped closed again.

"Aria," he whispered, dropping his head, then sniffed, lifting his eyes to the blood that seeped from my shoulder. "You're wounded."

I didn't answer him. I didn't even look in his direction. He'd forced me to move, jarring the injury to my shoulder. He stood, walking to the front of the tent, speaking to someone in his language before returning to sit in his chair. His gaze slid to the blood dripping down my arm, the wound's sting creating a pulse in my shoulder.

Brander entered the tent, placing his medical bag on the table before hunching down in front of me, looking at my face. Sapphire eyes slid to the shoulder of my white dress, now a bright crimson.

"I'm going to need to look at your shoulder." Brander watched as my head nodded with permission.

Brander stood, moving around behind me, and slowly pushed the dress aside to reveal the scabbed injury. He hissed, finding the flesh mangled.

"Your shoulder had healed," he pointed out, and Knox rattled low in his throat, seeing what had happened. "It looks as if blades removed the skin."

"What the hell did you do, Aria?" Knox demanded angrily.

"I removed your mark because it offended me," I admitted in a deadpan tone.

"It doesn't work like that," Brander grunted, shocked at what I had done to myself. "You'd have had to cut the flesh to the bone—which is why it hasn't healed yet," he admitted. "Bloody hell, Aria."

"You can't just remove a mark. It doesn't work like that," Knox growled, his eyes boring a hole into the side of my head.

"Apparently, you can. If the mark was ill-placed or it offended both parties. It's removable so long as you rid your body of the marked flesh."

"My mark upon your skin did not offend me,

woman."

I stared at the daylight pouring in from outside the tent. My heart thundered in my chest as I refused to respond. Knox didn't merit a reply since it hadn't been about him. Brander touched the raw, bleeding flesh, and I didn't react to the pain.

"Who was offended by the mark on your shoulder, Aria?" Brander asked.

"My creature and I decided it was vile, and we detested it marring our flesh. King Karnavious placed it there under false pretenses; therefore, we removed it. Mistakes happen, and while at the time it seemed right to allow the king's mark, it wasn't, and so we amended our mistake."

"You cut your shoulder to the bone to remove Knox's mark?" Horror that he couldn't hide etched Brander's tone. "Tell me you didn't do this, woman."

"I did." I nodded to the place in the dirt where I'd hidden the skin and tissue that would have alerted Knox to what I had done if we'd stayed here.

Knox walked over to the dirt, kneeling to brush it aside, exhaling when he found several chunks of my tissue. He swore under his breath, turning to look at me with an expression that screamed anger and betrayal.

"Why would you do something like that?" Brander demanded.

"Because it felt vile, and I detested it as much as Lord Andres's mark on my body," I stated, standing. "Am I to ride in my cage, or shall I find where the trash belongs?" I asked, my voice as dead as I felt while I stared at Knox with no emotion exposed.

"You're not trash, Aria," Brander whispered before his angry eyes slipped to Knox, who hadn't spoken since I'd told him he was no better than Lord Andres.

"No, that's right. I'm just a prisoner who is only wanted for what lies between her thighs and the power she holds. I'll be in my cage if you need my vagina or magic, Master," I laughed soundlessly, fixing the shoulder of my dress. I slipped from the tent, finding Lore, Greer, and Killian all watching me warily.

"Aria?" Lore called, but I ignored him as I walked to the cage, secured and magically enhanced to hold me.

Greer called to my back, but I didn't care anymore. While relief that they'd both survived rushed through me, I didn't respond to either. I'd been put through hell and was exhausted. None of them cared about me, only about what I could do for their side of this war. To them, I was a weapon to be wielded and used at their leisure. To Knox, I was someone to warm his bed when he desired it and a whipping post when he needed that, too.

I opened the cage, smiling at Siobhan and Soraya. Both women watched with unease and worried expressions as they took in the fresh blood soaking my dress. I pulled the cage door closed until it clicked, lifting the blanket from the floor to wrap around my body. I glanced up, finding the men staring at me from outside the tent before I covered my head and closed my eyes, getting comfortable for the ride.

Eventually, we started moving, and hours went by before I'd woken and peeked out from the blanket, finding Knox riding beside the cage. Turning away from him, I sat up to look at the countryside that we traveled through. I could feel his stare burning into my back. His anger pulsated through me, and yet I didn't care. I was too damn exhausted to worry or think about him anymore.

I understood that what I'd overheard forced him to look at painful things, but that wasn't my fault. If what Lord Andres and Kristal said was true, someone had planted a witch in his home, disguised as his perfect mate, forcing Knox to fall in love with her.

The deceit and horror he had to have felt as the words left my lips, well, it probably undid him. Hell, I'd have argued about it and lashed out if I were Knox. Not to mention, he was waging war because of those events, and he'd have to accept that his entire marriage was a lie. His wife, a tool used to get to him, but that wasn't something he wanted to face, and I didn't blame him. Who wanted to admit their enemies had schemed and planned his entire life for their benefit?

Knox had lashed out to protect what little remained of his heart. But I'd been kidnapped, hurt, and molested, and he'd still assumed the witches had planted me to make him change his mind about this war. Those facts alone made me want to rip his heart out because you'd have to be one heartless bitch to use something like that against another person.

Knox had struck violently with words, and they'd cut me deeper than him trying to drown me in a shallow fucking tub full of bathwater. His words held barbs, ones that he'd embedded in my heart.

We went hard against one another; that much was a given. I could take the blows. I could take Knox's taunts and his physical strength, but he'd wrapped his hand around my heart with his words and ripped it out of my chest.

After all that I'd been through, he'd added salt to the wound. He'd rubbed it in until it burned so acerbically that I couldn't get the granules out of my skin. I felt terrible that Knox had to lash out in that manner, and then I felt like an idiot for feeling sorry for him.

Knox was questioning everything. It sucked to be him, but it wasn't *my* doing, and who knew if it was even true?

Witches were masters of manipulation; that much was a known fact. I didn't blame Knox for being angry or even accusing me of playing with his mind. I'd probably do the same thing in his situation had he told me the love of my life was planted and wasn't real.

"We will stop here to water the horses and rest for a few hours," Knox announced, turning to stare at me as I peered out over the landscape. "Get Aria out of the cage, and bring her to me," he ordered, dismounting his horse while a young kid grabbed the reins.

Brander opened the cage, and I slipped out, following Knox as he walked toward a wooded area. My heart thundered in my chest, slowing when he vanished between the trees. I could feel his men behind me as we entered the forest. Knox didn't stop walking until the sound of the army had diminished, and silence filled my ears.

He stopped, and I paused as our eyes locked. My chest rose and fell with apprehension at the look burning in his gaze. Knox slowly closed the distance between us, lifting his hand for mine. I stepped back, but he moved faster than I could predict. His hands wrapped around me, holding me in place as my creature stirred within me.

His soft purr sounded, and I blinked slowly. I did everything I could to ignore the pull to echo his sound. Knox's mouth curved into a smile. He stepped closer, brushing his lips against my ear, purring louder. His hand slid to the back of my neck, and his lips brushed against my throat, his mouth sucking at the racing pulse.

"You are strong, Aria, but not strong enough to ignore what you are." Knox held my shaking body, and my creature gazed at him with resolve while reinforcing my ability to ignore his noises.

"You're touching me again," I hissed icily, my tone cold and filled with loathing.

Knox laughed soundlessly, pulling my body against his heat. My softness sank against his hard edges, and he inhaled deeply, knowing my body prepared for him. It wasn't something we controlled, which I'd discovered while lying beside him on one of the many nights I'd tried to forget he existed. I closed my eyes as his volume rose, and his tongue danced over my pulse.

I could feel the others watching us. The heat of their stares burned my flesh while they took in Knox, trying to make me respond to his seductive purring. I opened my eyes, finding obsidian orbs with ember flecks staring back at me. My creature peered out, her sultry purr exploding from my lips while Knox's mouth tipped up at the corners.

It was as if our creatures were taking in one another,

learning each other even though Knox and I held control. My spine arched, melding against his steel as he lowered his teeth to scrape against my throat. My creature shook herself, detangling us from the spell they were creating while pulling us into the allure of their temptation.

He rattled low, and I fought to control my response. Knox watched me, his fingers slowly moving over my bare arms with the precision of a surgeon's butterfly fingers. I wanted to step back, but his eyes held me prisoner while his rattle grew in volume.

My stomach clenched, and my legs grew weak. Heat unfurled in my chest, gradually wrapping itself around my womb, begging to be filled. Knox's scent was intoxicating and addictively enticing. My nipples hardened with the need for his mouth to taste them. My body released its pheromones without permission, seeking to prove I was ready for him.

"There she is," Knox chuckled, lifting his hands to run his thumbs over my cheeks while peering into my unguarded soul.

I jerked back, causing his creature to rattle loudly, forcing me to my knees as a gasp of shock exploded from my lungs. His dominance was absolute, forcing my spine to bow as my ass lifted for him. My teeth ground painfully together to hold the urgent purr into my lungs. Knox kneeled, lifting my chin with his finger while his creature took in my submission.

Knox stood and walked around my prone body. I could feel the men's need to join, craving to taste my surrender while Knox and his creature assured themselves I was still theirs. He settled behind me, pulling my body against his while I glanced at Killian. His soft blue eyes slid to where my nipples pushed against the dress, dipping lower before the tic in his jaw started hammering with anger and need.

Killian was erect, his cock pressing against his trousers as he watched me submit to Knox. My creature purred within me, needing them all to join in and taste my need. It was exhilarating to know they all craved me and wanted what I was, on a level so deliciously dark that my legs spread for the male behind me.

Knox wrapped his arm around my stomach, and his other pushed the sleeve of the dress aside, baring my breast to Killian's heavily hooded gaze. Knox pinched my nipple, uncaring that Killian was aroused by the sight of him touching me. Knox was subduing my body to transfix my mind. Lips brushed my shoulder, and the sharp sting of teeth sent my entire body spiraling into panic.

My mouth opened, and a rattle exploded on a wailing cry that caused my eyes to grow wide and round. It echoed around us, just like it had when Lord Andres had sunk his blunt teeth into my shoulder. Killian's head shook as if waking up from a spell before he kneeled in front of me.

Knox rattled, jerking his mouth from where he'd intended to mark me. His hands continued to hold me. My hands slapped over my mouth in horror at the noise exploding from my lungs.

It was a loud, painful, and heartbreaking sound. Tears swam in my eyes as Killian held my face, whispering words of comfort with a horrified look like he wasn't sure what the hell was happening. Next, Lore was beside me. His hands were on me and in my hair as he promised everything was okay. Brander was touching me too, whispering reassurances while Greer held the world's strangest expression on his face. His eyes studied me before sliding to the men who all had dropped to their knees, comforting me.

Knox continued to hold me from behind, his rattling purr comforting more than the others touching me had achieved. My heart raced, uncertain about how to turn off the heartrending sound that was coming from my creature. Greer stepped closer, and the men all snarled at him before he stepped back, searching their faces, then settling on mine.

"Help her," Knox snarled, his words coming out as if his mouth were filled with serrated teeth. Killian's eyes had turned a blueish green with golden embers floating in them, and his mouth had filled with rows of sharp, terrifying teeth.

I felt a hand moving down my belly, and the wail grew in volume, causing the men to slip back a tiny bit. Not men, monsters. My eyes slid around the group, noting each one's eyes had filled with midnight orbs and fiery embers. Greer turned, noting more men coming through the forest to investigate the sound.

"It's a distress call," Greer groaned, holding my stare as the men continued stroking me.

My body had never had so many freaking hands stroking it or touching it at once. It wasn't sexual either; it was a desperate need to stop the noise I was making from continuing. Knox kissed my neck, purred into my ear, his sound changing, growing painful to hear as if wounded by the shrieking rattle escaping me.

Killian leaned forward, his lips touching my temple as he purred, wiping away my tears, promising I would be okay. Brander groaned, yanking me toward his body, and Knox rattled a warning. My heart slid into my stomach while I shuddered from their scents oozing into my nose, intoxicating me until I feared my body would respond in violence.

It was too much all at once.

My creature chuckled, and I stiffened. She was humming in my head, and yet she held my scent within me, protecting me from the men I was sure would lose their shit the moment it slipped free. My head dropped against Knox, and he growled through gritted teeth, stroking my exposed breast while Killian awkwardly helped him.

"Greer, what the fuck is happening to her?" Knox demanded.

"She's in distress because you intended to mark her flesh by force," Greer explained, hiking his thumb over his shoulder to where more of his men kneeled on the forest floor surrounding us. "They seem to want to help, but luckily Aria has the strongest alphas around her, petting her like she's a kitten needing caressing."

"My mark stopped it last time," Knox argued, his tone sharp as steel while he slapped Killian's fingers away from my naked breast.

"You hurt her," Killian growled, and my eyes jerked toward his, locking with them.

"I saved her," Knox snapped crossly. "It's the noise she made when she called to me as Lord Andres assaulted her." Knox tilted his head and listened to the echoing cry that rattled within the noise I made.

"Because he terrified her," Killian whispered, unable to stop touching me. "She made that sound in distress because Andres was trying to force his mark upon her, and there were bodies all around them, indicating she'd watched them murdering her kind. It was traumatic and violent. He intended to mate with her forcefully, uncaring what she wanted. Now she's making the same sound, but it's because of you, Knox."

"My mark stopped it before," Knox repeated before turning me toward him, cupping my face. Pulling away from him, I fought to stop the noise from escaping. "Replacing my mark on her flesh eased her fear."

"It did, but then she removed yours too because it *felt* wrong. You tried to make her tell you where her family hid. You betrayed her creature and the shell that houses it by trying to drown her in her bathwater," Killian explained, reaching forward and pushing my hair away from my face before wiping away my tears.

"I took it back. I rescinded the fucking question," Knox growled, spinning me around to stare at me as tears swam in my eyes. It was dizzying the way they continued to turn me between them, both trying to comfort me. I felt like I was in the middle of a pissing contest, crying like a baby because the noise wouldn't stop exploding from me. "Females don't scream for help when alphas are around! They'd sense they're safe, even if they're not. Our scent comforts them. There are enough alphas here that Aria shouldn't need to make that sound, yet she fucking is."

"Our females don't rattle and purr either, but Aria does. That noise has me needing to defend her, and I don't actually *like* her, but it doesn't matter much at the moment. I *need* to protect her and comfort her, Knox. Look around. Her distress call brought every beast to her, feeling the need to protect her from what's upsetting her."

"I can't leave her unmarked. It isn't safe for Aria to be around us without my mark, protecting her from others that would fight over her. Take her back to the cage, Greer. Killian, find me something to murder, now."

I listened as Greer escorted me back, still echoing the sound without the ability to shut it off. I hadn't been afraid of Knox or his damn bite, so why the hell was I making the damn noise?

"You can't turn it off because the noise is coming from me. He'll fucking earn us before touching us again. You were right; he's a dicker."

I blanched, realizing my creature was continuing to make the noise to fuck with Knox. It wasn't something I would do, but it had gotten his attention rather quickly, along with every male I passed, who moved forward as if they *needed* to help me.

"What call are you sending out?" I pried carefully.

"The one no male ever wants to hear. Greer is smart. We cried for a protector, and we just had the entire camp of alphas on their fucking knees! His beast won't allow it again, so use it wisely. Also, maybe suck his dick, so we'd smell like him because everyone wants us now. I like dick, but you won't want this many in us at once, or even close together. Paint us with his scent. Consider this your warning. He hurt you, and no one hurts you without dealing with me too. Together, right, Aria? But

he's a man, and men are dumb. Use him for protection because you are soft and hurt easily, but I am hard. I hate it when you hurt. I wished to kill him when he hurt you. He is stronger than us. Now his dumb male pride is wounded, and he will kill shit and come to us to prove he is a man. Let him do it before everyone proves they are a man. Although, our vagina would be happy and me too," she chuckled darkly, even as the pained rattling continued echoing through my throat, annoyingly.

"Knox said we were only worth the scent our vagina makes. He doesn't get to have us anymore!"

"Then we choose another because I'm losing control of hiding our scent. You don't eat, and I need feeding. I weaken, Aria. I sleep too much, and I'm a growing girl. Feed me, fuck him, and then we will fight them all."

"You're insane! You know that, right? I'm not sucking his dick!"

"Then choose Killian's dick because he's second-in-command. He's a good killer, and I bet he'd fuck hard, too. He's got anger issues, and anger works when taken out on a vagina!"

"I am not fucking Killian, you dirty bird! Shut this noise up!"

"Aria?" Greer called.

His use of my name caused me to escape my internal conversation. He held the cage door open, peering at the men who surrounded me nervously. I slipped inside, watching as he sealed it behind me, stepping back as the sea of men moved closer.

"Are you okay?" Greer asked as the men crowding

the cage pushed him out of the way.

Purring erupted all around me, and I shivered while glancing around the cage. The men crushed each other to get closer to me, sending fear ripping through me, sounding through my call. My cry stopped the moment another entered the clearing. My body arched, alerting me to who rattled, sending the other men to their knees.

The rattle grew in volume, forcing the crowd to move back. Knox slid through the mass of bodies and gazed at me through the bars, glaring at the way I trembled. He reached through them, placing a bloodied flower on the blanket before turning, leaving me to ponder what the hell it meant. I picked up the white rose, holding it against my nose as he turned, watching me inhale its fragrance before he purred softly.

"We're moving out," he snapped to the crowd, sending them crashing into one another in their rush to obey.

Knox still stared at me as I studied him. He was covered in blood. Momentarily, I feared it was one of the men's until they exited the woods, laughing together, also covered in blood.

They carried a bloodied deer-like creature between them, causing my stomach to rumble with hunger. My lips and nose scrunched up at the idea of chowing down on it, but it smelled divine. I dropped the flower, sliding closer to the edge of the cage. My hands gripped the bars tightly, and my teeth slid free. Knox studied me, following my stare at the animal before moving back to me, narrowing his eyes at my response.

A lopsided smile played on his lips as he went to the

animal and ripped off a chunk of meat. Walking to me, he held it just out of my reach. Saliva filled my mouth as I took in the meat, lifting my eyes to lock with his as my stomach growled ravenously. I reached for it, and he pulled it away. Frowning, I whined low in my throat.

"When's the last time you ate fresh meat?" he asked, and I shook my head. "I asked you a question, Aria. When is the last time you ate *anything* to sate your creature's hunger?"

"I don't remember," I whispered, eyeing the meat in his hand while turning up my nose at it. "That's disgusting."

Knox smirked boyishly, holding his hand out and lowering his eyes to the chunk of meat. I lifted my hand, accepting it from him. Yanking it through the bars, I sank my teeth into it as a moan of pleasure rushed through me. I wanted to throw up at the fact I was eating raw meat, but I also was in danger of coming undone at how good it tasted. I sighed, devouring it, closing my eyes at how amazing it tasted on my tongue.

My eyes opened, and my gaze held Knox's, dripping blood down my chin while he and his men watched me. Brander ripped another chunk from the animal, handing it to Knox, who stepped closer, giving me more while I gulped down the first piece.

I accepted the next chunk, purring low in my throat. Studying Knox from beneath my lashes, I silently tore into the meat as he shook his head, snorting. "I forgot you needed meat, Little Monster. No wonder your creature wants to eat me. You're starving." He ran his hand over his mouth, uncaring that we were both covered in the blood of his kill.

"You want more?" Brander asked. Knox growled, turning to pierce him with a feral look. "To feed her with, asshole. You killed the damn thing, so feed your girl, Knox. When a bitch is hungry, you feed her. It's what men do."

Knox exhaled, turning to look at me as I sat back, eyeing him carefully while considering what the creature within me had said. She'd known he had hurt me, and she'd let me choose our path until he'd tried to mark me again.

We argued a lot, and we disagreed on most things simply because she had basic needs, and mine ran deeper. Knox had the same issue, which meant he fought the same internal battle, yet he made it look easy. My monster and I were a work in progress, trying to find common ground.

I now knew he could force me to disclose my family's location and that he'd always had the ability. It was the one thing he could have used to control me, but he hadn't. Why not? He hadn't used it because he knew it would hurt me deeply. In his own way, he didn't want to see me hurt unless he needed something to inflict pain upon me when he was hurting.

Knox wasn't as ruthless as I'd assumed him to be. He had limits to what he was willing to use against me. He hadn't ever forced me to fuck him, and it was as simple as rattling until I begged and pleaded for it to happen. He'd pulled back from physically hitting me because if he hadn't, it would have inflicted actual damage. Knox would have caved in my head had he used his full strength, but he'd barely tapped me.

This creature was more complicated than I wanted

to admit. When Knox softened, he got harder to protect himself. He blamed himself for betraying the memory of his wife and son. And hurting me wasn't just to force me to back off. It was to hurt him, too. He needed to remind himself what was happening, which meant I was getting under his skin, chipping through the wall he'd erected to entomb his heart.

I smiled at him, causing his lips to tug into a frown while his eyes narrowed to slits.

"That almost looks like she's imagining eating you next, doesn't it?" Lore asked softly.

"It's not an innocent smile, that's for sure," Knox agreed.

"It's almost sinister," Killian whispered as if I couldn't hear him. "I'd hide your cock for a bit, Knox. She looks like she is going to shred it with those pretty fangs."

"Dude, she can eat mine. Dislocating jaws are so hot." They all turned to stare at Lore as if he'd said something wrong.

I pulled the covers over my head while they were distracted, settling into the mess I'd made. The blankets offered me comfort with Knox's scent clinging to them. I was about to sink my claws into his freaking heart and make him face reality.

Whatever was between us, it went past bare-bones, right into the genetic make-up of our beings. It was as if I felt the man to my soul, and he felt me back. I was about to rattle his world on an entirely new level he wouldn't see coming.

If he thought all he had to do was feed me, he was dead wrong. He needed a reminder of who and what I was. I wasn't some basic-bitch you fed a cheeseburger to make up. I was a monster, like him.

So what if he was questioning his marriage, his reason for going to war, and, well, basically his entire life? I hadn't been a part of it, and I was done being his punching bag. I was about to punch back, and being a woman, we had so many ways of getting beneath a male's skin. I released the hold on my scent, allowing it to drift to him. I heard his rattle and smiled, pulling it back, making it seem as if I'd slipped up instead of tempting him with it on purpose.

Game on, asshole.

Chapter Ten

We made camp before darkness settled over the area, and much to my displeasure, they erected no tents. Knox's men had built fires and placed bedding surrounding them as the wagons packed with tents moved ahead to the next location they planned to camp. Knox had spoken little, but he offered me more food and whiskey, which I accepted silently.

"How long have you craved raw meat?" Knox asked, and I noted the others around us went silent, pretending they weren't listening.

I downed my whiskey, and he refilled my cup. I skipped the raw, bloody meat that smelled divine. Tipping the glass up, I swallowed it, moaning at the hint of citrus and aged wood that danced over my tongue while burning its way down my throat. I placed the glass onto the ground by the fire and scooted closer to its heat, forcing my shoulder into Knox's view. His eyes narrowed, still irked that it was bare of his mark and had finally healed back to smooth skin instead of scabs.

Staring into the fire, I closed my eyes. My fingers ran over the soft column of my throat, and I opened my eyes, noting that his gaze followed my fingertips, tracing the curve of my neck. I shivered from the intensity in Knox's stare, which he mistook as the night air chilling me. He stood, pulling off his cloak, before placing it over my shoulders, settling closer to me. Knox stared off into the fire for a few moments, slowly turning to look at me.

"I understand that you're disappointed and angry with me, but this isn't how I had imagined you behaving."

"And how did you see me acting after you abused me? How should I behave after being told the scent of my body is the measure of my worth and accused of trying to hurt you, deceitfully?"

"I'd just returned from finding an entire army of decent men slaughtered, Aria. I feared that you or your family had considered the men expendable to your escape. I found you missing, and then when I got you back, you threw yourself into my arms, which is out of character. You seemed to have forgotten we're enemies. While I admit I am guilty of the same, what you told me in that tent sent anger, unlike anything I'd ever felt, rushing through me."

"Can I fuck Killian tonight?" I asked, causing Killian to sputter his drink as he coughed. Brander patted him on his back, chuckling.

"She does that sometimes," Brander grunted.

"I acted poorly," Knox continued, grinding his teeth together, studying me, while ignoring my question.

"So you did," I replied, turning to stare at Killian. He glared at me, and I offered him a saucy smile with heat pooling into my eyes. His glare turned hooded, and he swallowed audibly. I purred huskily at Killian, causing Knox to rattle a warning. I assumed that was for Killian's benefit since it did not affect me.

"Absolutely fucking not happening," Knox snapped, peering at my unmarked shoulder once more.

"Brander, then?" I asked, lifting a brow in question.

"No," Knox replied harshly.

"Lore?"

"No fucking way, Aria," Knox groaned, running his hand over his face before turning to glare at the men beside us.

"Well, Greer doesn't do pussy, and mine needs painting rather badly tonight," I pointed out, and Greer's gaze swung to mine before lowering it to the region of my body in question.

"I do pussy, Peasant, I just prefer meat," Greer growled, flipping me off from his bedroll.

"You're sleeping with me," Knox whispered huskily. "End of fucking discussion about your bodily needs, woman."

"Yeah, sorry. I'm just not interested in you anymore. I'm going to pass on that offer." I shook out of Knox's cloak, carefully folding it up, before handing it back to him. "I'm going to need you to find me someone I can fuck, King Karnavious. My vagina needs feeding too, and the bitch is hungry." I stood, moving through the slumbering bodies to the wooded thicket for privacy as all the men watched me leaving camp.

"Did she just say her *vagina* was hungry?" Lore chuckled before making a pained sound deep in his throat.

"She's surprisingly brilliant for one so young," Greer snorted. "Shall I follow her to ensure the men give her privacy while she tends to her personal needs?"

"Fuck off, Greer," Knox growled as he stood, starting after me. "She needs a reminder about who the hell she's messing with."

"Should we worry for him or her?" Lore asked, needing clarification regarding who was about to get their ass handed to them.

"Him," they all stated together before chuckling.

I smiled wickedly as I entered the woods, finding a large boulder. Climbing onto it, I sat gazing up at the multitude of blinking stars. Knox entered the small clearing but stopped to lean against a tree, watching me as I took in the beauty of the Nine Realms' solar system. Unlike the human world, there was no pollution here, so you could clearly see the night sky.

It was a thing of beauty how the world highlighted the night sky as if the designer had wanted nothing else to mar the scene but stars. They shot through the heavens, creating a glow that followed close behind them.

Turning to look at where Knox had been, I frowned, finding the spot empty. Swinging my gaze around the clearing, I caught his scent, forcing me to look right in front of me. My heart kicked into overdrive with his nearness while the air refused to fill my lungs.

Knox studied me, closing the distance between our lips. I turned before he reached mine, staring up at the stars once more. He rattled softly, forcing my eyes back to his. Gradually, he pushed my dress up to expose my naked thighs, watching for any sign of fear or that I wanted him to stop.

He pressed his thumbs against the inside of my thighs, causing my lips to part as he carefully removed my panties. He ran his finger through my heated sex, slowly rubbing his thumb against my clit. Breathing became an effort, escaping my lungs in short, heavy pants. Moaning, I leaned back, lifting my legs while spreading them apart, placing my feet flat against the rock as my arms braced my body.

His finger pushed into my core, which clenched hungrily against him. He purred roughly, watching me rocking against his hand. Knox added another finger, stretching me while his gaze heated with lust, finding me wet and needy. He slid his attention to my core, inhaling the arousal painting his fingers as he withdrew them, sucking them clean.

I flinched, and he paused, staring at me before lowering his head, pushing me back against the rock. His mouth descended against my need. His heated kiss removed all unease from my mind the moment his tongue slid through my sex, rattling his approval. His heated breaths whispered promises against my flesh. My hands slid to his hair, and my ass lifted to allow him better access where I needed him. I used his mouth to push my body toward the edge, feeling the coming storm it created as pleasure rushed through me.

Knox pushed his fingers into my body slowly. He

twisted and bent them within me, finding the place connected to every nerve ending. Lips clamped against my clitoris, and Knox drove me toward the orgasm with precision. His tongue flicked against me, forcing pressure onto the silken nub, even as he pressed his fingers deeper into my body. My skin heated with the impending orgasm. It grew within me as my body moved against his mouth, uncaring that I wantonly used it for pleasure. The noises escaping my throat were loud, unabashed, and filled with the need he created.

Knox noted every emotion playing on my face. I moaned loudly, crying out as light exploded in my sight. The surrounding stars moved, shooting across the sky as if they shared in the bliss he'd given me. Knox lifted his head, purring as he moved to undo his pants, but my foot caught his chest, shoving him back. I pushed the skirt of my dress down as he watched through narrowed slits.

"Aria," Knox growled huskily. He shoved his fingers through his hair, frustration straining his face, and I knew that if I walked away from him, he'd allow it.

"Shut the hell up, Knox," I hissed huskily, running my eyes over the bulge in his pants.

Sitting up, I slid off the rock and grabbed him, pushing him back against the rock where I'd been. I unfasten his pants, pushing them down before wrapping my fingers around his thickness. He hissed through clenched teeth while I ran my fingers over the sensitive underside of his shaft. Cupping my cheeks, he watched as I lowered to my knees, stroking him slowly before my tongue jutted out and carefully licked the glistening tip, continuing to hold his dark, seductive stare.

My lips brushed over the head slowly, pushing

his cock up to work my way down his thickness until I reached his balls. I squeezed them gently, and his eyes grew hooded while seeing me pleasuring him. He threaded his fingers through my hair, rattling softly while I worked my way back up his shaft, pushing him between my lips. I leisurely ran my tongue over it, noting the way his breathing hitched, and he gasped while swallowing the noise.

He used my hair to guide me, but I jerked back, grabbing his hands to press them against the rock. The warning in my eyes was silent, but Knox understood it well enough. Both of my hands worked him slowly, knowing I couldn't take more than a few inches into my throat, as he was well endowed in all the right ways. My jaw burned while it stretched to accommodate his girth, tears escaping my eyes from forcing him into my throat. Knox purred, observing me as his hands fisted against the boulder, wanting to touch me.

I swallowed, and he groaned, staring into my eyes. I forced him deeper as he cried out, sending hot spurts of his scent down my throat. Swallowing the release that I took from him, I purred softly. I stood, stepping back to stare at his still hard cock, and frowned. I grabbed my panties and slipped them back on, fixing my dress while he righted his pants, watching as I started back to camp.

"Aria?" he called when I reached the trees.

I turned, using my thumb to wipe his arousal from my lip, sucking it clean as his gaze slid to it, forcing a purr to escape his chest. "I'm sorry, did you need me to suck your dick some more?" I canted my head to the side as his eyes widened while his mouth dropped open. Snorting, I continued through the sleeping people until

I reached the bedroll we'd share, knowing the others listened as I spoke.

"Aria, what the hell was that?" Knox demanded as he reached me.

"I sucked your cock, which should have been rather idiot-proof as to what *that* was," I stated, hearing Killian cough to smother the sound of his laughter.

"Cut the shit. What the hell do you think you're doing?"

"Doing? Nothing. What just happened? You ate my pussy, and I sucked you off. I have your scent, and that was what I needed from you. I mean, it's pretty much all you're worth to me now. It worked out perfectly, I thought. If you need to cuddle or some shit to make yourself feel less dirty or used, we can do that too. I'd rather not, though. It's honestly needy, and you disgust me."

Knox's eyes narrowed to angry slits, adding it up in his head. "You used me?"

"Yes, Knox. I did. I needed your scent, and I'm a greedy bitch, so I let you get me off first. I fail to see why it would bother you unless you thought I'd want you for more than your scent, which would make this rather awkward, wouldn't it? Honestly, I tried to fuck three other men before choosing you. That I looked elsewhere, then had to settle on you should have told you how desperate I was."

"What the fuck," Knox growled angrily.

"Oh, I'm going to need crayons to draw you a map, aren't I?" I smirked, as his anger pulsed, closing the distance between us while everyone secretly listened.

"You're playing with fire."

"I'm fireproof," I whispered huskily, grabbing his cock. "Need another go? I'm game," I said, sliding to my knees, and the men lifted their heads to watch. "I do enjoy the taste of you buried in my throat."

"Daddy wants one so badly," Lore groaned, shoving his knuckles into his mouth to bite them.

"Is that how you want to play it, woman?" Knox asked, searching my face.

"I don't want to play anything. Your scent was weakening within me; now it's not. It is what you said, right? I need your scent or your mark, and well, I don't want your mark on my flesh anymore, Knox. I took the other option, and it tasted fucking delicious. So what is the problem? It was an easy enough fix to suck you off to get your scent. It worked out well for you in the end, didn't it?"

"The next time you take my scent, it will be because I'm coming in that tight, needy body, Aria."

"Hard pass," I laughed soundlessly with challenge burning in my gaze. "My poisonous pussy is off-limits to you unless you're eating it, Knox. I don't intend to allow anyone to use it who merely thinks it is my total worth. The next man entering my body will be my husband, asshole. You don't get to fuck me anymore." I tucked myself into the blankets before dismissing him, frowning as he stomped off toward the woods, throwing a king-sized tantrum.

"Peasant, you're not stupid. I know you're not.

You just pissed off a king by sucking his dick. That's an oxymoron situation that shouldn't ever happen to a man. They normally rejoice from that sort of thing. You're not playing with fire; you're baiting a monster that has basic primal needs. Fuck, fight, and feed."

"You've forgotten, Meat Suit. I, too, have the same basic needs. Knox told me he didn't want me and that the only reason anyone would ever want me was because of my scent. So what is the fucking difference if I suck him off to get his scent, or he uses my vagina?"

"A pretty big one, actually," Brander grunted as he answered. "One ends with your womb filled, and the other is a waste that ends with you drinking him down. His beast needs the womb filled to feel satisfied. The other only sates the man's hunger. You just put man against beast, and the beast is a lot more primal and carnal than the man, Aria."

"My creature just wanted me to suck his dick," I announced, and the men snorted, then chuckled as if it were cute.

"Your beast is basically a horny teenager, and his creature is ancient. Yours wants to play, his needs to own. Yours is cute and cuddly, his is a fucking monster," Killian groaned, sitting up to look in the direction where Knox had vanished.

I sat up, peering toward the woods. "You guys have seen my beast kill shit, right? She's not cuddly. Not at all," I argued. "In fact, I'm not even sure she's mentally sound to make choices. She has traded places with me as she was eating dick before, literally."

"She's fluffy compared to our beasts," Killian

laughed, observing me with something akin to lust burning in his gaze.

"Should I go find him or something?" I asked, getting to my knees.

Rattling exploded from the woods, and we all groaned, bending to the power that flooded through the camp. Even those who were sleeping, woke, turning to bow their heads and backs toward the beast. I peered into the shadows as Knox emerged, locating me as he rattled once more.

It wasn't his usual rattle; it was violent. My legs parted, spreading wide as Brander groaned behind me, forced to smell the arousal that drenched my panties as Knox's beast threw down a challenge. Pain gripped my clitoris, and I whimpered as my nipples pebbled into hard peaks. An orgasm danced just out of reach, demanding I give in to the beast, desiring it from me.

"Aria, whatever the fuck you do, do not come in the middle of the camp. That's not a request; that's a plea for the lives of everyone close enough to smell your scent." Brander's tone was aggravated and filled with apprehension.

I moaned loudly, purring to the beast who watched me from the trees. My body unfurled, and everything within me *needed* to answer his call by coming for him. I purred while fiery eyes approved of my response.

"That is easier said than done," I whimpered loudly.

"Do not do it, woman," Killian growled through clenched teeth. "That isn't Knox. That's his beast showing you who you just pissed off. Tread carefully, for the lives of anyone close enough to smell your desire is about to end up meeting him in battle."

I gritted my clenched teeth together, forcing my body to calm down before it tipped over the edge. Slowly, I lifted onto shaking legs and started toward Knox. I moved away from the others as he tracked me. I made it a few feet away from him before black eyes slid to blue, and Knox exhaled loudly, glaring at me.

"I didn't come, Knox. Don't hurt them. They did nothing wrong."

He laughed soundlessly, shaking his head as claws retracted from his fingertips. His body trembled with power and anger that was palpable between us. "Good girl," he snorted.

Knox grabbed my hand, walking me back toward the makeshift bed. Once there, he folded his body around mine and fixed the blankets. Leaning over, he brushed his lips against my forehead. His knuckles brushed against my cheek softly before his thumb pushed into my mouth, forcing me to suck it. He leaned over, whispering against my ear.

"You look so fucking pretty on your knees, taking me into your tight throat, Aria."

"I think that might be the sweetest thing you've ever said to me, Knox." I glared up at him as Brander groaned loudly.

"Can you two assholes go to sleep so the rest of the camp can as well? Every male here is hard as fuck right now because you just made Aria *very* wet. We're all waiting to get off with our fucking fists the moment she's asleep and can't hear us being pathetic assholes. So, if you don't mind, Aria, close your pretty lips and eyes and go the fuck to sleep," Brander shouted, and the surrounding men grunted their agreements.

I snorted as Knox did the same, staring into my eyes. I sucked my bottom lip between my teeth, smirking at him. "Night, guys," I whispered, pushing my head against Knox's chest. He placed his hand over my ear, tightening the blankets around our entangled bodies.

"You like the taste of me?" Knox asked, and the men groaned, standing before stomping off toward the woods.

"Go to sleep," I scolded, kissing his heart as my eyes grew heavy while he held me against his heat.

I forced my smile to remain hidden. The sheer horror that I could use him had dumbfounded him. You'd think as King, he'd be accustomed to people using him for his status, but to consider his prisoner, his sworn enemy at that, and that had left him feeling dirty and used? Well, he hadn't liked that feeling one bit. Good, because I wasn't done with him. Even if I'd rattled his beast to reach the man, I would sink my claws into his heart and show him he still had one that beat among the land of the living.

Chapter Eleven

We'd moved to a smaller camp with more people, making it overcrowded. I'd been unable to escape Knox, and he was hell-bent on twisting me inside out. He'd been training for three days, each of which he'd been shirtless and covered in sweat. His scent drifted to me nonstop, and whatever control he'd held over it, he'd thrown aside and let it suffocate the air surrounding me.

Today he'd been training in front of me with Brander. Both men dressed in nothing but pants as they fought with swords. I'd skipped my usual wandering around the camp aimlessly to twine sage for the coming Beltane ceremony, which was where we were heading.

I worried my lip with my teeth as my fingers worked skillfully, having twined and threaded sage a million times before into smudge sticks. The sound of Knox and Brander's swords crashing against one another, mixing with their grunts as they collided, filled the silence of the camp.

Knox dodged an attack, and every sinewy muscle in his body pulsed as he spun, disarming Brander easily with an upward swing. Knox caught the blade before it hit the ground, handing it back to Brander. Turning toward me, Knox grabbed a jug of water, pouring it over his head, and I swallowed hard on a groan as his eyes sparkled in victory.

I set the sage down, running my fingers over the sweat beading at the back of my neck. Unable to look away from the water droplets that ran in slow motion down Knox's abs, I exhaled a shuddered breath. Closing my eyes, I released my lip from my teeth as a moan escaped my throat before clamping my mouth shut. I grabbed the table, fighting the urge to strip naked and mount him like some wildling in heat that didn't know proper etiquette.

"Are you okay?" someone asked, and I turned, opening my eyes to stare at Siobhan. Her voice sounded far away, yet she was directly beside me, wide, worried eyes studying me. Okay? No. I wasn't okay.

"I'm great," I mumbled as a rattle slipped from my chest. "Couldn't be better," I said in a high-pitched tone that caused Siobhan to frown and for Soraya to match her expression.

I turned as Bekkah moved into my line of sight, slipping her hand over Knox's bare chest. The purr that slid past my lips was loud and very, very unfriendly. Knox's lips twitched, tipping up in the corners as he leaned over, whispering something against Bekkah's ear. His hand played with a strand of her hair, and Soraya screamed, "Fire!"

Smoke billowed up with the thick scent of wood

and sage surrounding me. I watched Knox and Bekkah through the smoke with narrowed slits as anger shot through me. Turning away, I dismissed them, noting that Greer looked past me toward the table.

"Breathe, Peasant, before you burn everyone up," Greer warned, staring at the table of sage, now fully engulfed in flames. "Some of us aren't fireproof!"

"Noted," I growled, moving away from the others with my hands still burning.

At the edge of the camp, the guards stepped into my path. Looking over my shoulder, they moved out of my way, allowing me to pass. Heading to the stream, I didn't bother to strip out of my dress as I dove into the frigid water. I sat beneath the surface, gathering my composure before emerging from the depths as steam covered the top of the creek, billowing into the air.

Masculine laughter forced my gaze to the bank. I found Knox kneeling on his haunches, smiling at me as his eyes dropped to the sheer top of my white dress. We glared at one another for several moments before he brought his hand up, rubbing his lip slowly with his thumb. His eyes remained locked to my very erect nipples pushing against the soaked dress, lifting and falling with my labored breathing.

"Wet?" he asked, and I tilted my head to the side.

"Very." Knox stood, removing his pants. He entered the water gradually, allowing me to see his naked masculine perfection in vivid detail. Knox was all hot tattoos and muscle that made my brain go stupid. There should be a law against men with bodies like his being allowed to get tattoos. It left a woman defenseless and disarmed.

I danced away from Knox as he smiled mischievously. "You set the camp on fire, woman. You burned enough sage to ward against demons worldwide from entering it should they have attempted. Not that they would want to with this many of our kind gathered together in one place."

"Oops, my bad," I whispered huskily. Knox stood in front of me, using the water to wash away the sweat from his body, caused by his training with Brander.

"You're a little overdressed for bathing, aren't you?"

I swallowed before glancing down at the see-through dress, slowly lifted my gaze back to his piercing stare. "There was a bug on me."

His lips twitched, and his eyes danced with merriment as he crept closer. "Was there? Is it gone now?"

"I assume so, yes."

His hand lifted to my hair, pushing the wet strands away from my face. "Maybe I should check beneath your dress to be certain?" I hated it when he touched my hair because it left me without walls of defense against him.

I blinked and shook my head, dispelling whatever was happening with the alpha big dick energy he was throwing toward me. "I don't feel anything beneath it."

"You sure?" he countered, pulling me against him as his lips brushed against my ear. "I'd hate for you to get bitten by anything that wasn't me." The heat of his breath warred with the iciness of the creek, sending a shudder through my body.

"Is that so?" I brushed my cheek against his. Heat

rolled through me, and my body tightened against the scent oozing from his pores. My apex clenched, reacting to his nearness as his body pressed against mine.

"It would be a travesty for anything else to mar your gorgeous body, Aria," Knox chuckled, brushing his nose against my shoulder, causing my breathing to hitch and get stuck in my lungs.

He kissed my shoulder, and my hands slid through his hair, pulling his mouth to mine, claiming it hungrily. His tongue pushed past my lips as his hands lifted me, forcing my legs to wrap around him.

Knox devoured me until I was mindless with need. Purring exploded from both of us, our bodies unable to get close enough as he claimed ownership with his kiss. He lifted my dress while my legs wrapped around him together, rocking my sex against his. I needed him inside of me with a wild desire that drove me past the brink of coherent thought, and he knew it too. His fingers pushed against my opening, and I felt his cock aiming for entrance, uncaring that we were within sight of the camp.

"Does this mean we're not fucking then, My King?" Bekkah asked from the shore, and Knox groaned.

I pulled back, unable to stop the rattle that exploded from my chest, sliding down his body, before shoving him into the water. Anger slithered through me while my eyes moved to the bitch on the shore, who smirked coldly.

"Have him," I grunted, walking past Bekkah. I headed toward the tent to change out of the wet dress, preparing to go back and fix the mess I'd made of the sage.

"Aria, get back here now!" Knox demanded.

I muttered beneath my breath. "Demons, huh? Too bad sage doesn't repel assholes!" I shouted over my shoulder, catching sight of him glaring at me from the water. Bekkah grabbed the hem of her dress, intending to join him, and I snorted in disgust.

My eyes swung to Knox with loathing, swallowing past the tightness in my throat. Shaking my head, I moved faster to reach the tent before tears could break free. No sooner had I entered and stripped out of the wet dress, Knox barged in, still naked, his eyes finding mine as he rattled.

"Go get your basic bitch, asshole." I covered my naked breasts with my arms. He crept forward, his hands fisted at his sides like he didn't appreciate being told to get fucked.

"I don't want a basic bitch, Aria Primrose," he hissed, holding my stare with the sparkling depths that promised me pleasure. "I crave you more than I care to admit."

"So don't admit it then, Knox," I shrugged, glaring angrily as he surveyed me. "I need something to wear since I'm *so* wet and still need to clean up my mess with the sage."

"You can wear me, woman."

"I don't think you're a good fit," I snorted, shuddering at the rumbling growl that escaped from deep in his chest. "You chafe me in delicate places, leaving me a little sore."

"I relish leaving you sore, Aria. I enjoy knowing I fucked you so hard your pussy swells from what you allowed me to do. You let me go to war against that soft body, and you savage me right back, don't you?" He stepped closer, and I danced back a step.

I swallowed thickly while considering how to talk myself out of that one. So naturally, I blurted the first thing that came to mind. "I've heard it can swell if it's an STD, and come to think about it, the way it leaks when you're near. It's possible I picked something up somewhere in this crazy world. I mean, let's be honest here, I've been in a lot of water lately. What if it is one of those little suckers that swim up your urethra?" Knox's lips twitched as he moved toward me, fighting to contain his laughter.

"It's not an STD. The arousal your body creates for me is because my cock is rather large, and you're very tiny, Aria. It's your beast preparing to take mine because these forms cannot tell the difference. If my beast were to take you, he'd need the slickness of your arousal to fit into those tight places you boast of, to prevent damaging your tender body."

"Oh, that actually makes sense," I whispered as he cupped my face between his hands.

"I want you, Aria," Knox bowed his head, kissing me softly, which sent a flood of emotions rushing through me. It wasn't a demanding kiss. It was a seeking kiss that curled my toes and knocked the wind out of me. "Stop fighting it because it is going to happen whether we want it or not. I'd rather this be our decision, instead of our creatures forcing it, and us regretting it or unwilling when it happens."

I pressed my hands against his chest, pushing him back, which he allowed. I looked into his eyes, and he accepted that this wasn't the time. "I'm not ready, and my creature knows it. I have some things to work through, some rather vile things, and that is something you and your beast need to give me time to accept and move past." Knox stepped back as if he'd overstepped, and I grabbed his hand, pulling him close to me. "I still need something to wear, and I know I said I wanted my own tent, but I don't. I need you to keep the nightmares away, and you do it somehow. You hold them at bay for me, and I don't want them to reach me anymore. So, if I can, I'd like to sleep beside you."

Knox smirked mischievously before pressing his lips against my ear. "I wasn't letting you leave my tent anyway since I enjoy you pressed against me too much. You're not sleeping alone unless you wear my mark on your flesh, so you may wish to consider that too. I know you want it, and I do too."

"And you'll wear my mark?" I asked, knowing I was pushing him away. Knox tensed, and I snorted as anger rushed through me, heating me with the intensity of it. "That's what I thought. I changed my mind. I want my own tent after all. I prefer nightmares to your company."

"It's not happening. An unmarked female is fair game, Aria. It isn't up for discussion. You may have my scent on you, but it isn't the same without my mark on your flesh. Before, when I placed my scent on you, my mark reinforced my claim."

"Then have Brander or Killian mark me." Knox rattled, spinning on his heel to dress before leaving the tent, shouting that he was going hunting.

Within the next two hours, I was fairly sure the forest's wildlife population had dwindled to near extinction. Meat stacked higher than I could see over, sat in front of the tent's opening. Peeking around it, I found Lore, Brander, and Killian all glaring at the forest as if it was the offender that had angered them.

"This is fucking ridiculous," Killian snapped.

"You think?" Brander groaned, turning to where Knox was stalking back into camp, dragging two large animals behind him as he glared at me. "We are going to need more salt to preserve the meat."

"Try a fucking salt mine if he continues this shit," Lore joked.

I broke off the leg of one animal, and all the men turned to glare at me. My attention swung to Knox, tossing the newest animals onto the pile, glaring at me. I purred, smiling slightly as his stare slid to the blanket that covered my naked body.

"You're an excellent hunter," I said huskily, stalking back into the tent. He growled, and I smiled at the sound of the men's groans. Knox rattled, the noise leaving camp as he went hunting, to kill more things in his rage at being denied what he wanted most.

Chapter Twelve

We still hadn't moved, which forced us to rearrange camp as more and more troops arrived to follow the army to the palace. I'd spent hours today playing with the children, arranging flowers in their hair, and teaching them simple things they should have already known, based on their age.

It seemed the basics of witchcraft were no longer taught to our daughters and sons, choosing instead to forego learning any magic or attack and defensive spells by the high king's order, whoever he was.

I was still braiding a little girl's hair when Knox's scent hit me from across the camp. Lifting my head, I searched him out in the crowd. I found him standing with men who had shown up earlier, nodding at me with a soft smile on his lips. Pink spread over my cheeks, and my body heated indecently as if it sensed his need from his scent alone. Swallowing hard, I chewed my bottom lip, returning my focus to the little girl's hair, or tried.

Knox had a way of reminding me he was here without even gazing at me. I felt him the moment he returned to camp or bed at night. The subtleness of his scent and the gentleness of his purr calmed my fear of another male entering the tent we shared. We'd fallen into somewhat of a routine, and his flirting was contagiously rakish, disarming my defenses.

He had remained distant, though, flirting with me from afar. It was both sexy and endearing, considering Knox could demand it or take what he wanted. If he did so, there was nothing anyone would do to stop or prevent that from happening. Ever since I'd pointed out that I was still processing my assault by Lord Andres, Knox had allowed me to heal, which spoke more about his character than anything else since meeting him.

I moved on from hair to teaching the girls about stones and crystals while Knox continued to observe. I taught the young witches what each stone represented as they held them in their palms, feeling their magic. They laughed and giggled while I recanted some of their uses. I avoid discussing their darker uses, keeping their more sinister and sexual nature from the girls' innocent minds.

One of the teenage girls argued over a crystal. At least she had until realizing that I was trying to protect their innocence. She settled for making a crude gesture that had us both howling with laughter. The sound drew Knox's attention, and I laughed harder. I was considering adding some stones to the bed when I finally allowed him to have me. Sucking my lip between my teeth, I stilled the laughter, and heat pooled in my eyes while I took in Knox's smoldering gaze.

One girl held up a rose quartz palm stone, and I

smiled as she handed it to me. "What does this one do?" she asked softly.

"This one will help you find love and bring forth your heart's greatest desires," I announced, holding it between my hands.

I closed my eyes tightly, and my lips tipped into a grin. My smile grew while I listened as the girls giggled and laughed. Inhaling Knox's scent, I slowly exhaled. Tilting my head, I imagined his lips against mine and opened my eyes to find him inches from my lips.

"What is it that your heart desires most, Aria?" Knox whispered huskily, causing the girls to giggle harder while others listened with curious interest.

"Occasionally, the crystal messes up. Or the heart is just an organ, and the crystal is just a rock," I whispered to the girls, fighting the urge to lean into his lips and kiss him soundly.

"Is the fierce, beautiful princess too afraid to admit what everyone else already knows she desires?" he asked, cupping my cheek, and leaning closer to brush his lips against mine.

I cradled his cheek with my hand and sucked his bottom lip between my teeth, enjoying the hiss of sound that expelled from his lungs. "She knows who she wants. She's only ever wanted one man, but he's a stubborn beast. He's the king and her sworn enemy, and they're on opposing sides of a war. That's difficult on them, knowing right from wrong. Yet, even so, they meet on that line where war rages and the battle drums echo through them. She yields to his battle cry, and he melts into her curves, but his heart is too broken to mend easily. He's buried too deeply within a tomb even though his heart beats loudly to the steady rhythm of hers," I whispered, kissing him softly before I stood, leaving him speechless as the girls followed me to gather more flowers under the guard's watchful eyes.

"Some wounds cannot be mended, Aria."

"Stick some fucking duct tape on it. That shit fixes everything." I spun around in time to see riders emerging from the forest at a breakneck pace. Grabbing one girl, I pulled her out of the way, and Knox rattled in warning as we narrowly missed being trampled.

"Aria, get inside the tent, now." Knox stepped forward, and his men moved in behind him while one rider stared at me coldly. Stunning, crystal blue eyes locked with mine. The iciness of the stare sent a chill racing down my spine. "Lord Carter, glad to see you made it here in one piece. We assumed you had gotten sidetracked," Knox announced, pulling the man's attention from me.

"I was gathering intel on a keep besieged by murderous whores," Lord Carter stated, sliding his attention back to me. "A silver-haired witch. Tell me, My King, is she the Hecate witch you captured?"

The lord dismounted, moving swiftly toward me. He grabbed my hair, wrenching my head back to press his fingers to my forehead. Pain shot through my skull as his eyes glowed. My claws extended, grabbing his hand to remove it as a low purr escaped my lungs, and his eyes narrowed.

"Amazing. So the rumors are true? Freya Hecate slept with a beast and made a bastard creature?"

"Get your fucking hands off of me, now," I hissed, dropping his hand, and his eyes widened with my warning.

"Have you not taught this bitch her position?" Lord Carter asked, moving to strike me, but Knox grabbed his hand, preventing the man from backhanding me. "You protect her?" He ripped his arm away from Knox, scowling.

"Not only I, but others in the resistance want her alive, and until I know who and why, Aria is to remain unharmed. She is under my protection, so see that your men understand and obey me."

"Never thought I'd live to see the day that King Karnavious protected a Hecate witch," Lord Carter sneered, grabbing my chin before Knox could stop him. "I'm going to kill your entire family, witch."

"You and everyone else, but you'd have to find them first." I smiled as his eyes narrowed. "You'd also have to go through me, and I may look small and harmless; however, I'm anything but. Touch me again, and I'll bite your fucking cock off and kiss you with it, asshole," I snorted, moving out of his grasp, heading toward the tent.

The other witches collected the children, rushing them away from the newcomer to safety. A shiver raced down my spine, feeling his hate-filled gaze on my back. Entering Knox's tent, I turned to close it, but Knox followed behind me, pushing me onto the bed until I bounced in front of him.

"Never challenge one of my lords in front of me again, witch," Knox snapped, his eyes searching my face as I struggled past the anger.

"Then get your lords under control, Knox. The last one betrayed you and tried to rape me. This one touched me after you explicitly told *him* not to. It isn't me disrespecting you; it is them. I won't allow him to abuse me, and you shouldn't expect me to accept that behavior."

"It's not that easy, Aria. This world isn't black and white. It's gray and filled with corpses of those who weren't strong enough to survive the beginning when the witches first made a play to take control of the world. They murdered Lord Carter's family, and it was brutal. They hung his family from trees unto death, ripping his children into neat little piles, and leaving their remains beneath his naked wife as they raped her in life and death."

"And again, I'm to blame for that too? I wasn't even alive when it happened."

"In the Nine Realms, if one inflicted terror, we punish them and the rest of their bloodline. It doesn't matter if you were alive or not, Aria. The blood that runs through your veins condemned you."

"That's unfair and not right," I whispered.

Knox kneeled between my thighs, placing his hands on them, smiling up at me with heat burning in his eyes. "Welcome home to the Nine Realms, where nothing is fair, and life is a battle to survive. I need to see what Lord Carter discovered about the keep taken over by the dark witches. Be a good girl for me and don't bite anyone's cock off and kiss them with it. I rather like knowing that your lips have only ever touched mine in such a manner."

"Whatever you want, Knox." I exhaled slowly. He leaned over, intending to kiss me, but I refused it, turning away before he could succeed. "Your lord is waiting for you."

"Indeed, he is. Lore will be in to make sure you're tucked in tightly tonight. I'll be busy for most of the evening, if not longer." Knox stood, moving to the chest at the end of the bed.

I watched him as he dressed for battle, his armor placed anywhere a blade would find purchase. Once on, he reached in the chest and grabbed a small box, placing it on the table. Opening it carefully, he retrieved a silver crown with black and red gems on the tips. Pulling his visor up, he placed the crown into the setting and turned, staring at me.

"Stand and fucking kiss me, Aria."

"Why would I want to do that?" I asked, standing slowly. Walking toward me, Knox wrapped his arms around me carefully, without removing the wicked-looking visor.

"Because I'm trying to be patient, but it isn't in my nature to be so. I have watched you laughing with others, braiding hair for little witches. I have never been jealous in my life until I heard you laughing with another person who wasn't me. It pissed me off that I have never heard you laugh as you did with them before today, woman."

"I have laughed with you, Knox," I argued, uncertain why I felt the need to do so.

"So you have," he smiled tightly, adjusting his visor to cover his mouth, but I reached out, grabbing his arm, which gave him pause. "I need to go."

I pulled him back to me, lifting my hand to push his visor away from his mouth. Claiming it softly, I whispered my goodbye with my lips. His hand rose, chafing my skin to caress me with the gauntlet covering it. He smiled against my mouth, gripping my lip between his teeth, and I gasped softly at the unexpected pain.

"Be good, and don't give Lore too much hell, Little Monster. I'll return as soon as I can," he promised, leaving me as he exited the tent.

It hadn't really hit me that Knox was an honest-to-gods king. Not until he wore his crown, sending butterflies rushing through me. I knew he *was* the King of Norvalla, but he didn't wear his crown or flaunt his title or importance in my face. I'd been here for months and never saw him wear it until today. I had glimpsed him wearing it once in Haven Falls but assumed I'd imagined it all. Now it was going to be hard to ignore who and what he was.

Lore entered the tent, and I smirked as he danced his way in, smiling. "You and me, and that damn jaw, *all* night long, pretty girl!"

"Lore!" Knox shouted through the side of the tent, causing us both to jump.

"*Fine!* No jaw time, Knox," Lore yelled back through the tent's opening, overly excited. "She excels at other things too!"

Knox entered the tent glaring at Lore and then noticed Lore was smiling, and I was hiding my grin behind my hand. Knox's eyes heated as he shook his head at me. "Don't make me bite Aria to ensure your teeth stay to yourself, asshole."

"Dude, I think her teeth are bigger than mine. I'm not claiming that ass. She'd own me. I'm not into domination."

"Good, remember that." Knox walked to me, brushing his mouth against mine again. "Be good, beautiful."

"You said that before when you left a minute ago. Miss me already, Knox?" I teased playfully, and he smiled, brushing his lips against mine passionately.

"Actually, I'm trying to get my scent on you, so you smell like me. I'm about to leave you with my youngest brother, who would hump a tree if it was wet enough."

"I would not hump a tree. Now, find me a wet woman and game on, *bro*."

I grinned at Knox, who closed his eyes against Lore's teasing, then opening them. I lifted on my toes, kissing him hard as his hands ran down my spine. Grabbing my ass, Knox growled in approval.

"Now go be kingly or some shit," I smirked, and his lips twitched. "I don't know what it is I'm supposed to say here."

"That works perfectly." Knox turned on his heel, and he vanished from the tent without another backward glance.

"So, you and me, sugar."

"You and me, Lore." I sat on the bed while he poured whiskey into a glass, bringing it to me.

"Cheers to being left behind as the army marches on without us."

"What?" I whispered, and my stomach dropped with his admission.

"They're going to slaughter witches tonight. I'm stuck babysitting because I'm still mending. You know, I saw you take out the witch with the arrow aimed at me. It was poison-tipped, and that alone would have sucked. It wouldn't have killed me, but fuck if it wouldn't have hurt like hell healing. You keep protecting me, Aria Hecate. You're supposed to be evil. You put flowers in the hair of little girls and laugh at their jokes, even if they're not funny. You hold babies while looking at them as if you want one of your own someday. You have hope, and this world hasn't had that since before I was born. Knox won't ever love you; he's incapable of it. He'll flirt, and he'll be whatever you need him to be, but he can't love you. Don't fall in love with him. Choose someone who will love you back because you deserve to keep your hope for the future."

"Why are you telling me this?" I asked carefully.

"Because you saved my life once, and you tried to do it again, even at the cost of your own. Evil doesn't care about the loss of innocent lives, Princess. You do, so consider it a fucking freebie and drink because I'm thirsty, and I hate drinking alone."

"Cheers to not dying in this bloodbath of a land you guys love so much," I muttered, downing the drink and holding it out for a refill.

"Damn. My kind of woman," Lore smiled, refilling the glasses to the rim. I smirked at his endless flirting as Greer entered the tent.

"Men are assholes," Greer announced.

"Amen," I snorted, smiling at Greer. He tilted his head, dropping on the bed beside me as Lore stood to grab another glass for him. "Pull up a pillow, Meat Suit. Tell me all about it."

Chapter Thirteen

Knox

I peered out over the blood-covered field with anger burning through me. Lifting my blade, I sent it down rapidly into the body of a minotaur. The moment his body dropped, I spun and swung the sword wide, sending his head across the field. Raising my blades, I crisscrossed them as another unwanted beast lunged toward me. His body severing into pieces before I followed it down, sending my sword to remove the head before the body hit the ground.

Brander jumped, flipping toward another monstrous beast. His blade sliced through the shoulder, turning his body as he sent the other creature in the opposite direction, removing the head in a fluid motion. Killian took down three at once, his body created for battle. His blades cut through the air, singing as they found their mark. Dancing, Killian spun low, severing legs from bodies and then heads as all three went down at once.

I tasted the coppery tang in the air, sensing the magic that flooded the field, thick and powerful. The magic was familiar, one I'd felt long ago and wouldn't ever forget. Sweat clung to my forehead, dripping into my eyes, stinging like tiny vipers. The sound of blades cutting through air sang around me, and the witches we'd brought sent energy and defensive magic rushing against the monsters.

Dark witches covered the wide, stone battlement, sending wave after wave of magic toward us. That wasn't what I'd felt, though; it was weaker, less potent. Blood thundered deafeningly in my ears, pounding louder than the drums announcing our entrance onto the battlefield.

A creature ran toward me, and I lifted my blades, twisting my body before it reached me, sending pieces of it flinging across the field. Facing the stronghold, I watched more men lining up to die. My stomach tightened, taking in the faces of the young boys prepped for slaughter. Exhaling a shuddered breath of unease, I turned as Killian and Brander ran toward me, their armor painted red with blood.

"This is a distraction," Killian snapped.

I nodded, unable to look away as the soldiers' swords on the battlement swung, severing head from body, then kicking or pushing the deceased from the high walls.

The dark witches had demanded we bring Aria to them and send her into the stronghold alone. It was a ruse to free her because the magic I felt smelled like the Hecate bloodline, and I knew that stench intimately. The scent had surrounded the carriage I'd found Lore swaddled in, with no sign of my parents, and then again clinging to Liliana on our marriage bed.

"Bring me Siobhan and the other witch, whatever her fucking name is," I snapped, moving across the field, pushing my blades into their sheaths. I lifted my hand, sending power rushing through the beasts that moved toward us, and they shattered into shrapnel that shot into men, tinkling against armor.

"Soraya? The herb brewer?" Brander asked.

"She's fucking lying, and we both know it, Brander. Soraya's a fighter down to her damn soul. It's in her eyes, which is why she's kept them hidden," I grunted, turning as booming footsteps rushed at us. I raised my hand, sending the large, dog-like creature to the spikes bordering the battlefield, impaling it.

"You think she's a spy?" he countered.

"We're about to find out." I turned on the edge of the field to peer up at the evil bitches, still sending waves of magic toward the fighting warriors. "These witches have threatened to kill one hundred men every hour we haven't brought Aria before them. They've just killed children, boys who hadn't ever taken their first woman to bed. I feel Hecate bloodline magic on this field, which means they plan to use a Hecate witch to free Aria from my hold. It's a member of her family or the high queen," I elaborated. "Someone is willing to slaughter an entire village and stronghold to get to Aria."

"You think Aria would approve of this method?" Brander asked, his dark eyes studying me.

"It doesn't fucking matter. Tell me you can't sense that magic, Brander. There would only be one reason for it to be here, and whether Aria was privy to the plan or not, she's still responsible. If she accepts the summons of the dark witches or defends their actions, she will be guilty of the lives lost here."

I turned, watching as Killian walked behind Soraya and Siobhan, his blades drawn. He appeared ready to defend them when, in reality, he prepared to end their lives if they lied. I took in the smaller girl, her dark blond hair sticky with sweat from making healing herbs. Her eyes lowered demurely. There wasn't a coy bone in her fucking body, and I knew it. I sensed the fight within her, noting the way her magic clung to her like second nature.

"My King, you sent for us?" Siobhan asked.

I didn't answer, letting my gaze slide down her gentle curves as heat filled her cheeks. Siobhan was a gentlewoman and skilled lover. She'd allowed me to take her inside the potion tent several years ago. Her soft moans had been pathetic, but I'd gone hard on her— *Once*. I had never craved another taste of her after I'd finished.

"Tell me what you sense." I looked at Soraya. Siobhan opened her mouth, and I glared at her, silencing her with a look filled with warning. My attention moved back to the other witch. Soraya closed her eyes and opened her palms skyward. She tensed, lifting soft green eyes to mine.

"It can't be," Soraya swallowed, and I looked at Killian, who canted his head, tightening his hand on his blade. "I feel Hecate bloodline magic, but it isn't powerful. It's muted. However, there's an underlying current to it. It's seeking, searching for something, or maybe someone." Her attention slid to the woods beside the keep. "It's coming from there, in the woods."

I shook my head at Killian, who stepped back, waiting. My gaze slid to Siobhan, who nodded softly, her worry washing away as Soraya spoke the truth.

"How many are out there?" I asked, directing my comment to Siobhan.

"Three, but two are further out. They're Hecate witches, Knox. They're watered down, unlike Aria. That doesn't mean much, considering Hecate magic is absolute power."

The sound of the howling shrieks on the battlement forced my attention back to where the dark witches were releasing black, poisonous magic. Their shrilling screams were barely audible over the cries and sounds of steel meeting steel on the battlefield.

"Collect a war party, and let's go hunt down some fucking witches," I growled, watching bodies being tossed over the side of the wall to join the others on the ground. "Soraya and Siobhan, you're coming with us."

"I am only a potion maker," Soraya lied. I smiled cruelly, tilting my head as Killian's blade touched against her throat.

"You lie to me again, and that blade severs your head, witch. I suggest you contemplate your next words. When you took that mark onto your wrist, you pledged your loyalty. That includes honesty about what you do and who the fuck you are. So, Soraya, who the fuck are you?"

"I have spent my entire adult life running from Ilsa. She built the Palace of Vãkya in my hometown and unleashed monsters within it as their prize for joining her forces. I served on my back for years, and then I escaped, and I've been running ever since. My bloodline isn't the most powerful, but we are fighters who learned to hide what we are from your people. My mother, father, and sisters didn't get out of Vãkya, and I wasn't much help while chained to a bed for pleasure. By the time I escaped, there wasn't anyone I recognized, either due to torture or because Ilsa had added them to the power grid that sits outside the palace. I was alone. I survived in the wilderness, but I wasn't always successful in that endeavor. I trained myself to fight because I didn't want to die or end up added to the high queen's grid to use until death, drained to nothing more than a husk of flesh and bone. If you're asking if I am powerful, I am. If you're asking if I can fight, I can. You're the first one who hasn't forced me to serve on my back or beaten me. So I serve you, and I do so willingly."

I frowned, hiding the emotion her tale stirred within me. I wasn't blind to what other lords had done to the witches, but then I only saved those I thought I could turn and use against the dark witches. Those that survived and had been through hell, needing somewhere to grow stronger, I'd taken them, too, because once they saw what we fought against, they willingly stayed to help. War created monsters, but monsters had no limit on how far they went. I drew the line at harming women and children, unlike most of the other kings and queens of the Nine Realms.

"Lower the blade, Killian. If you turn against me or you use your magic to hurt anyone under my protection, Soraya," I paused, staring at her coldly, "I won't hesitate to end your life."

"You hold the true Queen of Witches, King

Karnavious. The Hecate witches are here because you hold her, and they want her back."

I smiled tightly, sliding my gaze to Siobhan, who swallowed, averting her eyes. She nodded, not willing to meet my stare, which pissed me off. Most people wouldn't hold it long, not like Aria did with a challenge and dare to push her fucking buttons shining within them.

"How do you know that, Soraya?"

"Because when she touched us, we felt her to our soul. It is Aria Hecate's destiny to kill Ilsa, and she knows it. So do you and everyone standing here. She needs training for war because she's not a fighter. Aria's too fucking soft, and her heart is on her sleeve. Ilsa will tear her apart mentally, and then she'll shred her fucking soul until she lies down and dies."

I frowned at Soraya's words as the men gathered around us. Issuing orders, we moved toward the woods to surround the Hecate witches. I prayed I was wrong, that it wouldn't be Aria's sisters inside the forest, hiding and watching a slaughter unfold. If they sat on the sidelines as the dark witches massacred children on the battlements, then they weren't worth saving.

I hit the jetstream as my men joined me, rushing through the woods. Siobhan and Soraya moved from one direction while we landed in the other. We turned, staring into the woods as a siren released her call. I frowned, shaking my head. Drawing my blades, I moved into the heavily wooded forest while my men spread out.

Magic rushed toward me, and I hit the ground, waiting for Siobhan and Soraya to send theirs back in the direction it had come. The moment they did, I lunged, slamming my fist into the face of Aria's sister, Callista, watching her body go down hard and limp.

Crouching, I stared at the blood rushing from Callista's nose, holding my hand out for the gag Brander tossed to me. My lips curled into a cruel smile, considering what Aria would give me to secure my word that no harm would befall her sister. The satisfaction didn't come, and uneasiness filled my chest. There was no joy in capturing Callista or for what I intended to do with her.

Standing, I backed away as Brander moved closer, binding Callista's hands against magic, securing them and her body so he could carry her back.

"What happens now?" Siobhan asked, her eyes holding mine with concern.

"Now we put Callista in a cage, and I retrieve her lying sister. They're here because of Aria, all of them. This entire stronghold and everyone within it died to free Aria Hecate. Whether or not she knew it, they're all here for her. Now we find out why the high queen wants Aria and what her intention is for her."

"My guess, she wants her dead and buried. Aria is killing her foot soldiers, and leaving bodies piled up isn't something Ilsa would allow to continue," Soraya offered, her word carrying truth. "She's left a huge body count in her wake, and that's had to have been noticed by Ilsa."

"And how the fuck would you know that?" I asked, observing Soraya.

"Because she's an evil bitch, and anyone who isn't on her side is against her. Aria hasn't even gotten close to the Palace of Vãkya, which is a slight against the queen. I am a witch, King Karnavious. I know the price for disobeying the queen and breaking her rules. If you're not beside Ilsa as her puppet or on her grid, you're against her. It is widely known that the silver-haired witch with pretty blue-green eyes brought Lady Asil's keep down. Some whisper she's a monster, and others say she's an angel in the guise of a witch come to free us of Ilsa's terror. I say she's both, and we've yet to see her true power. I fear that once we've seen it, this world will never be the same."

I smiled, hating that Soraya had pegged Aria right down to her pretty eyes that changed with her mood. Swallowing past the turmoil within me, I nodded to Brander and Killian, walking with them back toward camp.

"What about the others in the woods?" Siobhan asked.

"I only need one member of her family to make my pretty witch promise me her devotion."

Chapter Fourteen

Aria

I studied the young witchlings that rushed through the camp, squealing as older ones tried to tag them in their game. They'd been at it all morning, and it was a welcome distraction from worrying about Knox not returning. It had almost been an entire week of silence, which Greer assured, was perfectly normal. Knox had to deal with taking back the strongholds the witches took from the Nine Realms' lords and ladies, so his silence was a good thing, according to the men.

Either Lore or Greer was on babysitting duty while Knox was gone. They barely allowed me to bathe or do anything other than move around the camp, unwilling to let me out of their sight. They didn't let me get close to Soraya or Siobhan without Knox here, nor had I seen them. Admittedly, the people here worked well together. Everyone had their parts to play, and they did it effortlessly since they'd done it for a lot longer than I'd even been alive.

"Penny for your thoughts, beautiful maiden," Lore chuckled, tossing a piece of grass at me to gain my attention.

"Just wondering how many of the witches are willingly here." Frowning, I sat up on the grassy knoll, noting that the older witches seemed happy. The younger ones, and the ones my age, well, they seemed lost here.

"I wouldn't know that answer."

"So what happens if they don't join Knox willingly? Do they end up like the inhabitants of that village we passed?" I snorted, hating that I was in a sour mood because it had worried me.

"Knox didn't kill the people in that village, Aria. You assumed he did, which makes you an ass. In the beginning, it was brutal. It was a full-on war, and yeah, we lost innocent lives. War doesn't care who dies, or if they're a part of the fighting." Lore gazed silently out over the camp.

"Knox knew I thought he'd slaughtered them, yet he chose to let me think the worst of him." I hated that Knox didn't care what I thought about him.

"He's Knox, and he doesn't owe anyone an explanation for his actions. He doesn't explain it to you because you wouldn't understand. You weren't here during that time."

"Who killed those witches and the villagers then?"

"Your family did," Lore admitted, plucking more grass to toss at me. "Your family, although royalty, were ruthless. If witches escaped their rule or laws, they handled it swiftly and without mercy. The wards on the doors were for witches, along with one for the forbidden witch. When Hecate was alive, she was selfish and vengeful, and the witches beneath her rule either fell in line or died. She didn't ask people to join; she demanded they do it or face the consequences of the merciless Goddess of Magic. So, to answer your question, your grandmother ordered a swift death for those who betrayed her for love or wished for peace within the mountain villages."

"Witches killed witches at the start of this war?" I asked cautiously.

"They did. Thousands of witches who refused to bend to the new High Queen of Witches died without warning or cause. At first, no one thought anything of it, other than it was a problem the witches needed to work out amongst themselves. Those who stood back and allowed the witches to fight assumed it would end with them. We were all horribly wrong."

"How did Knox offend Hecate?" I wondered if Lore would tell me since he was chatty at the moment.

"Knox refused Hecate's offer to fix Norvalla during a council meeting. He also turned her down for something more sinister. Within a few weeks of him doing so, the King and Queen of Norvalla went missing, their heads discovered outside Hecate's tomb. Someone went to a lot of trouble to display them as a gift to Hecate, who had recently gone to her eternal slumber. The problem was that only one creature was powerful enough to murder the King of Norvalla."

"Hecate," I said, swallowing hard as Lore nodded.

"Knox argued at a summit with her once, and being

Hecate, she didn't take kindly to a mere prince shooting down her proposal. She wanted him punished for his insolence, but our father refused her request. Knox was training to become king, and he'd stood his ground against the goddess. I've been told that our father couldn't have been more proud. Hecate took issue with it and tried to seduce Knox to her bed, but he refused her again. Knox had no interest in her or any other witch. He'd just met Killian's baby sister and fell in love with her at the same summit which begun their courting. Knox and Liliana were the perfect couple. Liliana was everything he desired, and she besotted Knox. They were to wed soon after returning home. The kingdom rejoiced at having a princess. She was the perfect image of demure and silent strength, and what every queen should strive to be."

I fought the sting of jealousy that reared its ugly head at the sound of longing that entered Lore's tone as he spoke of Liliana. His eyes smiled as he recalled her, and I wrapped my arms around my legs before adjusting the skirt of my dress.

"The Nine Realms leaders summoned my parents to a meeting before the summit ended, leaving Knox in charge while returning to the kingdom. He'd just finished his knighthood with Killian and Brander days before the tragedy struck. To celebrate his coming nuptials and knighthood, they all got drunk, and the soldiers sent in women to entertain them. A courier notified Knox that the king and queen had gone missing before ever reaching the meeting. It forced Knox to stand in as king until our parents were located. They were already dead; he just didn't know it yet. They found the carriage with me still inside, but there was no sign of the king or queen. They'd vanished into the mist without a trace."

"Knox was young, then?" I asked, and Lore turned, nodding slowly.

"But not by your standards. Our knighthood is a rite of passage. It takes five hundred years to achieve in Norvalla. It's an act of dedication and devotion to protect and better the realm. The day the patrol discovered our parents' heads, Knox vowed revenge against those who murdered them. The problem was that Killian was impatient for Knox to take his sister as his bride, so she wouldn't have to wait to wed him when they went to war. Killian didn't want the responsibility of caring for two sisters during that time since he'd raised them after his parent's murder, years before ours died. Knox married Liliana, and the kingdom found some relief knowing he had found his true mate. It eased the grief our people felt at the loss of our parents."

I swallowed hard, looking away from Lore, whose gaze drifted, lost within his memories. "I imagine Knox and his wife were the perfect power couple."

"Liliana was weak and feeble. She suffered horrible headaches once a month. Knox loved and adored her, but Liliana was gentle, and he was savage. Knox worried about her obsessively to where he wouldn't sleep in the same bed with Liliana for fear his beast would take her and harm her during the night. They never shared a bed, and he hardly touched her, worried he would hurt her with his need to mark her."

"Knox does bite rather hard, but it only hurts for a moment. I'm sure she didn't mind it once it turned to pleasure," I muttered, hating the jealousy that wrapped around my stomach, hurting at the thought of Knox marking his true mate.

"Knox never marked Liliana. She was far too delicate for something so savage to be done to her. He tried once, and she sobbed, stating she feared it more than anything. I think if Knox could have, he'd have allowed someone gentler to take his wife to bed if it kept her safe from harm while securing an heir for the kingdom. He devoted himself to her. His need to protect her was unnatural considering the nature of the beasts we house. None of us understood it since Liliana was like us. Her scent was the same as ours, but unlike Killian or Kalyria, Liliana neither rattled nor purred, and she was old enough to do one or the other. She was so beautiful, delicate, and petite. Her disposition was Knox's perfect match, docile and submissive when his temper rose, and yet the soft queen that the people needed and craved after losing our gentle mother."

"Knox does like submission," I frowned, hating that Liliana was pretty much everything I would never be. No wonder he thought I needed to be caged.

"You're nothing like her."

I swallowed, staring at the playing children, hiding the pain Lore's words caused. "I'm neither docile nor demure."

"No, you're savage as fuck. You go to war against Knox, fighting him and making him earn your submission. He isn't worried about hurting you because you take his jagged edges and aren't afraid of getting cut. Knox has never allowed another woman to remain in his bed overnight, yet you don't leave it. Knox isn't soft, and he has no problem fucking a camp follower and kicking her out when he's finished with her. I've never seen him with the same woman twice."

"I'm so glad he doesn't care about how much he hurts me," I grunted, turning angry eyes on Lore, who shook his head.

"You misunderstand my point, woman. Knox can savage you, and you take it. He goes to war against your tight, soft body, and you tell him harder. You're not afraid of his creature, and you should be. The creature inside Knox holds absolute, ancient power that not even the strongest man could stand against, not even our father. It's why Knox is the King of Norvalla. He would have eventually taken the throne from our father, the most powerful creature within the Nine Realms, until Knox matured and his beast awoke. Most people can't hold eye contact with Knox for more than a moment, and you don't look away. You meet his stare dead-on, challenging him with a fire burning in your eyes. We've seen nothing like it before, and considering your heritage, Aria, it's a dangerous thing. It's especially risky for Knox's emotional state, given how much he desires you. He should terrify you."

"He does!" I watched Lore stand, tilting his head to the side to peer down at me.

"Really?" He pursed his lips together, smiling wickedly. "Because from the first moment your beast woke up, you were after that dick. There was an entire room full of monster cock, and in walks this little silver-haired beauty with her tits up, shoulders out, ass all perky and shit. And fuck, you were the hottest thing I'd ever seen in my life! You looked around a room full of rattling alphas and found them *lacking*! Up the stairs you went," Lore grinned, pointing toward the clouds. "Knox, I need that good dick." He rocked his hips, mimicking me, using his hand to make a crude gesture as I laughed behind mine. "And we were all like yes! These mother-fuckers are about to rock the staircase right in front of us! And lord above me, your sweet scent was like the most divine fragrance I'd ever smelled, Aria! But then Knox got all defensive, and he hid your tight body in the shadows. The house started shaking because you two were fucking it to the ground!" Lore slammed his hand toward his crotch, making another crude gesture as he mimicked us. "Oh, Knox, give me that dick! Fuck me now, harder, deeper, destroy me, alpha! Burn this house down with that good dick!" Lore screamed in a high-pitched tone that had people turning to watch as he drew a vivid picture of what he assumed had played out in the hallway on the day I'd gone into heat for the first time.

I fell back laughing, holding my stomach. Lore continued screaming, pretending to be me as Knox fucked me. His eyes were alight with humor as I lifted from the ground, giggling. The shadow behind Lore gave me pause, causing my laughter to still in my throat. Knox stood there, staring at me through a narrowed gaze as Lore continued.

"Oh, Knox, fuck me harder, deeper! You take this fucking alpha dick, Aria! You take it deep into that tight body. That's right, you dirty fucking Little Monster. You take it all real good, Little Witch!" Lore paused, looking at me. I blushed while watching Knox's brow lift in silent question. "He's right behind me, isn't he?"

"Yes," I whispered past the longing in my tone. I slid my gaze over Knox, looking for injuries, and felt a rush of relief when he only appeared to be dirty rather than wounded.

Lore scratched his head, slowly turning to Knox, who had yet to look away from me. "Yeah, we were playing Pictionary or some shit, bro."

"Were you indeed? And did Aria comprehend that you'd watched me fuck her that night, Lore?" Knox asked, studying my face as it fell. "Judging by the look in her eyes, I'm guessing not. Get up, witch. Your Queen has summoned you to the battlefield."

"I don't have a queen." Knox snorted, holding out his hand to pull me up, and the iciness in his eyes sent shivers rushing through me.

His demeanor was chilly. The way Knox watched me said he didn't trust me further than he could see me standing. Swallowing hard, I waited for his command to follow to avoid conflict. We'd been making headway until he'd had time to think.

"You do. You're a witch, aren't you? She just slaughtered over five hundred soldiers and will continue to kill more until we present you to her representative, who murdered an entire village and castle full of innocent people in your name and honor. The dark witches will slaughter everyone to free you, Aria. I'd say that sounds like something a Hecate witch would do, don't you?"

"That's not my fault, Knox," I whispered thickly, hating that he assumed I had something to do with anything so cruel.

"Strange request, don't you agree? Unless this was how you intended to escape me, which is the only thing that would make sense," Knox growled angrily, sliding his attention to my unmarked shoulder blade. "Lore, secure Aria in her cage while I order the camp moved to the battlefield. You better hope this isn't your doing because I have vowed to protect these people, and if you're guilty of the loss of their lives, your pretty head will follow theirs to the grave."

I shivered as Knox turned, moving through the camp. He spoke his language in a low tone, passing people who stopped working and began disassembling the camp. Lore nodded toward the cage that sat outside of the tent I'd shared with him and Greer for the last few days. I exhaled, marching toward it silently before climbing in and closing the door. Fuck Knox and his mood swings. I was over them. It seemed any chance he got time to think; he would over analyze and come back believing the worst about me.

Chapter Fifteen

I'd never seen a battlefield with wounded or dead soldiers. Considering that my fights were rather one-sided, and my army was already dead, it had been easy enough to skip the surreal elements. It wasn't like the one we'd just left with happy people packing up camp.

Fires were lit on the borders of camp while glowing quartz powered by Knox's witches sat brightly around them on each corner. Men helped the wounded to the large medical tents that sat in the center of camp, filled with the screams of the injured or dying. Men stood with bandages covering parts of their bodies while others cried, holding amputated stumps. Bile flooded my mouth, and my stomach tightened from the brutality inflicted on the warriors.

The scent of death and blood filled the air, tickling my nose with the coppery tang. Screams and cries echoed through the field, filling my head. My hands gripped the bars of my cage as I watched the lifeless bodies of witches moved from the frontline.

Unlike the men and warriors, the dark witches had savaged and melted the flesh of the marked witches' skin. Their lifeless eyes stared heavenward while men carried many bodies on large, wide stretchers, adding them to a pile that made my stomach flip, needing to empty its meager contents.

Trembling with apprehension, I pressed my face against the bars as the horse moved me in the cage toward the biggest tent. People rushed all around us, turning to glare at me as they passed my rune-covered cell. Knox had recharged the wards, taking the time to ensure no one could remove me except for him.

Screaming erupted, and men howled, forcing me to cover my ears with my hands. My stomach sank, knowing it had taken us hours to reach the battlefield and that the queen had kept her promise to kill more of Knox's men until he handed me over to her. I could smell the blood in the air, so thick it coated my tongue as I swallowed past the dryness of my mouth. My eyes closed, and the sound of my heartbeat mirrored the war drums as night descended on the camp.

The wagon jerked to a stop. I held my hands against my ears, squeezing my eyes closed. I felt the magic brushing against my skin, bitingly strong within the surrounding air. Power radiated from the keep, churning unease and doubt that I may not be powerful enough to handle whoever was within it.

The cage door opened, and Knox grabbed my arm, pulling me out and pushing me toward the tent nearest where we'd stopped. Instead of moving the cage away, he shoved me into the tent moments before it followed us inside. I looked around, noting that Knox had moved here, leaving me behind. His trunk sat at the foot of the bed, which looked unkempt as if he hadn't slept well in it.

"Strip and get changed," Knox ordered, and I paused, noticing he'd brought my bag.

I silently brushed my fingertips over the semi-sheer tulle dress laid out for me. Peering around, I frowned, turning to where he silently observed me. He wore full battle armor, and the chest plate etched with ravens glowed from the candle's flame.

"I have nothing to wear beneath this, Knox," I admitted softly, and the lines of his eyes creased, narrowing on me.

"Put the fucking dress on now. No one cares what you wear beneath it, or if you wear anything at all, witch."

I swallowed hard, giving him my back. Reaching up, I untied the pink dress I'd worn, revealing nothing beneath. It wasn't like they had a shopping outlet in the Nine Realms where I could go pick up some panties. Lowering the clean dress, I stepped into it, pulling it up and over my curves before straining to zip it. If Knox noticed my struggle, he ignored it, choosing not to offer help.

The dress was A-line with thin sleeves, and a flowing skirt adorned with beaded flowers reflecting the light. A long train flowed from the shoulder straps, giving it a regal appearance even though the back was low hanging, barely covering the base of my spine. I silently spun to face Knox. He ignored the dress, glaring into my eyes, standing closer than he'd been when I'd turned away from him.

"If you try to run from me tonight, I will capture you again. Then, I will hold you in chains for the rest of your days. I will decide how many of those remain, and only me. I don't know what game you're playing with your act of seduction, but it ends here. I'm no longer concerned about who marks you or eases your ache. You've crossed the line this time."

"I didn't do this, Knox. I don't know why the queen wishes for me to be here, but I had nothing to with it. I wouldn't end anyone's life to get free from you. If I wanted to escape, I'd have called my sisters to me and vanished with them, harming no one in the process. It would be a simple matter of calling them here while you're distracted by the fighting, allowing me to escape while you're otherwise occupied. I could have had them hiding in the woods and ran away while you stood on the front line." His eyes turned cold as steel, and his mouth went tight in an angry white line. "You want to assume the worst of me. It makes you feel better to hate me, doesn't it? It allows you to paint me as a monster, and then you can hate yourself a little less for wanting me. And for the record, I wasn't seducing you. You were trying to seduce me, and you fucking suck at it." I righted my shoulders as he reached for me, yanking me toward him and twisting my arm.

"I have something I want to show you before I remove your cuffs." He paused, smiling coldly, forcing me to look at him. "And if I wanted to seduce you, Aria, you'd be putty in my fucking hands, and I'd be buried in that tight body before the end of the night. The thing is, I just don't give a shit to put effort into bedding a witch who is nothing more than a prisoner. And definitely not one I rattled to her knees, begging me to take her so easily that a simple noise was enough to get her panties wet. I'm the fucking King, and I don't seduce anyone, let alone my enemies."

I didn't speak because I couldn't past the lump in my throat. Knox studied my face, smiling as he leaned in, brushing his lips against mine. I pulled away from him, stepping back, needing distance as my heart cracked, and tears swam in my eyes while victory shone in his.

"No snappy comment? No witty comeback taking a jab at inflicting pain against me this time, Aria?"

"What's the point, Knox? You're nothing but a fucking heartless corpse who should have lain down and died with your family." His eyes narrowed, threading his fingers through my hair and yanking me closer as he smiled coldly. My heart thundered against my chest and fear spiked into my soul.

"I can't wait for you to see what I found outside the castle, deep in the woods. Imagine my surprise when I found the last thing I expected, standing sentinel, adding power to the assault unfolding here," he whispered, as my heart began beating painfully against my ribs.

Knox pulled me from the tent, forcing me to run to keep up with him. He moved us through the people who milled about, rushing to help the others or heading toward the frontline. Knox didn't bother talking to anyone who called his name or shouted for his attention over the sound of marching feet or the cries coming from the large keep. Torches high on the battlement blazed as archers let loose arrows, and more screams echoed through the camp. Once we reached one of the wagons, he ripped back the cover, and my heart stopped beating.

Everything went silent around me. The world stopped turning as I shattered into tiny, broken pieces. My mouth opened, but no sound escaped other than a broken sob. Callista turned, shielding her eyes from the light before they widened on me. She leaned forward, wrapping her hands around the bars of the cage as she stared at me.

"Callista," I whispered, barely loud enough to hear. My lips quivered, and I stepped forward to touch her with shaking hands. "Are you okay?" I asked, and she shook her head, looking over my shoulder. "Say something, please?"

"She can't," Knox grunted, watching me with a sarcastic smile playing on his generous mouth. "I've had her spelled to remain silent so she couldn't cast. Unlike you, she's a nymph who sings a siren's song with her words. Your sister will remain alive as long as you behave. Do you understand me, Aria?" When I silently nodded, he chuckled. "I found her outside the castle, deep in the woods. Her magic was pulsing through the battlefield, and my guess is, she was here to get you out of my grasp. You mentioned how you intended to escape, didn't you?"

My eyes flicked to his, knowing I'd told him exactly how I would have escaped his clutches, which coincided with how he'd captured my sister.

Exhaling, I held Callista's hands while she stared at me. She leaned her head against the cage, tightening her grip on my hands. Her eyes pleaded as her lips moved with the word sorry repeating from them.

Tears streaked down my cheeks, and Callista reached through the bars to wipe them away. Shock rushed through me, pain tightening and slicing around my heart after having done everything within my power to keep my family safe, they'd still ended up caged by Knox.

"The others?" Callista's eyes narrowed, and she shook her head, lipping safe to me. I reached into the cage, cupping her neck, bringing her closer, before kissing her forehead. "I will keep you safe, Callista. I promise," I whispered thickly, watching as she sat back, glaring at Knox, who stood stiffly beside me.

"The cage Callista is in isn't like yours, Aria," Knox explained emotionlessly. "If it senses magic trying to release her, it will send spikes through her body before blades release, removing her head. If I were you, I wouldn't try to save her when I remove the cuffs from your wrists," he warned, and I swallowed past the bile the imagery caused.

"I understand," I whispered, unwilling to even look in his direction.

"It's not personal; it's war. You needed the motivation to assist me when I require you to do so. I told you it was only a matter of time before I discovered where your family was hiding. Even if I have to locate them one at a time, I will. Now come, the hour is almost upon us, and every time more of my men die, I want to murder more witches. As I understand, you've got even more secrets you haven't told me. There's an entire keep filled with witches, one you've promised would remain protected from my blade. It's causing quite the stir in the witch community, and it turns out that it was created by none other than Aria Hecate herself, or so I have been told."

"I understand," I stated, feeling Knox's grip tighten on mine. I repeated the only words that would come out as everything within me screamed and cried for my sister, Callista. She was a gentle soul and wouldn't do well in a cage trapped like an animal.

"Look at me, Aria," Knox snapped, turning me before grabbing my wrists and freeing them from the cuffs.

My eyes remained on the ravens that covered his chest plate, unwilling to look him in the eye. He pinched my chin, lifting my face to look at me. My blood rushed to my ears, echoing deafeningly as I exhaled my rising panic. Knox had my sister, which meant I'd do anything he asked of me, even sell my soul to the devil who was apparently the monster in which I had sex.

"The queen's representative asked for you by name, which means she is aware of who you are and what blood runs through your veins. If you are in on this, do nothing you will regret. You will hear what she has to say, and then you will stand back and allow us to finish this battle. Do not engage the dark witches and do not fight against them. Do you understand me?"

"I understand," I repeated, and his eyes narrowed on me.

"Where's the fire in you now, Aria Hecate?" he asked snidely.

I stared through him, turning to look back at where Callista watched us. Knox turned to look at my sister before sliding his gaze back to mine. Snorting, he pulled me with him to where the High Queen of Witches emissary awaited me.

Chapter Sixteen

At the front of the line, chaos ensued as Knox pushed me through the men moving away, forcing me forward. Once we stopped, I stared at the dark witches who all turned, glaring at me coldly as their heckling echoed through the now empty field between us. Magic rushed through my veins as one stepped forward, her eyes the shade of freshly spilled black ink. I could feel the dark magic flowing through her veins as she smiled, revealing rotten teeth.

"Aria Hecate," she hissed, and the other witches tossed back their heads, howling into the night, causing fire to leap from the torches. "The queen wishes to meet with you, murderer of witches."

"I understand," I whispered, and Knox tightened his hold on me.

"Whore to the murderous King of Norvalla, shame be upon you," she hissed, and the witches behind her echoed it as if forced by the noise she created.

I felt their dark magic seeking mine, assessing it, and yet I didn't stop them. I remained in place, hearing what they had to say. It was oily, oozing, dark magic that slithered against my soul, touching and testing me. I didn't reach for my magic, allowing them to assume I was defenseless.

"The queen requests your presence. What say you?" The witch walked closer, strangely, as her body gyrated and twitched. She moved like it was a struggle to walk like a human because of the darkness within her.

"I understand," I repeated.

"The blood that runs through you is pure, yet you spread your body for him? You murder our sisters for him? You're a traitor to our people, and the queen will see you dead, Aria. Blood for blood of yours is light. She intends to drain it and turn you to the night."

The witch lifted her hands, and Knox and those who were behind me all shot backward. A barrier stood between us, leaving me with the dark witches while everyone else was on the other side, unable to reach me. I didn't move to attack or pose any danger on Knox's orders. I stood motionless, uncaring that they intended to end my life.

I wasn't afraid to die.

Dying was easy.

Living was terrifying.

Not knowing if my sister would survive was horrifying, and that left me frozen in place.

"Aria!" Knox snarled, and I turned, staring at him. "Bring it down now!"

"I can't," I admitted, turning to look at him over my shoulder. "I can't bring it down."

His eyes searched mine before lifting toward the witches and slowly coming back to lock with mine. I was going to die here because he had my sister. I couldn't fight back and chance him losing it and harming her. I swallowed the bile that the thought induced as magic hummed behind me. Slowly, I turned toward the witches who approached me with harsh looks burning in their eyes, along with madness.

I felt them growing their combined magic, pulling it from one another as the men they'd captured screamed in warning behind them. My eyes scanned the men for injuries and magic, finding them safe other than behind a line of cankerous, evil witches. They were the bait to get me here. The barrier that trapped me once I'd reached the camp was meant to be my tomb.

The first wave of magic sent my body slamming against the barrier. Pain ripped through me as I screamed, howling until it had washed through me. Slowly, I rose from the ground. I no sooner had reached my feet when another, more substantial wave struck me.

I screeched from the intensity of the magic, dropping to my knees as my ears popped, and all sound dimmed. I covered my ears, holding them while pain ripped through me, raw and brutal as wave after wave of magic continually slammed into me.

When it stopped, I turned, facing the witches, only to scream in pain as an arrow sliced through my shoulder, bouncing off the barrier. Lowering my head, I gritted my teeth against the agony. As I ensured it hadn't done too much damage, another one impaled my arm. My hand shook as I ripped the arrow from my arm, screaming as I got to my feet. More arrows were let loose, and I dropped to the ground, lowering my head as they peppered the surrounding dirt.

"Aria," Knox whispered. I lifted my head, finding him at the same level as me. His eyes searched mine as I spat out blood.

"I thought you said she was the most powerful witch you'd ever encountered. She seems rather disappointing, King Karnavious," Lord Carter snorted beside Knox.

"Fight," Knox growled.

I stared at him, knowing that I could end this here. I could be free of the pain he and this world wanted to give me. Knox searched my eyes, seeing the indecision dancing within them. His worry-filled gaze lifted as I heard the volley of arrows sailing toward me. All I had to do was let them reach me, and it ended. However, I wasn't done yet.

I spun and lifted my hand, stalling the arrows' descent toward me. They froze in place, hovering in the air, and the world went silent around me as magic flowed through my veins, igniting the power of the Nine Realms rushing to heed my call. I sent the arrows flying toward those who released them, smiling as their screams echoed through the keep.

I turned my hands, pointing my finger before twirling it, producing a portal that opened in the middle of the field. Dropping my hand, I used the other to force the warriors standing behind the witches into it, hearing their cries as they exploded through the other side of the barrier and into the hands of Knox's army.

Slamming the portal closed, I smiled wickedly at the witches. Silently, I walked toward them, flicking my finger, forcing the leader to land behind me against the barrier in front of Knox. Both of her knees shattered along with her pelvis as I twisted my lips into an evil grin.

The witches called more magic to them, and I allowed it, pausing midfield to prevent it from reaching me. The moment they sent it toward me, I unleashed my anger and frustration from the moment Knox had caught me until I'd entered this barrier.

The ground exploded directly in front of me, rushing toward the dark witches until their bodies imploded, sending blood into the air in clouds of pink mist. The castle trembled from my fury. Fiery stones rained from the sky as my scream ripped through the clearing, rushing toward it with the magic I'd stored over the past several months.

The men assisting the dark witches on the battlements splashed against the ground with a popping sound. The wind sent the flames leaping toward the heavens, and I screamed until I was hoarse. Giant meteor-sized balls of fire continued slamming into the stronghold until reduced to ruins. I didn't stop the fiery assault until satisfied that nothing else was alive within the keep.

Explosions erupted from within the castle, sending shrapnel of the fiery rocks sailing toward me. I didn't move, didn't feel fear at the moment, then peace settled in my soul from creating chaos. A smile played on my lips. The soothing inner peace from raining down hell on evil sent a rush of warmth through me.

Lightning crashed, slamming into anything that still

breathed. All sound sucked out of the barrier, and my heartbeat echoed loudly in my ears as my blood pulsed. The ground rumbled, drawing the remains and wreckage of the keep deep into the earth, ripping a hole where the once magnificent castle had stood. In its place were fresh soil and the fire that continued to burn with my rage.

I whispered a spell to expel the flames. Then I whispered another, watching as flowers grew, budding and blooming with beauty. Trees pushed through the ground, filing the meadow, appearing as if they had always been part of the forest, untouched by man. I silently took in the beauty before a shrill scream pierced the serenity I found in creating beauty.

Turning, I glared at the dark witch, knowing my eyes danced with flames. I walked toward her as fear filled her obsidian gaze. My hair floated around me, and no mark marred my forehead, just the power bestowed to me by the Nine Realms and those who had created the monster I was becoming.

"Tell the High Queen of Witches I will see her soon and that I am coming for her fucking head," I snarled, ripping the dark witch's head from her torso with the anger still rushing through me. I turned, glaring at Knox and the silent army that all stared at the flowering field behind me.

I tossed her head at his feet the moment her magic dropped, and the barrier fell. His eyes lowered to the head before slowly sliding to take me in, unable to look away. I closed the distance to him, holding up my arms for his magic nulling cuffs.

"How the fuck did you do that?" Knox whispered.

"Easy. I simply imagined a world where my sisters no longer existed, and I decided I'd rather burn it to the fucking ground than allow it to continue without them. That was merely a sliver of my power. Don't make me show you my true strength. You have my attention. Do I have yours, King Karnavious?" I whispered so softly that I wasn't sure he had heard me, but then the entire battlefield had filled with silence at what I'd done.

Knox replaced the cuffs, lifting his eyes to the field before slowly sliding them back to mine. A single tear slid from my eye to roll down my cheek. "I'll be in my kennel, Master," I whispered, moving through the crowd that parted quickly, fear etching their faces as I walked by them.

Knox's marked witches stopped whispering to bow as I passed them, uttering blessings to me. I ignored them, unwilling to bless anything. They spoke my name in awe and horror, fear etching their tone at the taste of the power I'd unleashed to show Knox precisely what I'd been holding back from him.

Pausing before I entered the tent, I slid my attention to Callista, who watched me with wide, horrified eyes. Her confused stare moved back to the meadow that still had flowers blooming throughout it, pulling from the blood that had dripped from my wounded shoulder, feeding the land my power.

I could destroy this world, but I didn't want to do that. I wanted to fix it, but if Knox or the dark witches thought fucking with my family was an option, I had to show them what happened if they did. I had to show just how badly that mistake would end for them and the entire Nine Realms.

"I love you, Callista," I whispered, knowing she'd hear me.

Her hands touched the bars as she leaned against them, nodding her head. Soft blue eyes filled with silent tears while she stared at me from her cage. She mouthed the same, her hand moving to her heart as silent tears rolled from my eyes.

Five minutes.

It had taken me five minutes once Knox had freed me of his command to end the fight they'd been battling for almost seven days. Could I do it again? I probably could if he pissed me off enough to bring the same rage to my soul. Considering it was Knox, there was a high probability.

If Knox or anyone else killed my family, I'd bring him the ending he craved. I'd set the entire world on fire and watch it burn to ashes, letting him live in the chaos of the remains.

Chapter Seventeen

One of Knox's men pulled me from the cage and sat me at a table where people celebrated the battle's victory. I wasn't celebrating shit with them. A woman poured whiskey into a goblet and pushed it in front of me, but I refused to drink with them. My anger and fear hadn't dissipated, nor would it until I knew Callista was free and away from Knox's rage.

Knox silently studied me, along with the others who sat with us at the table. I stared through them to the cage that held my sister. I felt no hunger or need. My magic had drained, and I fought the need to still the trembling within me. It was dangerous to drain so much of my power, but I wasn't stupid. I knew Knox would never release me now, not after seeing the destruction in which I was capable.

I'd held back, forcing myself not to expose the true force of what I could unleash, in case anyone was watching. Now he knew. He'd witnessed the fiery storm that rained from the skies upon my call, the anger that I released from fear and frustration. Knox knew he not only held the strongest Hecate witch, but now he knew my other half relied on fire.

I could call down the stars to burn the worlds to nothing more than ash if I felt like it. What surprised me and everyone else that witnessed my destruction was that I had tapped into the Nine Realms' power. That power enabled me to rebuild and restore the meadows, creating life from blood and ash.

"Drink. You've earned it, Aria," Lore chuckled, bumping my arm while smiling from ear to ear.

I turned my gaze on him slowly. He went silent the moment my eyes locked with his, finding nothing in them other than cold detachment. Lore swallowed, swinging his gaze to Knox, who continued to stare at me and then back at the field in which we sat.

Men piled meat on the table, glancing at me before walking off. Lord Carter sat beside Knox, his eyes still wide like an owl's as he studied me from where he sat across from me. I placed my hands on the table, and he jumped backward, falling from his chair, which should have caused some joy, but it didn't. Instead, I felt only fear and emptiness for Callista's future.

"Do not raise your hands at me, witch!" Lord Carter snapped, climbing from the ground, staring at where I'd simply folded them on the table.

Knox took in the position of my hands before turning to look at Lord Carter, who was a pretty shade of green. Knox looked at the plate in front of me and lifted his eyes to hold mine.

"Eat, Aria," Knox demanded.

"No, thank you, Your Majesty." I slid my eyes away from his, staring toward the covered cage, unable to look away as the fear of it activating slithered through my mind.

"Eat your food," Knox insisted.

I reached down, grabbing the plate and tossing it over my shoulder, hearing someone grunt behind me. The goblet followed as Knox, narrowing his eyes on me as if he was searching for something to say. Instead, he slid his eyes back to where the castle once stood, frowning.

"Would you like anything else to eat or drink?" Greer asked, and I glared at Knox.

"No, thank you, sir," I whispered demurely, and Knox frowned at my tone.

"Drink with me, Aria," Lore whispered, leaning against my shoulder.

"No, thank you, sir," I repeated, and he exhaled as Knox stood, moving around the table to grab my arm.

He yanked me from the table and pulled me behind him to the tent where he turned, closing the curtain, spinning around to stare at me. "You blew up an entire fucking castle. How the hell did you do that?"

"I told you." I waited for him to speak again.

"Get on the bed," Knox ordered. I reached for the straps of the dress, but his hands captured mine, holding them. "Leave it on, Aria."

"As you wish, Your Majesty." I walked to the bed, standing beside it. "How would you like me positioned?"

Knox stared at me, pushing his fingers through his hair.

"Sit down, woman." He glared at me as I sat, crossing one leg over the other, looking up at him. Knox sat beside me, placing his hand on my leg, and I stared at it like it was a bug I couldn't remove. "Callista is safe from harm. Her cage doesn't move unless I make it. Do you understand me?"

"I understand," I replied.

"Say something else, woman."

"Whatever you wish," I muttered.

"Ride me," Knox commanded, and I swallowed as anger slithered through me.

Silently, I stood and removed my dress as he watched. The garment pooled on the ground at my feet, and I stepped out of it. Knox leaned back, crossing his arms behind his head as I bent down, unbuttoning his pants while he allowed it. He waited for me to straddle his body before rolling us, and I peered up at him, offering a deadened stare of boredom.

He lowered his mouth, kissing me slowly even though I failed to kiss him back. Lifting his head, he stared down at me with heat burning in his eyes.

"Kiss me, Aria," he stated, and I lifted, placing a soft kiss against his mouth before spreading my legs.

"Get it over with quickly. I am tired, Master," I whispered, turning to look away from him as my hands fisted the furs on the bed, and tears slipped from my eyes.

"Is that so? From my viewpoint, it took you less than ten minutes to decimate an entire castle, and with it, over five thousand enemies, along with powerful dark magic witches." Knox sat up, staring down at me.

"Five minutes and ten thousand," I returned without a trace of emotion in my tone. "They had filled the two lower levels with reinforcements. The witches weren't powerful, but the witch controlling them was. Behind the castle were more warriors who had only just arrived."

"You can't possibly know that." He ran his fingers over my stomach before dipping his head and clasping his teeth over my nipple.

I gasped, closing my eyes as his fingers trailed through the arousal coating my sex. His finger pushed into my body, and I closed my eyes, forcing myself not to react, which was easier said than done. Knox lifted his head, finding my face scrunched up while my chest rose and fell from the emotion slithering through me.

"If you're going to rape me, just do it," I hissed as my throat swelled with frustration.

"Get up," Knox growled angrily, grabbing my arm to pull me from the bed. He moved to the chest, withdrawing a sheer nightgown that he tossed at me. He retrieved the whiskey and his sweatpants, nodding at the table for me to sit. "Get it on and sit down, Aria."

I pulled the gown over my head, sluggishly moving to sit before facing him. He searched my face and rubbed his eyes. He poured two glasses of whiskey and pushed one in front of me, sitting back to observe me.

"Drink," he ordered, and I lifted it, downing it in one long gulp. He refilled it and nodded, narrowing his eyes on me as I drank it too. He did this several more times before he slapped the glass from the table, leaning over it to look me in the eye. "In about five minutes, the time that it took you to destroy an entire stronghold, you're going to be fucking drunk. I want to fuck you, hard. I want to bend you over and pound into your naked core so gods damn hard they hear me back in your human world as I go to town on that tight body of yours. That's what I want to do in five minutes. Instead, I'm going to walk you outside of this tent, and we're going to go release your sister."

"What?" I asked softly, lifting my eyes to hold his.

"Here are my conditions because her release isn't free, Aria." Knox studied my face, frowning as he grabbed my hand, pulling me closer to him. "You're going to kiss me as you did in that healing pool." I blinked, frowning at his request.

"That's all you want?" I questioned with disbelief, my brows pushing together while I studied him.

"Not even close. I want your help to free the keeps between here and Norvalla. Once we reach my kingdom, you will fight this war at my side, on my side, Aria Hecate. You'll be mine to do with as I wish."

"I'll be your slave?" I snorted, knowing I should have realized he wouldn't ever just want a kiss.

"Don't think of it like that," he growled, eyeing me.

"That's what I'd be. I'd be your whore to fuck whenever you needed to get off and a weapon to wield against your enemies, which are my people. You are asking for everything you want with the release of my sister."

"You offered to sell your soul to the devil to keep them safe. I'm your devil, Aria, and as such, I want to know the location of the keep where you're hiding the witches you've promised safety from my sword. You shouldn't make promises you can't keep."

"That's something I won't tell you, Knox. You may find the keep, but you will never get past the stone walls shielded by the magic of the Nine Realms. Since you're concerned about empty promises, I won't guarantee that I won't try to escape you."

"I know, and I wouldn't expect you to do so." Knox placed his elbows on the table, assessing me. "I also don't intend to allow you to escape me. I thought you were powerful for a witch, but you're not. You're a fucking game-changer. You could help me make this world a better place."

"I would willingly fight at your side if you gave up the need to kill all witches, Knox. If you vowed not to murder the ones who have done no harm, and my family, I'd fight this war at your side while riding your cock into battle like a stallion."

His lips twitched as his eyes sparkled, shaking his head. "That can't happen." He frowned, watching the way I shook my head. "Come kiss me and seal the deal. You better make it believable, and I better feel your soul touching mine when I taste your lips."

"I'm not finished negotiating with you." His mouth opened and closed before he smiled, sitting back, crossing his arms over his chest.

"Let's hear it, Aria." Knox pushed his glass in front of me, smiling, running his thumb over his lip as I followed the path. I accepted the whisky, sipping it while watching him over the rim. I set the glass down, sucking my lip between my teeth, causing his eyes to lower.

"I'm not sleeping with you," I announced, and his hand dropped from his mouth. "Not because I don't want to, but because mentally, I haven't healed, Knox. I am strong and lethal, but I'm only twenty-five years old and nearly been raped twice since coming here." I reached up, wiping a tear, looking away from the pain that filled his eyes. Exhaling slowly, I struggled to contain the pain the words caused.

"I will help you, but not if innocent lives are in the way. I'm not willing to carry that blood on my soul. I'll never stop trying to escape because I'm not a fucking pet that you can cage. If you intend to mark me, I have to agree before you do it," I continued, noting the way his eyes narrowed at my last condition. "I'm not saying it won't happen. I just have to be ready for you to do that to me again."

"Because it's so fucking vile?" Knox snorted, grabbing the bottle of whiskey to down it while staring at me.

"No, Knox. Because it's a significant thing for me to allow you to mark me," I whispered as he paused with the bottle halfway back to the table. "To you, it may be a mark of ownership or alpha badassery to claim my body. To me, it seemed deeper and more meaningful. It meant something to me to allow your mark on my flesh. I liked it there, knowing it was yours, but you changed that. Removing it felt wrong, but leaving it there wasn't right either. Not after what you did to me, thinking the worst of me and what you thought I could do," I said carefully, lowering my eyes from his. "I felt as if I was ripping out a part of my soul when I removed it from my shoulder."

My hands fidgeted in front of me as he exhaled.

"It meant more to me, too," Knox admitted after a moment had passed in silence.

"Deal?" I lifted my tear-filled eyes to hold his from the admission that his mark had meant more than just an ownership tag. I hadn't expected him to say it, and his words sent warmth flooding through me.

"I'm not done," he said with a playful smile on his lips.

I snorted, scrunching my nose while I held his gaze. "What else could you possibly want from me?"

"Beltane is approaching. I want you to be my partner throughout the festivities. I want one night where you lower your shields and give yourself to me. I want the real, unguarded, unprotected version of Aria Primrose Hecate. No walls between us for twenty-four hours. Just you and me, with no impending war, no future, and no past between us," he whispered, his eyes holding something I hadn't ever seen—fear of rejection.

"You don't get turned down often being King, do you?" I asked, and he covered his mouth before retrieving the other glass, filling them both.

"I've never been told no in my entire life until I met you, Aria." His eyes held mine, watching me chew my lip silently.

"Really? That explains so much," I laughed soundlessly.

His lips twitched, and his head shook as he placed my glass in front of me. "I'm the King, and no one says no to a king or a future king." He held out his hand, and

I stared at it for a moment.

"I'm considering it still. I have conditions."

"You're a better negotiator than Killian. Maybe you should do his damn job."

"One day with no walls, no ghosts, and since it is Beltane and things—*happen* during Beltane," his smile turn wolfish while his eyes sparkled with laughter, "if we end up in bed together, it has to be my choice. I have to be ready for it, mentally and physically." I stood, slowly moving to where Knox sat, straddling his lap. I lifted my arms, resting them around his neck as my fingers pushed through his hair. "Deal, King Karnavious?"

"You'll bless the ceremony?" he asked huskily, staring at my mouth.

I licked my lips slowly, tilting my head to the side. Adjusting on his lap, I shivered at the feel of his erection through his sweatpants. Heat unfurled within me, and I wallowed past the lump in my throat as I smelled the arousal that oozed from him with my nearness.

"Is the land purified?" I countered.

"It's purified, but no one has brought it to life in over four hundred years. I just need to provide my people with a semblance of hope of fertility. The ceremony gives them that, even if it is an empty hope."

"What is wrong with the fertility of your people?" I asked, noting the slight twitch in his jaw.

"We believe Hecate cursed us to become sterile soon after we conceived Sven. He was among the last of our young to be born to our race."

"Of course she did. She was seriously one evil,

sadistic bitch," I muttered as he smiled. "What? Don't you think I know she was evil? I spent the first fifteen years of my life told how perfect and selfless my grandmother was. How she'd spent her entire life trying to better the Nine Realms, yet there was no proof of her deeds or anything to back it up, other than chaos and destruction left in her wake. They wanted us to ignore those things because, to find peace, one must first burn the world to the ground and rebuild what they desired. If that had happened, people would have suffered, and yet there was no talk of those who had lost everything because of Hecate's plan to take control of all Nine Realms. Nobody asked those questions except for me, and they punished me for it. If you asked me, anyone demanding all Nine Realms learn about how giving and amazing Hecate was, has to have been one self-absorbed cunt."

Knox smiled wider, and I swallowed. The air left my lungs at the beauty of something so rare and unguarded that it knocked me stupid, sending my body into a downward spiral that threatened to take my breath away.

"Are you sure you're a Hecate witch, Aria?" he asked, narrowing his eyes on me.

"I am, I'm afraid. We have a deal, but considering who I am and things I have set into motion, your people might want to be careful." His eyes narrowed. "I'm not saying what I did, so don't ask me, Knox. I won't chance jinxing it because too much depends on my plan, and too many people deserve it to become their reality. I used a lot of power to achieve what I have so far, but it also got me caught by you because I put the people before myself." I studied his face for a moment. "So do we have a deal, and Callista goes free?"

"Kiss me," he whispered thickly.

I leaned over, placing my lips softly against his before deepening the kiss, putting everything I had into the act. The kiss turned into something deeper, more turbulent. I moaned against him, whimpering as he gripped me behind the neck, holding me to his heated lips. His hands lowered to my hips, and I rocked against his hardened length. He devoured me until I was panting as he pulled away.

"Let's go let her out," I whispered breathlessly, and he smirked.

"Callista's already gone, Aria. I gave the order for Killian, Lore, and Brander to escort her away from here. Siobhan and Soraya have opened a portal for her to put distance between us. She's on her way back to your family."

"But..." I paused as my stomach tightened. Worry entered my mind as his eyes narrowed, and something cold passed beneath his stare.

"I only needed her long enough to show you I had her. I needed your word that you would willingly help me and light the fires at Beltane. You're not the type of woman who gives her word and then goes against it, Aria. You have a rare honor code that I respect. Today, I saw you kill with your grief, and I saw myself in it. I won't make you into the monster your family has turned me into unless I have no choice. If you ever harm my people, I won't hesitate to return it tenfold, but I won't reach for your family unless that happens. When the time comes to handle them, I will do it without mercy because

I made a promise to end your line, and I will keep that promise."

I stared at him as my mind replayed the time we'd been in the tent and that he'd already released my sister. I swallowed hard, narrowing my eyes on him as my heart kicked into overdrive, thumping against my ribcage to get free. I'd enjoyed matching wits against him, lost in the sexiness of his bartering and negotiating that I hadn't considered what could be happening here.

"You released Callista so you could find out where they are all hiding," I whispered through quivering lips.

"Of course I did, Aria. I'm not a fucking idiot. You're in over your pretty head, little girl. The first rule of negotiating: always have a visual of what you're negotiating. Second, always make sure you have the upper hand within the negotiations and cover your bases. You never even considered I would send a magical tracker home with Callista. You should have realized how far I will go to get to them. I promised you that no matter what happened between us, my end goal wouldn't ever change."

"So why negotiate at all?"

"Because I want you, and I'm a selfish prick who isn't above cheating to get everything I want, and I did. In the next forty-eight hours, I will know exactly where they are and how to get to them. I only need one alive, and that's you, Aria. If I were you, I'd start working on your negotiating skills and a way to remove their magic, so I don't have to make you into a monster like me. I'm open to hearing what you're willing to offer me to spare their lives." His eyes slid down my body leisurely as a sardonic smile played on his mouth. "Now, get your tight little body into my bed because I still have shit to do tonight. Unfortunately, you're not on that list." He crowded my space, lowering his eyes to my trembling lips.

"You're a bastard," I swallowed past the tightening in my throat, hating the tears that slipped free of my hold as fear slithered through me, wrapping around my heart.

"For research purposes, how rattled are you right now, Little Witch?" he asked, lifting me as he stood. Holding my waist, he set me on the ground, tilting my chin to peer into my eyes while I internally screamed at what had just happened. "I'd say you finally understand that you're out of your league, wouldn't you? You may be powerful and the most gorgeous woman I have ever seen in my life, but you're a Hecate witch, and that's a big problem for me."

"I wish I'd never met you, Knox," I whispered, wiping the tears from my eyes. "I'm trying to right the wrongs that my people did to you and the Nine Realms, and you're just trying to destroy me."

"No, Aria. I don't want to destroy you. Just your bloodline and those who follow it blindly," he whispered, holding my chin in place, watching the tears roll down my cheeks. "You, on the other hand, I just fucking want at my side. I'm willing to do whatever it takes to keep you there, and I wish it were as easy as saying you're mine. You're anything but easy and everything I shouldn't want, and still, I crave you. Do you even know the difference between a white witch and a dark witch?"

"One practices light magic. The other follows the darkness into death for the power it offers them."

"We own one, and they cling to the light. The other, the dark witches, they're your people, witch. The dark witches within the Nine Realms are what's left of the Hecate bloodline and the ones who still follow your grandmother's rules. You're the bad guys, Aria. Maybe stop feeling sorry for yourself. Get to know the other witches in camp. Ask them about those who held on to your laws and what happened to them. Ask your people what transpired and why they fled from the crown that should have protected them. After all, you're here to take that crown, aren't you? You don't even know what it means to hold a crown, and yet you're so willing to help Aurora get it from the High Queen of Witches. That will only exchange one evil bitch for another. You're not here to change the world, Aria. You're here to put Aurora on the throne, and you're too fucking blinded by love and devotion to see what is right in front of you."

"I don't want the crown."

"No, you don't. But your family does, and you are their pet, one who jumps when they tell you to jump," he laughed hollowly. "Aren't you? Do you think I'm the only one using you? Wake the fuck up, Little Monster. You're in over your head and playing with people who have had lifetimes to arrange their chess boards, cementing their plans. You're just a little girl skipping blindly around the gameboard, assuming everyone has a heart. Spoiler alert, Aria. None of us have that useless organ anymore because your bloodline ripped it out and ate them."

Chapter Eighteen

I woke alone in an empty bed. Turning over, I surveyed the tent, finding no one. Sitting up, I yawned and stretched my body, feeling the magical residue that flittered through me, itching to be used. Unfortunately, the cuffs prevented that from happening. Frowning, I noticed a cup of water on the table and the single flower placed into it. I scooted from the bed, padding on bare feet to pick up the flower, dropping it immediately.

My lips pulled down into a deep frown while my brows pushed together. Holding up my fingers, I stared at the pink burn that had seared my fingertips. *Asshole.* It had been a long time since I'd seen a hemlock flower bud. I looked at the bushel that held tiny white flowers spreading from the stem.

Knox had zero seduction skills, and even if he pumped them up, I'd be hard-pressed to give a shit at this point. He was lucky I was magically neutered after his little shit show last night. He wanted to battle with his wits, showing me he was more skilled than I had thought. I hated that it had impressed me. Luckily, I'd been too floored and in shock to give him the response he'd wanted. Instead, he'd once again left me cold and confused.

He'd had time to think, and when he had that time, he thought the worst of me. Knox wasn't just broken; he was shattered. He was in pieces he fought to hold together, and if they faltered, he clutched them tighter. I was beneath his skin, under it, so to say.

Knox didn't want to hurt me, protecting me in his own way. If I was in danger, he fought hard to ensure I was safe and unharmed, even at the cost of his safety. He held me through the night to keep my demons away, but when the sun rose, so too did his walls.

I stepped away from the table, smelling the hemlock-laced water. Grabbing my bag, I pulled out the only clean dress left. It was a halter dress with two lengths of cloth that covered my breasts, with an open back, and a front that flowed into a tulle skirt that was wispy and delicate.

Pulling out the brush, I combed through my hair, working it into a braid that went around my head, appearing like a crown of smooth, silver hair. I used the diamond embedded pins to hold it in place, finishing the look with the silver chains that adorned my waist, neck, and ankles. I looked regal and born to be a witch in the soft, baby-blue dress.

Exiting the tent, since I hadn't been ordered to stay inside, I looked for Brander to get some cream to stop the pulsing burn on my fingertips. Soldiers stepped into place behind me as I headed for the extensive medical tent, assuming he'd be within it. Discovering he wasn't,

I frowned, absently chewing my lip while looking for someone to ask his whereabouts.

"Do you know where Brander is?" I asked a soldier who watched me in silence, ignoring my question. Snorting, I walked toward the witches. Reaching Siobhan, I smiled, but she dropped her tonic vials and stepped back, worry etching her wide eyes. "Do you know where I can find Brander?" I asked, watching the color drain from her face before she turned, walking away from me. "Thanks!" I called to her retreating back.

I went to the warriors, and they cleared a path to avoid being near me. I almost wanted to smile, but the burn that had merely been on my fingertips had now reached my wrist. Hecate witches were more than sensitive to hemlock, and a single touch could leave us writhing in pain for days. I was about to have a painful reminder of why it was so toxic to us, and it would not be pretty.

I approached the guards sitting on the camp's edge, knowing they couldn't leave their post to escape me. Smiling, I noted the loathing and worry filling their glares while I closed the distance between us.

"Gentlemen, blessed be," I smiled tightly, aware they'd worry at the blessing shit. Non-witches hated that saying, and we used it often, simply because we fucking could. "Have you, by chance, seen Brander?" I asked, hating that I needed to figure out where he was.

"He's in the woods, witch," one stated, hiking his thumb over his shoulder toward a trail.

I frowned, wondering if the guards would try to stop me. Stepping over the protection barrier, I waited for them to sound an alarm, and when they didn't, I started toward the forest's entrance with a quick thank you.

My guards were close behind me, and I could feel their fear oozing from their pores. I guess it took an act of rage to force a little fear into Knox's people. Lost in my thoughts, I moved deeper into the woods. When I heard a loud moan, I stopped in my tracks, and the sight of Brander's naked ass came into view.

The descent thing to do would have been to look away from the really sexy, really nice ass thrusting forward. I, however, was in dire need of Brander's help right now. A woman was in front of him on her knees, her naked body moving as he used her mouth. His noises sent heat into my cheeks, forcing me to swallow down the need blooming in my center.

I stepped back, and a twig snapped beneath my feet. Brander's head turned toward me, his eyes locking with mine. Heat pooled in them, filling with obsidian as he watched me, not stopping the thrusts of his hips as he continued pushing into the woman's mouth. I turned, hurrying back through the guards toward the trail, when Killian stepped into my path, blocking my exit from the licentious scene I'd observed.

"You're not supposed to be out here, witch," Killian snapped, peering over my shoulder to glare at the guards.

"I needed Brander," I swallowed.

"He's busy," he countered, lowering his eyes to my dress.

"I really need Brander, Killian," I whispered, fighting against the urge to rush toward the water I could hear, pushing my hands into it to ease the burn.

"He's fucking busy. You'll have to wait."

"I can't," I stated, holding up my hands. "Someone left hemlock in the tent and laced the water in which they placed it. I touched the flower and smelled the poison."

He examined the burns creeping up my arms and exhaled, glancing back into the woods. Killian didn't speak, not until he started toward camp, staring over his shoulder when I didn't move.

"Come on. We'll get the ointment and start. Brander's not coming yet," he grunted, and the guards laughed behind me at the lame pun.

I followed Killian to a large tent, stopping outside to collect the strength to enter alone with a man who literally wanted my head removed. Inside were rolled-up bedrolls and small tincture bottles. Killian pulled out a large bag, searching through it before pointing to a chair, indicating I should sit. I silently took a seat, holding out my hands.

Killian settled in front of me in a crouched position, looking into my eyes before he removed the small cork and grabbed my hand. I hissed, and he muttered an apology. His hands were rough, and yet he was gentle as he tended to the blistering burns with a cream that offered instant relief.

"You could have killed us when we captured you," Killian pointed out carefully. "You could have killed us several times over while we were tracking you down. Why didn't you?" He lifted his cerulean eyes to hold mine.

"I didn't want you guys dead. I've never intended to hurt Knox, but I also won't allow him to keep me as his slave, Killian. He's done nothing to warrant death yet. He's flirted with it, skated the line a few times, but he hasn't truly wanted me hurt. I can't undo what my family has done, but if I could, I would. There's no magic, and no spell to undo deeds of the past or to rectify them."

"Knox intends to kill you," Killian reminded me without hiding the look of loathing in his eyes. His hand brushed against my thigh, and he lowered his head to stare at the exposed flesh. Killian lifted his hand, gripping my thigh as my breathing grew labored. "He will eventually have to take your head, no matter how much he craves you. Knox has never broken a vow in his entire life, and this one means the most to him."

I swallowed as Killian's hands trailed up my thigh, stopping in the middle to push his fingers against the inside. Dumping a drop of the cream on the burning flesh, he massaged it into the area where the flower had touched me as it dropped.

"I know he will, but that isn't today. He plans to use me against his enemies, and we've yet to figure out who here wants me alive."

"You're not his mate either," he growled, and I smiled sadly.

"I know," I exhaled slowly as Killian continued rubbing the cream into my flesh, working it deep into the tissue to ease the pain.

"You're like us, and probably one of our mates, or someone within the kingdom. You need to let him go, Aria."

"Aden," I announced, watching Killian's eyes lift to hold mine.

"The man inside the cavern is your mate?" he asked.

"He's who I plan to choose," I answered, hearing someone snort beside me. I turned, seeing oceanic-colored eyes that glared down at me.

"I don't think so," Knox growled. His stare slid to my hands and thigh, where Killian still worked the cream into my burn. "What happened?"

"She said someone left hemlock in your tent," Killian stated, his eyes lifting to meet Knox's stare. "I'm done. You're a witch. You should know what the fuck hemlock looks like when you see it. Be more careful."

"Get up, Aria," Knox demanded.

I rose from the chair, turning to stand before him as his gaze slid down my dress. I didn't ask if he'd found my family because, honestly, I feared the answer. He was Knox and a skilled hunter. He enjoyed hunting things down and capturing them. That's probably why he didn't use the brand on my leg or insisted that I tell him their location when he forced me to take truth serum.

Moving toward Knox, I noted how he looked over my shoulder at Killian. It was tense, and the moment we stepped out of the tent, we all walked in silence toward the one I shared with Knox. Inside, there was no glass of water or hemlock. I swallowed, moving toward the spot I'd dropped the flower as the men watched.

"It was here," I stated, watching their nostrils flare.

"I smell nothing." Knox eyed me instead of the hand that pointed toward the table. "What game are you playing, Aria?" Knox asked, and I snorted in reply, rolling my eyes as I held my hands up in the air.

"You think I'd do this? Do you have any idea what hemlock does to me? To us? It burns through the tissue, soaking into the bones. If left untreated, it would make me horridly sick, slowly killing me. But sure, let's say I'm playing games. I get off on Russian roulette and playing with my life, especially when you've locked away my magic, and I can't save myself." I crossed my arms over my chest and stared at Knox, who, in return, looked at Killian, who frowned.

"Her burns were real," Killian said, nodding at my leg. "Her thigh was burned as well, which backs up her story of dropping it with her dress choice, which is rather open in that region."

"They're called thighs, Killian," I said pointedly.

Knox looked between us and snorted, shaking his head. He lifted his arms, crossing them over his chest as Brander entered the tent, unannounced.

"Who the fuck let Aria out of camp?" Brander demanded.

"You were out of camp?" Knox asked, his eyes narrowing to slits.

"I was looking for Brander, and the guards at the edges of camp said he was in the woods. No one stopped me, not even my guards."

"Did you enjoy the show?" Brander asked, heat banking in his stare.

Knox rattled, turning angry eyes on me. I groaned, rolling mine, placing my still, very red hands on my hips, glaring at him.

"I needed medical help, and Brander was rather—

busy. My life was literally on the line, yet I still walked away instead of disturbing the show. Are you accusing me of trying to off myself, or what are you thinking here? I woke up to flowers on the table and water in a glass. I picked it up, still half asleep, and then realized what it was. I didn't drink the water. I dressed, left the tent, and asked Siobhan if she knew where I could find Brander, but she rushed away. I asked other guards, and they bitched out and away from me like little girls. I knew the guards stationed at the edge of camp literally could not run away. I asked them where he was, found him, turned my ass around, came back to camp where Killian discovered me, and then tended to my hands. You came in, and now we're here. So, pray-tell, what the fuck are you thinking I did now?"

"You're a witch who willingly touched hemlock," Brander stated.

I nodded because I couldn't argue with that fact. "Do you know how rare it is to find hemlock in a flowering form in the human realm? It's only grown in certain locals, and we made damn sure it didn't grow around us. Not that it stopped my mother from growing it in an attempt to murder me," I muttered. "Just take my fucking head already. It would be so much easier than the accusations and the bipolar King of Norvalla, who intends to do it, anyway."

"Aria, go find Greer and sit with him," Knox growled.

I threw my hands into the air before rattling in frustration, hearing three answering rattles as I exited the tent. Moving through camp, I found Greer beside a table, watching warriors train.

"You're such a hussy, Meat Suit," I stated, and he peered over at me.

"Oh, are you talking to me now, Peasant?" he asked.

"You're on babysitting duty, along with them," I announced, hiking my thumb at my silent guards.

"I see Knox didn't strangle you in your sleep. Pity that." Greer teased. I sat beside him, resting my chin in my hands while we watched the men train.

Chapter Nineteen

As night fell, we moved to sit beside one of the bigger bonfires. Greer watched me, moping in silence even though he'd tried several times to engage me in conversation. Men and women milled about, and witches watched me openly as if they expected me to attack or start a revolt at any moment.

"I welcome your silence, but I feel as if you're hurting tonight, Peasant. You've had a lot happen to you in the short time you've been here, and I worry that at any moment, all your emotions are going to come out, causing asteroids to land on us all."

"I prefer meteors. They're easier to control," I mumbled as Greer snorted.

"Are you okay?" he asked, and I turned, rolling my eyes for maximum effect.

"Is anyone Knox liked ever, okay? I mean, I totally get the one-night stand thing that's happened because one night of him is enough to drive you insane."

"Wounded creatures will attack whatever touches their injuries or hurts them." Greer sat back to stare at the dancing flames. "They attack first and then regret it afterward. Knox's wounds are deep, and you're digging into them, whether by choice or by just being you. He doesn't know how to let anyone in. He's had to remain strong for his kingdom and his family. He's had no one rattle him before, you know. He's never faced something like you, and it can't be easy wanting something that goes against everything he's been fighting against for five hundred years."

"That wasn't my fault, Meat Suit. I get that he's hurt, but why am I punished for something that happened a very long time ago? I wasn't alive, and I don't want to hurt Knox. I wanted to do what I came here to accomplish, but he's fought me every step of the way. Something happens, and he grabs onto it with everything he has and holds on. He's given me whiplash," I admitted.

"I have an idea."

"On how to treat whiplash in this hellhole?" Greer stood and moved to a bag on a table adorned with glasses near an enormous whiskey barrel.

Greer pulled out a silver iPod and walked over to a shirtless warrior. Pointing at it, Greer lifted his hands into the air and leaned closer to the guard, running his finger over his chest. The guard smirked, and I turned away to glance over the flames, finding Knox, Brander, and Killian taking a seat on the other side of the bonfire. My eyes held Knox's for a moment before dropping back to the flames. Greer grabbed my hand and bowed low at the waist while I looked around at those who had turned to watch him.

"Greer, did you, by chance, take drugs?" I whispered in a hushed tone.

His head lifted, and his ancient blue eyes held mine. "I'm asking you to dance with me, Peasant."

The iPod played *Talk to Me* by Stevie Nicks, and I frowned as he stood looking at me oddly. He smiled, moving to the beat as the music grew louder. I spun toward it as the man held the iPod in the air, and waves shot into the sky. Turning back to Greer, I watched him dance.

"Oh, Meat Suit, you got moves, mister," I said, watching him. My eyes took in the large crowd observing us as if we were aliens that had just shown up and announced we were taking control of the planet. "Everyone is watching us."

"Who cares? I'm a meat suit, and you're a peasant. We can do whatever the hell we want," he announced, rocking his hips as he held out his hand for me.

Smiling, I accepted, lifted my arms into the air, danced with Greer, rocking and moving until the middle of the song. He dipped me back, holding me there, then slowly brought me up against his body. He smiled, taking in the warm glow of my eyes from the dancing.

"Thought you might enjoy something familiar," he chuckled. "You get one more song, so pick well, Peasant."

"Ava Max's, *Kings & Queens*," I said, smiling as he nodded.

"Your taste in music sucks, but luckily I have it."

Greer nodded at the guy holding the iPod, and my eyes slid to Knox. He studied me, sitting back in his large chair beside the bonfire.

When the music started, we danced, and I made a point of singing the lyrics loudly, so Knox caught the meaning. I was halfway through the song when a little girl tugged on my dress. Her big brown eyes were fixated on me until I bent, picked her up, and began dancing again, only slower so I didn't drop someone's kid on their head.

When the song ended, I smiled unguardedly at Greer and moved closer, kissing his cheek. "Thank you, Meat Suit. I needed that," I swallowed, returning the little girl to the ground, only to notice more of the kids had gotten closer to me.

One held a rose into the air, so I kneeled, accepting it with a smile before I kissed her forehead and thanked her for it. The entire camp went silent as the music cut off. Lifting my eyes, I found Siobhan observing me with Soraya beside her. The children moved forward, crowding me, and with a smile and wide eyes, they touched my dress with dirty hands. I laughed as one lifted a strand of material to her nose, and then more did the same.

Standing, the children bowed, and the surrounding witches kneeled, causing my stomach to churn with unease. I stepped back as their heads lowered to the ground. Spinning on my heel, I left the fires and walked to the tent, my throat tightening until I thought I'd die from asphyxiation.

Stopping in front of the tent's opening, I paused, feeling someone behind me. I turned, staring at Lord

Carter, where he watched me from the shadows. Swallowing past the swelling in my throat, I turned, giving him my back and straightening my shoulders, repeating what Knox had done to Aden. Killian and Brander stepped from the shadows at the sound of Lord Carter reaching for my exposed back. I didn't wait to see if they hurt him since I was merely a witch, and my life was forfeited.

Inside the tent, I retrieved the nightgown I'd worn the night before, carefully stripping out of the dress and placing it back into my pack. I tilted my head, noticing the scent of Knox. Turning, I took in the lust dripping from his eyes, but there was uneasiness there too. He came further into the tent, running his fingertips over my spine slowly.

"You're charming the witches," he admitted.

"I was just trying to dance, Knox," I argued, turning to look at him.

He smirked, slowly sliding his hungry eyes down my body. I spun, but he grabbed me, kissing my neck before running his lips over my shoulder, holding his mouth against the spot that had once held his mark. We didn't speak, but then we didn't need words to know that we both wanted this, and yet we wouldn't let it happen.

I shifted away from him, and he allowed it as I retrieved the nightgown, slipping it on. Knox moved toward me, and my heart kicked into overdrive as he turned me, removing the jewels from my hair and my body, handing them to me.

"Thank you," I swallowed, climbing into the bed as he shed his clothes and joined me.

"You deserve to be treated better, but five hundred years of betrayal and treachery isn't something that fades away. You dream of the nightmares you've survived. I dream of Sven, holding him in my arms through one thousand deaths. I relive each one, and they always end the same way. I bury him, and then I bury his mother next to him. I'm not a forgiving man, Aria. I am waging war to free the Nine Realms from the evil your bloodline released onto it. I made a vow, and I don't break them, ever. You're a Hecate witch, the same bloodline who murdered my son and wife. I didn't ask to become a monster, but I am what the Nine Realms needed. You expected me to trust you, but you've not earned my trust. I have not earned yours either. I know you're not evil, but evil never starts that way. We become what the world molds us to be. That's how I became a monster. You're in a war, Little Witch, and there are two sides, yours and mine. You need to decide which side you're on soon. Try looking at it from both views before deciding. You should also make sure you're choosing the side you believe in and not choose based on blood. Blood changes; it evolves and can be easily swayed. Callista was adding strength to the witches who were slaughtering innocent beings. Whether by accident or because she was aware, she helped them slaughter the stronghold."

I shivered, shaking my head. "You're wrong. Callista wouldn't do that."

Knox exhaled, turning his back to me as I stared at him, considering what he'd said. If Callista had done what Knox said, it wouldn't have been out of malice. All of my family were working to slaughter the dark witches and take back our kingdom. Helping the witches within the battlefield didn't fit into that plan. My stomach tightened as tears burned my eyes. I turned away from Knox, pulling the covers up around me tightly as I closed my eyes.

Chapter Twenty

I woke to Knox kissing my neck. His hands slid down my side as he moaned loudly, pushing his cock through the arousal coating my apex. Arching into his touch, I was unable to stop the subtle curving of my spine as his rattle filled the tent. Teeth skimmed over my shoulder, and I purred, fighting the heaviness of sleep that fought to keep me in its peaceful embrace.

He cupped my breast, squeezing it hard, causing a gasp to escape my throat. Groaning, he whispered something in his strange, foreign language that sounded sexy as his cock continued sliding through my parted sex. Rolling me over, he kissed me hard, pushing my hands above my head, deepening the kiss.

He lifted away from my lips and continued speaking while running his steel length through my apex, creating enticing friction that had me moaning louder. After a moment, I understood his words and smiled through the sleep he removed, staring into his eyes that looked through me.

"I love you, Liliana," Knox whispered against my lips, causing me to tense, and I fought to push him away.

His cock moved against my opening, still brushing it erotically. Anger spiked through me, and I bucked my hips to unseat him. Rattling low in warning, he slowly pulled back, still peering through me as if I didn't exist. He moaned loudly, shifting as he aimed his cock at my sex, even though I was moving it to keep him away from my core. He fully intended to bury his need within my body, thinking I was his dead wife.

His eyes opened, and he looked down at me, slowly letting his sleep-filled gaze settle on where his thick head had pushed against my core. I rattled again, growling as my nails extended, intending to remove him forcefully if needed.

"Get the fuck off of me, Knox," I demanded through trembling lips, watching the narrowing of his eyes before slowly sliding back up to my face.

Knox tensed while holding my stare before rolling over. He sat on the edge of the bed, glancing back at me over his shoulder with a peeved look in his eyes. "I didn't mean to molest you, Aria."

"Well, at least you can remember my name when you're awake," I snorted coolly, pulling the blankets up to cover my body, using them as a shield. That he'd said he loved me stung deeply with his wife's name attached to the sentiment as an afterthought.

"Excuse me?" he asked thickly. "What the fuck has gotten into you now, woman?"

"You almost got into me," I whispered vehemently, uncaring that my lips quivered with the anger I felt. "I think I should sleep someplace else or with anyone else. You don't have enough room for me in your bed with your ghosts joining us."

"Whose name did I call you, Aria?" he asked softly, his back tensing as he waited.

"You called me Liliana, right after you said you loved me as you prepared to fuck me. I can accept many things, but hearing another woman's name as you push your cock into my body isn't among the list. I'd rather sleep in the cage than be a substitute for who you really wanted in your bed."

Knox snorted, dropping his head into his hands. "I didn't mean to say that to you."

"I got that from the '*I love you* part,'" I exhaled a shuddered breath as he shook his dark head. "You could always allow me to change someone *else* to appear as your dead wife. That way, you can have a night with her instead of me," I offered coldly. "Obviously, you'd prefer her in your bed."

"I didn't enjoy fucking my wife, Aria."

I tensed as he turned to stare at me. "It hurt Liliana to be with me, and when we made love, it was never for pleasure. Liliana was delicate, and my size made it painful for her to endure being with me. We were only together to create an heir for the throne, as required by our union. So no, I do not prefer my deceased wife in my bed. I prefer you because I can destroy you, and you'll take it, begging for more. I'm sorry that I said her name in my sleep. I must have been dreaming."

"And woke up to a nightmare," I grunted, kicking off the blanket before turning away from him.

I hadn't expected him to grab me or pull me to him. He swiftly rolled my body beneath his, pinning me to the bed with his weight. Knox peered down into my eyes, searching them briefly before his mouth lowered, claiming mine in a soft kiss that caused a storm of emotions to tear through me. He grabbed my wrists, pinning them above my head as he lifted his body, smiling wickedly.

"You're nothing like my wife. If I told her to do something, she'd never have thought to argue or defy me. You argue about everything because you're the most infuriating, stubborn woman I have ever met. You defy me at every turn, and you have no fear of whom or what I am. I am a born king who has seen wars and ended thousands of lives, and you don't allow that to faze you. You have no fear of me, Aria. There's not a timid or docile bone in your entire body. I hate that I admire you and your brazenness. You would make a fierce queen."

I didn't speak because I wasn't sure what to say. Knox had loved his wife, and I was just fun. He could abuse me and enjoyed that about me. I looked away as he exhaled, rolling from the bed to open the chest at the foot of it. He tossed me a dress and shoved his legs into dark pants that hugged his powerful thighs.

"Get up," he said roughly, his eyes noting the sheerness of the nightgown I wore. "We have a long journey ahead of us today. We might as well start now. I don't think either of us could go back to sleep. Unless, of course, you need your pretty pussy painted?"

"Pass," I whispered, turning and slowly sliding to

the edge of the bed, standing to dress.

I hooked my fingers through the hem of the nightgown, lifting it over my head and reaching for the dress. I turned my back to him to get dressed as I began pulling it on. Knox grabbed me, lifting me in his arms, and parted my legs as his mouth met my flesh. I gasped, screaming as I fought the dress and pleasure he sent radiating through me all at once.

Knox held me in the air, lapping hungrily against my core. He'd forced my legs over his shoulders, hooking his hands around my thighs, devouring me without mercy. His tongue slid through my sex, slurping greedily as I gasped, moaning while fighting the dress that was covering my head, blinding me.

"Knox," I moaned loudly, hearing his throaty laughter. He ignored me, continuing to suck and lick hungrily against my pussy. The noises he made were fierce and primal as he brought me to the edge of orgasm, forcing me to dance along the giant cliff before he dropped me onto the bed, and I bounced. "You ass!"

"Eventually, you're going to be so fucking worked up that you attack me," he chuckled as I pulled the dress over my head as he licked his lips clean with laughter sparkling in his eyes.

"Yeah? You do know you may have been my first lover, but I can self-pleasure without your help, right?" I lifted a brow at the snort that escaped his lips.

"I'd like to see you try to come without me right now," he challenged huskily. He crossed his arms over his seductively tattooed chest, staring at the arousal covering my sex. "Let's see you fuck that tight body with those clumsy fingers, woman. Right now, right here. Make it sing so I can hear your sweet noises."

I sat back on the bed, slowly spreading my legs wide. Knox's eyes heated and grew heavy with naked desire banked within their darkening depths. My fingers smoothed down my stomach, sliding through the sleekness of my sex, and a moan escaped my throat at the slight contact.

Knox grabbed a chair, taking a seat in front of me as his eyes noted everywhere my fingers touched. I lifted a hand, cupping my breast, squeezing it while the other sunk two fingers into my body. I curved my spine off the bed, lifting as his eyes rose to hold mine.

My heart raced at a rapid crescendo as my body neared the edge, already worked up from being denied by him. My thumb found the swollen flesh of my clit, rubbing small, slow circles against the nub. The orgasm slowly built into a storm that whispered its nearing presence. My fingers moved faster, and I could not tear my eyes away from the heat churning in his as my orgasm threatened to unleash.

His lips twisted into a grin before he captured my hands, pinning both against my belly with one of his. Knox slapped my clit softly, repeatedly, until I was trembling with the need to come. It was within reach, and yet each soft slap against my sex had it slipping away from me. He continued, only for him to rub my clit softly while holding my eyes.

He was creating a storm that threatened to swallow me entirely. However, every time I even got close to unraveling, he would stop again, preventing the orgasm from reaching the tiny cusp it needed to give me relief.

His dark head lowered, clasping his teeth against my nipple as I whimpered his name, fighting to free my hands to finish what I'd started.

Knox lifted his head, and his tongue darted out, assuaging the hardened peak he'd just nipped. "You come when I say you can, Aria. If you come before then, I'll bind your hands behind your back and make you ride my face until you're insane with the need to come. I'll edge your body so fucking hard that you'll scream and beg me to fuck any part of you so you can come for me. Do you understand?" He smiled as he took in my clenching sex, knowing that I was close to combusting and exploding into a million tiny pieces. When I didn't answer him, he slapped my sex, causing me to yelp as I writhed beneath him, searching for his hand. "Do you understand me?"

"Yes," I whispered through trembling lips.

"Good girl. Riding a horse for hours today should be quite a challenge." He stood, pulling me with him until I was inches from his cock.

I grabbed it as he watched. A dark look burned in his stare while I ran my fingers over the thick, velvety steel. The muscles in his stomach tensed, tightening as I slowly stroked his magnificent cock. I stood slowly, moving my mouth to his stomach, raining soft, heated kisses down his belly until my breath fanned against his tip. My tongue ran over the edge causing him to hiss, pushing my hair away from my face while he watched me tease him.

"If you're planning to torture me as I have tortured you, know that I have been hard every night I have slept beside you. I barely sleep because your soft body rubbing against mine has me in a perpetual state of need that never abates or lessens. When I do sleep, I dream of your lips, and you are choking on me as I fuck your throat, or your tight, sleek body while you clench down, holding me in firmly as you drain me dry."

My nails slid over his cock, and he growled low in his throat in warning. "Unless you're dreaming about your wife, whispering that you love me as you try to fuck me with her name on your tongue. Because if I am in those dreams too, well, that would be awkward as fuck, and I don't share my toys well, Knox."

The twitch in his jaw pounded, and his eyes took on a darker, sinister look as he snorted. Turning away, he pulled his pants up and grabbed a shirt, yanking it on over his head. Knox moved to the chest, withdrawing panties that he tossed at me, along with a corset.

"Put them on," he ordered angrily.

"A corset?" I snorted, holding it up in my hand while studying the anger etched in the lines of his face.

"You're in the Nine Realms. It's time you began dressing for your station. You're a princess, Aria; fucking act like it." He grabbed the dress I'd planned to wear, replacing it with a turquoise blue one that matched my eyes.

"You were the one dressing me. I have my own clothes, you know?" I snorted, staring at the corset with unease. I'd never worn one since they weren't the most comfortable thing to wear.

Pulling on the panties, I frowned at where the corset sat on the bed. I reached for it, but Knox pushed me aside, holding out a slip as his attention lowered to the pink, swollen nipple he'd nipped with his teeth, reddening the surface around it.

"This goes on before that," he explained, watching as I slipped on the thin material.

Glaring at him, I tightened the corset and then grabbed the dress, pulling it over my head, fighting with the ties on the back so it would stay on. Knox snorted, moving behind me as he tightened the lace straps securely, adjusting the slip to hide beneath the outfit's outer layer. He pressed his lips against my throat, dragging them slowly to my shoulder before kissing where his mark had been, sending regret to my heart that it wasn't there.

I brushed my fingers across the spot as a wailing rattle slid from my chest. Knox's rattle echoed the sound as if his monster felt the loss as mine had. They were disappointed in both shells that fought against the need to allow the animalistic parts of them out to play. Fear sliced through me without warning, and Knox pulled me against him, purring into my ear as if he'd sensed the oncoming panic attack.

"I don't know what is happening to me," I whispered thickly.

"You're going to be entering the last phase of your heat cycle soon. Your beast just warned mine. Somehow, they're communicating their needs without using us anymore. Some can warn their... another beast when the time is nearing for their cycle. They do it to protect the host from being away during their time, so they may tend to her alone. It's rare for them to do so without carrying a mark."

"How is that possible if mine is so young?" I

narrowed my eyes on him as he turned me, cupping my face between his hands.

"Your creature is very young, Aria. She's not stupid, though. She realized you were in danger, and she protected you. You're still young and soft. She depends on you as you do her. They're a part of us. A very large part of who we are is what they are. I knew your cycle was nearing the last stages because of your sweet taste, which is why I taste you so often. Your creature probably thought I hadn't noticed the state of your need. Have you named her yet?" Knox asked through smiling eyes.

"Oh my gods, are we supposed to do that? I thought she was like a personality disorder kind of thing."

He studied me and nodded slowly as his lips twitched. "I call my creature Lennox since it was my birth name. My parents preferred Knox. It prevented confusion since it was my father's name and his father's name before him."

"I am not naming her Freya," I stammered, leaning my head against him, deeply inhaling his calming scent. "I am a horrible host."

"You're not a host. You're her face so that people don't freak out when they see her true form and nature. Our creatures are not like us or anyone else within this realm. What we are, Aria, they were lost to this world hundreds of years ago. Our creatures are unable to take their true forms anymore and haven't in over five hundred years. I doubt you'll ever fully meet her, but I bet you can pick out a perfect name for her."

"Ember," I whispered, hearing the purr escaping my throat. "She likes it," I stated, biting my lip as Knox watched me with smiling eyes.

"Yeah, Lennox and Ember have a good ring together."

I rattled, and he echoed my sound as if our inner monsters were agreeing. "I'm kind of terrified that they're talking when all we do is fight and argue. Are they more advanced than we are?"

"Much more advanced."

"Why won't you just tell me what I am? Or what you are? I mean, we are having sex, and that can lead to babies. I'd like to know what might come out of my vagina."

"I can't have children, Aria," Knox growled, turning to put on his armor. "Get your shoes on. We're leaving. The camp is awake and waiting for us."

"I'm sorry," I whispered.

"For what?" he snapped frostily.

"That you lost your family and cannot have more children."

"Can you just get your fucking shoes on like I told you to, witch?" he hissed, shoving his armor on while I backed up, turning to do what he'd asked.

Once my shoes were on, I slipped out of the tent without waiting for permission. I met Brander's sapphire stare and a silent head shake, knowing he'd heard everything happening within the thin tent.

"Ember is a pretty name for your beast, Aria." Brander reached out, tucking my hair behind my ear. "You should probably ask Knox for a hairbrush. You look freshly fucked, and it's distracting when you're such a beautiful creature already."

"It would probably be treasonous to ask him for something so simple," I whispered thickly, moving past him while he stared at my back. "I'm just a worthless witch. Who gives a shit what my hair looks like, right?"

Chapter Twenty-One

The entire army was loading up and waiting by the time Knox reached where I stood, glaring at me. I fidgeted from the state of my ramped up libido he'd created along with the emotions rushing through me. I was a mix of chaos. He smirked, fully aware that I was on edge and could implode at any moment. Fidgeting from foot-to-foot, I rubbed the back of my neck, beaded in sweat.

"Get on the horse, and if I were you, I'd ride side-saddle, Aria."

"I'm walking," I announced with a look of defiance shining in my eyes. I didn't want to be anywhere near Knox this morning, let alone close enough where he could stoke the burning need that was becoming an inferno.

"Come again?" Brander asked, pausing mid-mount and turning toward me.

"I'll just walk," I repeated, crossing my arms over my chest to glare at Knox. "I'd rather not be close to your brother, Brander. He is entirely too unpredictable."

His bipolar mood swings were tiring, as was feeling like I always had to walk on eggshells. I danced enough around what he allowed me to talk about that I wished I had a hand guide to help me navigate Knox, which wasn't forthcoming. Knox stared at me with a look of annoyance, his lips curving up into a sinister smile that made apprehension slither down my spine.

"All witches can walk with Aria, then." He mounted his horse, and my heart dropped to my stomach. "That's an order," he growled, heading toward the lords who watched curiously.

Everyone was giving me a wide berth minus Killian, Greer, Knox, and his brothers. The witches began lining up as guards shouted for them to move forward. I closed my eyes in frustration, then opened them, leveling Knox with a lethal glare.

One witch stepped beside me, her eyes wide with panic as she carried a toddler on her hip and a newborn in her arms. A woman followed behind her with another child, trying to hand the babe off to the woman who already had both arms full.

"What's happening?" she whispered, looking from me to the lords.

"I'm an asshole," I grunted, staring down at the toddler who hid in her skirts, watching me. "I'll help carry them since we're walking."

"Why are we walking?" Wide, blue eyes held mine as a frown creased her brow.

"Because I pissed off the king by refusing to ride with him," I admitted begrudgingly, pursing my lips as I took in the situation. I swung my gaze to Knox, who smiled, expecting me to suck it up and ask him to reconsider my course. Fuck that. I smiled tightly, turning to the woman as she spoke again.

"I have three babes and another child who can barely walk," she explained.

"It's okay. We can handle this. We're witches," I smiled at her tightly, and she looked at me as if I was insane. Bending, I ripped scraps of fabric from my dress, and Knox's eyes narrowed to slits as I destroyed my princess outfit, much to his vexation.

I tied the torn material around my chest, securing it to me like a sling. I accepted the babe, laying her in the cloth and adjusting her. I bent again, ripping another section of my dress, kneeling to coax her toddler out from her skirts with a smile.

"You want to go for an adventure with me, little one?"

The child nodded, and I smiled brightly. Pointing to my back, I waited until she was close to me, securing the fabric in a manner that allowed her to sit harnessed to my back. I tied the material over my chest, ensuring it didn't harm or bother the babe.

I stood, and the mother smiled, shaking her head. I removed more fabric from my dress and helped her position the babes she carried, just like I had done for the other two children. Packed with babes, we were ready to move. A small hand slipped into mine, and I looked behind me, staring at the witches who all grinned at the wild set up we now wore, covered in children. The chilled air slid over my bare legs, and I exhaled slowly.

"Are we ready then, ladies?" I asked, and they smiled and nodded. "Let's do this," I muttered, starting forward, and Knox snorted as his eyes bore a hole into my back.

The babe fussed, so I bounced, causing the child on my back to giggle. The one holding my hand started skipping, and I laughed. My eyes slid to Brander, who studied me with a soft grin, laughing soundlessly as he shook his head.

The army marched down the road at a slow pace. I was certain Knox didn't move quickly because I'd refused to get on his damn horse. I would not allow him to torture me anymore today; that much was a given. No one offered to help us, but then we didn't need their help, anyway. Witches were creatures of nature, and we preferred the earth beneath our feet and the wind in our hair.

I lowered my head, brushing my nose over the babe's forehead, inhaling her scent. She smelled of lavender, sage, and newborn. My eyes rose, locking with Knox's as he frowned, looking away from me.

"Did you make her shampoo?" I asked softly, causing the woman to turn toward me with confusion stamped on her face.

"Babes cannot use shampoo, Princess Hecate," she whispered demurely before bowing with her slight burdens.

"My name is Aria," I offered, watching her eyes widening in horror. "I prefer to be called Aria. Princess makes me sound delicate."

"Pardon me, Aria, but I do not think anyone assumes you are delicate after your display of magic and power the other night. I made the soap for the babe since someone abandoned her and left her infested with lice bugs. The king found her and the others in a keep he took back a few weeks ago. They had left the poor wee thing for dead. Bless him for sparing the wee beings and bringing them back with him."

"He saved them?" I asked, lifting my gaze to where Knox rode ahead of us.

"The king saved all of us," she admitted with a genuine smile lifting her lips. "We're given the option to join him or to have a few days' headstart running from the army and those who would capture us and hang us from their walls as a warning. King Karnavious has proven to differ from most of the lords."

"He's saving you guys," I whispered, barely above a breath.

Knox turned, smirking as he watched me. Frowning at him while holding his stare, my foot hit a rock in the road, and I almost tripped, righting myself before checking the sleeping babe.

We'd been walking for hours in silence when I finally pulled out of my mind. Knox was literally saving witches. He was offering them a place in his army, even the babies. The babes wouldn't be able to do anything until they matured to at least fifteen years old, and then it would be iffy, depending on their magical precision and parentage. He was spending resources to keep them alive, which meant he wasn't an asshole. Correction, he wasn't as big of an asshole as I'd thought him to be.

I'd been arguing that we could save some witches, and he was already doing it! He was taking in children, feeding them, clothing them, and keeping them safe within his army as he marched them toward his palace. He was taking them to his home and offering them a new life.

"Does he save all of them?" I asked absently, turning to look at the woman, balancing the sleeping toddler on my shoulder while the babe sucked on my fingertip.

"Not the dark ones, as they're evil," she murmured, bouncing the other babe in her arms. "I mean, not all of your line is evil."

"Why do you say *my* line?"

"Because the high queen is of the royal blood," she said, eyeing me peculiarly. "She's a watered-down version, but all Hecate bloodline witches are now dark. When your grandmother went to her entombment, the line began changing. With none of the royal bloodline inside the Nine Realms, Hecate's power faded from the line. Knowing they were weakening, your bloodline reached for the darkness to maintain balance and to remain the strongest race in the realms. It happened right before the king's son got sick."

"When my mother and her sisters left to take the Tenth Realm," I frowned, wincing as the babe grabbed my hair. "Ouch, that's still attached to my head, little lady," I cooed, bouncing as the babe howled, causing me to smile. I made a shushing noise, and she blinked up at me with sleepy eyes.

"She's probably a bit hungry," the woman stated,

turning to hold her arms out for the infant. I paused, trading her babes, watching with wide eyes as she whipped out her boob and began feeding the child.

"Oh, yeah, I can't do that trick," I chuckled nervously, tucking the other babe into the sling, starting forward again once the woman was ready.

"I lost a babe a few months ago, so I offered to help with the ones abandoned. It isn't often that we have little ones anymore. When they come, those of us who could, shared in feeding the little witchlings."

"I'm sorry for your loss," I stated, turning at the sound of someone moving toward us. Lore jogged up beside me, picking up the child that had been hanging on my skirt, trudging through the trail that was becoming more rugged. "Thank you," I whispered as he chuckled.

"You're stubborn. What did Knox do to make you walk rather than ride with him?" Lore asked, helping the child onto his back.

"It's a rather inappropriate conversation for innocent ears," I muttered while heat blossomed in my cheeks.

"So he primed that flower, and something prevented it from reaching pollination?" Lore asked, lifting a platinum brow, watching my face turn red before he laughed outright at my expense.

"Something close to that," I admitted, turning back to the woman who was smiling while pretending she wasn't overhearing our conversation.

"Are you telling me we're walking because the king didn't get you off?" Siobhan asked, coming up to stand beside me. At my reddening face, she began laughing.

The women behind us did the same, and all conversation came to a halt so they could hear my reply.

"Yes! Well, no," I amended. Siobhan laughed louder, following along with the others. Knox turned around, finding my face bright red with a horrified smile playing on my mouth. "It wasn't like that. Okay, so it was something like that, but not from lack of trying. It was an outright ploy to induce a state of arousal without allowing the end goal to happen."

"He edged you, didn't he?" Lore hooted. At my look of frustration, he started laughing as the women joined him, much to my mortification.

"You guys are assholes," I mumbled, chewing my lip as Knox's eyes narrowed to slits, taking in the group of witches walking, who laughed while staring at him.

"What is edging?" the witch beside me asked, and I realized I didn't even know her name.

"It's a thing you do to bring a woman right to the precipice of orgasm, and before she reaches it, you prevent it from happening. You can do it for days or even weeks, and when she finally comes, it's violent and beautiful." Lore turned, nodding at the ladies who all whispered behind their hands, staring at him. "That's right, come to daddy. Daddy knows how to edge a bitch right good, ladies!"

"It's cruel and unusual punishment," I snorted.

"Only if he doesn't finish," Siobhan supplied.

"Yeah, tell me that in a few days after he's finally gotten into those panties, Aria. You'll scream so loud that you'll bring the dire wolves down on our heads. Which hopefully doesn't happen," Lore muttered, shivering.

I almost tripped again, righting myself before face-planting on the ground. Rubbing my neck, I ignored the burning in my legs and the ache in my back from the sleeping child. I turned to the woman, intending to ask her name, and ran into something solid. Knox righted my body, looking down at me with something dark and wicked in his stare.

The crowd behind me went silent as he slid his eyes over my head, reaching behind me to pull the toddler off my back. Silently, I watched him settle in next to me, holding the child as we started walking again.

"What are we talking about?" Knox's lips twitched when I turned my attention toward him.

"It looks like rain. Wouldn't you agree?" I swallowed audibly as he lifted his eyes to the cloudless sky, dropping them back to study me.

"The last time you said that people exploded, Aria."

"Those weren't people, Knox," I frowned.

Studying the way he held the sleeping toddler as if he'd done it a million times before, I smiled tightly. It was easy to forget that he'd had a child and was accustomed to carrying them. My brow furrowed as I looked away, fighting the pang of regret in my chest as my beast tried to force my eyes back to the sight of Knox with a babe in his arms. Her jealousy was palpable.

Knox didn't answer, choosing to ignore my comment as he continued walking. More and more men dismounted, picking up children until pretty much they all carried a child, and walked with them, or just walked.

Knox stopped, and we all halted to see what had made him pause. I looked around us, realizing that everyone was off their horses, all the way down the line.

"We're taking a break at the next watering hole," Knox snorted, looking down at me with sparkling eyes, shaking his head at the lunacy of the situation. He leaned over and brushed his nose against my ear, smiling against my neck. "All these people are walking because your pussy got edged, and they're all aware of it because you can't whisper worth a shit."

"I'm very aware of my whispering issue. According to the whispers in the back of the line, most assume *you* couldn't get *me* off. If you listened closely, they're wondering about your prowess in the bedroom now."

"The fuck they are," he snorted, looking back over his shoulder. I smirked, hiding it in my shoulder as the woman beside me observed with wide eyes. "Why would they even think something so insanely untrue?"

"Because that happens when rumors spread, I guess. So much for your seduction skills," I laughed, enjoying the horror displayed on his face. "They're all assuming you're a minute-man."

"You realize if I were to turn on the seduction, you'd end up dripping like the waterfall you took us over when I caught your pretty ass."

"I'm sorry, but I don't think you could seduce a limp leaf off a tree in a hurricane, Knox," I snorted, watching his eyes narrow on me as if he was calculating what to say.

In fact, he looked like a man planning to go to war against my vagina. And it was a vagina already in a state of emergency, preparing to wave the white flag of surrender. His lips twitched, and my eyes rounded as people moved aside to let a wagon through. I stared, mouth opened at the stack of pineapples that wobbled as it moved ahead of us, taunting me.

"That's your dinner because I'm planning to eat that pussy, and you taste much sweeter when you've eaten some," he whispered, smirking roguishly. "And I guess we'll see if I taste better after eating it as well, won't we?"

"I surrender," I groaned, turning to watch the humor dancing in his eyes.

"What?" he laughed loudly.

The sound of Knox's laughter caused Lore to turn; his mouth open in shock at the sound. It saddened me his laughter was such a rare occurrence that it shocked his brothers and best friend. A quick look at Brander and Killian, who mirrored Lore's shock, confirmed it, and I snorted. Greer, on the other hand, smiled at me mischievously.

"Nothing. I take it back. Game on, Sir Seduce A Lot."

Chapter Twenty-Two

I stood in the creek, soaking my sore feet in its chilled depths. Knox played with the toddler, holding her hands to keep her up as she entered the water and began splashing with her feet. I waded in deeper, uncaring that I was about to get drenched with a child in my arms. Hunching down, I wet my hands to cool my neck with them. Knox watched me, lowering his eyes to the child asleep in the carrier at my chest.

Men approached us, and Knox turned back into the king the moment they spoke. Called away, Brander took his place, sitting on a large boulder, peeling an apple as he pretended not to watch me.

Splashing started, and I cried out, turning toward the shore as everyone laughed at my expense. The children played in the water, splashing me. Turning toward them, I sprayed them back, protecting the babe's face from getting wet. I squealed while they continued to douse me with water, giggling hysterically when I made a face of horror as they all began splashing me together.

Siobhan moved in beside me, holding her arms out for the sleeping babe who had protested as an unwilling participant in the water fight. Carefully supporting her head, I handed her off before turning, smiling as the children screamed in excitement. Laughing, they started running through the water to escape me. I hiked my skirt up to give chase, even as I grabbed one, preventing her from slipping on the slick bottom of the creek.

"No!" I shouted, and they spun around, forcing me to do the same. I leaned toward the water, cupping it in my hands to send it back at them. They squealed, laughing freely while we soaked one another.

Brander sat with a slice of apple halfway to his lips. His eyes dropped to the dress where my nipples responded to the ice-cold water. I waited, slowing down as the children prepared to drench me again, scrunching up my face. Flattening my hands, I turned to soak them, and peals of laughter exploded when I slapped water toward them, enjoying the sound of their happiness before something dark slithered against me.

"Get to the shore now!" I screamed loudly, turning to look at the water as something lunged from its depths without warning.

My nails extended, and I rattled, raising my arms and spinning to sever the head of a slimy, long body in one swift, calculated move. I was certain I'd had nothing to do with that since the rattle escaping me was all monster and no Aria. A large, very dead snake floated on the surface before sinking into the water.

Brander was beside me in the next instant as a dark

figure walked down the embankment on the other side of the creek. A dark veil hid her face, and her bare arms were black, covered in pulsing glyphs that increased her power.

"We have heard your challenge, Princess Aria. The witches of the Nine Realms have answered your call. Your blood is impure, your heart tainted, and your body loose for your enemy's cock. Our queen, however, still wishes to meet with you. Your challenge for her crown intrigued her, considering the blood running through your veins lacks the purity required to sit upon the throne."

"It wasn't only about blood. The law states that when a challenge is issued to the queen, each party must meet on the field of battle to ascertain who is more powerful and the rightful witch to sit upon the High Throne of Witches. I have enough Hecate blood in my veins to challenge Ilsa," I growled, watching as her eyes glazed from white to black, with ooze running down her face. "I hereby challenge you for the throne, you evil bitch. You betrayed Hecate, and I am your executioner. Meet me on the field of battle and fight me."

"You're an abomination, Aria Hecate!" the witch hissed as spittle escaped her lips, mixed with black discharge.

"My mother called me much worse, Ilsa, High Queen of Vākya," I snorted, unimpressed with her display of power.

"I will murder you, Aria!"

"I'm right here, come get me bitch," I challenged, holding my hands into the air.

"You do not understand my reach or even the power

that runs through my veins, you stupid child. I have been the High Queen of Vãkya since Hecate herself placed me on the throne!"

"Then I'd say you're long overdue for a vacation. Hecate never allowed witches to touch darkness; for once they had, the darkness took their souls. Face it, you're old news, and I'm here to replace your cancerous ass. You betrayed the witches of the Nine Realms, forcing them to reach for darkness! You could have let the magic go, to return to the land, replenishing it. Your greed sent our people into ruins! You suck as a ruler, and you *will* face me!"

"Says who? You've been gone a long time, little witch, and so has Hecate. We've changed the laws. The witches bow to me, or they die. You have no claim to my throne. You're not strong enough, not even close. I have the power of the darkness, and you're still soaked in the light. I deny your challenge and your right to the crown."

"Did she just tell me no?" I asked, creasing my brow, turning to find Brander glaring at the witch.

"No, she can't, per the laws of the Nine Realms," he said.

Magic rushed toward us without warning. Holding up my hands up, I chanted in the ancient language of my ancestors, pulling her toward me while she struggled to remain in place. The magic slammed against me, and Brander grabbed my wrists, freeing my magic as the children behind me screamed in fear.

I focused on the witch, forcing her light to the surface. I didn't stop, not even as she began howling in horror at the feeling of purity slithering up from her rotting soul. Her eyes changed to a startling blue as the blackness sucked back into Ilsa, who held control while I freed the witch she wielded like a puppet. The screaming intensified as the witch's skin turned unmarked, and her soul rose to the surface, forced by the magic I was drawing.

I shouted the chant louder, continuing the words while she hissed, begging for me to stop. Sweat beaded my brow, running in rivulets down my face from the energy I used. I forced the oily, evil magic out of her, pushing it back into the source, following it to Ilsa's location. I was moments away from removing it when a blade slid through her throat, and her head went sailing into the water, floating beside the serpent's head.

The connection to the magic broke, and my knees gave out. I sank bonelessly into the murky water. Brander placed the cuffs on my wrists, staring down at me with worry-filled eyes. I struggled to stand, only to fall back down, until Brander helped me up.

"What the hell is happening to her?" Knox yelled, moving closer to us from the opposite bank.

"You broke the connection," Siobhan stated, walking to where I gasped for air. "You sent the magic Aria was using off with the High Queen of Witches, giving her an extra kick of magic. That means your witch is drained, and the queen isn't. You need to get Aria someplace safe because right about now, Ilsa knows your witch is a sitting duck. She will call upon all dark witches to come for her now because she's defenseless against them. We need to go now."

Brander reached down, dragging me fully out of the water before trudging toward the shore. Knox appeared from thin air in front of us, pulling me into his arms. He lifted me, shouting orders to the surrounding men while they grabbed the young witches, rushing toward the wagons with them. I moaned, pain slicing through me with the abrupt emptiness of my magic. My soul felt drained along with the magic Knox had just spoon-fed Ilsa.

"We're using horses now, woman," Knox announced. I nodded weakly, wrapping my arms around his neck, allowing his body to heat mine. "You should have warned me about breaking a connection."

"I'm not used to anyone helping me fight, Knox," I admitted, leaning closer to him. He brushed his cheek against my forehead, handing me off to Killian to mount his horse before accepting me up into his lap. He adjusted my legs to wrap around his waist, pulling his cloak off to warm my trembling body.

"Get used to it. You're not alone anymore, Little Witch. Head to the Killamore Keep, and meet us there," Knox shouted to the other lords, most of whom were busy gathering the children who had scattered at my cries to move. "Let's go," he growled, forcing his horse to take off quickly. I held onto him tightly, pushing my face into his soothing scent, purring while rushing me toward safety.

"She just challenged the fucking high queen," Killian snapped beside us, keeping pace as the men formed a circle around Knox's horse.

"She's Aria. She just does shit like that," Lore snorted, keeping pace with Knox, who didn't bother answering them.

"You don't get it," Killian snarled, voice tinged with worry. "She could challenge Aria's challenge! If she changes her mind, the high queen can summon Aria to her for that challenge, Lore."

"She won't," Knox stated without hesitation. "The evil bitch hasn't come out of hiding in over five hundred years. She won't come out unless she's found and forced to expose herself. Aria has to challenge her where others hear it. The only way to call out the High Queen of Witches is to shout the challenge where her people gather to worship the whore. If she looked weak in the eyes of those who followed her, she'd be forced to face the Hecate witch challenging her, or look too weak to hold her throne."

Something shot past us, and Knox jerked his horse to the left seconds before it would have struck. He turned, peering in the direction from which the bolt of magic had come. I lifted my head from his chest, turning to glare at the witch slithering out of the tree line. Lore appeared behind her, twisting his body as his blades rushed down, cutting through her throat and torso with one well-placed move that made my eyebrows lift.

"Go!" Lore shouted, turning as another witch came up behind him.

"Killian, stay with him," Knox yelled, forcing his horse forward.

"You can't leave Lore behind," I whispered, and Knox shook his head. "Knox, he's your brother!"

"He's seven hundred years old and knows how to dispatch witches, Aria. They're not after Lore, they're after you, and you're mine. No one hurts my girl, not when we can prevent it from happening," he growled, rounding a bend as a huge, dark castle came into view. He increased the pace, pushing the horse as something slammed into its side, sending us both sailing through the air.

I cried out, and pain rushed through me when I hit the ground. Blood coated my forehead, and I pushed up from the ground, groaning as magic filled the clearing outside of the castle. Knox lifted his head, finding me with a look of fear in his eyes. He turned toward the incoming witch, sending ravens rushing toward her as if they'd come from his flesh. Only it was an entire flock of the feathered fuckers.

Brander swore vehemently, leaping from his horse midair as a dark shadow sailed toward us. He flipped, bringing a blade down on the witch's throat, sending blood splattering over my face. I crawled on the ground, moving to Knox, who stood, cracking his neck. He reached behind his back, producing dual blades, stepping in front of me while Brander slid in behind me.

"Ready, brother?" Knox asked, turning to look at me over his shoulder.

His face changed, and black lines escaped from his eyes, changing the color to freshly polished onyx as his features sharpened, becoming more defined. His nails lengthened, and his teeth pushed through his gums. The lines around his dark pupils turned fluorescent blue, and his head tilted. The smile that spread on his lips was sinister.

Brander rattled, lowering his head before he turned, smirking at me with long teeth that mirrored mine and Knox's. Lore and Killian prowled into the clearing, similar sharp features and protruding serrated teeth pushed from their gums as their nails lengthened.

I slowly stood, rattling as my teeth slid from my gums, and my nails pushed through my fingertips while the men rattled with approval. Growling low, I purred as they lifted their blades to attack as the witches approached the tree line surrounding us.

Knox and his men didn't move away from me, choosing to form a circle around me as oily magic slid into the field. The witches vanished behind a veil of magic, sending thick fog into the clearing. I closed my eyes, forcing my senses to seek their position.

"Fuck," Killian snapped.

"I know where they are," I whispered, holding my focus while the witches moved closer.

"They're fucking invisible," Lore growled.

"No, they're magic, but so am I," I chuckled coldly. I felt the sliver of magic before they attacked. "Left," I whispered, and Knox swung blindly, sending black colored blood sailing through the air. "Right." Lore swung, severing a head as a body tumbled to the ground at his feet. "Far left," I hissed again. "Low right." Killian swung, and we continued with me calling out their location and the men swinging blindly, unable to sense the witches coming toward us.

By the time we'd finished, I was drained. I slid to the ground on my knees between the men, holding myself up as they turned, taking in my crumpled form before looking around at the decomposing bodies. They'd swung deftly, attacking without questioning me while I helped them to escape injury.

More witches entered the clearing, and I chanted on my knees, covered in sweat. Still wet from the creek, I shuddered at the chill of the fog. My chanting dropped the veil that held the witches beyond the men's sight, and the moment it was gone, they lunged forward to attack.

I watched from between their legs as they danced to a battle drum only they could hear, moving fluidly. They severed heads, limbs, and torsos until too many witches surrounded us for them to fight.

Power slithered through the clearing, and I felt the land answering the call as bodies began exploding, shattering like glass as Knox whispered words of a language, not his own. The echoing words sent a shiver rushing through me as he destroyed the dark witches with magic he'd pulled by force from the land around us.

Hundreds of witches escaped through the woods, and no sooner had they reached the tree line, they shattered as if they were antique porcelain dolls placed into an oven. A tremor of unease ran up my spine as I lifted my gaze. Slivers of red lines rushed through Knox's forearms as if he'd stolen embers from a fire that powered him. It was similar to my hands turning black; only his were red. Once the numbers dwindled, I sagged in relief. My eyes closed as Knox lifted me into his arms, moving toward the castle.

"Light it up, Lore," Brander snapped, and Lore's palm erupted in flames as he lowered it to the ground. I watched as fire shot across the keep, sliding up the wall to light the torches, igniting them all at once.

The gate made a noise, and the chain lowered the portcullis. Knox didn't stop, leaping onto it before it had even fully reached the ground, sliding into the castle's heavily lit courtyard as the men followed behind us.

"Killian, handle the wall and alert us if they try to attack. Lore, get the wards up, Brander, come help me with Aria."

"I'm okay, Knox," I muttered weakly. "I just have to rest for a while and recharge."

"You don't look okay!" Knox snapped with fear etched in his tone.

"I am, though, promise. You won't get rid of me that easily. I'm actually hard to kill," I whispered, leaning my head against his shoulder, smiling at him. "Add wards for rodents and critters that can breach the walls easily. They'll use them to watch us from the shadows, to learn our plans and weaknesses. The vermin and cats can bypass wards and reach us where the witch's corporeal forms cannot."

"Are you spilling secrets, Little Monster?" Knox asked softly.

"Only theirs, but I can tell you one of mine if you want to hear it."

"And what would that be, Aria?" he asked, turning to ensure the men weren't met with difficulties as they took their positions.

"I'm still horny, dick," I whispered, which apparently wasn't a whisper at all because all the men started laughing, turning to look down at us.

Knox exhaled and shook his head slowly. "If the war depends on your whispering skills, Aria, we're all fucked."

"At least someone is, right?" I exhaled slowly, and my eyes closed as he moved into the castle.

Chapter Twenty-Three

Soraya

We rushed into the castle, staring at the beast upon the walls that watched as we entered. My heart raced, knowing that Aria had almost called light back into a soul. This meant she could bring Julia back from Ilsa's oily magic that filled her and locked her in her mind.

"Pay attention, Soraya," Siobhan growled when I ran into her back, displacing the child in her arms onto the ground.

I bent, picking the babe up to bounce in my arms as I looked at Brander, who watched me through narrowing eyes. I kissed the babe's head absently, dropping my stare immediately from the look in his eyes as heat filled my cheeks.

Aria had nearly fucking freed a witch of the darkness! We'd spent countless nights trying to free witches, only for them to wither and die in our arms. Thousands of them had expired before we'd given up on ever finding a cure.

"Did you see it?" I asked, unable to prevent the words from tumbling out of my throat. Hope was a dangerous thing. It made people think they could turn this hell back into what it was before Ilsa, and the dark magic had spread like a plague through the Nine Realms.

"Quiet. They're listening," Siobhan murmured, turning to give me a pointed look.

My heart was racing, and the skin on my neck rose. I turned, looking back at Killian, who glared at me, slowly following behind us. His cerulean-blue eyes were sharp and filled with mistrust. My mind closed down, and I pushed everything away from me to steel my features.

It wouldn't be a shock for any of us to be excited about what Aria had done. There was no one within the Nine Realms who hadn't lost someone to the darkness. I believed Esme's story after seeing what Aria did with her rage by unleashing a fierce hailstorm of fire and almost fully removing darkness.

I handed the babe off to Dana, smiling before moving toward the old crone who handed out chores and bedding for us to use. Smiling, she glared, rolling her eyes and folding her arms over her chest.

"What ye be after, Soraya?" she asked, and I smirked.

"Where am I sleeping tonight, ya old bat?" I asked teasingly, noting the way her eyes slid over my shoulder. My stomach tightened and churned as power sizzled over my flesh. I closed my eyes, then glanced over my shoulder, finding Killian behind me.

"Come with me, witch," he growled, starting forward before I'd caught my breath.

Unlike Brander, Killian scared me. His persona was hard and filled with loathing for witches. I knew who he was and what we'd done to him, and while I didn't blame him, I also feared him. His pace was hurried, and yet he paused to speak in his language to a guard. Killian stepped to the side, revealing a room, holding his arm out to show I should enter.

I was supposed to be sneaking off to a room to contact Ilsa, but I was pretty certain Killian was about to interrogate me. I moved past him, examining the room that held a single table and two chairs. My heartbeat thundered in my chest, and I silently waited for my head to leave my body.

Inwardly, I screamed while Killian stood behind me quietly. Turning, I discovered him directly behind me, and he smirked, lifting his hand to push the dark hair away from my face. He didn't speak, and it was unnerving. Heat slid into my core with how he studied me like he was working to figure me out while I stood, silently screaming inside my head.

"How can I serve you, My Lord?" I whispered, unable to stop the trembling in my lips.

Men flooded into the room, and I slid to my knees, bowing my head. Lowering, I placed my palms up as my forehead brushed against the floor. I trembled, wondering how many had come to rape me. Everything within me screamed as a silent sob rocked through my body. A hand touched my shoulder, and I whispered what they had trained me to say.

"I am here for your pleasure and entertainment, My Lord. Please take what you want from me," I said through quivering lips.

"Bloody hell, woman. Get up," Brander growled.

"Did I displease you?" I asked, slowly lifting my eyes to find his filled with understanding and compassion. "I can be better."

Brander kneeled, brushing his knuckles against my cheek. "You're here to look at a fucking map. You don't submit to anyone who hasn't earned your fucking respect and trust. I know they trained you to be submissive, but let's be honest here. You're not submissive, you're wounded—here," he said, touching my forehead, "and here," he pointed to my heart.

Brander held his hand out, and I stared at it for a moment before looking around the room, finding witches and men watching me with the same sympathy and understanding that Brander had shown.

"I assumed…"

"You assumed we planned to rape you. We're not those types of people. If you sleep with someone here, it's because you want to do so. Come on, stand." he said, pulling me up with him.

Killian narrowed his eyes on me with something akin to worry. Shaking his head, he walked to the table as a male pulled out a rolled-up scroll, unraveling it on the tabletop.

It was a map of the Nine Realms, and on it were places crossed out in red ink. My eyes slid to Siobhan, finding her studying me with regret and compassion. I knew she'd been spared at a young age, but she'd been raped and harmed before serving the King of Norvalla. Her family was slaughtered, and he was her savior.

"Aria was here when we found her," Brander stated, pointing at one of the weaker keeps. "Then she moved here, decimating it easily. Afterward, she turned herself into a Trojan horse and gained entrance into this keep, which is where Aden's men first found her."

"You said they had silver hair and turquoise eyes?" Siobhan asked.

"They looked as if they had the same fucking parents, but we all know that's impossible with the Hecate line. Only one appeared sexually interested, and Knox gave him a show. He marked Aria in front of him, showing that Aria submitted to Knox and only him. It should have stopped them, and yet they're trailing us to Dorcha. We've seen them outside of camp, hiding where they thought we wouldn't notice. Today they were closer, but Aria was in danger. They didn't intervene to protect her. I think they want her for the same reason Lord Andres did. They intend to breed her. She's not the final product of whoever created her. She's their first step in creating an unstoppable monster. Aden only wants her womb. Luckily for us, she can't smell shit past Knox's scent."

"I can't ward against them reaching her if we don't know who or what they are, Brander," Siobhan admitted softly, her hand pushing the map out further. "Aria's magic, it's unhinged and unimaginable. She rained fire from the heavens, and it didn't fucking weaken her. I've seen nothing like it, or her. The king goes hard against her, and she pops right back up and doesn't carry a grudge against him for long, from what I have seen."

"You forgive someone until you can't forgive them anymore. Once you reach that point, there's no forgiveness within the well to offer. The king will push Aria too far, and she won't forgive him," I whispered, causing all eyes to turn toward me.

"If that happens, she's dead. We can't chance Aria attacking us," Killian grunted. "She burned everything to the ground, eliminating any trace that life had ever been within that stronghold. It took that girl five minutes to slaughter an entire army and remake the land to what she wanted it to be. Curiously enough, she sprouted hemlock with her magic. Witches eradicate the plant since we can use it against them. Aria grew an entire field of it, and then some asshole tried to kill her with her creation. I want to know who it was and why."

I swallowed, lifting my eyes to Siobhan. She held my stare and turned to Killian. "I did it because Aria should be immune if her beast half is dominant. She wasn't immune."

He tensed, staring at Siobhan. "You tried to murder her?" Killian growled.

"No, the glass only had hemlock outside of it. It wouldn't have killed Aria, but it tested my theory. Brander had the antidote in his medical tent for the burns, so I knew it would heal her quickly. You're not hearing me, Killian. Aria doesn't have a dormant half. Both are active and thriving. The thing is, she's not even figured out how to tap into her Hecate magic yet. She relies on her beast and the magic she pulls to her from the land. Hecate witches are always magic dominant, which means she hasn't reached her full potential yet. Aria rained down hell on earth, and the world trembled in her presence. What happens when she taps into her magic and wields it?"

The men swallowed past the unease of Siobhan's words. I trailed my fingers across the map, skimming over the Kingdom of Vãkya's location. I knew what would happen when Aria gained her magic and what it would mean to have her at her full potential.

"That's easy, Siobhan. Aria walks into the Palace of Vãkya, and she removes Ilsa from the throne. We assume she hasn't figured out how to wield her magic, but Aria's not stupid. There's intelligence in her eyes that shines from within." The door opened, and I paused as the king entered to stand beside his brothers.

"Continue," the king stated, peering down at the map.

"Aria isn't like us. She depends on her creature to guide her. I've watched her, knowing that she was created or born to be our queen. Aria almost succeeded in removing the darkness from the witch on the bank. No one else within the Nine Realms has ever come close to completing such a feat. What if she's already tapped into her magic and doesn't need it because the magic within her is so powerful that adding more would become unstable?"

"Too much magic is never a problem," Siobhan snorted.

"Not if it is just magic. Aria pulled magic to her from the Nine Realms, raw, undiluted, powerful magic. Add Hecate bloodline magic to that, and you'd have one hell of a monster. It would be too much magic. No one within the Nine Realms wields two types of magic at once. It becomes unstable, and Hecate murdered those born to two breeds that housed their own type of magic. Why?"

"Because they were more powerful than the Goddess of Magic," Knox stated, leaning his body against the table. "What if Aria wasn't created to use against us? What if she was created to destroy the witches?" he asked, turning blue-green eyes on Siobhan.

"That would explain why she wasn't to be murdered," Killian answered.

Knox nodded, snorting as he looked at the map which marked each castle, keep, or stronghold Aria had decimated. "It would explain a lot, but it would also create a lot more questions."

"Is Aria a phoenix?" I asked softly, watching their eyes turn to me.

"We don't know, but killing her isn't an option to find out if she is," Brander stated, holding my eyes with something burning within his. Curiosity or interest? Both terrified me.

"They died out long ago, and there's been no trace of them since Hecate decided their fire was too dangerous to allow them to remain in the Nine Realms. Aria called flames from her rage when she screamed in pain from the assault. She was a fire. You said something moved in her spine? What if it's wings? Phoenix women had wings, and yet they held their human-like form as Aria has. They nested, and they birthed litters. It's possible they went to ground. Some could have escaped Hecate's genocide on their race, but they've hidden so long it wouldn't make sense to return just to breed one daughter. I could see a son. Aria is a woman inside and out," Siobhan stated, and Knox snorted, his eyes filling with need. "Stop thinking with your dick, King Karnavious," she murmured, heat filling her stare while he narrowed his eyes.

"How do you control both?" Lore asked, and my eyes slid to the soothing golden embers of his gaze. "You claim it, and you make it yours."

"May I ask you a personal question?" Siobhan asked, peering at Knox.

"That depends on the question, woman," he said with a guarded expression.

"You know Aria will become High Queen of the Witches; that's a given. You know she has Hecate's blood within her veins. You realize she is like you, or very similar to what you house. Have you not considered marrying her, claiming the crown, and her before she reaches her potential? No Hecate witch has ever married or allowed a male to rule her throne. The reason being, once they have, they give up their power to their husband, combining two lives into one power source. I know what you can do, but can you imagine it combined with what she can do?"

"I've considered it," he stated, stepping back to glare at her. "And rejected it because what runs through her veins murdered my child. I made a vow, and I have never hesitated to keep it. Keep those words out of your mouth, Siobhan. This meeting is over. Return to your post." The king glared at her before turning and leaving the room with Killian and Lore behind him. I started toward the door, but Brander's words stopped me.

"Stay, Soraya," he ordered, and Siobhan stopped too.

"Leave, Siobhan. Return to the witches." Once the door closed behind her, he smiled and snarled. "Submit." I hit the ground, spreading my hips as my forehead touched the floor.

Brander moved around me, his feet the only thing I could see before he kneeled in front of me, ripping my head up by my hair, pulling me up with him.

"Why the fuck did you submit?" he asked, his hand simply holding my hair back until I forced my eyes on his.

"You said to submit," I swallowed past the fear he created.

"Have I earned your respect? Have I earned your submission?" he asked, releasing me.

"No," I whispered through trembling lips.

"Submit!"

I dropped to the floor, returning to the pose. Brander snorted, reaching down to yank me back up.

"Why the fuck are you on your knees?"

"You said to submit," I cried, fighting the fear that filled me until tears pricked my eyes.

"Yet I have not earned your submission, have I?"

I shook my head, and he shouted it yet again. I dropped, refusing to bow my head. He kneeled, lifting my chin with his finger. Smiling cruelly, he slid his hand around my throat and yanked me up by it, forcing me to walk back until he slammed me against the wall. His hands collected mine, pushing them above my head.

"You don't fucking submit to anyone unless they've

earned it," he whispered huskily. "Are you afraid, or are you excited?"

"Both," I admitted, watching as he leaned closer until his mouth was a hairbreadth away from mine.

"You're body reeks of need and fear. You're wet, and yet you tremble with terror," Brander growled, clasping my bottom lip between his teeth. Releasing it, he crushed his lips against mine, pushing his other hand down my body. Lifting my dress, he slid his hand against my apex.

I moved against him, kissing him with a hunger I'd never felt before. He growled against my lips, pushing my panties aside, slipping his fingers through the wetness between my thighs. Knuckles brushed against my clit, and I whimpered my need for him. All at once, he stepped back, watching me with a sinful smile on his seductive mouth.

"You don't submit to anyone ever again. You don't fuck anyone else, you understand? Turn around and face the wall." I swallowed, spinning to do as he ordered, spreading my legs for him. "Did you just fucking submit to me?"

"No, I turned around because I wanted to see what you would do with my body if I obeyed," I swallowed, placing my head against the wall, daring him to play with the chaotic darkness that lived within me.

"Not until I earn your respect, woman," he whispered, and I turned as his footsteps moved across the floor, and the door closed behind him.

I didn't move, holding my pose until the door opened once more, causing my lips to upturn into a smile. I turned, and Siobhan tossed quartz around me. Stepping into the circle, I tilted my head.

"Spit out whatever it is you want to say," she demanded. "You have less than five minutes before they sense the crystals and realize we're both not who they think we are."

"Why the fuck are you telling him to marry Aria?" I demanded, watching her eyes narrowing on me.

"I'd rather he entertain the idea of marriage to that girl than extinguish her fire. For goddess's sake, she danced with orphans in front of a bonfire and carried them on her, uncaring that they weighed her down and discomforted her. If Aria is stronger than Ilsa, we may survive this war yet."

"You saw what she did, Siobhan. She can undo the darkness and rain down fire from the sky," I said while holding her stare.

"She failed. We can't know if it would have worked without having seen the witch afterward. And Knox took her head. Brander is an excellent lover, but he's a one and done kind of guy, as are the others. They like to show us they're alphas. If I were you, I'd keep my distance. Now, who the fuck are you, and why are you here, Soraya?" Siobhan demanded, and I swallowed, canting my head while studying her.

Aria wasn't just any witch. She was the promised witch, the one that Ilsa feared being born into the Nine Realms. I'd heard her speaking to the shadows, demanding we hunted down those with higher volumes of Hecate blood in their veins. Now I knew why. Aria would set the Nine Realms on fire, and I intended to be right beside her when she did because she was the key to freeing Julia from Ilsa.

I'd planned to release her by murdering her. I couldn't stand the idea of Julia being an eternal power source for Ilsa. No one deserved to be, but without another witch strong enough to face her, we were all forced to deal with the reality that it was inevitable. No more. My eyes slid to the sun that was setting as Siobhan swore beneath her breath, removing the quartz.

"I'm not your enemy, Siobhan. I'm your ally."

Chapter Twenty-Four

Aria

My eyelashes tickled my cheeks as I woke, slowly sitting up. I stretched my arms wide as a yawn escaped me. My attention swung to the body brushing against mine. Staring at the naked chest that rose and fell in slumber, I licked my dry lips. Knox looked peaceful and sexy as hell when unguarded. He shifted, causing me to turn away, so he wouldn't catch me gawking at his naked body. When nothing happened, and no noise came from his side of the bed, I slowly slid my heated gaze back to his body.

Knox was built for war; every inch of him was hard, sinewy muscle. Where most men had a six-pack of abs, he had an eight-pack that my tongue itched to taste while tracing every single one of them. The ravens on his body moved under his skin, which was something I'd noticed the more I was around him. Today, they were scattered in different varying poses of flight, and I counted them. I now knew they could leave his body and attach to mine, which intrigued me.

He shifted again, and the blanket slid lower on his hips, revealing the silken tip of his cock. My lips parted, and I leisurely moved my attention to his face, finding him still lost to sleep. One arm rested behind his head. The other stretched out where I'd been sleeping on it. Gliding my gaze down his tattoo-covered ribcage, I wondered what the words said or meant. I needed to learn to speak in his language and adapt faster to the world around me.

Knox's scent was seductive, forcing my body to tighten with need. Erotic pheromones filled the room, his and mine fighting for dominance as my spine arched. I felt my body preparing for his, as if my creature was trying to help me ease into seducing him. She sucked at giving subtle hints, not that I listened when she spoke. *Obviously.*

Silently, I leaned over to inhale Knox's masculine scent into my lungs. My hand slid over his abdomen, pushing the blankets away from the thick, velvety length of his cock that lifted the moment it was freed as if sensing my curious stare. I swallowed thickly, turning my head, ensuring he was still asleep through my leisurely exploration of his body.

My lips brushed against his abs to taste him, slowly traveling lower to the bead of come that graced the rounded tip. A soft moan of need slipped from my lips, and I sat up before I reached it, slowly running my hands down my body while feasting on Knox's perfect masculine form. My fingertips danced over the swollen nub of my sex. Closing my eyes as my other hand found the weight of my breast, pinching my nipple just like he'd done.

I sucked in air as my fingers pushed through my arousal. Lying back, I turned away from the slumbering male, trembling as pleasure ripped through me. My fingers moved quickly, thrusting into my body, while the other moved against my clit. Hands grabbed mine, causing me to cry out as they pinned them above my head. A very awake male stared down at me. I rolled my hips unabashedly, uncaring about stopping him from ending the painful denial he'd forced on me the day before.

My legs dropped apart, showing him the current state of my body, begging him to devour it. Knox wasn't gentle when he owned a body. He was brutality mixed with primal male that shed inhibitions and destroyed the ideology of what a woman should want.

Ocean-colored waves moved through his stare, locking them with my turquoise eyes. He rolled over, placing his body above mine before sitting back, taking in my needy disposition. Knox silently leaned over, clasping his teeth against my nipple. The action stole a cry of need from my lips as he growled hungrily against it. His tongue worked the tip between his teeth, and his hands released mine, allowing me to push them through his hair, holding him to me.

His thickness rubbed against my core, coating the silken flesh in my scent. Chuckling, Knox released my nipple with a soft groan before studying the heat burning in me. Sliding his attention to where I rocked against him, Knox rattled softly, approving of my wantonness. Smiling, he watched me using his cock to rub my need against my clit as my orgasm built to a boiling point. Right before I could reach it, he rolled us, lifting my hips into the air.

"I need you, Knox," I whispered against his mouth, claiming him in a searing kiss.

He smiled against my lips, lowering my body once again until I was grinding on his shaft. I moaned loudly against his mouth, whimpering before purring exploded from my throat. My skin danced against his, need ripping through me as Knox allowed me to taste his kiss, devouring me even though I was on top.

Knox didn't kiss. He destroyed. He ravaged, leaving ruins in his wake as he consumed my mouth, warring against my tongue. The orgasm danced to the surface once more, and I whimpered loudly. Lifting my rear, I intended to push my body down on his, but he held my hips up in the air where I couldn't reach his silken length.

"I need you now," I whimpered huskily.

"I know you do, Little Monster," Knox muttered through a layer of gravel that seemed to scrape over everything within me.

"Fuck me, Knox," I growled breathlessly, staring down at where he watched me through sparkling eyes. "I need you to *fuck* me right now."

"I'm aware of what you need from me."

"I'm asking you to fuck me."

"I heard you," he laughed roughly, watching my eyes narrowing to angry slits.

"It aches, Knox. I'm permitting you to fuck me here."

"I know I have your permission, Aria. I got that from your slow, hungry exploration of my body when you woke up this morning."

"Then why isn't your cock inside of me?" I snapped, frustrated past the point of reasoning.

My body was a ball of nerves that wanted the high that came from what he did to me. I *needed* to feel him buried within me. I *needed* him to stretch me as my body clamped against his, sending the delicious whisper of pain while taking him inside of me. His pupils dilated, his cock rock hard, and a glorious display of his masculine body was below me, just begging to give me what I craved, and he wasn't.

"Are you sure you want me to fuck you?" he asked carefully, his voice dripping and promising sex. I nodded vigorously, but he continued holding me in the air above him as if I weighed nothing.

"That's what I am saying. Fuck me. Destroy me. *Use me.* Just please do it now," I begged, nodding enthusiastically as a sinful smirk played on his lips. Knox chuckled, lowering his eyes to where my hips continued to gyrate as if he was already within my welcoming heat, and it was *so* welcoming.

He tossed me down on the bed, pushing himself between my thighs, gazing down at the need and arousal coating my sex. His jaw flexed as if it pained him by having to wait. I rocked my hips, moving my hands to slide them down to my needy core. Capturing them, he pinned them against my stomach. Knox held my eyes while lowering his mouth, pushing his tongue through the need he discovered there, moaning as he tasted me. He was moving painfully slow. So slow, and I couldn't do anything other than rock my hips, trying to drive him to the swollen nub faster.

His attention shifted, and a wicked smile played on his lips. Knox lifted, pressing his cock against my opening. I moaned, knowing he was past the point of denying me what I craved, what we desired. His cock slapped down against my clit, causing my eyes to widen as he chuckled.

"What the hell?" I demanded, watching as he sat back, holding my wrists captive still.

"What's wrong, Little Monster?"

"I need you," I growled in frustration, fighting to get control to take matters into my own hands since he was enjoying playing with me. "I'm about to bust out some crayons here and draw you instructions on how to fuck me!"

"I know how to fuck you, Aria."

"Then why aren't you inside my vagina yet, Knox?" I huffed way past frustration and into sheer desperation.

"Because I've decided I enjoy you needing to be fucked. I intend to watch you suffer a little longer before I give you what you're begging me for."

"*No!* No, Knox, I need you to fuck me *now*. You're hard! I'm wet! You want this, and I want this. It's the perfect set up here. I know you want me because you keep saying it! I'm right here, spread for you. I ache, and my body is ready for yours! You don't even need foreplay because I am soaking wet!"

"You're right. You are *very* wet," Knox purred, pushing his fingers against my opening.

"You need this too!"

"I do. I want nothing more than to push into your needy flesh and feel you clenching against me as I stretch you, forcing my way into your tight body. But, I also enjoy knowing you're thinking about fucking me, needing me to act on your desires."

"You can't walk away from me. You want this more than I do!"

"Do I, though?" he asked, smirking as fire danced in his eyes. "I can outwait you, woman. I am a *very* patient man."

"You don't need patience, Knox. It's ready and willing. You want me, and I want you. It's pretty much idiot-proof."

"Is that so? Too bad neither of us will be coming today then, huh?" He pulled me with him as he moved to the edge of the bed. "As I said, I rather enjoy you sexually frustrated and unable to reach down and stroke that swollen clit, which I could so easily do. One stroke and you'd sing so prettily for me, wouldn't you?"

"Yes," I mused, watching the heat sparkling in his eyes. "I can beg. I'm not above begging." I ground my teeth in frustration as his lips spread into a wicked smile.

"I'm going to *pass*," he whispered, and my eyes bulged. "You see, I have waited much longer to get fucked before, and I'm very aware that you're in need and won't be able to say no soon."

"I'm not saying *no,* now," I pointed out because I was starting to agree with my creature. He wasn't smart.

"My wife couldn't take me often, and in the first

fifty years of our marriage, we had sex twice. I can count how many times she and I were intimate on my fingers. I was married to Liliana for two hundred years." I deflated at the mention of his wife, swallowing back the anger that he'd compare us until I calculated the math within my sex-starved mind.

Knox released me, sensing the unease his words caused. I stepped back, frowning as Knox rested his arms on his legs, scowling. He had ten fingers, and they'd been together for two hundred years?

"I never strayed from Liliana for pleasure. I respected her body's limits, knowing that every time I took her, she screamed and begged me to stop, and I did. I was a virile male who couldn't fuck my wife because my cock hurt her delicate body. So I can wait because I have waited longer than this to feel the pleasure that I craved and wanted Aria."

I moved closer to him, cupping his cheeks as he lifted his head to stare up at me. "If you were mine, your cock wouldn't ever get out."

"Out of what?"

"My vagina," I elaborated. "I'd want you in my body every moment of every day. You are an amazing lover, generous, and very giving. I'm also very greedy and needy for you. I wish you wouldn't have told me how patient you are. I'm pretty sure my vagina is weeping at the idea of waiting for you to get into it now." I closed my eyes against the look burning in his. "Ten times in two hundred years? And you never strayed because you loved her that much," I swallowed, moving away from him as he reached for me. "No, don't," I exhaled, grabbing the clothes laid out for me.

"She was my heart, Aria."

"I'm aware. I'm also aware of why I'm here too. My bloodline took your family, and I'm a *sit-in-bitch* until you're finished waging war against the witches. Once that is done, I'll be disposable. I know it, yet I'm too stupid to understand the magnitude of what is coming. I keep thinking that if I try hard enough, and I fix the wrongs of what my bloodline did, I can make this world a better place, and then people would forgive us. I can't bring back the dead, though, and therein lies the problem. I can't fix it because I can't give people back what they've lost. I can stick a Band-Aid on it, but wounds fester. I'm such an idiot. I honestly thought I could make a difference, but everyone wants us dead. Not just you, *everyone*. That's why I've ended up with the two options I could take. I could cave to reality and give this world a massively gothic makeover that ends in fire and brimstone, or I could walk away, compliant to what this world turns into, and become nothing."

"What are you talking about?" Knox asked softly, still seated on the bed from the sound of his voice and the distance from me.

"Taren showed me two paths of what I would become once I have finished fixing this world. I can be the cold, calculated witch who enforced the wielding of no magic within the Nine Realms, or I become something soft and loving. He didn't show me enough. There was a child, but I don't know if he was mine. I assumed he was, but what if he wasn't? What if there is nothing?" I turned, staring at Knox as he watched me quietly working through my mental breakdown.

"If I rise to be the high queen, there would be no

more magic within the Nine Realms. I would murder witches for using it, making magic forbidden. If I don't rise, I think I become nothing. I don't get to be a mother, and I don't get a mate. I get to help others, but I give up everything to make it happen for those who deserve it." My body trembled with the realization of what was going to happen.

"You doomed me to become a vile monster or nothing at all. Because what I do now won't change anything or anyone's mind. I can't undo the past for you. I can't bring your wife back or your son. I'm just the monster this world intended to make me into because nothingness for me would be a hard pass. I am going to become the High Queen of Witches. I'm going to slaughter them all," I frowned, fighting tears. I dropped my head back, staring at the ceiling.

"I have already set these events into motion because I'm an idiot. I thought I could change the world by fixing what is and has happened while forgetting the past. People don't move on from grieving. They just learn to live with the pain, as you are now, Knox."

"You will never sit on the throne as high queen, Aria. I won't allow it to happen." Knox moved to where his clothes were set out. "You won't become a mother or find a husband because you're mine. I can't love you because of who and what you are. That would mean admitting I was capable of loving the creatures that murdered my wife and child. I will, however, ensure you're never harmed and that you never want for anything as long as you live."

Knox slipped his pants on, padding across the stone floor in bare feet until he paused in front of me. His eyes searched my face, finding the pain his words caused, etched in my expression before snorting and shaking his head.

"I will escape you. I will find a mate and be a mother." I balled my hands at my sides, staring at him with defiance burning in my eyes. It was bad enough he'd brought up his wife, but he'd just basically told me I'd never get anything I craved in life.

"Liliana carried my child, which means she was my mate. I won't be able to give you children. I won't allow you to carry anyone else's child in your womb because the thing inside of me would go insane. Whether you or I like it, Lennox thinks you belong to him. If you escaped me, I would always find and get you back. There is no world where you are not mine and at my side. The sooner you accept it, the sooner you can move on from thinking that children are a possibility for you or your future."

"You expect me to accept never being a mother because *you* said I couldn't be? You're not the only man within the Nine Realms who wants me. Dimitri *wants* me, Knox. My creature wants a child. She *will* settle for a mate who can provide it for us. There are other men, too, like Aden, who would accept me for who and what I am without calling me trash because of my bloodline. I am not ugly. I have a good heart. I am not cold and lifeless like you are, Knox. I am not buried in the ground with my dead!"

His hand snaked up, gripping my jaw as his breathing grew labored and pained. His eyes burned with regret and something much deeper, something I didn't understand or could grasp. He dropped his hand as mine lifted, intending to take my anger out on him, but he captured it. Holding my other hand in his, he pushed me against the wall, brushing his mouth against my bare shoulder.

"What's the matter? Don't you like the monster your family created? I don't like him either, Aria. However, I knew we needed a monster to fix what your line allowed to move through our land like a plague of darkness, reaching into the light. The dark witches stole all the prettiest things first and then cried foul-play when we finally fought back. I vowed to your grandmother that if she harmed Liliana in her tantrum, I would bring down hell on every Hecate witch ever created or born. Am I supposed to forgive their sins when my family lies in a crypt, dead from that evil bitch's fit because I wouldn't bed the whore or bow to her demands? I opposed her coming into my realm to sink her poison-tipped claws into our land! I vowed to stay the course I set before me. I am the head of the rebellion, Aria. I have over five-hundred thousand troops counting on me to follow through with my promise and end the witches' reign of terror so that this world can begin to live again. I can't change that for one girl whose company I've enjoyed."

I swallowed, struggling against his grip while Knox watched me through narrowed slits. He chuckled, chewing his bottom lip as I looked away.

"I wish I could give you everything you wanted, but to do that, I'd have to let you go. That isn't something I can do, especially now that I know how powerful you are. You exposed your power to a witch hunter. The one who craves to end powerful witches until none remain. Lord Carter would make it his only task to hunt you down and end your life before you ever fought against us." Knox's free hand came down, gripping my chin, forcing me to look at him.

"Carter is the one who brought me your mother, your aunt, and her daughters. He is very powerful and one of the few males who can siphon magic from witches, rendering them powerless against him with a single touch. Every lord within the Nine Realms agreed to this happening. There was not a single objection to the genocide of witches, Aria. Not a single one."

"I am against this," I growled, jerking my chin away from his touch. "I will escape you, and if Carter makes a play for me, I'll end his life before he's even seen it coming. I will fall in love and become a mother. I will let my husband fucking wreck me whenever he wishes. And you? You'll be left with basic whores to warm your bed and ride your dick. Maybe your wife's ghost can ride that cock without it hurting, now that she's dead. Her spirit can keep you company while I am off making babies with someone who wants me for more than my dripping sex."

Knox slammed me against the wall, wrapping his hand around my throat, pressing his lips against my forehead. "I know you want me to hurt you because my words cut deeply. You are just like me. I cut you; you cut me right back. I wrapped my fingers around your heart, and you're digging your fucking talons into mine. You forgot one thing, little girl. I don't have a heart anymore because I ripped it out and buried it beside my son. Now cover your pussy because we're leaving, and you smell fucking delicious."

"I'm certain my mate will decide how delicious I am. He's the only one ever tasting me again. *You?* You and I are finished. Keep your teeth and your dick away from me, asshole. I don't want you anymore. You and I are enemies, and enemies don't fuck. You should have taken me when I offered myself because I won't be offering it again."

I shoved Knox away, turning toward the dress as he rattled. My spine arched as he continued, growing in volume until I gasped, dropping to my knees. My ass lifted and lowered as if he was behind me, fucking me. My hips spread, and my nipples pebbled. I gasped for air from the absolute control he held at that moment. Moaning loudly, I bucked for him to mount me, begging him with the scent my body released. He kneeled beside me, laughing coldly as my body pleaded for him to take what it offers.

"What's wrong, Aria?" Knox asked huskily, pushing his fingers through my hair before forcing my head back, glaring into my eyes. "You need to be fucked, don't you? Can I have what you're offering me?" he laughed, letting his stare slide down the curve of my spine to where my ass lifted, and arousal escaped to run down my thighs from the rattle he made.

His fingers slid through the mess slowly, the tips pushing against my slit, causing a silky purr to escape my lips, moaning with need. It was a violent need, all-consuming, to be taken by him and only him. Knox didn't alleviate that need, choosing to remove his fingers instead. He held the arousal coated fingers to his nose, breathing in before placing them near his mouth, licking them clean as he moaned.

"Do you know what you taste like, Aria?"

My body trembled from the way his pupils had

fully dilated. His need for me shone from within the stormy depths while he held my stare. He replaced his fingers against my sex, watching as I pushed my body onto them, using them to calm the storm he'd created. The need was primal and instinctive. It was like he'd bypassed me and went straight to the animal within. I shivered, glaring up at him, rubbing my core against his fingers. He slowly slid them against it for me to use, holding my eyes prisoner.

"This is mine, and if you ever allow anyone else to touch you, know that you're signing their life over to me. I won't even kill them, Aria. Instead, I'll make him watch me take you, seeing your full submission as you beg me to fuck you. At night, I'll whip him so you can witness him bleeding out. You would know that he died while you lay in my bed, curled around my body, drained from being fucked until you were too exhausted to argue it. I am the fucking King, but more than that, Little Monster, I am the strongest and the most primal monster in all Nine Realms. I am stronger than you even. I'm not only fireproof, my sweet little witch. I'm immune to dark magic, which is why I am the head of the rebellion against you and your bloodline. So be a good little girl, pull your shit together, dry your pussy off, and behave for me. I'd hate to have to assert my dominance over you and your infant creature in front of my army. You want to take a shot at me? I'll take a shot at you. Leave my fucking wife out of your mouth. She's suffered enough because of your fucking bloodline, and so have I."

I didn't speak, didn't move from the floor as he rose, moving away from me. I fought a sob that was building in my throat as tears of anger and frustration burned my eyes. Pushing from the floor on wobbly legs, I fought to remain upright. Knox chuckled from behind me. Grabbing the panties, I slowly bent forward to step into them, but he made a tsking noise, forcing me to pause. He turned me around and lowered himself, and I lifted my eyes, staring at the ceiling.

Knox didn't touch me as I'd assumed he would. Instead, he used a soft wet cloth to remove the arousal coating my thighs. He pulled up my panties, standing to brush his lips against my shoulder, before slowly sliding his mouth to kiss the pulse at the hollow curve of my throat, ignoring my labored breathing.

"You want a monster? Here I am, Aria," he growled, watching as I refused to speak or look at him.

He grabbed my hair, forcing me to face him. His smile was cocky, knowing full well I could hardly move from whatever his rattle had done to me. It hadn't been like any of the rattles he'd used on me before.

Knox reached behind me, grabbing the slip. He placed it over my head before sliding it on, pushing my arms through. I stood there, glaring at him, unable to move. Next, he pulled me against him, wrapping a red corset around my waist, tying it in front. He slowly threaded the ties together as his fingers continually touched against the thin slip pressing against my breasts. Leaning over, his mouth touched my shoulder, and his teeth slid against it. A soft rattle escaped his throat as he finished, reaching for the outer dress and pulling it over my head.

Knox backed away, slowly looking over his dressing job before he tilted his head, grabbing for something behind me and placing it on my head. I narrowed my eyes on him as he adjusted my crown.

"Perfect, Queen Aria Hecate."

Chapter Twenty-Five

Knox escorted and handed me off to Brander to stay next to him while my body still fought to overcome whatever he'd done to it. Brander frowned, lifting his eyes to follow Knox's stiff back before sliding his gaze to me. His attention focused on the crown, shifting to the tears, silently rolling down my cheeks.

"Bloody hell," Brander groaned. "You brought her down with your rattle, didn't you?" he called to Knox's back. Knox stiffened and dropped his head before turning to glare at Brander.

"If she continues threatening to breed or fuck other men, I'll do much more to her than that. My creature won't allow her to continue pushing him. It's better for Aria that I rattle her sweet body than for Lennox to use it. He'd be much more brutal getting his point across. Considering Aria keeps offering him that sexy fucking throat of hers, I'm surprised she hasn't been more than subdued. Try reasoning with her, Brander, because she has no fucking idea with whom she is dealing. If you think you can get it across her fucking thick skull, go for it."

Knox stormed away, leaving Brander and me staring after him. He lifted his hands as he reached the doors, shattering them, causing me to flinch. The entire castle trembled from the intensity of Knox's magic, filling it with a smothering amount of power that I was certain he'd wanted me to feel.

Brander's hand touched my cheek, his thumbs pushing away the tears. He righted the crown on my head, which had shifted when I'd recoiled from Knox's magic. Like me, Knox's magic was from the land. Only when he'd used it, it hadn't answered. He'd taken the magic by force.

"Your body needs a few hours to recover from the rattle, Aria. You should think of Knox's beast as the ultimate killer. Lennox is a hunter with only a few basic needs. Smelling a woman in heat drives his need to ease her ache by gaining access to her womb. Normally, he wouldn't hesitate to take her by any means necessary. The only thing that prevented Lennox from claiming you brutally, the way he wanted, is Knox. He's been at war with his monster since the first scent of your body in Haven Falls, and it hasn't eased. Knox has protected you because his beast wants to pin you down and fill you with his scent, marking you so fucking deep that you won't ever escape. It knows little else other than to claim its prey in the most violent way possible. Lennox is a brutal, lethal predator, which you're very aware of, having met him. He is the strongest creature ever to be born within the Nine Realms. No other male would challenge Knox for you, Aria."

Brander pulled me with him, slipping his hand into mine, but I pulled back, stopping him. "I need a minute before going out there," I whispered, forcing the mumbled words past my swollen tongue. "What the hell kind of rattle was that?" I leaned against the nearest wall, and the crown slid down my head. Brander caught it before it fell to the ground.

"The sound made by a king when he's proving his absolute power and wants you to be very aware of that fact. You're not in your world anymore. Here, the strongest is king. The rattle you just heard was that of the High King of the Nine Realms, and he's the one who placed a claim on you, Aria. Now, fix your pretty hair, dry your eyes, and walk out of here like you own the fucking place. You just challenged the high queen, and she has eyes everywhere. You can't afford to look timid, weak, or uncertain about who you are."

"Knox is the High King? I saw two people inside Gerald's throne room, Brander. The King of Norvalla, and the High King." I narrowed my gaze as he smirked, lifting his eyes to lock with mine.

"You saw Killian posing as the King of Norvalla, and Knox in the back prepared to murder everything and everyone inside the room where you hung. Knox was out of his fucking mind when we figured out where you were. When we reached the party, he was a little unhinged and had to hang back so he wouldn't murder Gerald. He wanted to march in and bring the entire kingdom down because he thought you were dead or that monster had raped you. His beast won't accept you talking about breeding with anyone else. He's claimed you, which is troubling, considering the blood running through your veins. You have to stop taunting him."

"I want to be a mother, Brander. I want to hold my babe in my arms and love it. Knox is going to take that away from me."

"He's not going to, Aria. He already has. You're marked with his name on your thigh. He can find you at any time and place. He was toying with you because he wanted to see where you went and what you did when you arrived here. His ravens are on your flesh, mixed in with yours. He watched over you, protecting you while he learned your mind."

I shivered, realizing that the mark on my thigh was a lot worse than I'd first assumed. I nodded, understanding what Brander was saying. I would not escape Knox anytime soon, but there was always a way to undo the magic. You just had to figure out how to counteract it, and I was powerful enough to do that.

"Are you still weakened?" I pushed off the wall, and Brander snorted at my irritated frown. "From Knox breaking the connection when he took the witch's head," he clarified carefully.

"No," I lied, and his eyes narrowed as his scent caught my attention. I leaned closer, drinking him in until a loud rattle slithered into the empty room. My eyes slid to the door, finding Knox standing in the shadows observing us. "I'll be fine."

Ignoring Knox, I tried to slip past him, walking out of the room until he stopped me. He held his hand out, and Brander handed him the crown. Knox replaced it on my head, standing back and offering his hand. I stared at him for a moment before placing my hand into his, hating the butterflies that erupted at the simplest touch.

"Smile. You're a queen now," he whispered, pushing my hair away from my face.

"Hecate queen's wear black obsidian crowns with smoky quartz. You got me a basic bitch crown, and I'm no basic bitch." I glared at him, plastering a fake saccharine smile on my lips. I walked beside him, and the witches kneeled when I passed them. I paused, feeling my stomach churn with uneasiness.

"All Hail the Queen," Knox whispered, smiling wickedly. He pulled me from my stupor, moving me toward his horse. "We'll be riding for a few days to put distance between your people and us, Queen Hecate."

"My name is Aria," I said thickly, sucking my lip between my teeth as he rattled in warning.

"Indeed, Queen *Aria* Hecate. As I said before, you interrupted me; we will be riding straight through, sleeping only when there's cover from your people. We can't have you harmed because you're willing to lie and say you're healed when it's obvious that you're not. If you were, you could walk and wouldn't have gone down so hard at my rattle."

Knox turned me around when we reached the horse, pulling off our crowns and slipping them into the saddlebag. He effortlessly mounted his horse and held his hand out for me. "Up we go, Your Majesty."

I slipped my hand into his, yelping as he pulled me up with no help. Sliding his arm around my waist, he yanked me against his body, and I shivered. Unable to prevent it, arousal coated my sex from the aftershocks of pleasure slithering through me.

Our horse moved forward, and his men slipped in around us, creating a barrier while the army followed. I stared back at the castle, watching the rodents as they converged on the battlements, scurrying along with us until we reached where they could no longer follow.

"The high queen is watching you, which means she's afraid. That's a good sign."

I didn't reply, choosing to ignore Knox, eyeing the countryside until Lore sang a rendition of AC/DC's *Big Balls*. The other men began singing along as we continued traveling at an easy pace. When Lore reached the lyrics, '*And everybody comes and comes again*,' Knox leaned forward.

"Everyone comes but you. Isn't that right, Aria? How's your clit feeling? Swollen yet? I could turn you around, push deep into that needy pussy, and I bet you'd let me."

"Pass," I snorted, leaning forward only for him to pull me back, slowly sliding his hand lower as he smiled against the curve of my shoulder.

"I warned you not to taunt me. I've asked you to leave my wife out of your mouth, and I've tried to be patient with you. You're my enemy, yet I still care that you're not in pain or treated poorly. I am not a good man, Aria. I am your devil, but we don't have to always be at odds. I can make this easy on you, or I can make it hell. That choice is one only you can make."

"I'd take hell over you any day. It would be much easier, Knox."

Chapter Twenty-Six

The rain was relentless, causing us to continue through the night until we finally found an abandoned keep. Knox had demanded I remain outside with the others, which ruffled my tail feathers. He'd told me to sit and behave like some pet he held control over.

For three entire days, Knox had given my body hell, bringing me to the edge and leaving it in a heightened state of need. He enjoyed the fact that I found no relief, even though I'd tried several times to achieve that end goal alone, uncaring that he listened and felt me doing so.

Knox chuckled and whispered against my ear, telling me I made the sexiest sounds of frustration when I didn't get what I wanted. As if he knew that it was futile even to attempt it, but allowed me to try, anyway. There was further frustration when he touched me, and my body lit up like Christmas lights finding a plugin during the first sign of snow.

Explosions sounded from within the keep moments before dark shadows escaped through the large doors. I braced for impact as they sailed directly at me, only for Knox to appear before me, swinging his sword in a wide arc that severed a head from shoulders, sending it smashing against the courtyard wall.

He turned his head, smiling coldly at me as his men exited the keep next, their swords held at the ready as piercing shrieks filled the space in which we stood. I hit the ground, jarring my body the instant my knees slammed into the wet grass.

Dark witches materialized to attack, sending magic rushing into me before they reached me. Black lips and eyes opened as they let loose a deafening shriek that caused my ears to pierce with pain.

Knox slid his blade into his scabbard and lifted his hands, pushing magic toward the witches. I watched as they shattered as if created from delicate glass instead of blood and bones. He didn't stop there, sending more power rushing through the abandoned ruins, sucking the air out of the space, creating a vacuum that stole the sound. Lowering his hands, it all came rushing back at once, causing my body to double over with the intensity of the magic he commanded.

"Get up, Aria," he whispered, crouching to push my hair away from my face as I continually gasped for air to feed my lungs.

Knox pulled me up with him, shouting out orders. He didn't wait to see who was obeying him as he moved us swiftly inside the castle, past the grisly remains of the dead witches. He hadn't even batted an eye at destroying them. There hadn't been a single flicker of hesitation before shattering them into tiny pieces.

I'd thought I was special in making witches explode, which admittedly was rather messy and included the use of a raincoat. He, on the other hand, had shattered them without causing a single droplet of blood to escape their bodies. He showed me who was more powerful, and I knew that I'd lose horribly if I went to battle against him.

Inside the keep, I peered around at the empty interior as Knox directed me to a seat in front of an enormous fireplace. Brander was bent in front of it, holding his fingers against large logs that crackled as the flames roared to life. Pulling off the wet cloak, I shivered as the heat from the fire offered a reprieve from the spring rain that had soaked a chill into my bones.

"Sit, and don't move," Knox ordered, pushing me into a chair before he took the cloak from me, hanging it on another chair beside me.

"The women are seeing to the rooms and preparing a bath for you," Brander told Knox, who nodded, moving away from us.

More men entered the large room carrying meat and barrels of whiskey while forcing the witches to wait with the camp followers, which was just a nice way of saying, 'whore,' I'd learned from Soraya. They followed the army to offer services while earning coin. I stood, hearing Brander groan as I moved over to take the crying babe who had to be miserable with the wet blanket concealing her.

"Give her here," I stated, watching the relief play on Siobhan's face. I took the slight burden from her, walking back toward the fire as the smaller ones followed me to the heat source.

Brander tossed me an irritated look over his shoulder, still getting the fire going. I took my seat, pulling off the babe's wet clothes before gently rocking her. My dress was soaked, but there was little I could do about that at the moment. Greer walked to where I sat, handing me a blanket of rough wool, which I used to swaddle the babe within, making cooing sounds as she continued to cry her discomfort at being cold.

Once she was warm, her cries continued. I sat back, placing my lips against her head. I sang softly, *Rescue* by Lauren Daigle, to calm the tiny thing while I stared into the flames that danced seductively. I shut the room out, singing to her as she watched me. A tiny fist entered her mouth, and she sucked greedily against it while staring up at me through pretty brown eyes.

When the song was over, I turned, frowning deeply when I noticed the entire room watching me. Swallowing past the uneasiness that lodged in my throat, I took in the bright eyes of the tiny witchlings. I lifted my stare to Knox, who had leaned against the wall, his arms crossed over his chest as he'd listened to me comforting the babe. I swung my attention to Brander, grinning at the silent babe before his sapphire gaze slid to mine with a smile burning in them.

"You have a calming nature for something so chaotic, Aria," Knox murmured, turning as men approached him.

"The king's room is ready, and a bath prepared for him and his witch," a soldier announced. I stood, turning to find Dana beside me with a soft smile playing on her lips.

"I think the wee beastie enjoyed your singing, My Queen," Dana muttered, accepting the content babe from me before smiling sheepishly.

"Just Aria, please," I swallowed, doing my best to ignore the title and the witches who curtsied as I moved past them, heading for Knox, who continued to watch me silently.

"We will eat first, woman," he said as I stood awkwardly before him.

Knox nodded toward the table, set for dinner and moved from the wall, making his scent waft toward my nose. I silently followed him as he pulled out my chair, allowing me to slide into it before he pushed it in and took the one beside me. Knox had impeccable manners for being such a caveman. He'd kept me as dry as he could while riding, holding me against him to keep me from becoming chilled, and at night, he gripped my body tightly to ensure I wasn't cold.

It was crazy how one minute we were enemies going at each other's throats, and the next, we were civil and protecting one another from the elements. At night though, he'd stoked my fire until I was nothing more than mush with a pulse, leaving me that way before falling asleep with his arms cradling me like I was precious to him. It unnerved me, creating confusion, which I was certain he did on purpose.

Women brought warm food to the table, and I closed my eyes, inhaling the freshly cooked meat and vegetables that someone had whipped up out of thin air. Servers moved around the table, loading dishes full of steaming hot food while others poured whiskey into glasses. They offered it to me, but only when Knox nodded to the servers, which I refused to acknowledge since he allowed me alcohol and meat.

Everyone waited for something, so I sat there with my hands in my lap, watching the people around the table. The castle was in a state of readiness, and yet no one had met the army or been present to welcome us.

"Knox," I whispered, leaning over toward him. "Where are the people that live here?"

"Dead, murdered by witches," he stated, lifting his fork to take a bite of meat, which signaled that everyone else could eat.

"That's sad. It's a beautiful place."

"So were the people murdered for simply being in the high queen's way," Knox muttered. He reached for his glass, and my eyes slid over the people who were watching me silently, which unnerved me. "Eat, Aria. We will retire shortly."

I reached for my glass, turning to find one of the little witches had moved behind me. Turning in my seat, I smiled at her as she tugged on my dress. She held out a small bag, and I accepted it, frowning when she didn't look up.

"Is this for me?" I asked, and she nodded, her eyes still downcast to the floor. "Thank you," I whispered, opening the bag to find a tiny hand inside of it. "What is this? Where did you get this?" I demanded thickly, emotion and fear tightening in my throat as she finally lifted her eyes.

Black ooze ran from her eyes and nose as she smiled, revealing a black tongue as well. "I heard you like children, so I sent you a gift."

"No," I whispered as Knox grabbed me. Her other hand lifted with a needle-like blade, stabbing herself in the chest. A scream ripped from my throat as Knox yanked me back, and the Lord beside me fought to take it, only for the high queen to toss him around with the magic she wielded within the child's body.

I sobbed, fighting Knox to get free as women's screams filled the keep. Pandemonium ensued as magic sliced through the room, creating barriers between the children and us as they took their own lives, forced by the evil queen who wanted to hurt me. The moment the tiny body dropped to the ground, I shot forward to hold the wounds closed.

Brander ran around the table, but something across the room captured his attention as he slowly exhaled. Giant sobs rocked my body as I fought to stop the blood from flowing, noting the black lines of hemlock that rushed through her tiny body.

Hands grabbed me from behind, but I fought them, struggling to get free. I screamed, uncaring that everyone was watching me fall apart as blood spread beneath the tiny body. I was hefted up and cradled in powerful arms as purring sounded against my ear. Knox rushed me down a long hallway with the sound of feet echoing behind us as my sobs escaped unchecked.

"Get the quartz and count the witches. Find out how many died tonight and which bloodline they were from for the record books," Knox ordered, entering a room with me as he instantly started ripping the dress off, revealing hemlock burns on my arms and hands. "Brander, get the ointment and make sure the others have enough. Hemlock laced all the blades. There will be burns on those who tried to prevent the children from bleeding."

Knox placed me into a tub, and before I could argue it, he climbed in behind me, still dressed in his clothes. He purred loudly, and Lore and Killian echoed the sound while I continued sobbing at the injustice of what she'd done. She murdered children! Who could be so cold, and so evil to murder innocent lives to reach me?

Knox kissed the side of my head, holding me in the cradle of his body as he continually made soothing noises to ease my sobs. I trembled with rage and denial. He held me tighter, pushing my hair away from my face until Brander returned, grabbing my arms to apply the salve. Knox held me, helping to slather ointment onto the blisters that the trace of hemlock had caused.

Brander purred soothingly, his eyes never moving over my nakedness. He worked the salve into my skin, forcing the hemlock to become neutralized, to absorb through my flesh. When he finished, he dropped back on his knees, frowning as Knox spoke to him.

"How many?" Knox asked.

"We don't know yet, but it was only children. No adults were hurt or killed."

"Evil bitch," Knox whispered. His throat tightened with emotion as his words slipped past it. "Bury them. Make sure they're on sanctified ground. Allow the witches to bless them and burn the sage. Have the men assist them if they need it, but tell them not to intervene unless needed or asked for their help."

"I'll have whiskey brought in for Aria. She'll need

it to numb the pain," Brander stated, lifting to move out of the room.

"Wait in the hallway," Knox said, and Lore and Killian left the room as well.

He waited until they left before lifting me from the bathtub. Slowly, he sat me on the bed, cupping my cheeks, and staring into my eyes. "I'm sorry, Aria."

"You didn't kill them," I whispered on a soft cry I couldn't prevent.

"No, I didn't. But I knew she would make a move for you. I failed to predict that your love of the children would be where she struck against you. I declared you high queen and didn't consider the lengths she would go to hurt you. For that, I am sorry. Crawl into bed. My men will be in soon to place smoky quartz and other crystals around us for protection, and I'd rather them not see you like this."

I nodded, staring at him as I lifted on my feet, kissing him chastely before I moved onto the bed, crawling beneath the covers. Knox stripped from his wet clothes and moved onto the bed, wrapping me up in his arms. He continued to purr softly against my ear, easing the pain of the loss, even though the moment he stopped, that pain would return.

"Who could be so evil to use children to send a message?" I whispered, and he snorted.

"Witches," he uttered, tightening his hold on me. I started to turn around to argue that not all witches were evil. "In this world, you never show your weakness to your enemies. You love no one or anything because it is the first thing they strike against to hurt you the deepest.

The high queen watched you singing a beautiful song to a babe and discovered your weakness. If she saw what I saw, Aria, she saw how much you care about the children of your race regardless of their bloodline or stature. She watched you having a water fight with giggling girls and boys and singing to a babe of lesser blood, and she struck hard and fast against you."

"I showed her a weakness, and she used it."

"Just as I loved my wife and son and got them killed for allowing others to know what they meant to me. Love is a weakness. You can enjoy someone, and you can use them. But loving them makes them a target. You never allow your enemies to think you have any feelings for anyone other than to use them for your cause."

"Anything or anyone I fall in love with would be cursed. You would kill them or torture them while you fucked me in front of them, as you promised. And if I loved you, the high queen would move against you."

"I can hold my own against her, Aria."

"It's disturbing that you didn't argue the first part, Knox."

"I can't argue the facts or my own words."

Knox's men entered the room to place the crystals, and he rattled in a low warning. The sound soothing as mine echoed, reinforcing his without me having to think about it. It was as if the creatures within us were warning the other men together. Knox chuckled against my ear, noting it as well. Once the men exited the room, we purred together, my eyes growing heavy as I fought sleep, still filled with grief.

"Has anyone ever refused to follow your orders, Knox?" I asked into the silence of the room.

"Not and lived, Little Monster," he mused. "No one except you, and you fight me. I find I enjoy battling you in more than just the bed. You challenged me when no one else would dare."

"I'm going to kill the high queen, and I'm going to do it with the entire world watching."

"We're going to kill her together because you're not strong enough to do it alone yet. Together, there would be nothing strong enough to oppose us."

Chapter Twenty-Seven

I awoke to my body being ravished and consumed by an inferno of heat. I arched my back, lifting my need to the mouth, licking me awake. Fingers pushed into my body, building a sultry moan in my lungs that slowly escaped. I could not get Knox deep enough into my body to sate the burning need he was setting ablaze.

I dropped my knees apart, fisting his hair, knowing that when I got near, he'd pull away and leave me edged on the never-ending cliff he'd had me dancing on now for weeks. Knox chuckled against my sex, devouring it hungrily while I rode his face. I whimpered louder, using his hair to direct him as the orgasm slowly built within me, begging to find release.

The noises he made were sexy, that of a starving beast unable to get enough of what it craved. His fingers slowed, and I groaned softly, whimpering when they escaped my body, and his mouth started to pull away.

"Dimitri, I need you to make me come," I whispered,

rocking my body. I felt Knox go rigid as I cried out for another man. "Come on, My Love. Finish me and stop the ache that monster created. You make me come the hardest, my Sweet Wolf."

"Get the fuck up, Aria," Knox roared, lifting from between my thighs. He glared down at me with his hair going every which way from sleep, and his mouth covered with my arousal painting his lips.

"I don't want to get up yet. I was having the most amazing dream," I groaned, turning over and stretching as his rattle sounded, growing in volume while I purred softly to soothe his anger.

He landed on top of me, pinning my arms above my head. Knox ground his large, very hard erection against my clit and belly. I growled, opening heavily hooded eyes to peer into his, which threatened to swallow me whole in their angry waves. I wrapped my legs around him, smiling up sleepily.

"Morning," I whispered huskily, silently taking in his tight lips and angry glare. "Are you mad at me again?" I lifted, brushing my mouth against his, finding him unresponsive. "Is something wrong?"

"Do I feel like your fucking lover who makes you come the hardest?" he snapped crossly, his brows pushing together before he rattled more.

"Yes?" I replied in a husky tone. "Is that a trick question?"

"You ever call out another man's name while I'm with you, and he'll fucking regret it," Knox hissed, lifting to stare at my body that tightened with need. I could feel my sex swelling from being denied an orgasm for too long without relief.

"Excuse me?"

"Who were you fucking in your dream, Aria?" he demanded with gravel coating his tone, causing my body to clench with need.

"I don't remember, but it was truly an amazing dream," I lied, enjoying the jealousy burning in his sea-colored depths. "Was it you?"

"Would I be pissed if you were screaming *my* name as I licked the arousal from your body, woman?" Knox sat back and slapped my clit, causing a pained cry to escape my lips before he rubbed it slowly, replacing the sensation of pain with pleasure. "This is mine and only mine." He lifted his hand, slapping it again before he leaned over, biting softly against my nipple, running his tongue over the swollen peak teasingly. "Mine," he hissed furiously, sliding his attention to the other, lavishing it with the same pleasure. My legs dropped open, hearing his darkly erotic laughter at my eagerness. Knox rose, claiming my lips roughly, the kiss one of ownership as he slipped his hand behind my neck for full control of my hungry mouth. Pulling back, he whispered hoarsely, "Mine, and only mine, Aria." He slowly kissed his way down the slick arousal covering my sex, running his tongue through it as if he owned it.

"Knox, please," I whispered, needing to come more than I needed fucking air in my lungs.

I slid my hands to his hair, threading through the dark, silken strands, fighting to hold him where I needed him. His seductive whisper danced over my apex before he pulled away, staring at my swollen nub, "You think you can scream out another man's name while I'm giving you pleasure? I was fully intending to wake you up by pushing into your tight haven. Do you think I'd still fuck you?" My clit was a solid throb of pain with its own pulse, needing release. He lifted his hand as I sat up to attack him.

Laughing, Knox easily caught me, rolling us on the giant bed, and held my hips up, away from his body, "I was going to stretch you full of me this morning. Waking you up to the strongest orgasm of your life, but you went and cried out for *Dimitri*. Why is that, Aria? Has he tasted you? Has he pleasured your body?"

"No," I replied honestly, knowing that I'd have to give up my ruse and admit that I'd meant to cry out his name before Knox went hunting a wolf to feed me tiny morsels slowly.

"No? Then why the fuck are you dreaming of Dimitri then?" Knox moved from the bed, grabbing his pants and angrily shoving his legs into them before running his fingers through his hair. "Killian, get in here!"

"Knox, you're obtuse."

"I'm the fucking King! I am the one your *beast* craves, and you go and shout another man's name while I'm literally tongue deep in that pussy. A pussy I fucking own! I made you a woman. I am the only man who knows how you taste! How your sweet body feels around mine, clamping against it hungrily. So why the fuck would you scream *his* name while I am devouring you?"

"It hurts, doesn't it?" I whispered angrily, pulling the blankets around me as the door opened. Killian walked into the room, noting the tension immediately, pausing to watch us.

"What the fuck does that mean?" Knox growled angrily.

"Now, you know how I felt when *you* were about to enter me, and you whispered your wife's name and told me you loved me while attempting to push into my body!" I snapped, and he paused. Killian's mouth dropped open while his eyes moved between us faster.

"Good morning, Killian. Want to fuck me? Knox isn't able to finish, it seems, and I need a man who wants to get me off."

"Get out, Killian," Knox growled, glaring at me.

"Morning, Aria. Morning, Knox. We have completed the burials, and the witches have asked to wear the mourning clothes to honor their dead."

"The baby?" I whispered barely above a breath, struggling past the emotion that ripped to the surface without warning.

"You don't want to know, Aria," Killian said carefully.

"I do. It's important to me. She was just a baby."

He looked to Knox, who frowned, moving toward the bed to purr softly as if he was aware of how bad it had been.

"We found her remains and buried her with the other children. It wasn't pretty, Aria. There are some details you just don't need to know."

I covered my mouth with my hand as nausea churned inside of me. I jumped from the bed, rushing to the bowl on the dresser, emptying my stomach violently. Tears burned my eyes as Knox moved across the room, wetting a cloth before he brought it to me, holding it out. Accepting it, I wiped off my mouth, fighting to control the imagery playing out in my head of what Ilsa might have done to the baby.

"She suffered because of me," I whispered, hating that Knox and Killian purred. More men entered and immediately began purring, sensing my unease. "That evil bitch murdered the baby because of me. I got her killed," I sobbed brokenly, holding my stomach that threatened to empty again.

"Aria." Killian's voice beside me caused me to jump. He wrapped a blanket around my naked body. Knox took it, and held it over my trembling form. "I don't know if the babe suffered, only that it was her hand in the bag at dinner."

"Thank you for telling me the truth," I replied, turning into the heat of Knox's body, drinking in his scent greedily to calm my frayed senses. "What are mourning clothes?" I questioned. We'd only ever lost Amara, and we hadn't had time to mourn her loss.

"It's a black dress that marks the passing of the dead, accompanied by a black veil that covers their faces to hide their pain." At Knox's words, I nodded against his chest. "Would you like to wear something similar? I have nothing like it for you to wear, but you have a black dress in your bag."

Greer brought in my bag. His eyes filled with worry as they settled on me. My grip tightened on the blanket as the men exited, leaving me alone with Knox. He didn't speak as I dropped the blanket, accepting the glass of whiskey he held out to help calm my nerves. I swished it in my mouth, spitting it out in the bowl.

"This is what we go through, Aria," Knox said with a tremor in his voice that caused my chest to tighten with regret. I started to move away, but he prevented it, pulling me against him tightly. "I'm sorry that you're getting a crash course through this world. I am also sorry for whispering my wife's name in *our* bed. It wasn't a good feeling this morning."

"I know it wasn't," I admitted. "It was difficult to make you understand, though. You're very rough around the edges, and they easily cut me. You're used to getting what you want. I understand that being King comes with certain perks, but I am new to this world. There's also the fact that Ilsa will target my family now because they're my greatest weakness. What she did last night showed me her reach, which I'm sure was the point. She bypassed the wards you set, and she got to those I cared about." That terrified me because it wasn't hard to figure out my family was my world. "She will go after them next, my family. I'd sell my soul to the devil himself to protect them. So, King Karnavious, this is me, asking what you want from me to protect them. I'm offering you my soul here, Knox. I can't let Ilsa hurt my family because of what I have done."

"It's not that simple, Little Monster."

"It is, Knox. You tell me what you want from me to keep them alive, and I'll do it. I'm standing here, bartering my soul for theirs. Tell me what I can give you to protect them, and I will make it happen."

He lifted his hand to push the hair away from my face. Knox's eyes closed, and he leaned his forehead against mine, whispering his words softly as if they hurt him to say out loud. "I want you, pretty girl. I want you to marry me. You'd be my wife, but only in the aspect that I will rule it through you when you take your throne. You will be a silent queen who has no authority and no power. You will never sit on either of the thrones, Aria. I cannot allow you to rule over Norvalla as my wife because that would be the biggest slap in the face to my actual mate, who your people murdered. You won't ever have children because I cannot create them with you. You won't ever take another man to your bed or share your body with them. You will carry my mark and will only ever know my touch so long as you live. We will strip your family of their powers and send them to the Barren Islands, where they will remain far away from this realm, which I will control through you."

I moved my attention to the bowl, fighting the urge to throw up again. Knox watched me, snorting, before he shifted away to grab his shirt, his back tensing as he pulled it over his head.

I could save my family's lives, but the cost would be my life. If I didn't agree to Knox's terms, it would leave my family in his and Ilsa's crosshairs. If I accepted this deal and he captured them, it would force him to keep his word. Knox was the High King, which meant he was above all else. This deal would also ensure Knox's lords were beholden to uphold his word. Ilsa, on the other hand, would have to get past Knox and my magic to reach for my family.

"Where are the Barren Islands?" I asked, watching him dress.

"Does it matter? You'd never see them again. They'd

be free to live their lives without the threat of death. That is more than the warlords, kings, and queens of the Nine Realms would allow them."

"And you'd ensure they made it there alive?" I continued, causing him to turn around and stare at me. Tears rolled from my eyes, and his throat bobbed before he spoke again.

"I would, Aria. I give you my word on that." Knox placed his hands on his hips as if it took effort not to comfort me while I negotiated for the protection of my family.

"This would depend on if you found my family, of course," I swallowed, watching his eyes narrowing to slits as a wicked smile slid onto his lips. His smile made my heart thunder with what it meant.

"I will find them, Aria."

"I know you will, Knox. If you haven't already, it would only be a matter of time. This deal would have to be explained to them once they're captured. They would need reassurance that I had agreed to become your wife, or they won't believe it to be true."

"That is a given, woman." He crossed his arms, staring at me pointedly. "Are we negotiating? Because I was pretty sure you asked what *my* terms were."

"This is the rest of my life you're asking for, Knox." I swallowed past the lump in my throat, wiping away the tears while he watched me closely. "Am I the only one who will be faithful in our marriage?" I asked as he curled his lips into a wolfish grin that tugged at my ovaries.

"Are you asking me to be faithful to you, Aria?"

"I don't know," I whispered through the confusion playing in my mind. "I don't know if I should say yes, and chance it, or take my chances fighting. I'm not weak. Not by any means, and you know that. You want my forever, but you don't even like me. Sometimes I think you hate me, and other times I think maybe you like me, but that it hurts because of the past. I'm afraid to say yes and end up broken by you, Knox. My heart is still soft and wouldn't survive if I fell in love with you, and you didn't love me back."

"I don't hate you, Aria. I've tried, but you're a hard woman to hate. I push you away because I don't want you to get cut too deeply on my jagged edges, which, as you mentioned, are sharp. Marrying you would be easy, as would being faithful to you, considering how hot we burn together. I will even agree to save other witches who aren't influenced by dark magic, but like you, they'll belong to me and the army I am continually building."

"You're good at this king thing, aren't you? You make it sound so easy. I don't even feel like I am offering my soul to my enemy right now, but I know I am. My husband won't love me, and I won't hold my child in my arms. I will be nothing to no one, other than a tool to be used and someone who warms your bed. I am what you want and what's needed to gain access to the Throne of Witches, and once you have it and have won this war, what happens to me? Do you lock me up? Chain me to a wall in a dark dungeon? Remove my head?"

"You'd remain my wife, Aria," Knox moved to stand between my legs, running his fingertips over the outside of my thighs. "Even if you weren't the strongest Hecate witch, I'd still have come for you and claimed you. Even if you weren't the key to the throne, I'd still want this deal." He swallowed hard as if I should understand the gravity of what that meant.

"I won't help you catch my family. I won't fight them, ever. I will take my life before I am ever pitted against my sisters or my aunt for you. If I marry you, I want the illusion that you're only mine. If you take another because you tire of me, I'd want you to do it silently. Sex would be a mutual understanding and agreement between us. It wouldn't be promised, Knox. We would both need to agree to the act. I will have heat cycles, and you'd need to soothe that ache. Since my body would never reach its goal of creating life, I may have more than most, and you'd need to handle them so I can uphold my end of this agreement. You will treat me with respect and tender hands. I deserve that from you. I deserve to be respected by my husband."

"What are you saying, Aria?"

"I'll marry you, King Karnavious. I will give up my life to protect those I love more than I love myself. You will protect them from harm, from your lords, the other kings, queens, and the High Queen of Witches. I'm not an idiot, Knox. You don't really want me; you just want the throne. I am just your key to unlocking the kingdom for you to ascend as King of Vākya. When you've won the war, and there is no longer a need for us to be together, you will either remove my head or set me free." Leaning forward, I kissed him with trembling hands, and tears ran from my eyes while he watched me in silence. "You're carnal sin and the beast of my dreams. I'm not your beauty, though. You had your perfect mate, and we took her away from you. How ironic that my dream guy is the one that can never want or love me back," I said through the swelling in my throat.

Wiping away the tears, I stood, forcing him to do the same. I grabbed my pack, pulled out the thin lace panties, nylons, and garter, changing into them. My dress was a dark shade of midnight blue, but the closest thing to black I owned. The long skirt touched the top of my feet, and silently I stepped into it, securing the swooping neckline behind my throat. Reaching into the bag, I withdrew the soft silk cape that went over my naked shoulders, completing the outfit.

I'd marry Knox to ensure he couldn't murder my family because the tremor in my spine told me he would. I would use it as my backup plan. He wouldn't harm them if I were his wife, forced to protect them from the High Queen of Witches until we could figure out a way to remove their magic. Considering what magic ran through their veins, that wouldn't happen. You couldn't remove Hecate magic from a witch. It just wasn't possible until their death occurred.

Knox was silent while I finished placing the simple chains onto my wrist, throat, and waist. Pulling out the actual crown I'd retrieved from Hecate's tomb, I set it on my head and slowly turned, finding Knox sitting on the bed, watching me.

"You're not five steps ahead right now." Knox frowned, standing to move in front of me. He stared at my crown before pushing my hair behind my ear and leaned over to brush his lips against my cheek. "You won't escape me, woman. I won't ever agree to let you go. You are my beauty. I may not love you, but you're the most gorgeous creature I've ever encountered. Liliana was ethereal, and everything graceful. You, Aria, you're the fire that ravages through me that I pray is never extinguished. I don't know what it is about you, but my beast demands we claim you. That alone should terrify you because you're wrong. My beast wants yours, and he thinks you're the most perfect being he's ever come across in his entire life. Lennox never acknowledged Liliana, and I wanted him to so badly that I ached with that need. You're the only woman we have both wanted. What that means, I don't know yet, but I want to discover it with you. I recognize it's strange that my enemy is my perfect idea of a mate. That alone makes it impossible for me to believe you're real. You're too perfect, Aria. You are everything I want, and that seems too good to be true in a world of magic."

"You're right. I am not five steps ahead, because unlike you, I can admit that I misjudged you. I thought you'd be easy to deal with, but you're nothing like what I assumed you'd be. No one designed me. I am real. I bleed, Knox, and I have wants and needs that have nothing to do with anyone else. We house monsters that seek to accomplish our desires. Have you ever considered the fact that while we may hate one another, our creatures could be mates?"

"No, because I bred with my wife," Knox snorted, moving to dress in his armor. "What I am, my race, we mate once in a lifetime and create our children through that union. I don't care what anyone else says. I craved my wife and her scent, and we created life. That means she was *our* mate, and I have yet to die. My beast wants yours, but that doesn't mean he wants to mate with her, Aria. He's a primal male, and your beast is an alpha female. Lennox likes to be challenged, and you and your creature have openly challenged him many times. Now, get your shit because it's time to go. We're marching a mourning party into Norvalla's border to the Beltane Circle. If you agree to my terms, you'll become my wife on Beltane. If not, you'll be opening the ceremonies and keeping the first deal you made for the release of Callista."

Chapter Twenty-Eight

I stood inside the keep's doors, staring at Knox, listening as he spoke to a group of men that looked haggard and dirty from riding hard to reach us. They were exhausted, dark circles marring the otherwise bronzed flesh of their faces. Knox listened, his head moving as anger ignited, his body tensing at whatever they were saying to him. Oceanic eyes turned to me, and the entire group slid their attention to where I stood, clothed in the finest dress I owned, with the actual Hecate High Queen crown adorning my head.

He exhaled a shuddered breath, slowly moving toward me. My heart lifted to my throat as my stomach plummeted to the ground. Knox brushed his hands over my cheek the moment he reached me.

"There was an attack on a stronghold this morning," Knox rumbled, grimacing.

"Let me guess. You think I had something to do with

it again?" I snorted, watching his eyes sparkling with something dangerous.

"No, not this time," he frowned. "It seems there was an attack on one of my strongholds bordering my lands. The witches holding it have asked for you, or they will attack more keeps, killing more people until you are on your knees before the High Queen. They've openly declared war on you, demanding your life for the lives of anyone who isn't on the side of their queen."

"What?" I gasped, shaking my head.

"You were with me, and I know you weren't communicating with anyone while in my arms last night, Aria. They're using old tactics because you're new here."

"Ilsa's going to murder people unless I surrender?" The heaviness in my chest caused my stomach to somersault. "Then, I will surrender, kill her, and end this now."

"The dark witches are using tactics they've employed over the past five hundred years to lure you in. You won't surrender because your death doesn't end this war, and I won't chance Ilsa getting her hands on you. You're much too powerful. I need your answer to what we spoke of inside the room. I need it before we reach the stronghold, Aria."

"I told you I would marry you," I whispered, and my words caused the hall to go silent as people turned to listen.

"You said you would marry me, but you also asked me to release you after the war, and that isn't possible. In our world, marriage is forever, Little Monster. There's no divorce, and I wouldn't do it, anyway. If you marry me, you do it intending to be my wife and no one else's. In the Nine Realms, it is until death do we part. If you agree, Aria Primrose Hecate, you will always belong to me. I will be yours as much as I can, treasuring the gift you're offering me. I can't promise you the things you want from a husband. I can't do that with you or anyone else. I can promise that you'll never go hungry, and I will always protect you. That's my vow to you. That's what they left of me when they took my son and ripped my heart from my chest."

"So what you're saying is that you'll make me a sandwich and hold me at night? I don't need your protection. I'm not some damsel who needs saving. I'm the fucking dragon who eats prince charming and picks my teeth with the bones of my enemies, King Karnavious. I asked for you to be faithful in the public's eyes and not murder my family. Give me your word that they won't be hurt, and when I am in heat, you handle that need without making me endure the pain it creates. I'm not naïve. I know the longer I hold out, the more painful it will become until I am mindless with need and bordering on insanity. When I am in heat, that need is primordial brutality trying to achieve the end goal. I don't want anyone else to handle my needs, Knox," I stated without wavering, my eyes holding his with the intensity of my words.

"I agree with that, but on the condition that your family doesn't murder innocent lives. If they do, I won't be able to sway the other lords from their course against them. I am the High King of the Nine Realms and the King of Norvalla. My promise as High King was that any witch who inflicted harm to the Nine Realms would die by my hand without question. When you are in heat,

Aria, I will gladly handle your body's needs, and then some. I promise never to leave you wanting or needing any other man. Satisfying you won't be a hardship by any means. I will hold you in my arms as you sleep. When you fall, I will be the strength that picks you back up, fixing your surprisingly familiar crown."

"It's a family heirloom. Which I know you're well-acquainted with, considering what Hecate wanted from you," I snorted, glaring at him.

"Loren has a loose tongue, which I should probably tie up or cut off," Knox stated coldly, turning to stare at Lore, who watched warily with the others. Lore winced as I replayed what Knox had called him over my head.

"Loren? It sounds almost girlie," I whispered, hearing him groan at Knox.

"Does dumb-shit, Loren, get dumb prizes," Knox snorted. "Tighten your lips, brother."

My eyes slid through the group, noting the unease that played amongst them. They listened to us negotiating my future in silence, tensing while they waited for my answer. Killian looked pissed, but Brander didn't look worried. It had been Brander who gave Knox the stupid idea to claim me as his bride in the first place. Greer looked troubled, his mouth tightening into a white line as if he wanted to speak but stayed silent. Lore seemed uneasy, his golden stare sliding between Knox and me.

"I still won't promise that I won't run from you. Not that hiding from you would do much good, considering your name on my thigh allows you to locate me. I also can't promise that I won't try to find a way out of this arrangement. You've made promises to your people, and

I respect that. I made promises too, and I'm going to need you to understand them as well. I know you won't respect them, but my word is all I have here, and you know that means something to me."

"I'm honored that you have agreed to become my wife," Knox whispered, kissing my forehead.

"It's a facade, Knox. Don't pretend otherwise. I don't intend to pretend any more than necessary to convince our people it is real. I am the key to a door you need to open, and that is all I am to you. You're my relief in my time of need, and I yours. Don't romanticize it or try to sell it for anything other than a business arrangement between two people who can barely stand one another on their best days."

His mouth tightened into a tight line at my words. Lore sputtered, coughing as he turned away from us to hide his shock. Killian's gaze narrowed like he just realized it wasn't a love match, which should have been obvious. Brander scrubbed his hands over his face, worry etched in his expression. Greer, on the other hand, smiled like an idiot as his worry melted away.

"I told you she was extremely intelligent for her age," Greer pointed out as the other men grunted. "Argue it all you want, but it worked out as you intended, Brander. Knox didn't even have to use Beltane as an excuse to perform a handfasting ceremony without her knowledge of it happening. I don't know which of them is more brilliant. I can't say I've ever had to question that with Knox in the equation."

My gaze zeroed in on Greer before swinging back to Knox, who smirked wickedly. His eyes sparkled with amusement, enjoying the anger burning in my own at Greer's words. Had he planned to trick me into handfasting him? Dick move.

"Having the key to the door is much easier than setting siege to a kingdom, Aria," Knox shrugged, holding his hand out for mine. I placed my much smaller hand into his, and he adjusted his visor to cover his face while the men flanked our sides.

Outside, Knox's witches waited, their faces covered in a simple, sheer, black layer of lace that didn't shield who they were from the eyes. They cried openly, each feeling the attack on the children to their very soul, the same as I had. At the opening of the doors, they'd worked to still their tears, but that only made mine join theirs.

We moved into the courtyard, and I pulled my hand from Knox's grasp, lifting my dress's skirt to go stand with them. They quieted at my approach, noting the crown that sat atop my head, then curtseyed.

"Dry your eyes." It wasn't a suggestion.

"She killed the babies!" Dana wailed, her chest heaving with sobs.

"Ilsa hit us where it hurt the most. She doesn't value life as we do, nor does she care to follow our laws anymore. She's done pretending to be the rightful queen and is revealing who she really is. The high queen's job is to protect the next generation. That is our job now, and we will protect others from this point on, together. But we don't cry, Dana. We are witches. We get wicked, not wounded. We do not weep for our dead; we rejoice that they've moved onto something better. This world is brutal, and now these children are released from the tyranny of a mad queen. They are beyond Ilsa's reach and cannot suffer any more pain."

"They're with Hecate. Blessed be," someone in the back shouted, and I snorted.

"Fuck Hecate," I shouted, glaring at the woman, whose eyes rounded in horror at my words.

"That is blaspheme, Aria!" Siobhan whispered in a hushed tone.

"Where is she, Siobhan? Where the fuck is the goddess in our darkest hour? Hecate can rise using any bloodline witch she wishes, and yet as Ilsa slaughtered the babes, Hecate has refused to rise. She is the reason the Nine Realms is in this mess, to begin with! Where the hell is she? Your savior, your vain goddess who can't be bothered to wake up and fight with us," I shouted, moving down the line as they watched me. "Hecate could end this, and yet she has refused to come back for us in our time of need. My grandmother was the vainest, narcissistic bitch in all the realms. She demanded control, starting wars with anyone who opposed her. She murdered and destroyed kingdoms in a rage, uncaring of the innocent lives lost. Now her victims are taking our lives because of her actions. There's a mad queen on our throne. Ilsa is murdering witches who refuse to follow her, and for what? For not wishing to break the laws that she, herself, put into place? Fuck that and fuck her. Let Hecate sleep, unbothered by our suffering. We don't need her, do we?"

"You can't take Ilsa down alone, Aria," Siobhan snorted, her eyes moving to where Knox was slowly walking toward me.

"She isn't alone. Aria Primrose Hecate has agreed

to become my wife. If that doesn't tell you her level of devotion to you and the other witches, nothing will. I will wed her during the Beltane celebration and make a Hecate witch my wife. I will secure her throne with her, and we will rule it together," he lied, and I stifled an eye roll that would have caused the bell at the back of my head to ring.

"You're marrying the high king?" Siobhan asked, searching my face before narrowing her stare on Knox.

"I am, and before you think it is something other than it is, I love his cock," I announced, causing Knox to laugh as he pulled me against him. "It's a really nice cock."

"Indeed, it is," she snorted, glaring at me. "You aren't marrying the king for his dick, though. You're marrying him to give him the throne, meaning you're selling us out before you ever become the rightful queen."

"I am not selling anyone out. I am doing what is needed for our people. I, alone, can't save us. I know there are good witches out there, and they don't deserve to die. Any bitch who can slaughter our sons and daughters doesn't get to be my queen." Tears slipped free as I stepped away from Knox, moving to Siobhan. "Any woman that can murder an infant by tearing her into pieces to cause pain is the evilest of beings," I whispered thickly through the emotion as she watched me, her own eyes filling with unshed tears. "I intend to make sure Ilsa feels a thousand deaths, in a thousand ways, reserved for only the evilest of creatures."

"That is what your grandmother did for King Karnavious, Aria. His son suffered that fate, and he was merely a lad of seven years. If you think it will be easy to sway us to your side simply because you're a Hecate witch, think again. We've lived in this war zone your bloodline created. Your legacy *is* Ilsa because you and your bloodline placed her on our throne."

"I know that I have a lot to atone for, Siobhan. I don't expect blind devotion. If you could blindly follow someone, then I don't want your loyalty. I intend to earn your respect and to prove who I am. I am unlike any witch within the Nine Realms. I am a witch and a monster, and these days, my monster is much louder than the magic within me. I am a Hecate witch, but hear me now. I do not need your magic or your strength because I have my own. I will never ask you to feed me your magic because the Nine Realms fuel me. I require nothing of you, other than your support for my throne, and to help me protect others like us before they share the same fate as the children last night."

"Prove it. If you're so powerful, then undo the curse your grandmother placed on us. Undo the curses against the other races. Prove that you are really seeking to atone for what she has allowed! Hecate muted every race, their strength and power held hostage by *your* line. Our power feeds you magic, draining us every time the high queen casts a spell."

"I am working on that, but as you know, it isn't a simple spell. I took the power of the Keeper of Lightning. I freed it for all witches to call upon who've remained within the light. I did it *alone*, with the help of the Nine Realms. This world brought me back from the brink of death, meaning that it found me worthy of leading. Lifting the curses won't be as easy as bringing back the full power of our people to use against the mad queen, as we shall call that dirty bitch from henceforth."

"You're serious, aren't you?" Siobhan whispered through trembling lips. "You're going to give us back our powers and help us undo the damage?"

"I cannot undo the past, but I can ensure that the future belongs to us. That we're not under the thumb of the mad queen, and that I can free those who are there unwillingly. I am not my grandmother. I don't crave power, and I don't hunger for a throne. I know my family has a lot to atone for, and we're here to do that now. My vow to you is that I won't ever stop fighting until we are all free again."

"I will follow you, Aria Hecate. Not blindly, but beside you against Ilsa, because you're right. She is evil, and she isn't my queen." Siobhan swallowed, nodding as she stepped back.

I lifted my arms, hugging Dana, who continued to cry silently. "Dry your tears. The children are free of the flesh that housed their beauty. They feel no pain and know not the horrors of this world anymore, sweet girl," I murmured. "I know you loved them, but you have to free them so they can go where they belong."

"I wasn't enough to save them from Ilsa," Dana admitted.

"I don't think anyone was. No one expected Ilsa to strike against children because it is forbidden to harm them. We are commanded not to murder them. We protect them at all costs."

"No, Aria," Knox snorted, watching as I turned to take in his anger. "Some of us knew how far witches would go to hurt others and that no life is precious in their eyes."

Siobhan had mentioned his son's death, and I'd brought up his thousand deaths. We used the curse on those who trespassed against our children, but never on another's child. Hecate had chosen the worst death we could give, using it against Knox.

How much pain had Knox endured while watching his son die one thousand times? I'd been unable to watch one child die, but he'd endured holding his own through each death, according to Lore. I silently walked to Knox, sliding my fingers through his as he watched me with a coldness I knew well.

"Let us go take back the castle and show them we are together, King Karnavious. Beltane comes, and if you intend to give your people a proper mating ritual and ceremony, I prefer we do so while Bel can visit and bless our fires."

"Indeed." Knox pulled me against him, kissing my forehead before he left me standing there while he issued orders in a sharp, clipped voice.

Knox was deeply wounded. So much so that it would never be healed. It was something I was learning to recognize. When he hurt, he lashed out at me. Unfortunately, I was the nearest thing in his path that he could blame for his pain. It wasn't right, but grief didn't have a time limit or make sense. Knox only had to think of his wife or son, and I was where he took out his pain. The thing was, I would not accept it anymore. I was fighting with him, and while admittedly, I didn't plan to fight on his side; we wanted the same thing. We both were trying to end the terror of one mad queen.

Chapter Twenty-Nine

The dead covered the castle walls. Silently, I noted their bowels unraveled from their stomachs, hanging from them like ropes. Nausea swirled through me, pushing against my throat as it threatened to spill the little food I'd been able to hold down today.

Knox and his men pointed toward the battlements, and I noted the dark shadows moving around on them. Each shadow hid behind a pillar that jutted into the sky, offering them protection from being seen. Flags adorned the battlement, and one stood out more than the others, a single white flag with the decapitated head of a unicorn beside a skull with the mark of Hecate. The background of the flag showed a rainbow with what appeared to be castle ruins on the ground.

"Peasant," Greer whispered, causing me to jump with his sudden appearance. "I'm glad to see your ability to die of a heart attack by my sudden appearance hasn't lessened any. What is that hideous flag?"

"I believe it's supposed to be my flag. It's a headless unicorn with a rainbow behind it," I frowned. "Do you find it offensive?"

"I'm not gay, Peasant. I am bisexual and just happen to prefer men over women, which I have repeatedly explained to you. I can go either way, though, really," he snorted, tilting his head at the same moment I did. The flags turned, lifted by the breeze, and Greer smirked, "I do take offense for the poor unicorn that didn't deserve to lose its head."

"I take offense," I admitted. "My flag would be a full unkindness of ravens poised for battle on a skull with the mark of Hecate burning in the middle of it. It could be white, but it would need to represent me, and I didn't own that raincoat. It belonged to my sister."

"An unkindness?" Greer asked, staring at me strangely.

"A flock of ravens is often called an 'unkindness' because they are associated with bad luck. In mythology, they are trickster animals. Did you know ravens are among the smartest birds? Probably of all animals if you consider their history and events in which they played a role. They never forget, and they study their enemies and even those they don't think of as foes. They're amazing creatures."

"You do know that the high king's flag has twin ravens, both perched on the skull of a Hecate witch, right?"

"No," I frowned, shaking my head, pursing my lips. "I assumed it was only on his armor and that it was the flag of Norvalla that held ravens."

"You're honestly the most brilliant, stupid person I know, Peasant."

"Ouch, that coming from a suit of meat actually makes me give a fuck. No, wait. That wasn't a fuck. It was indigestion from eating the last fuck I gave," I snorted, and Greer chuckled. "You do realize that I am only twenty-five and have no idea what I am doing, right? I'm winging this, which is pretty much the story of my life."

"You're not doing too badly, Peasant. Or shall I call you the High Queen of the Nine Realms, now? Or do you prefer I wait until after the joyous occasion has occurred?"

"I'd prefer you to call me Peasant, because it is something that has remained steady, to keep me grounded, Meat Suit. I will never be a real queen. Knox won't allow it. I will be a joke to the people, one whispered about behind their hands. You and I both know that. I could be more, but not with the high queen and high king hunting my family to use against me. So the princess has become a pawn for them both."

"It does sound pitifully hopeless when you put it like that," he muttered, leaning his head against my shoulder. "Knox is wounded and has been for so long that he doesn't know any other way to be. Change that, and you may change the man. You're more fire than ice, and he's the ice to your fire. Melt through his frozen heart, and breathe life and fire back into him, Aria. He's good at concealing his feelings. That lesson was beaten into him when he was young. I know because I watched his father teach him that a great king feels nothing. For hours and hours, King Lennox beat his son. The child lifted from the ground as nothing more than a bloody pulp, staring down a king. Knox told the king he hit like a lady of the court, even while spitting out blood. He told King Lennox that his mother had often struck him harder than that for peeking up the skirts of maidens at court."

"Knox wasn't ever a child," I grunted, turning to stare at Knox as he frowned at something Brander said beside him, pointing at a location on a map.

"Oh, but he was. Prince Knox was a bright child. One filled with dreams of making the Kingdom of Norvalla a place others respected and could love as he did. He had these smiling eyes, and you could see the brilliance within them, burning to get out. His parents directed his entire life to become the next king as the firstborn son. He never found joy in training to become king, but there wasn't a choice. Knox loved learning and would spend hours hiding in the Library of Knowledge that only responded to him. Knox was something else, this kid who wanted to teach himself everything, devouring books that no one else cared or thought to look twice at."

"You were his teacher," I noted, watching Greer smile from the memories.

"Indeed, I was. I've been with Knox since he was born. I was there for his greatest feats and defeats. I was with him as he held Prince Sven in his arms, begging for his life. I am the one who found Queen Liliana on his bed and tried to prevent Knox from entering the chambers. I watched a once carefree king become cold and calculated. The boy I knew wouldn't have hit you, even if it was a knee-jerk reaction to your taunts that forced him to relive memories of his wife and son. I know you did it because you wanted him to feel pain, and he did. I heard it in your voice when you said the words. I've also seen Knox watching you, and I have caught glimpses of that boy in him through you. You're his equal in every way, Aria Hecate. The world took his wife and son from him, but it gave you in return, and for whatever reason that happened, only you two can discover the answers together. Admittedly, I thought he would have murdered you, not kept you."

"Wow. That's deep, Greer. Wait, you actually thought Knox would murder me?"

"I'm being serious here, Peasant. Knox is broken, but broken things can be fixed. You are a rarity, and he craves you. I don't think he even realizes how much he does. I've seen Knox around hundreds of women, and never once has he cared about them or kept them close. He can't seem to get enough of you. He planned to fuck you and be done. You fucked him, and it was game on. He enjoyed chasing you, like a kid hunting down his first wild beast. He's stared at you when he thought no one was watching, and there was pride in his eyes, which shouldn't be there for an enemy. Knox could learn to love again, but only if someone was willing to fight for him."

"You seem to have forgotten he wants my family dead and hates what I am. That isn't something I can change. You can't paint stripes on a horse and call it a zebra. Nor place a horn on a horse and call it a unicorn."

"Neither of you are those things, Aria. You are the glue to his broken pieces. You're the missing flame, and he can't see it because his grief has had five hundred years to fester within him. He started a war with it, and he won't break his vow. You must bend to him and show him what he will lose if he cannot meet you halfway. There are four creatures within this relationship, and two are fighting to be together. The other two can't seem to see past what others have expected of them. You're the key to the locks that will turn the tide in this war. Together, you become everything this world needs."

"That makes about as much sense as the flag they created to represent me," I grumbled, jumping when Lore patted my backside, pointing at the flag.

"Are you two talking about that hideous flag?" Lore snorted before crossing his arms. "Hey, gorgeous. My tent later?" he called to a woman walking by who made a mock purring sound.

I purred low in my throat as his gaze swung toward me. A smile curved my mouth as Lore's eyes grew hooded, and he dropped his head back, swearing into the night.

"You need to give me mercy, woman. Those noises make me ache, and my blood boil. It's such a waste that you're ending up with someone who won't even take advantage of those things. If you purred for me, I'd never let you out of my bed."

I swallowed past the lump his words caused, turning back to the bodies that hung on the wall. One moved, and I gasped. I walked closer, only for both Lore and Greer to intercept me.

"They're alive?" I whispered in a horrified tone.

"They're immortals," Lore answered cautiously. "They won't fully die unless we remove their heads. They awake to die again, but immortality prevents their true death from occurring."

"That's so wrong."

"Welcome to the Wicked West of Vãkya, Aria," Greer muttered.

"Lore, Greer, we could use some help," Knox snapped, watching as the lord and lady slowly succumbed to death.

Once they'd finished dying, I reached up to wipe away the angry tears. Making my way to the table outside of our tent, I sat where Knox pointed. The men at the table turned to glare at me, and I frowned before dismissing them. My head tilted as Ember calculated the heartbeats present, silently humming before turning my head to listen to something within the walls.

The men all spoke the same language, ensuring I wasn't included in the conversation or preparations for the attack they intended to wage on the castle. Knox listened, taking what the others said into consideration before asking someone else their opinion on the matter. He gave each lord equal time to express whatever it was they were trying to convey.

Greer settled in beside me, frowning as he noted they spoke in a language I couldn't understand. He slowly folded his hands together, turning to look at me.

"Knox, have you considered including Aria in the conversation? She may be able to help end the issue at hand," Greer announced, causing Knox to turn and offer him a disgruntled look of irritation.

"No, because she can't know how many people are inside the castle or how many enemies are on the battlements and within the courtyard. She wouldn't know how many dead bodies lay within or where the children of the keep ended up when the slaughter began."

"Ten thousand enemies are waiting for us to breach the gates within the stronghold. Of those, most are unwanted beasts of some kind. On the battlements are two hundred and three witches, all of which are dark magic wielders, and none are young or inexperienced in their craft. That is why they're able to mask their presence. In a room beside the main hall are children. Mostly crying or whimpering, yet they're trying to be brave while reassuring one another that they will make it out of this alive. Somewhere beneath us are more people, but they're weakening, as if the air source or their injuries are lowering their heart rate. Behind the castle is another group of witches, but they're not here to fight. They're here for me in the event that they win this battle."

"How the hell can you know that?" one lord asked, his murky brown eyes sizing me up as I sat in my sundress, smiling.

"Because I am a witch, but also, the predator in me is starving, and she is counting potential prey within her grasp. Some of those creatures could be a potential donor or dinner. Bitches need feeding, and when they don't get an easy kill, they stalk what's available and within their grasp. We're rather crafty and creative in fulfilling our needs when they haven't been met. There are ten thousand potential meals behind those stone walls, and my creature knows it. She can smell them, but she can also hear their hearts beating erratically with excitement, which differs from those beating with fear. That removes them from the equation of those she'll be allowed to consume for supper. Does that explain it on a level you can understand, My Lord?" Brander's lips curve into a grin. Killian shook his head, silent laughter in his eyes as he turned to Knox. "Does that help end the issue? Because the people on that gate are about to come back to life, and they're suffering needlessly."

"They're immortal, and they've probably endured much worse than what is currently happening to them, all things considered," the lord stated, glaring at me. "Your kind enjoys torturing people and excels at it, whore."

"*Whore?* Of all the slurs you have at your disposal, that's what you choose to use? Let's put that to rest, shall we? Your King is the only man who's ever touched me sexually, and he intends to marry me, which means he will be the only man I will ever know in that way. Am I a whore? Of course, I am, but only for him, and only when he's earned it. I'll be in the tent where I'm wanted, apparently, being a whore," I laughed soundlessly, the men watching me as I left.

Inside the tent, the chest containing Knox's things caught my attention. It hadn't been closed and was never left open, but it was now. Moving to it, I stared at an image, realizing every time he opened it, he was reminded of what he'd lost—his family.

On the inside of the chest was a painted portrait of Knox's wife, holding their son in her arms. Her eyes sparkled at whatever stood beside the painter. My eyes zeroed in on the amulet she wore, having seen something similar before. I bent, staring at the necklace as fear sliced up my spine. A rattle forced my eyes to lift to the entrance of the tent, finding Knox standing there watching me.

"I'm sorry. It was open already," I admitted.

Knox moved into the tent, slamming the lid closed. "Keep your fucking nose out of where it doesn't belong."

"As you wish," I said stiffly, moving to the table to pour whiskey into a glass, ignoring him while I swished it in my mouth.

"My dirty little whore?" His tone filled with anger, and I easily dismissed it since I was becoming desensitized to it and him.

"I'm whatever you want me to be. Remember the deal? So far today, your people have called me the king's whore, his slut, and his personal pleasure pouch, which was my favorite. Oh, and let's not forget, the vilest Queen of Norvalla to date, who is nothing but a mock queen to be erased from history when my uses run as dry as my body after you've finally taken my head. So, at this point, Knox, I honestly don't care what I get called or what they think. I signed up for it, knowing exactly what I would get in return."

"You're not my whore," he exhaled slowly, moving to the table. "Are you hungry?"

"No," I replied, polishing off the whiskey. "When do we attack?"

"Within the hour. Are you still weakened?"

"Very much so," I admitted. "With your cuffs on, it takes me ten times longer to refuel the magic within me. I expelled a lot when I attacked the last keep, raining down hell for your benefit. I've had very little time to recoup the magic and won't be very strong in this fight."

Knox sat before me, steepling his fingers in front of his mouth, watching me through narrowed eyes. "It's

Liliana and Sven. I was preparing to leave for a meeting of the kings, and she gifted me the chest before I left."

"It's a beautiful and thoughtful gift."

And she was wearing a tonic amulet, which meant it was given as a gift, or she'd acquired it on her own. Most amulets like that were gifts from only the most powerful witches. I hadn't mastered the ability to place a spell or enchantment into one yet, and I wasn't a weak witch. However, I kept that knowledge to myself as Knox watched me.

"That's it? That's all you have to say about them?" he demanded, sitting back to cross his arms over his chest, stretching out.

"They were beautiful, Knox. He had your eyes. I'm glad you had him for the time you did and very sorry you lost them." He stared at me, narrowing his eyes slowly. "What do you want me to say here?"

"I don't know," Knox admitted, snorting before he eyed the whiskey. "You only poured one glass, woman."

"Your arms work just fine, Your Majesty." I watched his lips twitching. "In fact, I happen to know they're very powerful arms that can hold my weight as you do very naughty things to me." His lips tipped into a dazzling smile as he laughed, inspecting me.

"Indeed, they are," he chuckled, grabbing the whiskey and pouring us both drinks.

"Thank you." I lifted the glass, taking a long pull as he spoke again.

"I enjoy your pussy dripping down my chin, tasting your arousal as I drink your pleasure, woman."

I choked, spitting whiskey all over him, sputtering much to his amusement. "That was a cheap shot," I complained, rubbing my nose where it burned.

"Yeah, but it turned you on, didn't it? I can smell it on you. Your body responds to the sound of my voice when I am aroused. Mine does the same with yours as if we're highly aware of the other's needs."

I blushed, watching his smile lift across his mouth. Knox moved to the front of the tent as Brander's voice announced his presence. I studied how Brander entered, inhaling, then stepping back as if he, too, could discern the state of my body by scent, guarding his reaction to me.

"This is all I could find on short notice," Brander stated, holding out a miniature version of Knox's armor.

"I don't wear armor. That stuff cannot be comfortable," I snorted, grabbing a cloth to wipe the whiskey from the table.

"You have her cleaning your tent already? I am impressed, brother," Brander chuckled, watching as my eyes narrowed on him, noting he was joking.

"I discussed how I enjoyed her arousal dripping down my chin. Apparently, she isn't immune to her own medicine of being surprised and choking on drinks."

"I don't know, I find it rather refreshing to have a woman hand the king his balls with her wit," Brander laughed. "Aria has a way with balls, though, doesn't she?"

I rolled my eyes, fighting the smile that played on my lips as they teased me. I stood, accepting the lightweight armor, and frowned. "It isn't heavy like yours." I nibbled my lip, turning to look at Knox, who smirked.

"It's the armor of the queen. You'll have an entire set made once we reach Norvalla. You'll be a battle queen, after all. I won't chance you being injured or worse."

"You're not fully immortal yet, Aria," Brander pointed out.

"No, I'm not. I'm also not easy to kill, or my mother would have succeeded in one of the many times she tried to murder me."

"I wish I could bring her back, Aria," Knox admitted.

"Why the hell would you ever wish to do that?" I countered, staring at Knox, who smiled wickedly back at me.

"To watch you remove her head."

"That's actually kind of sweet of you. So, how do I put this stuff on?" Knox smiled as he slid his gaze down my body.

"I'll help you, Aria," Brander teased.

"Knox looks for any excuse to touch you, woman. Stop giving it to him and start making him work for it." Brander laughed as Knox rattled, and Brander rattled right back before ducking out of the tent, still amused.

"He isn't wrong," Knox whispered, pulling me against him, reaching for the armor.

"Is that so?" I swallowed hard as heat flooded my core, tightening with need and dark desire, wishing for the release he'd refused to give me.

"Careful," Knox warned. "Edging you isn't the

easiest thing I've ever done. Not when all I want is to be within the heat your body gives me. So behave, because we're about to slaughter some witches, and it's our first time working together. Watch my cues and don't fuck me over. I'm about to trust you with the lives of my brothers the moment we walk onto that battlefield. Which is more than I have ever done in battle for a witch," he admitted, studying my face.

"Noted, but I actually like your brothers, Knox." He smiled tightly, staring at me as he lifted the chest plate over my head, sliding it on and adjusting the sides. "How many brothers did you have when this war started?" I asked softly.

"Nineteen," he swallowed hard, lifting his eyes to hold mine.

"How many are left?" I asked through the tightening in my throat. He lowered his eyes, focusing on the armor while his jaw flexed, and the tic started in it.

"Seven," he admitted, swallowing audibly before stepping back, turning toward his armor. I followed him, grabbing it before he could.

"I'll help you into your armor since you helped me into mine."

"I can do that myself, Aria."

"I know you can, but I can't touch you if you're the one putting it on," I whispered, chewing my lip while staring at the armor. His fingers clasped my chin, pulling the heavy suit out of my hands. He tossed it aside, lifting me off the floor, before kissing me.

It wasn't the brutal kiss I was used to from him.

Instead, it was soft and meant to curl my toes and create havoc on my emotions. He allowed me to slide down his body, but I rose, nipping his full bottom lip. As I did, a rattle slipped free from my throat, his more dominant one filling the tent over mine, sending a shiver of longing down my spine.

"I'll set the camp straight on what they're allowed to call you, Aria."

"Don't do that. I will earn the respect of your people on my own, Knox. I don't need coddling, which I know is why you don't defend me against your lords. You know I can give them back anything they give me. If you didn't, you'd defend me. I don't need it, though. Thank you for noticing that fact about me."

"There's a lot I have noticed about you. There is a lot more I'd like to learn without fighting you to understand who you are. You stood in front of witches and defended the Nine Realms against a goddess. No one else has ever dared to do that before. They saw a queen taking her first steps toward her throne, and you were beautifully enraged when you spoke of what you believed. I wasn't sure you believed everything you said, but you did. You spoke with conviction and fire this world needs. You may be a queen only in name, but you will still be my Queen, Aria Hecate. Now, shall we go have some fun?"

"I like fun," I smirked, yelping as he slapped my rear end. "Do you do that to the other warriors?"

"No, but you have a sexy ass, and I enjoy slapping it and hearing your little cry of surprise," he chuckled.

"You're incorrigible."

"You should have noticed that by now, woman."

Chapter Thirty

By the time we reached the battlefield, torches were lit to create an eerie flicker highlighting the bodies dangling from the walls. I could hear Knox's witches chanting, harvesting power, and stealing it from the other witches within the vicinity. I lifted my hands, and Knox reached forward, removing the cuffs, moments before power slammed against mine, sending it rushing back toward the witches who tested us on the battlements.

Knox stepped forward with me, mirroring each move I made. He added his power to mine, lifting and lowering his hands surprisingly efficiently. Brander hadn't been lying. Knox had stalked me, learning me. Energy blasts shot toward us, and we dropped our hands together so I could absorb the magic like a sponge, fueling our power with theirs.

Men rushed forward, remaining right behind us. I deflected each shot the archers took while potion bottles exploded at our feet. I hissed, stepping back, and Knox grabbed my waist, pulling the pain from me as if he'd known exactly what to do.

It was a dance. I'd move forward, and he'd move back. If I moved backward, he moved forward. If I dodged, he defended. If I attacked, Knox added strength. Each move was precise and planned. He knew every move I made, which terrified me and was exhilarating at the same time.

If I took a hit, Knox took the pain. If I took power, he allowed it. He knew each of my moves before I made it, slamming my hands into the air to eject the potions they sent toward us with ease. Knox laughed wickedly behind me as the dark witches howled from the pain of their poisons thrown back at them. I stepped toward Knox when I felt the earth shift as ten thousand creatures started exiting the keep.

"Go to Killian, Aria," Knox growled, his eyes alight with the coming battle.

Magic rushed through the field, and I lifted my hands to push it back, but it slammed forward before I could stop it from reaching us. Sprinting to Killian, I searched the field for Knox, slamming into him as magic hit us both, sending us to the ground, hard.

Our army's witches hurried forward, placing their hands in the air to prevent the black, oily magic from reaching our armed forces. I watched as the dark witches opened their mouths, and more black magic escaped from them, sailing toward the crowd fighting below. Knox rushed a dark witch nearest to us, sending his blade in a wide arch, removing her head.

Men moved forward, sliding through the witches as they flooded out of the castle with the unwanted beasts. Someone grabbed my arm from behind and threw me to the ground as men moved past me, fighting with blades. The witches within Knox's army started chanting loudly. I frowned, noting that the melee wasn't my strong point, and I was in the thick of it. A bolt of magic shot someone in front of me backward, sending me to the ground once more.

I crawled toward the horses, but men marched past me, blocking my path. Getting to my feet, I peered through the fighting until I spotted Knox's armor. His moves were precise and graceful as his blades cut through the air, severing limbs and heads smoothly. It was like watching a dancer move, but where they would swoop their arms, he wielded wickedly carved blades in both hands with murderous precision.

I shivered as three creatures rushed toward Knox all at once. He used a blade to sever the head of one, then spun to cut through the other's middle, lifting his blades to remove their heads effortlessly. Knox didn't stop. He moved through the masses that continued in a sea of bodies that rushed toward him.

Blood painted my face, and I turned slowly, finding Killian standing beside a headless body that dropped to the ground next to me. My eyes rose to his, and he lifted his blade as if I would be his next target.

Closing my eyes, I exhaled, waiting for the strike to come. Something bumped into me, and I turned, staring at the three-horned creature wielding a blade, only for Killian to deflect the blow before it could reach me. I moved back, my breathing labored and uneven while the coppery tang of blood filled the air, and the sound of metal meeting steel filled the night.

Three creatures joined the fight, and Killian deflected the blows easily, though they outnumbered him. I looked around the ground, grabbing a fallen warrior's blade, swiping it into the air while twisting my body to severe a head, spinning to shove it through the head of another. I watched it drop to the ground, only to lift my head as a sword blade touched my chin.

Killian glared at me, and I dropped the sword before he realized what I'd done. His eyes narrowed, but something moved behind him, and he spun, dispatching it. I turned back to search for Knox, finding him watching me with his head tilted while surrounded by dead bodies littering the ground, all headless. Shivering, I stared at the dark witches above that continued releasing black magic as I shuffled through the dead toward Knox.

I was almost to him when the dead started to rise. My hackles rose as power exploded through the courtyard. Turning around, something whizzed by me, and I winced as a blade struck my chest plate, sending me flying backward. I stared at the sky, pain throbbing through my chest.

A sword rushed toward me, and I rolled, pushing off the ground to stand. I drew a blade from the ground, frowning when I found no one there. I hated that I couldn't wield enough magic to matter as war raged around me.

I turned to Knox as a creature sneaked up behind him. I lifted my blade, and he watched me through the slits of his armor. I hefted it over my head, sending it sailing through the air as uncertainty filled his eyes. He sidestepped it easily, turning to look over his shoulder where it impaled his would-be assassin. Knox lifted his blade, and he removed the head in a swift swing that sent it rolling across the bloodied ground.

I stood there amid the battle without fear, lifting my eyes to the battlement where shadows moved in and out of sight. I rushed toward Knox, dodging blades. I watched him dispatching a giant as if it was nothing more than a nuisance.

The ground trembled, and I turned to see a large, winged beast rushing the gates of the stronghold. It had horns covering its head and screeched out a howl. Its skin was wrinkly, with a leather-like coat that appeared to have been in the water, way too long. Knox uttered a single word, which, I was pretty certain, consisted of four letters.

I lifted my hands and hissed before sending a burst of magic toward the creature, and when my magic hit it, it grew. Knox reached for my hands, aiming them at the monster, and it exploded into a fine mist. I stared with my mouth open, pulling back my hands, still holding Knox's, staring at them. Above us, the dark witches howled, and creatures began flowing out around us, cutting us off from the army. I turned toward Knox with worry burning in my eyes.

"Are you ready to stop playing around, woman?" he asked, gripping my waist as he yanked me up against him.

"I have decided that I am not great at melee fights," I laughed nervously, watching his eyes narrow on me.

"I thought you were rather great at it when you

were being tossed about, dodging attacks. In fact, you were very sexy, and while rather fucking clumsy, it was endearing to watch you try to pull it off and act badass while in your unicorn suit."

Growling sounded from all around us, sending the hair on my nape up in awareness of the power accumulating. I glared at Knox, slamming my hands down as he mirrored the action, sending his power down onto mine. Blood sloshed over the ground, painting it red as a wicked grin flitted over my mouth.

"Give me your power, and I will give mine," he urged.

I shivered, knowing exactly what he wanted. I knew it as a power merge, and if we were not compatible, it would go really bad fast. I opened my mouth to argue, but he shook his head. I lifted my hands, his mirroring mine, sending power rushing toward the enemies trying to gather around us.

"Trust me, woman. If anyone is compatible, it's us."

Knox placed his hands on my waist to lift my body against his. I raised my arms, swinging them around as he spun us, slicing creatures into bloody pieces. Knox noted how my hands shifted, and if they turned, he turned us while amplifying my power. Canine-like beasts exploded from around the castle, and Knox leaned back as my legs wrapped around his waist, holding my weight as he spun me again. Our combined magic slammed into the mutated dogs that howled before exploding, adding green goo to the field.

Knox pulled me up, cradling the small of my back as his power pulsed through me, heady with blood magic. It was the same magic he'd used to place his name on my flesh, sending lust rushing through me violently. I gasped as it entered my body, forcing my eyes to go hooded while he watched. Shadows moved around us, and Knox spun, using his magic. I adjusted to the pulsating feel of his magic rushing through me, losing focus on the battle while he became an all-consuming need that was building within me.

"Breathe, pretty girl," he urged.

I dropped back, sliding my hands together to clap as bodies burst into flames, painting the walls of the keep. Knox watched as I pulled myself up to claim his lips hungrily.

I didn't care if we were in the middle of a war. I needed him more than I ever had before. Knox pushed his hands through my hair, holding me to him, still spinning us in a tight circle while popping noises sounded all around us. It wasn't until the oily, dark magic brushed against us that we paused, turning to stare at the battlements and the ghastly witches above as I slid down his body.

Knox and I lifted our hands at the same moment, sending magic to search for the offenders. The dark witches shattered like glass when it found them, the noise a loud screeching howl that echoed through the valley in which we fought. One by one, we took down our enemies, clearing each side until we met in the middle.

A massive three-headed beast lunged from the battlements. I grabbed it with my magic, holding it in place as Knox slapped his hands together, threading his fingers before his magic ripped it apart. The shattered beast rained shards of glass-like pieces onto the ground, mere feet in front of us.

I lifted my hands once more, setting fire to the nooses around the bodies of the immortals strung up on the walls. They dropped, only to be caught by Knox and his men. My hands softened, threading organs back into bodies, righting the damage to the victims. I continued until sweat beaded on my brow, dripping down my neck. Once I had healed them, I stepped back, searching the ground before I started toward an empty spot, barren of grass.

Opening the ground with my magic, I stared down at the people who looked up at me from within a cavern that stunk of earth and filth, crammed pack with prisoners. I reached down, offering a lord my hand as a soft smile played on my lips. A flash of silver caught my eye before someone shoved me back. A sword pushed forward, and Killian growled, dropping to his knees as he stared at the blade protruding from his side.

Anger ripped through me violently. I screamed in outrage, reaching for my magic as the unjustness of what had just happened entered my mind. We'd saved them, and they'd killed Killian! I rattled threateningly, slowly walking forward, pulling more magic around me as I screamed in rage. My claws descended, teeth slipped from my gums, and magic rushed into my fingers, itching to be released on the people who had harmed one of our own. A hand touched my shoulder, and I turned, staring at Killian. My ears pulsed loudly with the blood pounding and coursing through my system.

"Let it go," Killian growled hoarsely, studying my face as I fought for control over the emotions churning through me. "They thought you were the enemy, Aria. I will survive. They're innocent," He grunted, tightening his hold on my arm.

"The only innocent people are the children," I whispered, staring into his dark blue eyes while fighting to reign in the emotion driving my anger.

So much power pulsed through me that my entire body trembled violently. Killian tightened his hand on my shoulder, grounding me to the present. I was fighting for control, and I was fucking losing. My eyes lifted to find Knox studying me with a guarded expression.

I turned, staring toward the side of the castle where freedom beckoned me. My mind raced with the thought of running, but I'd be running blind and alone in Knox's territory. The power I held diminished rapidly, and Killian's hand released my shoulder. Knox rattled low in warning, his eyes narrowing on me as he gathered his power, ready to defend his people from me. Or maybe he was preparing to hunt me down.

Swallowing, I turned around to find him slowly moving toward me, allowing me to decide my course. I turned once more, studying the darkened path to freedom, and whispered a soft spell instead, since running wouldn't accomplish what I was here to achieve.

Hands touched my wrist, and I looked up into oceanic eyes that studied me silently. We both knew how close I'd just come to murdering innocent people. I'd hesitated, but just freaking barely. I shivered as the power drain came from the cuffs that Knox returned to my wrists, feeling his men as they moved in around us.

"I have a fucking hard-on, yet I have never been so fucking terrified in my life! What the hell *was* that? You were literally making out as you *destroyed* people.

I mean, Knox was like *'come on up here, Aria, jump on. We'll spin and shit, murder some bitches while we're at it, yeah?'* How hot was that?" Lore demanded.

"Pretty damn hot," Brander snorted. "I do believe it is the first time I've ever watched couples dancing while destroying an army. I think our entire army felt that fight in their dicks."

I didn't speak, holding Knox's stare as his jaw flinched. He nodded to the men as they failed to grasp the gravity of what just happened. My breathing was labored as tears pricked my eyes, tightening my throat as I fought to control the reaction to what I'd almost done.

"She almost fucking murdered innocent lives because Knox's power became unhinged within her," Killian growled. "It was messy and reckless. Worse than that, she did it to defend me. Her anger was because they'd harmed me. She doesn't even fucking like me." Killian wasn't speaking in a language that I should have understood, proving my spell had worked as one ear heard their language and the other the English equivalent.

"She isn't at fault tonight. I am. I needed to know if she would live through our power merge. There's a healing spring close. If she'd been wounded from the merge, we could have gotten her there in enough time to stop her death. Get your ass to that spring, Killian. Lore, make sure he makes it there before he passes out from blood loss. We don't have time for him to heal naturally. This siege has already placed us behind schedule for my wedding, and we don't want the bride getting cold feet, now do we?"

I wrapped my arms around my middle, staring at Knox as if I understood nothing he said, right in front of me. His eyes searched my face, pulling me closer until his heat stalled my trembling. His magic scorched against mine, heating me from within.

"I'm going to marry a Hecate witch and own her pretty ass. How many other kings can say they've managed that feat? She has no idea that no other woman in her bloodline has given their vow to another, and yet she's offered me hers."

"You told her it's a vow for eternity, right?" Killian questioned, his eyes sliding over me as he held his bleeding side.

"Of course I did," Knox muttered. "She's one of the smartest women I have ever encountered. Her age limits her, but her innocence is genuine. She's a rarity and the strongest witch ever to grace the Hecate line, other than Hecate herself. She's going to win this war for us, and when it's over, I'll figure out what to do with her."

I should've run from him. I hadn't because Knox's magic had been pulsing through me. I wasn't convinced he didn't know that my mind was already implementing an escape plan, and I had thirteen routes away from him.

I just had to remove the bracelets, do what I'd come to do, and leave him to his grief while I created a new realm, untouchable by him. I didn't want a House of Magic anymore. I was raising a Realm of Magic. I was going to create an entire realm where witches could be free and not worry about being slaughtered by those within the Nine Realms. I was going to create the Tenth Realm. He could deal with the dark witches on his own, but me and my people, we would leave the moment I erected that realm and made it Knox proof.

"Are you tired, Aria?" he asked softly.

"Exhausted," I hissed, turning to leave him to wonder at my wariness.

He was exhaustingly confusing. Aurora thought I could reach him. The only real reach I wanted on Knox was my hands around his throat to shake sense into him. I'd done most of what I'd set out to do and only needed a few more things to fall into place before I could leave him and this arduous army behind. You couldn't reach someone who wasn't ready to reach back.

Knox wanted me beneath him, above him, around him, but not beside him. I was a weapon to wield, which was the same way Aurora saw me. I wasn't blinded by her intentions. The thing was, I'd offered to be her tool because she'd wanted to save the good witches.

But I'd felt her watching us tonight. I'd felt anger from a Hecate witch. I'd done what Aurora wanted me to do, so how could she be mad at me? Unless it was one of my sisters, but they were in on the plan too. It unnerved me to think my family would be here, within Knox's grasp, easily discovered.

We'd agreed upon what was required and made a plan. I executed that plan to the letter. I'd given Knox more of me than I'd intended, but to reach him, to break through the ice encasing his heart, I had to give an inch to get through the wall he'd placed around his emotions. I couldn't even blame Knox for holding me at arm's length or wanting to use me as a weapon.

I was a weapon, and everyone knew that now. I'd never find peace because of the blood rushing through my veins. I'd never know motherhood or experience anything I wanted in life because I was about to marry the one creature no one would challenge for me.

Worse, I wanted to marry the prick just to make him regret forcing me into it in the first place. So which one of us was more of an asshole? Him; still him. He was also way ahead of me on the scoreboard. I needed to up my game because I was playing the game master.

"Woman, stop for a moment," Knox called, but he'd used his language. My eyes peered up at the stars while I walked until lowering to find the camp was packing to move. I stopped in my tracks, staring at the tents being taken down, and I deflated. I folded my arms over the chest plate of my armor, glaring at the people messing with my sleep. "Aria," Knox whispered against my ear, causing me to jump before turning toward him. "Are you okay?"

"I'm fine, Knox. Just tired," I lied, turning back around before he saw the lie in my eyes. "Are we moving tonight?"

"The lord and lady don't wish you to be here because of who you are. We will leave here as soon as Lore and Killian return. We're heading to the Beltane Circle, where we will camp for a few days before traveling through the passes to reach my home in Norvalla."

"I just helped you save their lives, and they don't want me here?" I questioned, but he remained silent as I spun, leveling him with a chilling glare. "They don't want any witches here, good or bad, right? We're just all the fucking same."

"Considering what happened tonight, I am choosing to respect their wishes. I didn't want them to try attacking our witches or you in retaliation. You do not see the bigger picture, Aria. No one wants witches in the Nine Realms anymore."

"Not even you," I snorted, exhaling slowly.

I moved to the nearest table and sat, resting my chin on my palm to watch the warriors dismantle the camp. My stomach tightened with the reality of the situation my family had come back to correct. The Nine Realms was a bloodbath and unhinged, and it sucked big time.

"Do you want to talk about what happened tonight?" he asked, settling in beside me.

"I held too much unstable power within me. I think yours was too much, too soon. I went from horny to psycho in a nanosecond. It wasn't safe, especially with them harming one of our own with so much power still rushing through me."

"But you stopped before you acted out of anger. I've never met anyone who could use or wield my magic, and yet you did tonight."

"It's called a power merge, which normally only certain beings can do. Hecate tried it once and almost died. She hated anyone who could do what she couldn't achieve, even with her goddess status. Aurora mentioned it once, stating that the first creatures of the Nine Realms could do it, but only the true mates of the species. Luckily, we didn't merge correctly, which means we're not mates or even close to being anything similar. Rest assured, you will be able to walk away from me once we finish this war or whatever it is you're planning to do with me." I turned, studying how Knox swallowed as if he felt bad for the deception he was playing. "I mean, we'll be married still, but you'll be free of this wicked Hecate witch you're saddling yourself to."

"If only it were so simple, my little beauty. You're much too powerful to escape me. Not while breathing, at least. The only way out of this for you is death. I wish it were otherwise, or that I had the answer to what I intend for you, but I don't," Knox whispered in his language. He frowned, staring up at the stars, and then stood to head toward where his men were loading his things into a large wagon.

I silently watched Knox walk toward the army. I exhaled slowly, fighting the anger and pain that his word sent rushing through me. The man had more issues than any entire race within the Nine Realms combined. The thing was, Knox was the key to creating the new Realm of Magic, and I had to see this through to get to the one thing I needed.

Chapter Thirty-One

The ride into the Beltane Circle was breathtaking but terrifying, considering what was about to happen here. We'd entered a forest that spread deep into the mountains before opening up to reveal a heart-stopping view of ethereal beauty.

A long, winding trail took us out of the mountains and deep into a rolling valley of lush greenery. A vibrant sunset of violet, deep orange, and red hues painted the sky as a backdrop to an enormous, cascading waterfall. Its beauty caused tears to prick my eyes, overwhelmed by the unreal setting on which my eyes feasted.

We turned a corner on the trail, and Knox stopped the line. Dismounting, he held his hand up for me, helping me down from the large warhorse. I allowed him to drag me with him as a boy took the horse, leading it behind us while we moved forward with his men.

Knox paused, staring at me as my gaze slid over the crimson horizon. My breath caught in my throat as I stepped forward on the edge of the trail. Knox tightened his hold, turning my body in his arms to show me the giant Hecate-marked skull shooting water from its mouth into the air.

He smiled as my attention moving back to the mist, painting a rainbow in front of the skull. It was the size of a giant from legends, and in the eye sockets were huge golden healer crystals that looked like they'd trapped the sun within them, glinting and reflecting it.

In front of us was a gigantic statue of a male, his hand poised in the air like he held the sinking sun in his palm. A crown marked him as a king, and at each point of his crown were large banded carnelian boulders. Birds flew around them, filling the bustling valley with their song as hordes of deer ran through it, rushing away from the approaching army.

My attention slid back to the statue, noting the male's lack of clothing, and a blush filled my cheeks. Bel, Beltane's deity, who blessed fertility, watched over the valley where his celebration marked the coming summer months.

Several circular stone structures similar to Stonehenge's architecture sat throughout the widening valley. Unlike the human version, these rock formations had glowing tips with runes that reflected varying colors, starting at the bottom and rising to the peaks. The pillars sent the power of Beltane rushing through our party, welcoming us for the coming celebration. The largest set of structures sat beneath Bel's statue, marking it as the most powerful and important of the many circles. Inside the circle sat a raised altar. This altar wasn't for sacrifices but rather to beckon the deity from his slumber to power the valley and bless unions and couples for fertility.

Knox chuckled, forcing my eyes to slide toward him, where he watched me. "This is amazing."

"It's exquisite," he whispered, but his eyes were on me. His murmured words made my heart race, heating my cheeks with color. "Wait until you see the bathing caves and the beauty they hold."

Swallowing past the lump in my throat, I frowned before turning to look where loud sounds began echoing through the valley. My body hummed with peace while the singing bowl's song filled the entire place, cleansing the soul of those entering the valley.

"How does that work?" I asked, noting the people using ropes, dragging their slipper-covered feet over the top of the large rounded rock formation like acrobats.

"I sent men ahead with the witches, blessing the valley for our upcoming nuptials. I know that sage burning and the blessing of the bowls are important to your line. The bowls were also a faster way to cleanse the stones within the valley for Beltane. Usually, we arrive days sooner to prepare the valley for those entering a handfasting on Beltane."

"Not this time, though, because you were too busy chasing me?" I questioned, turning as the hypnotic sound of the singing bowl increased and my breathing intensified. The vibrations touched my soul, forcing a deep soothing purr to explode from my lips. "Ember approves."

"I was indeed chasing a rare, prized beauty around the Nine Realms, fully intending to capture her. You were worth the time it took to catch you. Learning you as a person while I followed you was also worth our late arrival."

His thumb traced small circles over my palm, sending heat rushing through me. I started forward again, lulled into a sense of peace by the deep pulsing hum that vibrated within me until I wanted to lean against Knox and just listen to the singing bowls. The sun continued lowering behind the mountains as stars became visible through the darkening heavens.

Once we were upon the flat ground, Knox pulled me toward the massive stone structure that had steam escaping through a hole in the roof. When we reached it, he smirked, nodding toward the men who watched us silently.

"We will be back in a few hours," Knox announced, his voice husky with lust.

"If you're not out within the next few hours, Aria is going to see more of us than she wants," Brander scoffed, wiping away the sweat on his brow.

"Who says I don't want to see it all, Brander?" I teased, watching Brander's lips twitch as Knox gave a loud jealous growl behind me. I winked at Brander as I turned, allowing Knox to pull me through the small, stone entrance.

"You're pushing my limits, woman." Knox turned back to look over his shoulder, smiling at me to assure me he wasn't serious. He pulled me closer, tossing Brander a look of warning before we entered the room, vanishing from their sight.

"I'm glad you noticed," I admitted, stopping at the first view of the cavern. "Maybe if I push you, you'll remind me why you keep saying I'm yours."

"I like this naughty side of you, Aria. The thing is, we must cleanse you before the wedding, which means I can't touch you yet. There's also what you said."

"And what was that?"

"The next man who touches you, and is within your tight body, will be your husband," Knox pointed out, smiling deviously. "You're about to marry me, which means I have your permission already."

"That's dubious and sneaky, Knox." Dismissing him, my attention went to the cave, and the air left my lungs on a whispered breath of wonder. "Wow."

The entire cavern was lit by thousands of tiny lights from a single crystal that sat in front of a torch. I felt the magic within the room slithering against my skin. The sexuality that pulsed through me was heady, driving me toward the crystalline water that exposed the fire and ice quartz beneath the surface. Moving to the water, I kicked off my slippers to test the temperature, which was heated and perfect for bathing. I turned, smiling at Knox as he watched me with a fire burning in his gaze.

Knox secured two candles, smirking impishly, and I slowly made my way to where he stood, waiting. He lit his candle from the largest one that flooded the cave. Leaning closer to the large candle placed on the altar, he ignited the wick before holding his candle out to ignite mine.

"Tomorrow, Aria, you'll become my wife."

"So I will," I murmured softly, watching him move to the side so I could add my flame to his. "Are you asking them to bless our wedding for fertility or victory in the upcoming war?" I asked carefully, a guarded look in my eyes as he smiled tightly.

"I am asking them for you to be happy with what I can offer you and that you'll be satisfied during our marriage." His eyes held mine, noting the tears that swam within them.

Stepping forward, I lit the candle, turning to watch the blessing spell ignite on the walls. The cave became even more illuminated, creating an enticingly seductive setting. Smaller torches burned around the water, lighting the way into a tunnel that fed the pool. I ducked, staring into the lit passageway before looking to Knox, finding something very masculine obstructing my view.

"What did you ask of the gods?" he asked softly, his eyes studying mine.

"To heal you from your pain. To ease your internal wounds and grief."

"You asked them to heal me, instead of to bless your womb you want to fill with a babe?" he questioned, swallowing hard.

"Some things are more important than what we want most. So we make sacrifices, and we put others before ourselves."

Standing, I allowed my hungry eyes to feast on Knox's muscular form. Turning away, I slowly stripped out of the dress I'd worn for days, covered in sweat, dirt, and dust, accumulated from traveling across strange lands and winding roads.

We were so close to Norvalla that I could taste

the change in the climate. I felt the air growing thinner and noted the animals were becoming wilder and more primal. As we continued toward it, the siren's song singed my blood, igniting a fire that I couldn't ignore inside of me.

"How many days until we reach Norvalla?" I dropped the gown, stepping out of it and folding it. I turned, finding Knox mere inches from me. He smirked, dropping his gaze to my nakedness.

"Are you in a hurry to get to your new home, Little Monster?" he asked softly.

"Norvalla isn't my home, nor will it ever be, Knox. Home is where the people you love are, and there's no one inside Norvalla who cares if I live or die."

I swallowed past the lump those words caused, heading toward the pool to escape his gaze. I silently made my way down the ancient stairs leading into the pool, pausing once I was waist-deep in the water. Knox picked me up and pushed me against the side of the pool, glaring up at me as I repeatedly swallowed, trying to keep the tears from breaking free.

"I will make it your home. I do care that you live, Aria. You're not just a weapon. You're this beautiful thing filled with chaos that turns me inside out. I know that I am hard to deal with. My cracks are many, and my edges are more than jagged, often cutting deeply. I know you want me, and I want you. That's more than most kings and queens have before entering a marriage agreement. I know I will please you in bed and that you will please me greatly in return. I'm taking everything you have ever wanted away from you, and I don't like myself for doing it. I expected to feel a victory over you, but you went and fucking cried and fucked that up. I hate your tears because I feel them in my soul, and I know I can't change direction. I can't undo what I started for you. I made a vow to my wife that I would bring the witches to their knees, and I fully intend to keep that promise."

"If you hate it so much, stop it from happening, Knox. Don't marry me for who you think I will become. We both deserve more than that."

"I want to marry you, Aria Primrose Hecate. I want to know that you can never touch another man so long as you draw air into your lungs." Knox rested his head against my breasts, holding my hips softly before he pulled back, searching my face. "That makes me an asshole, and I can't say I care. I have wanted no one else since the moment you mouthed off to me on that cliff in Haven Falls. I have craved nothing as much as I crave you."

"You literally have my vagina on speed dial. You call, it rings off the hook. You rattle, I experience random waterworks that would make a water company offer me millions for the rights to use, etcetera. You don't need to marry me to have me. I'm not the type of woman to move onto another man easily. I am blindly loyal to those I love, which you've pointed out numerous times."

"You don't love me, though, Aria." He pulled me down, lifting my chin to stare into my eyes, his words creating a maelstrom of emotions that ripped through me. His smile tightened when I held my tongue, knowing that this pool was spelled to elicit only truths. "Come, there's something I want to show you," he said thickly, threading his fingers through mine, pulling me toward the tunnel.

My fingers touched the runes, igniting them to a pulsing glow. I watched as they rushed through the tunnel, causing the water to glow a violet color. Knox turned, smiling at me as he yanked me closer, forcing me to walk in front of him.

At the end of the tunnel, we emerged into a large glowing waterfall that had ruins of a castle nestled behind it. I stared at the pool fed by the waterfall, noting the crystals lining it all the way around. Another fertility pool! Only this pool was enhanced for the King and Queen of Beltane. Swallowing hard past the tightening in my throat, I jumped into the pool before Knox could stop me. He chuckled the moment my head broke the surface, treading water to stay afloat.

"You should have been a nymph or water creature," he growled, leaping over the edge without looking.

When Knox entered the pool, the water turned the stormy color of his eyes, and the fire quartz crystals ignited. His eyes slowly took them in as a worried frown flitted over his mouth. After a moment of unease, he swam toward me, wrapping his arms around me as I settled against him.

"It approves our union, doesn't it?" he asked softly, leaning over to kiss my shoulder, his powerful body keeping us both above the surface.

"The pool approves of our marriage and mating. If it was possible, and we mated here during my cycle, we'd create life with the blessing of the Deities of Beltane."

Knox swallowed hard, cupping my face, smiling wickedly. "I am regretting bringing you here at this moment with the power this place is sending into my body. I am craving you something fierce." He rubbed me against the thickness of his arousal, watching as my mouth opened, and a loud moan slipped from my throat. "You make the most delicious noises for me, Aria."

"Did you bring me in here to fuck me or torture me more?" I asked.

His mouth lowered, kissing the pulse that raced in my throat. I shivered as he trailed his lips toward my shoulder, kissing it too, before slowly placing his lips against my heart.

"I'm undecided as of this moment," he whispered in a tone heavy with gravel. "I enjoy knowing you need me inside of you and that it's a violent need."

Chapter Thirty-Two

Knox chuckled softly, claiming my lips hungrily. His devouring kiss made me forget to tread water. Luckily, he held me above the surface. His slow, gentle kiss created a need of desire that rushed through me, tightening in my belly until my hands lifted, holding him against me. A loud, sultry purr escaped from deep in my soul, filling the cave. Knox broke the kiss, leaning his forehead against mine. He purred softly, echoing my violent need perfectly, like two parts becoming one.

I smiled awkwardly, uncertain how to kick my creature's ass without hurting myself. I could feel Ember within me, stretching out while flexing her pull on Knox's beast. Ember knew her noises drove them wild, and she wasn't afraid to use them.

"Do our creatures feel everything we feel when we're together?" I asked hesitantly, and when Knox pulled back, I tried to clarify what I meant. "When I am kissing you, is she kissing him? Or is it just us kissing, and they sense it happening? I'm not saying it right because you fluster me."

Knox smiled roguishly, noting that I was fumbling with my words, knowing exactly what he did to me. "They feel us, but they're not with us. They feel a watered-down version of what we're doing. Like when she took control because you were in heat, deciding you could withstand the pain. What could you feel of me when I was with her?" he asked, swimming us toward a bench created from fire and ice quartz, sending prisms of rainbows dancing over our bodies.

"I felt you were stretching me, but it was muted. I felt frustrated because Ember wouldn't make you move faster, and I couldn't control my body when she had control. I was a passenger in the backseat, watching everything. I could understand what was happening, but it felt more like an erotic dream. Then I woke up stuck to you like my body was a lock, and you were the key, and we fit together perfectly. I didn't know how to release you, though, which admittedly was awkward and the most embarrassing thing in my entire life."

"And do you know why Ember did that?" Knox settled me on his lap, leaning back to regard me through hooded eyes.

"Because she said you would end up dead if we didn't protect you. Basically, Ember thinks you're too stupid to live. She wanted to keep you safe by clamping down around you."

Knox laughed, and his eyes sparkled with amusement, watching me until he realized I was serious. "She's very young," he grumbled. "My creature thinks you're gorgeous and wants to pin you down and mark you everywhere so that the world knows you're ours."

"Mine wants to eat you most of the time. Pretty much right after we've fucked you, she's considering which herbs to feed you to enrich your flavor," I muttered, dropping my head to his shoulder before he jerked away from me, forcing my head to lift.

He studied my face, exhaling when he realized I hadn't intended to take a bite out of him. I tried to move away from him at the twinge of unease his denial created within Ember and me. Knox wouldn't allow me to mark him, but he intended to mark me. It was one-sided, and it bothered us. His hands tightened on my hips, preventing me from escaping his touch.

"This is where we speak our true feelings about the nuptials we are taking tomorrow," he swallowed, noting that my eyes narrowed while studying him.

"I don't think that is wise," I swallowed past the lump forming in my throat.

Ember's irritation at him flinching and recoiling from us slithered through me, making my emotions run high. Knox studied me, observing the way I had pulled back from him. I learned that half my mood swings were from Ember, and I felt them with her. I felt the overwhelming lust; it was both of ours mixed into one heap of confusion and longing we hadn't learned to control yet. Knox was right. We were young, but we weren't stupid.

"Marrying you won't be a hardship for me, Aria. You're brilliant, strategic, and absolutely beautiful. You're a fire that burns without a match. You still look at the world with the eyes of innocence I once had. You make being around you easy, even when you're mad. You forgive easily for things you shouldn't, and things that you realize have nothing to do with you and everything to do with my turbulent past. You understand my flaws and the shattered pieces of what remains of me, and you haven't tried to change them. You would try to glue me back together if you thought you could. You need to know that isn't something that will ever happen. You can't put something that broken back together."

"No, but you can rebuild it, Knox. You're still alive and breathing. Grief changes people. While it changes you irrevocably, it doesn't get to rule or decide who you become. You're not your grief. You're a very virile male who has needs and desires. You fight for wrongs wrought to those who didn't deserve them. You're the type of man I'd go to war for, but you *are* the war that I wage. I have to fight to remind myself who you are when you kiss me. I struggle to remember why I'm opposing you and that you will be the one who murders everyone I love, and eventually me.

"You're upholding a promise you made to your deceased wife, made over five hundred years ago. I am the unfortunate one you intend to use to achieve that promise, no matter the cost. That cost *is* me. You're sacrificing every desire I have ever had in life, and my life decided on by you, for the vow you made to your ghosts. Liliana is gone, and I am here and alive. I wanted to live a normal, boring life. I wanted babies that I created with the man I loved. I wanted that so much that it aches. Maybe that is my creature's need and something that she perceives as important, and I only sense that burgeoning need from her. I am giving that up for your vow to protect my family, and if you betray that, I will join the opposing side, even if I have to slaughter them and raise them again to be within my army."

"Careful, Aria," Knox warned huskily, tightening his hold on my hips. "You're encroaching dangerous territory. Tonight is for lovers who prepare for eternity together."

"Tonight is for truths, and I promise you it is a truth I speak. You're taking my future away for your promise to your deceased family. You had love. You had a child of your own. I will never know either. I get your broken fucking pieces and a warm bed. I get a promise for protection, one you've already failed to keep. Tomorrow, I will stand in front of *your* people, blessing the fruit of *their* unions. I will speak vows and promise you eternity, promising myself to you in front of *your* people and *your* family. I will tie the knot of unity, dance the maypole with you, drink the wine of celebration, leap over the firing logs, and become your wife. I will be alone through it all, with a man who will never love me. I will spend the rest of my days pining for a child to fill my womb.

"I will know pleasure, but the emptiness of what you're taking from me will always be there. You promised to make me a fucking sandwich and give me a dick when my womb aches to be filled. I will be alone until I either escape you or give in and accept the nothingness you offer. That is our truth, Knox. I will be your silent bride, who everyone mocks because while I'll take your name, I can never use it. I will be the Queen of Nothing, and I will be nothing more than a joke that your people will speak about behind their hands. You will be the King of Norvalla, Vākya, and the High King of all Nine Realms. You will have me anytime you wish to use me, as your weapon, as your whore. I will be something you loathe and crave to punish, and you will punish me every time something happens because I will be on hand and nothing more than your whipping post. I'll be there to take the blows of your anger for crimes I did not commit. Eventually, you'll tire of me, but you'll still do your duty because that is who you are. Maybe you'll tire of my body or just get to the point where you hate me enough to end this misery you've promised me. Either way, your life won't change any with the vow we take tomorrow. You can still find another to love, and while you won't be able to give her a child, she'll get to feel and be with you without the walls up every moment of every day. Me, I'll be the forgotten queen, who no one cares about. I'll be the witch who is caged and pulled out when it suits her husband to use her. I am what you said. I am nothing to anyone. I will never be more than a weapon or a body to use. That is my truth, right?" I pushed away from him, swimming toward the cave's opening as he watched.

Once I returned to the cave's entrance, I dressed and then hurried toward the opening. Knox grabbed my arm and yanked me back, glaring down at me with a fire burning in his eyes. His chest rose and fell with his anger, and yet he didn't argue the truth of my words.

"I take that as you don't want to marry me anymore?" he snapped.

"No, I really don't. I think I am better off taking the chance that you will not discover where my family is hiding. I don't want that kind of future for you or me, Knox. If I marry you, I want it to be because you have buried your ghosts and chose me. I'd want it to be because I'm something you want for *yourself*, not your army or your kingdom."

"Change your mind, Aria. Don't make me into a monster that has to force your choice. You won't like it any more than I will."

"No, I don't think so. I have to agree to marry you for it to be legal in the Nine Realms. I may be young, but I have read and been educated on the terms of unions for a very long time. A forced marriage isn't binding or legal."

"In that case, I have a wedding gift for you," he snorted, moving to his clothes. The blood drained from my face, and my pulse beat deafeningly in my head until I felt it between my eyes. "I think it might change your mind about marrying me."

I watched Knox dress with scenarios running through my mind at what his gift might be this time. Nausea churned in my stomach, threatening to empty its contents at the look of victory in his beautiful eyes.

Water dripped from my hair, drenching my dress. He'd given me a purity gown, made for a bride to wear the night before her wedding vows. Knox grabbed my elbow, pulling me with him as we exited the cave to greet his men, who watched us warily.

"Bring in her present. My intended bride has changed her mind," Knox snapped, and I turned, taking in his men's worried faces.

I shivered violently while Knox turned, studying me with a cocky smirk on his lips. Laughing sounded, and I narrowed my glare on Dimitri, who walked beside Killian and Brander, smiling. The blood drained from my face, pooling at my feet. The world spun around me, and my body trembled uncontrollably.

"Hello, Aria. Good to see he hasn't placed you in chains at his feet yet. I'm certain that is changing soon, what, with your upcoming nuptials and all," Dimitri stated, and it took everything I had within me not to vomit.

Dimitri was working with Knox. That meant he'd known where my family was this entire time. Knox had flirted, warning me he'd find Dimitri, and he'd know everything the moment we'd entered the Nine Realms. Tears swam in my eyes, and my heart clenched before my attention slid to Knox, who watched me with mirth dancing in his expression. This was going to end badly, and it was going there quickly.

"Say hello, Aria. You're being rude to you old friend," Knox chided, his mouth curving into a dark smirk that filled his eyes with an icy-chill.

Chapter Thirty-Three

"You've met the King of Wolves, haven't you?" Knox asked, his eyes noting the paleness of my face as the coloring drained. "Oh, that's right. I forgot to tell you I'd crowned him king before bringing his bitches home so his harem would be here when he and his men arrived."

"You bastards," I whispered, barely able to get the words past the swelling in my throat out.

"I told you. I've been planning this much longer than you have. Dimitri was already working for me when he entered town. I am the one who brought him back into Haven Falls, offering him a throne. All he had to do to earn it was get close to you and make your family think he was on your side. He got to you so easily, too, didn't he?"

"All I had to do was look interested, and you fell right into that trap," Dimitri said, clapping his hand on Knox's back. "Oh, don't look so sad, Aria. I would have fucked you if my King hadn't marked you. You did help me, after all, by killing Fallon. I'd drugged him, giving him enhancers that fueled his need for the best match to breed with at the gathering, knowing it would be you."

"You think Knox will honor his deal with you? You're a bastard. I saved you from him!"

"No, you didn't, actually. I was going for your sisters to catch them, needing to bring them back to Knox. The thing was, he never intended to murder Aurora. We only needed her to get you to play ball for our side. I was in that courtyard to keep her close, but then you went and broke us both out of his clutches. At that point, I remained in play to figure out where your family was hiding and the details of their plan."

"I'm going to rip out your heart and feed it to you, asshole."

"Such a blood, thirsty little woman, isn't she?" Knox asked softly.

"Indeed, she is. I wonder if she's figured out that you know where her family is and that you can easily get to them. I'm guessing she's adding it up right now because she looks ready to throw up," Dimitri stated, his sapphire eyes sliding over my face.

He was right, and worse than that even. Dimitri knew the location of the witches I'd hidden from Knox. My hands lifted, wrapping around my stomach as my head dropped. Pain punched through my middle, and tears burned my eyes. Knox had my weakness in his grasp because I'd trusted that Dimitri was on our side.

"You should have seen this coming, pretty girl. Did you actually think I'd be satisfied with being your bitch?

Running around the Nine Realms doing as you wanted? I am a born king to the alpha clan. I am no one's bitch, witch. Your family? They treated mine like shit, running us out of town until only my father and mother remained. I was last in line for a throne that was rightfully mine. Knox murdered those who stood before me, paving the way for me to become the rightful king."

"King of what, Dimitri? You're nothing more than a bitch Knox intends to rule and boss around. It's called being a puppet, which means you're nothing. You'll be less than nothing, actually. You'll be under his thumb because Knox is a tyrant."

"And you're his pretty pussy he gets to fuck while aiming you as a weapon at his enemies. You're his whore and his weapon. You are the same thing to Aurora and your sisters, only they're not fucking you, at least not in the same way he is. You should hear them speak of you. You're basically a pet they intend to sic on their enemies. A rabid bitch they plan to send in, so they don't have to get their hands dirty. Aurora laughs at you, speaking about how easy it is to control the monster that crawled out of her sister's womb. You think it was a coincidence she showed up the same day you were born?" Dimitri's laughter was cruel, and the ice in his stare only made me want to rip his eyes from the sockets.

"Think about it, Aria. Your aunt, who vanished without a trace to escape that rotten-to-its-fucking-core town, comes back the day your mother births a monster. Freya placed your tiny body onto an altar, begging the gods and goddesses to take you away. Aurora came back to get what she helped create, her weapon to use against her enemies. She knew she could easily mold into what she wanted it to become. Aurora protected you because you're her key to the throne that she isn't strong enough to take by force. Or, she wasn't, until you. Aurora was there during every attack from your mother, yet she didn't stop Freya from hurting you. She merely healed the damage, earning your undying love. You don't question the hand that heals you, do you? The entire town wanted you to be put down like a rabid, ill-trained dog. My parents voted to murder you, and I agreed. Your friends, your family, your lover, no one wanted you. You're nothing but a gullible bitch that is easily manipulated."

I stood silently before Dimitri, watching his smile turn cruel, and his eyes sparkled with amusement at the tears I couldn't stop from falling. My head shook after a moment, and my attention slid to Knox, who didn't look amused by what Dimitri had stated. There was coldness in his eyes while he watched me being ripped apart to nothing more than what I'd just told him I was to him in the pool.

"What? No sassy come back out of those willing lips, woman?" Dimitri continued.

"Shut the fuck up, Dimitri. You're done here. Leave," Knox snapped, his hands fisting tightly at his sides while he watched me, never taking his eyes from my face.

"As you wish, My King," Dimitri smirked, stepping closer to me as if to kiss my cheek.

My hand shot out, slicing through his chest without warning, removing his heart, which I tossed toward Knox. Blood covered Knox's face, and his eyes narrowed on me. I trembled with rage and fear, knowing that Knox knew where my family was and had known since we'd first entered the Nine Realms.

Dimitri's body dropped to the ground at my feet, and I exhaled slowly. I wiped my hands off on the white bride's dress, holding Knox's icy stare.

"Can't start my reign with traitors in our midst, now can we?" I whispered, demurely holding his stare.

Knox smirked, nodding at Dimitri's body while his men moved into the space in front of me, hefting the corpse to toss him aside. Blood dripped down Knox's face as he stepped closer to me, lifting my chin to force my eyes to meet and hold his.

"I know where your family is hiding, Aria. I've known since the moment you entered the Nine Realms. I've allowed them to remain in place because it hasn't benefited me to gather them yet. I captured Callista with Dimitri's help. I picked her because she was the softer one between her and Reign, knowing you were more attached to her. I placed a tracking spell on her, using it to send in one that would attach to anyone else she came into contact with that carried the same bloodline. I know about the sanctuary, and I have allowed it to remain running. Not because of you, but because you're gathering those witches with the promise of your protection, and they're amassing within it, which will, in return, make them easier for us to capture. All I have to do is say the words, and the warriors within their vicinity will change that. I can kill them all, simply by sending word to them. So, I'd be very careful with your next words because lives depend on them. Do I have your attention now, little girl?" Knox chuckled, watching the tears that slid from my eyes while I nodded, unable to get words out. "I expect an answer," he snarled, and I swallowed.

"Yes," I whispered hoarsely.

"Are you going to marry me, or am I going to give the word to murder your people?"

"I will marry you," I agreed, fighting to stop the sobs that threatened to explode from my lungs at what was happening.

"And what else?" he asked, lifting one brow with the question while searching my face.

"What else do you want from me?"

"I want you to give my people a show tomorrow. If you can't awaken the deity, you're still to dance for them and make it appear as though you have awoken Bel. When you prepare for our wedding, you will be the happiest bride this world has ever seen. You will make them believe our union is your choice and that you're excited to belong to me. I expect a beautiful, radiant bride tomorrow. I expect her to welcome me to her bed, giving me no issues with our wedding vows or wedding night. You will make the witches believe you are entering into this union to protect them, but that you're also with me by choice."

"You want me to pretend that you didn't force me to be your wife?"

"That's exactly what I want," Knox snorted. "I've been ahead of you every step of the way, Aria. I know that you were told to use your body to get to me. I know that you're playing hard to get, so I would be on my knees for you, begging for access to what you assumed I want most from you. Pretending to be attracted to me should be easy enough for you. After all, you're here to seduce me at the behest of your aunt, aren't you? Get close to the king and make him want you more than he wants this war. Wasn't that what she told you? And you, the obedient little bitch that you are, thought you were actually skilled enough to seduce me? I eat women like you for breakfast, turning them mindless and against the cold, heartless villains that sent them to me in the first place. You're not even on my fucking level, Little One."

"I wasn't sent in to seduce you, Knox. I have not tried to seduce you yet. Have I tried to show you I am not evil? Yes, a thousand times over. Have I succumbed to your touch? Yes, because whatever is within me, it wants what is inside of you. Seduce you, though? No. I'm just trying to survive you. You're too jaded, too broken, and too damn fucked up even to try to seduce. You see enemies where there aren't any. You give bitches whiplash as if they're standing in line backstage to meet their favorite boy band. I thought I could make you see that we're not all the same, but you already knew that. You allow witches to move about freely, and you don't allow them to be abused. You are saving them to add to your army. I came here intending to show you I wasn't evil, but you can't see past the blood that I didn't even ask for, which runs through my veins. You're punishing me for my parentage, which I had no more control over than you had of yours. Did I try to seduce you? No, because you're nothing more than a fucking ghost. You're haunting the Nine Realms as surely as if you were another casualty of a wicked witch that didn't care about the laws of our races. You can't seduce something that doesn't even realize he's still alive. I wasn't playing hard to get either."

"And you expect me to believe that, why? Because you're so fucking truthful, Aria?" Knox snorted, shaking his head. He lowered his mouth for mine, and I turned, denying him my lips. "You're Aurora's lapdog, one I fucking muzzled. I planned for you, Little One. I planned for your betrayal, for your lies, and that you'd use your body to get me to bend to your will. The thing about that is, the king does not bow to a queen. The queen bows to the king, and once she weds, she is silent and beneath his rule."

"You want a submissive queen? Shall I get on my knees for you now, King Karnavious? Is that what you want from me? You want me to bow to you by force? Of course, it is because it is the only way you will ever get me."

"I'll have you tomorrow night and every night after that. Who knows, Aria, with as much as we've done to procure fertility, maybe you'll get that babe you crave. Maybe your gods will smile upon you, and I'll place a babe into your womb. Wouldn't that be a fucking miracle?" Knox snorted.

"Oh, I don't want your baby, Knox. I never said I wanted your child. I said I wanted the child of the man I love. I never once stated that it would be your child that grew within me. Besides, I'd have to open my womb to allow you in, and the only way you'd get that is if you ripped it out of my body and fucked it without my help. Bel, on the other hand, can offer me a child by awakening him. If he chooses me, I can open for him as he fucks me in front of you. Wouldn't that be a glorious start to our marriage?"

"You're not to give him your womb, Aria," Knox

snarled, tightening his fingers on my chin.

"That isn't your choice, Knox. You don't get to tell me who I can open for before we're wed. My creature chooses who breeds us, and right now, she doesn't want you. We learned a lot about ourselves from almost being raped. Lord Andres wanted our womb too, and she wailed to protect it, but Lennox told her that only *we* decide who breeds it. That isn't you. You won't get it, and neither will your beast. You may mark me, and you may claim me as your puppet queen, but you'll never touch my soul or my womb. Those are things that you can't force open or demand access. You can hurt me, you can break me, but you can't touch me deeper than I'll allow. Your mark will be nothing more than an ownership tag. One I loathe and despise."

"If you give Bel your womb, I'll rip it out and eat it in front of you," Knox said, smiling coldly, sending ice rushing down my spine. "Brander, take my bride to the bridal bed. I am going hunting tonight. Secure her there and allow no one else to enter. Use the cuffs to secure unwilling brides before we changed the tradition, so Aria realizes her position within the room," he stated, releasing my chin.

"I'll go with you," Killian announced, but Knox turned slowly, shaking his head.

"I'm going with my ghosts. Tomorrow I marry my enemy. I need to be alone with them tonight. I need to tell them that I will never love her or allow her more of me than to feed her basic needs. That she's simply a means to an end for what I promised them," Knox swallowed, staring at me as he moved past, leaving me with his men.

"Aria," Brander whispered, touching my fingers. I

closed my eyes, fighting for strength as I stepped over the blood on the ground. "Come, I'll get you somewhere that you can clean up and get a drink before sleeping."

"Thank you."

We walked toward a large stone structure that sat in the middle of the sea of tents erected around the stone circles. Inside the small cabin was a single room with runes painted around the walls. Inside sat a bed piled high with clean linens and furs, and a large pole sat at the head of it for unwilling brides or sacrifices. I felt like both.

"Drink. It will help you," Brander stated, shoving whiskey toward me. "Tell me how to make this easier on you."

"Free me," I answered, staring at him.

"I can't do that, Aria."

"He's about to take everything away from me. If you can't free me, then you can't help me, Brander," I whispered, drinking the whiskey to calm my trembling hands.

"Knox gave Liliana a child, Sven. Knox was fighting in a war for several years before they conceived Sven. He returned from war a colder, harder man—one who didn't look closely at what was happening around him. Sven was born seven months after Knox returned. He wasn't small. Sven was a healthy boy. He didn't hold the gene to rattle or purr, and the land hadn't accepted him before he began his one thousand deaths. Our children are not born early. And with Knox's genes in him, Sven should have been consoled by his father's noises. He never was. Liliana was weak, and when the witches cursed Sven, her first instinct was to run from both Knox and Sven. Our women don't do that. They fight to protect their young, even if the cost is their lives. Knox called her weak and told her he wished it had been she who was cursed instead of their gentle son. Those were his last words to her. When he returned, Liliana was dead. It broke him. And I think you are opening those wounds. I also think you're healing them, and Knox is afraid that you can make him forget the pain."

"Why are you telling me this?" I asked, holding my glass out for more whiskey.

"Knox is my brother, and I love him with everything inside of me. I understand your need to protect your siblings at all costs. If you can unravel what I am saying without committing treason, maybe you can find at least one thing to get out of your marriage that you want, Aria. He will not make this easy on you, because to him, he's committing the biggest sin by wanting you. He's betraying the memory of his son and wife, who wasn't perfect. She was weak in mind and body. She willingly sought her mother's witch once a month to ease her migraines, among other things. It's the same witch who gave her the toxin that killed her. If what you said is true, and since you were beneath a truth serum when you repeated it, then give tomorrow a shot."

"He intends to marry me and give me an entire lifetime of servitude."

"He doesn't have to marry you to take that throne. He doesn't have to marry you in order to use you as a weapon. Knox doesn't have to marry you at all, and yet he is. Ask yourself why he needs this. You're brilliant, so put that brilliant mind to use."

"He doesn't love me," I swallowed, fighting the pricking tears that burned my eyes.

Brander exhaled, slowly shaking his head. "He doesn't, and he may never be able to love again. That creature inside of him, Aria? He won't let you go, so you might as well find the middle ground and force Knox to stand on it with you," Brander stated, nodding toward the bed. I polished off the glass. "Sorry, but I need to secure you to the pole."

I stood slowly. Stripping out of the dress, I slid into the bed, turning to look at Brander. His eyes slid over my body, slowly taking in every inch of me that was bared to him.

"It really is too bad you're his," he uttered.

"You could have changed that. You were too slow."

"I don't move fast, woman. I'm more of a slow, hard, and deeper man. I like to know that my woman feels me there hours after I've left her body. Some men move fast, and some go gentle. Others go hard and slow, making sure that things don't end up lost in translation."

"That was pretty smooth, Brander."

"Isn't he smooth, though?" Knox snorted from where he leaned against the door, watching us before he stalked into the room. He glared at Brander as he removed his bloodied shirt. "Isn't she seductive, brother? All she has to do is remove her clothes, and we become helpless but to want her. If I didn't know better, I'd say she was related to Aphrodite instead of Hecate, but we're more than aware of from whom she came. Now, if you're done trying to fuck my brother, Aria, you and I both need to rest for our wedding tomorrow."

Chapter Thirty-Four

I awoke alone and to a disturbance within the room. Rising from the bed, I peered around the darkness, sensing the oily taint of dark magic. Candles lit without warning, causing the dark shadows around the bed to take form. Swallowing, I leaned back against the mattress while taking in the soulless eyes dripping a black, oily substance down their cheeks. A deep shiver rushed through me. One opened her mouth, screeching, and I gasped at the dark magic coursing through me.

I pulled on my arm, secured by Brander, groaning at finding one still tied to the bed. Ilsa's witches were casting evil, dark magic, and my chest tightened. A scream ripped from my throat as a blast rushed through me. A dark witch lunged with a glint of silver in her hand, and my claws extended, sliding through her arm. The coppery tang of blood filled the air as the arm I'd severed slammed against the door.

"Traitor! Die!" one of the witches shouted through

blackening teeth. She flew toward me, forcing me to use my free arm to sever her head from her torso, fighting to remain alive.

"Kill her now!" another screeched. The door to the cabin exploded open, and men flooded into the room, weapons out and ready to engage the enemies within. "She cannot live!"

A dark witch rushed toward me with a dagger aimed at my heart, but a blade sliced through the air, inches from my face, blocking the strike. The sword cut through body and torso, swinging again so quickly that my eyes hardly registered the motion, removing the hand that held the dagger. Ocean blue eyes held mine, Knox's eyes moving to the next witch before swinging deftly and fluidly to dispatch her too.

My body sagged in relief, watching Knox and his men eliminate the dark witches. His attention returned to me, and he dropped his sword on the floor before moving onto the bed beside me. Knox grabbed me, searching for injuries.

"Are you hurt?" he asked, cupping my cheeks. Brander removed the cuff from my hand, releasing me from the bed. Knox yanked me into his arms when I was freed, examining the sore flesh on my wrist from the cuff.

"No," I replied softly, exhaling while he held me in his arms, against the heat of his body to still the trembling of mine. "I'm fine, Knox."

"I want the witches up and placing protection spells around this camp. This cabin needs extra protection. Every corner of the camp needs clear quartz and smoky quartz to keep the high queen's minions out of this valley while we finish our vows. I want armed men placed at the entrances, in and out of the valley. Check everyone coming in for dark magic," Knox snapped harshly. "I won't risk Aria's life to marry her."

I shivered against him, listening to the soft purr slipping from him, offering comfort he probably hadn't even noticed he'd given. His fingers rubbed against my neck, working the muscles that had strained from being tied to the bed so I couldn't escape the upcoming nuptials.

The moment the room was empty of the dead witches and his men, Knox placed his forehead against mine. He didn't speak, but I could feel his body trembling with both anger and fear at finding the enemy within the bridal room.

"I should have been here," he swallowed, kissing my forehead.

I pulled away from him, staring through narrowed slits as my creature observed him. He noted the changes as my nails extended and my teeth slid through my gums. Before I could ask Ember what she intended to do, Knox's eyes slid to obsidian, burning with fire in their dark depths as Ember forced me into the backseat of my body.

"What are you doing?" I asked carefully.

"I am negotiating for our vagina's needs. You suck at negotiating, and so does my mate's host. He's too stupid to understand us."

"Nope! No, not happening," I argued. *"None of that* mate *shit!"*

"My pussy is hungry. You've failed to feed it,

dicker," Ember snapped, slowly leaning closer to sniff Knox.

"I will feed you tonight until you beg me to stop," Knox whispered, touching my cheek as he fought Lennox for control.

"You play with us, and we don't enjoy it. You change your mind faster than Aria changes her wet panties when you're around her."

"She enjoys being edged, and I enjoy pushing her body to that precarious point. Tonight, when she comes for me, it will be violent and the best orgasm of her life, and yours, Ember." Knox leaned forward, sliding a piece of dead witch off of the bed, pushing us down until he loomed over us.

"I do not enjoy it, stupid male," Ember hissed, letting the scent of our need fill the room. He growled, lifting his body to run his fingers over our swollen clit. "You hurt her, and I will eat you. She forgives easily. *I* do not. You push her away because you are hurting. She knows it and forgives your stupid, useless heart for grieving another mate who was not even yours, dicker." Knox's eyes darkened, and Ember laughed, cupping his cheek. "Do not get mad. This is not Aria speaking. I am the mate to that which watches me from within you, and he feels *us* viscerally. So do you, but you refuse to admit what you feel. You know I am his mate, and you hate us for it because you are thick of skull and large of dick. Not that we mind, but maybe you should have added a dick to your skull so you would use it more. You hate that it betrays your ghosts, but Aria is not at fault for the mistake you made in assuming that woman was yours. It makes you the biggest asshole and her, a sad girl because she has not wronged you. You wrong her and me, yet you know the truth already."

"Can she hear us now?" Knox asked, narrowing his eyes to slits.

"No, I have severed her hearing. She can only see you right now," she replied, and I tensed from within her.

"I had a son, Ember. My wife gave life to a babe we created together. You're young, newly formed, and just awakened. We only create life with our true mate. I had that. I cannot give you what you crave. I can keep Aria protected, and I do want her more than I have ever wanted anyone else, *including* my wife. Aria is fire and chaos. I crave it from her so deeply that I will never allow her to leave me."

"You think she was yours, but she wasn't. I am your mate, idiot. I'm new, yes. I am young, but Lennox is mine. You and Aria? You are the pretty parts that shield the world from what he and I are. You're not what you think you are, Knox. You are like Aria. The only difference within you both, well, besides you being stupid, is your magic that heightens sex and feeling, among other things, you've yet to show her. You kill with that magic blindly, fueled by the same source in which she was born. Aria's magic is from the Nine Realms, forged within the fires that created it as a whole. Yes, she is a witch, but that part of her is so little that she had to learn to mimic her sisters to prevent it from being detected. You hate her because of the blood running through her veins, but she doesn't need to use that magic because her other half, me, is more dominant. You are the same as me, but I'm smarter and prettier. You see, Lennox and me, we're going to be together whether you or Aria want it. Stop hurting my girl because you're fucking delicious, and I'm a very hungry, growing girl."

"Lennox chose Liliana too, Ember. If he hadn't, we wouldn't have created life."

"*Did* you create life? Your wife wore an amulet around her neck. It's one Aria knows well and thinks about often. It was filled with scent and magic. A scent taken from the same woman who fought us, and I know you smelled it on her in that cave as you ate us to show Aden that we belonged to you. Lennox knew, but you loved her. We are merely passengers, as Aria calls us, and we crave your happiness. Aria, and I, Lennox's true mate, were not born yet, so he allowed you your happiness for a time. You think you know everything because you're ancient and shit. Our kind, we know, and sense when our mate is coming, and we're very aware of each other once we are close enough to be felt. You sensed us by the smell of our womb, did you not? You were drawn to Aria because Lennox sensed us there. You never felt that way for Liliana because your human heart loved her, but your beast didn't care either way. He never mourned her. He mourned *your* pain. Lennox strikes hard and fast when you are in pain, the same as I do when Aria is in a similar situation. Ask Dimitri, who now has no heart since he revealed it was filled with darkness. Lennox didn't mourn your son, either. Did he? You fought with him because he didn't rise for the death, but he rose for the vengeance because you, his host, felt pain and anguish like you never had before."

"Sven was our son!" Knox growled, grinding his cock against my body, his anger intensifying. Yet Ember didn't relent.

"Maybe yours, Knox," she whispered, wrapping our legs around him, cradling his growing cock against our arousal. "He wasn't my mate's son. I can feel Lennox itching to breed me, and he craves me as much as you crave my host. You fight this because if you don't, you will forget your reason for fighting this war. Aria understands, and she allows you to hurt her so that, she too, remembers why she is fighting against your domination. She craves you as you crave her, stupid. She bends for you and holds you against her at night to feel you. You feel her too. Admit it to me. Admit that you want her for more than just that which lies between her thighs."

Knox swallowed hard as his eyes slid back to Caribbean blue. "I want her, Ember. I want to hear her screams as I stretch her body full of my arousal. I enjoy her mind and body. She has a beautiful soul that is pure and untainted, but she is not who I love. I loved my wife with everything I had, and when Aria's people took her away, they ripped my bleeding heart from my chest, replacing it with stone. I will marry your host today, and she will become my wife. You and Lennox may like each other, but he won't take you or Aria unless I agree that you will become more, which won't ever happen. You don't understand what drives us and what makes us evolve. You're nothing more than a monster hiding in pretty flesh that doesn't understand how the world around us works. I am not your mate. Lennox is not your mate, Ember. If that were true, you'd already carry my babe in your belly. You'd open that womb because he'd have forced you to give it to him, but he hasn't forced you to do anything, has he? You offer Lennox your throat, and he kisses it, but he hasn't accepted it, and that is something that mates cannot ignore."

"I'm young, and my host has been through hell because of whom and what she is. You put her through hell, and he knows she is hurting. Mates sense the other and know their pain. I sense his unease, his need to take what I offer him, but he gives us space where it is needed and knows that he must be gentle when he takes us. He isn't a gentle beast. Lennox also knows you will fight what is happening between us. Brander was right. There are four of us in this relationship, which is why we're all at war. You punish a girl for the crimes of her bloodline, but you see her fighting them too. You crave the woman she is to become. You are marrying her because of who she is and because you need to know that she can never give another what you want from her. You felt pain and anger when she said she would find someone to love her. You went to war to remain in control of Lennox because he intended to claim her throat to keep it from ever happening. Tell me, I am wrong. Tell me you didn't fight the beast to remain in control when those words left her pretty lips, Knox."

"You're not wrong. I have placed pieces onto the board to ensure that doesn't happen. Today Aria becomes my wife and will never know another lover because of it. Aria isn't wrong. She's a forever kind of woman. She'll be my forever, and I will promise to be patient and provide everything she needs that I can give her. I won't be able to love her, but I will cherish her and give her all of me that is left to give. Do you hear me, Aria? Because I know you can hear us. I will cherish you and always pick you up when you fall. I will protect you from your enemies and keep you satisfied with anything you want. I will marry you tonight as the sun sets. I will lay you down on a bed of roses and cherish every inch of you, and you will give me your womb to fill."

"If your little swimmers don't swim, we will find someone who can give us a child. I will be a mother, Knox. Lennox will give us a child, or he will release me to find another who can breed our womb. If I were you, I'd try to get through to Aria because I won't open it unless she agrees to let you that deep into her body. You have twenty-four hours until the window on creating life ends, and if you fail, know that I will take control and find another monster that will. That's not a threat. That's a fact, stupid male. Aria and I want a babe, so either you put one in us, or we will find another who can. Brander, Killian, and Aden are all compatible with our womb, and they could mate us too. You think we can only mate once because your brain is slow. Some of our ancestors could mate more than once, helping our species to populate the world, and we are them. Your parents hid secrets from you, but Hecate knew what you were. Why do you think she fought so hard to claim you? When that failed, she removed the one thing that you loved most in the world from your life? Because broken things don't fight well, and they mess up. She knew broken things don't stop to think anything through. She also cursed your people so they couldn't breed. Why? Because you will create the monsters that end this war, but only with us," Ember whispered, nipping his lip before releasing more scent that caused Knox's eyes to grow hooded.

"You're wrong, Ember."

"Am I? It terrifies and excites you at the idea of Aria swelling and growing round with your child within her, doesn't it?"

He searched my face, lowering his mouth to my shoulder slowly. His cock slid over the exposed flesh of our apex, gliding over the slick arousal before he chuckled darkly. Teeth skimmed over the place his mark had once been, and he nipped against it without breaking the surface.

"Keep threatening Lennox with opening your womb for another man, and he will rip it out before he ever allows another to breed you. He is watching you as we speak, counting down the minutes until Aria is beneath us, screaming our name as she comes undone for us. I'm going to fuck her so hard that it imprints my name on her soul, and she feels me for eternity. You forget, your host is mine as you are Lennox's now. You are strong, but I am stronger. You're smart and conniving, but you now know that I have been ahead of you every step of the way." Knox lifted, rubbing his cock against my opening, and Ember moaned, pushing the generous tip into my body as he purred, forcing me to make the same soothing sound.

"You want that, don't you, Little Monster? You want all of me buried deep into this body that knows it belongs to me. I promise to destroy you tonight and to make you come until the only fucking words you can whisper are my name, and yes, please. I am the monster others fear. The strongest alpha within the Nine Realms, and tonight, Aria, you become *my* wife for eternity." Knox pushed into my body deeper, watching as we trembled around him. Ember rocked my hips while he watched us, trying to get off on his thick, hard tip. "That's right. You need that, don't you? This body knows who it belongs to, and tonight, I intend to prove it to you until you crave nothing else."

"You won't get our womb, stupid male."

"Aria," Knox whispered, resting his forehead against mine, watching me fight for control of my body. I lifted my hips to seat him deeper, but he laughed huskily, lifting his body to prevent it from happening.

Knox grabbed my hands, holding them above my head. He stared down my body, noting the blood covering it from the witches who'd tried to murder me. His free hand slid between my thighs, slowly running his fingertips against my entrance.

"Knox," I whispered, noting Ember had vanished, leaving me to deal with the very virile, very aroused male that was slowly torturing me.

My knees parted, and I lifted my ass for his touch. Rocking my core against the pleasure he offered, I moaned loudly, breathlessly. Knox hissed, and his fingers pushed into my body as it clamped down hungrily against him. He spread them within me, chuckling as I gasped and moaned loudly.

I didn't care what it looked like anymore. He'd edged me to where my body was in control of what it wanted and needed. He leaned his head over, clamping teeth around one pebbled nipple, growling loudly with approval of my reaction to him. A loud popping sound echoed through the room as he released it, withdrawing his fingers, slick with arousal, pushing them into his mouth.

"You taste like heaven, woman," Knox groaned, releasing my hands as he sat up, pushing the purity gown up to my hips. He slapped my pussy, slowly rubbing his fingers over it, doing it several more times, forcing the pending storm to lessen as pain mingled with intense pleasure. "So fucking wet for me, aren't you? I'm going to enjoy being your husband and fucking you anytime I want you. You want that too, don't you? You won't ever crave anyone else because this pretty naked flesh will be too sore to want for anyone else ever to touch it. That much I can promise you. I intend to stretch your tight body every morning and every night until it fits perfectly for me. I intend to lavish you with pleasure and keep you fed until you're content." Knox leaned over and ran his tongue around my swollen clit, never sucking on it because we both knew if he did, I'd come undone with the orgasm he had denied me for far too long.

His tongue slid through my sex, and the noise he made was feral, that of a starving beast that intended to indulge in a feast. "I suggest you get to the cave, get bathed, and seduce a deity so I can fuck you and listen to your noises while I make you my wife tonight. If you open your womb to Bel or fuck him, I'll rip it out of you, Aria Primrose Hecate. You are mine, and mine alone from this day forward. I will see you in one hour when I join you for our mating bath. You wash me, and I wash you to cleanse ourselves of the past and begin our adventure into our new life together."

"Wish that it would wash away the past so you could see the future you could have," I whispered huskily. "Or sage the shit out of your ghosts," I offered, sitting up to put distance between us.

"As of now, your facade for the people outside this room begins, Aria. Show them you want this, and I'll reward you tonight. Fight me, and I'll chain you to this bed and leave you unsatisfied as I fuck you. I am the master of edging your body, but I can also prevent it from reaching climax. Be a good girl for me, and don't fuck a deity in front of our people, Queen Karnavious."

"As you wish, *Master*."

"Careful, Aria. I like that name from your talented tongue."

Chapter Thirty-Five

The cave was filled with witches, all of who helped me get ready for the bathing ritual. Each added salt, herbs, and rose oil to my skin, preparing me to enter the water. Rose petals floated above the surface in varying shades of red and orange. They oiled my skin and hair and washed my hair with my shampoo and conditioner.

Knox had an unlimited supply of products I'd used in my life before coming here. As if he'd gone out of his way to gather items, I would need to be comfortable. In his mind, he'd already caught and claimed me. He sure prepared to catch me for a man who didn't want me, collecting everything I would need for the journey to his home.

I'd listened to Ember, noting what she had told Knox, knowing I could hear. She believed to the very core of the bones we shared that Lennox was her mate. She'd challenged Knox, gone toe-to-toe against him on things I wouldn't have dared to bring up. Ember was bold, if not a little crazy. I hated that she'd gone silent so much lately, but she told me she was growing when I asked. I was almost afraid to ask just how much growing she had to do before she'd be finished.

Siobhan entered the cave, stopping to light more candles before she clapped her hands together loudly. "The king is coming, everyone out. Aria, enter the water and prepare to accept your intended mate," she ordered loudly, handing me the cloth and ointment oil I'd be using to bathe Knox for the ritual.

The women all flooded out of the cave in a rush of motion. I slipped into the water to submerge my body, placing the oil and cloth on the side where a stone altar sat. On it was the morning dew, collected for Beltane. I submerged my body to my chin as Knox's men entered the cave, ensuring no one else remained inside. Knox walked in, smirking as he found me watching him from the water.

Brander issued orders for the men, turning sapphire eyes on me before he looked away. He moved to the altar, lighting a candle and whispering a prayer for the mating ritual, followed by Lore, Killian, and Greer, who apparently would stand witness to the wedding vows.

Knox lifted his shirt off over his head, revealing his rippling muscles and tattoos. Tattoos that turned, watching me like they recognized me. I swallowed as two of the ravens escaped his flesh, and Knox smirked, removing his pants to reveal his cock that, for once, wasn't hard. It twitched, forcing my eyes to his, finding heat burning in the smoldering depths. The ravens sat on wooden perches I hadn't noticed, turning to watch the entrance. The men slipped silently from the cave as

Knox made his way into the water.

Knox waded to me, boxing me in against the side of the pool, his arms rested on either side of me. His lips lowered to my shoulder, kissing it softly. I'd played my part with the women watching, but I had no problem ignoring him in private.

"Turn around, and I will wash you, Knox," I grunted, watching his eyes narrow on me at the iciness of my tone.

"I've been told my princess is delighted with our upcoming nuptials. She told the others that she anticipates an amazingly beautiful wedding. Yet I come in and find her unhappy with my presence?" Knox placed his hands on my hips as he lifted me onto the altar, locking his gaze with mine.

"The deal was to lie to the people. I don't need to pretend when it is only us present," I muttered, intending to retrieve the oil, but he stopped me.

"The king washes the queen first, Aria," he explained, exhaling slowly. "This is one of the few times I will ever go first in our relationship or a ritual."

"I could just wash myself, since you hate me." I frowned as he narrowed his stare, dismissing my words as he grabbed the cloth, soaking it in oil.

"I do not hate you. You have not listened to what I have told you, have you? I want to marry you. I want you, period. I enjoy you in my bed, which I have stated repeatedly. I enjoy your mind and the way it works to eliminate problems. You're educated, not because you attended a school, but because you took it upon yourself to read the words of scholars and poets. You love reading the written words of fiction and nonfiction. You prefer to escape reality into worlds that don't exist. In those tales, you learned to imagine yourself in the situation of the characters you've read and what you would do if it were you in their place. You've evolved faster than some creatures in this world ever had a chance to because you read and taught yourself how to be a better person."

Knox grabbed my arm, slowly washing it until it shone in the candlelight. His fingers slid over my skin as he lowered his nose, inhaling the scent of roses before moving to the other arm, repeating the steps.

"Do you know why we wash one another, Aria?" Knox asked, never lifting his eyes to mine as he slowly lavished my skin with the oil. He massaged it on, soothing my body's aches while making it throb with need.

"No, I don't. I only know we wash away the past to prepare for the future."

"The first people of the Nine Realms believed that when a couple washed one another, it cleansed their souls. It also prepared them to create life with one another. The man would wash his bride, cleansing her flesh to prepare for her to accept him into her body, placing his seed deep within her womb. The goddess of fertility would sense his desire to breed with her and make her womb fertile for their coming marriage bed. The bride would wash his manhood, asking the god of fertility to bring her a strong son to fill her womb. They did it to create life, and I chose this ceremony because I want you to know how futile it is to think we could ever have a child with everything we've done. My people have literally done everything they could think of and still no children. We have tried and failed to create life since your grandmother cursed us to be sterile."

"Mm, how nice of you," I whispered as he smiled tightly.

I watched him lift my foot, slowly washing my calf then moving up my leg while he held my stare captive. Once he'd finished washing one leg, he did the other, spreading them apart as he pushed me back. My breathing hitched as his hand moved toward my sex, cleaning it with the cloth before his fingers danced precariously against my sex, only for him to move on to washing my breasts and stomach. Knox leaned over, placing a kiss against my womb before he whispered in a foreign language, not his own.

He pulled me down, turned me around, and pushed my body against the altar. Slowly, he ran his fingers down my spine, forcing something beneath my skin to pulse, moving to escape his touch as he laughed huskily. His lips kissed my shoulder blade, peppering it with kisses before his hand started moving the cloth over my naked back. I swallowed a moan as it sent pleasure wrapping around me, clenching my core until finally, he backed away.

"Now, sweet girl, you may wash your King," he growled, trading places.

I swallowed down the urge to tell him he wasn't my King, but I wasn't willing to argue the matter. He knew where I stood, and his eyes danced with silent victory, which told me he was aware I was giving him this one. I touched his arms, using the cloth to follow the sinewy muscles, bathing him in sandalwood scented oil.

My body tightened with every path the cloth took, slowly running over his chest until I reached his cock, stroking it with my hand. He hissed, watching me as

I lowered my mouth, placing a kiss on the rounded tip before lifting my eyes to his, smiling as my teeth elongated. His eyes dared me to follow through as his claws lengthened, along with his teeth. Swallowing, I dropped my stare, moving back.

My head rose as he lifted his body to the altar. The slight movement created a mass of muscles that rippled as he hefted his body up easily. I grabbed one foot, slowly washing it and his legs before he pulled me against him, cupping my face.

"You're beautiful, my bride," Knox growled, running his fingers over my jawbone while staring straight into my soul. "I cannot wait to make you mine tonight, Aria Primrose Hecate, regardless of the blood that rushes through your veins. I will cherish you and respect your needs."

"I promise to escape you, as your wife or not, Knox Karnavious," I uttered, watching as his smile turned lethal, and he slid into the water. "I will not start a marriage with lies, even if it is a mock marriage. I won't lie to you about my intentions. You forced this, and you want me to act complicit for the benefit of the people and yourself. You made me look like a fool, chasing me around the Nine Realms, allowing me to think I was ahead of you when, in reality, I wasn't. You've known where my family hid, every step of the way. You knew what I was doing, but I don't know why you didn't make a move against my family or me. Why let me think I was ahead of you?"

"Because I wanted to know what you would do when you got here. Pretty eyes can hide the largest lies. And yours are so beautiful, Aria. Your family is your weakness, and I have had them and not used them other than to test your magic against my enemies. I could have killed them all by now. None of them have stayed in that tomb, yet I chose not to do that. I don't want to make you into the monster I am, but I will to keep you at my side. Your magic is unparalleled to anyone else in the Nine Realms other than my own. You took power from the Nine Realms, and you freed the King of Gargoyles. You freed Taren from a curse that your grandmother sentenced him to for eternity. If it isn't me trying to control your power, someone else will. It's as simple as that, Little One.

"Creatures within the Nine Realms hide their power because letting others know their strengths makes them into a target. Within one week of you being inside this world, chatter started. Not about the return of the Hecate witches, but about one beautiful silver-haired girl, who could take down an entire castle by herself. They began hunting you, and I hunted them before they reached you." He watched the tremor of unease rushing through me. "The sun is rising, and with it, the only chances of getting Bel to rise before you are my bride. He only accepts maidens who are unwed, and I am marrying you tonight."

"What if you regret it, Knox?" I whispered thickly, watching his mouth curve into a frown. He lowered his mouth to mine, claiming it softly as he cupped my face between his hands.

"I won't, Aria. That is one thing I am certain. Now, go dress because I, for one, cannot wait to see Bel brought to his knees by *my* woman."

"You're so certain he will pick me? All the witches

dance for Bel. He only chooses one out of the group in which to spend the night. Turning him down isn't an easy thing, Knox. He's the most beautiful male known to the world, with fiery eyes and golden skin. He is literally made for pleasure and offers it to the woman he chooses. Once I am in that circle, only I can choose my path. You won't be able to get inside of it, not without disturbing the ceremony."

"I am very aware of how this works, Little One. I know who you are and who I am marrying tonight. You may want a child badly, but you are not the type of woman who will sleep with a man just to gain his child. You're Aria Primrose, and you're not a basic bitch. You need chemistry and to want a man before you lie down with him. I know because I watched you struggle, thinking it was Brander who would make you into a woman, wanting it to be me. I enjoyed that inner battle within you, and then the acceptance that it would not be me because in your eyes was the proof of how much you wished it otherwise. I also watched the relief playing across your face as you found me behind you, entering your body. So am I worried that my girl would take a deity over me? No, because she's my girl, and she knows it, even if she doesn't like that she is."

I hated that Knox was right, but worse than that, I hated that he knew me. I exhaled, twisting my lips and scrunching my nose up. I exited the water, moving to the scented towel set out for me. I heard Knox leaving the pool but refused to turn around. Drying off, I reached for the white lace panties, silently slipping them on before I placed the tiny lace top over my breasts. It barely covered them and was sheer enough that my pink nipples were visible through the material. Grabbing the skirt, I pulled the thin material up my hips before adding the silver chains onto my waist, securing the carnelian. I turned, facing Knox, who frowned at the outfit.

I spun away from him, and his arms slid around my stomach. "I'll see you out there," he whispered, and I exhaled slowly as he placed a kiss against my bare shoulder. "You smell like heaven and hell. Born an angel, created to bring hell to men with the sin your pretty lips promise. Wear your hair down. It drives men wild with the thought of fisting it as they ride your sweet curves hard."

I swallowed, spinning to tell him I'd wear it up for our wedding, but he wasn't there. I peered around, finding only the ravens flapping their wings while they watched me. My heart raced as they left their perches, slamming against my naked torso. Power rushed through me, and I gritted my teeth until it turned to a gentle tremor of pleasure. I gasped, watching them as they moved through my flesh, settling on my shoulders. Power sizzled through the cave, and I rolled my eyes. Knox had a backup plan if I took Bel up on his offer of planting a son into my womb.

Chapter Thirty-Six

Similarly dressed witches escorted me to the altar before the statue of Bel. Frowning at the sensation of magic and the powerful scent of sandalwood that wafted against my senses, I turned, finding Knox watching me with a knowing smile. He sat right outside the stone circle, his gaze sliding hungrily down my scantily dressed body. I rolled my eyes at his naked desire, turning toward the bonfires that blazed throughout the valley around the circle in which I stood.

"Light the candles, and we will signal for the music to begin. It's best to start now and proceed with the ceremony as we progress into the day. It may be hours before Bel comes to select a witch for the night."

"As you wish," Soraya murmured.

Pounding began as drums started, echoing a heady beat throughout the valley. People gathered around us on the stone columns that flowed in a spiral around the structure. I could feel their stares, the weight of their hopes to increase their libido for tonight.

Beltane was basically one big orgy where everyone went at it, hoping to create life. Not even the animals were spared from the breeding ritual. Thankfully, I'd been oblivious to everything since they had extinguished all light last night to focus on the light for today. I'd smelled the sex in the air when I'd emerged from the cave, even on the witches, who were walking beside me.

I used a mortar and pestle to grind the herbs into dust for paste. The witches danced around me, drugged by the magic in the air that Beltane released. I could feel the pull to move, sway my body, and lure any male worthy of mating to me. I could hear Ember within me, humming along with the drums, her tone happy as if she hadn't just called Knox onto the battlefield and rubbed his nose in his shit. Not that it hadn't impressed me, quite the opposite in fact. But hey, she'd held her own against him.

Once I ground the ingredients down and added the oil, I moved to the male who clouded my mind as he watched me closely. I paused at the cusp of the circle, placing the bowl on the ground before I pulled my skirt up to my knees, kneeling before Knox, staring at him. I waited for him to grasp the meaning of what I was giving him.

"My King, the May Queen, would like to choose you as her consort for tonight," Siobhan explained carefully. "It is her personal scent. It will prevent her from losing you through the procession of tonight. It ensures her that if something else takes control, that it would allow only you into her bed tonight."

Knox's eyes narrowed to slits, peering down at me. He moved to where I sat with my palms up, my pose nonthreatening. My attention sharpened by the way his body tensed as he lowered. "What is expected of me to accept it?" he asked.

"She would place her scent onto your wrists. It would give her the ability to scent you from another when the celebration begins or when Bel arrives. Since Aria shares her form with another, this would ensure her creature only comes to you if she takes control. You'll also keep Aria grounded to this plane should Bel wish to take her to his own. You, My King, will be the focal point of her dancing, among other things." Siobhan stepped back, turning to go to the altar.

Knox held out his hands, placing his palms up. Slowly running my fingers through the scent of the oil I'd created, I placed it over his racing pulse. My eyes rose to his quickly, finding him watching me with a worried expression. It started a reaction within me, sensing his fear that fed my own. My chest rose and fell with labored breathing that hadn't escaped his notice.

"You're afraid Ember will choose Bel, aren't you?" Knox whispered so softly that I thought my ears weren't hearing him correctly.

"Yes," I replied, sucking my lip between my teeth. "You weren't wrong about me. I don't want a baby from just anyone. I'd rather none than the one that would be created on this altar this morning."

"You're *my* girl, Aria. Whether you like it or not, you're mine. You crave me as much as I crave you. Admit it to me, right here, right now," he whispered, and I leaned forward, claiming his lips as the crowd cheered around us.

"No, asshole," I announced against his lips. "I'll see you after I seduce a deity, and maybe you'll see the difference when I try to seduce someone. Watch and learn, King Karnavious. Then afterward, you can ask yourself if I've ever tried to seduce you. Believe it or not, I am trained in seduction, as are all witches."

I pulled back to see a wolfish smile curving his lips. Standing, I moved back to the altar as power sung through the air, and his hiss of pain brought a smile to my lips. I stood in front of the stone slab, waiting for Siobhan to ignite the power of Beltane. Knox hadn't removed my bracelets, which prevented me from doing the honor myself. Not that it mattered, since as long as a witch started it, the circle would ignite.

The moment it was lit around us, I lifted myself onto the altar, staring into Knox's heated gaze. My sheer top barely covered my rose-colored nipples, and the tulle skirt flowed to my ankles, exposing my thighs while covering the lace thong they had given me to protect my sex against a deity made for sin. I was certain Knox had added the extra layer as a precautionary measure. Not that it would work.

The dancing was endless, and through it all, I never took my eyes from Knox, rocking and swaying to the drums' heady beat. Sweat beaded on my brow, pooling between my breasts, causing the thin material to cling to my flesh. My thighs burned, aching from the fact that Bel hadn't arrived yet, after three hours of endless dancing. I slid my hands over my body, touching nothing inappropriate while praying Siobhan got fucked instead of me.

The moment KALEO's, *Way Down We Go,* started, I almost paused. It was the song playing within me, now filling the entire valley, and everyone stopped, looking to see from where it was coming. Power erupted behind me, and Knox's eyes told me Bel was there.

Black obsidian with burning embers replaced the blue as Knox's nails lengthened, and his rattle started low. I lifted my arms in the air, holding his stare. Arms wrapped around my waist, sliding up to cup my breasts, sending pleasure rippling through me. Bel yanked me back, kissing my shoulder, and I fought the tremor of desire that rushed through me.

Knox stood, even as his brothers yanked him back down. Bel turned my body, lifting me and forcing my legs to wrap around his waist. Bel wasn't just pretty. He was the type of man that they sang ballads about, and angels pined to duplicate. He had thick blonde hair with matching golden eyes and bronzed skin. A full mouth leaned toward me, smiling as he claimed my lips in a kiss that sent everything within me, rushing toward the "O" zone.

Bel's hands held my hips, forcing my apex against a large, very male organ that promised me pleasure. He pulled his lips from mine and opened his mouth, revealing perfectly white, blunt teeth that deflated the creature within me. I lifted my hands as he slowly lowered me to the ground. My body still moved as if on autopilot, rocking and swaying against him as he loomed over me, watching me.

"So pretty, but not witch entirely," Bel crooned, leaning over to claim my lips. He chuckled as I chased them the moment he started pulling away. He took me down onto the altar as I continually moved, slowly luring him to me.

The pleasure his body gave was the shit of legends. He could send you into orgasm merely by contact against his skin. He slowly rocked his hips, watching me as if he was trying to place my species.

"You're a burning fire, Little Silver," he hissed. Leaning up, he watched me slowly rubbing my body as his eyes heated to pools of liquid gold. "Your flames beckon me. You're something the world hasn't seen before, aren't you?"

Bel fisted his thick cock, watching me with a hypnotic look burning in his gaze. He pushed it against my apex. I fought the lengthening claws that sought to tear loose. He leaned over once more, biting my nipple through the sheer fabric, which caused a cry to escape my lips. I shot up, taking him to the ground onto his back before my mouth crushed against his. He laughed, excited about my need to take him.

Ember purred from within me, but it wasn't friendly. It was a low warning that radiated through me, exiting my throat. Bel stared up, watching me through narrowed slits. He started to speak, but my hand pushed through his torso, and my fingers wrapped around his throat as a rattle exploded from my chest. I withdrew my hand, holding his heart, and my eyes lifted to the scent, keeping to my wits. Knox was my focus. His blue eyes held mine as Siobhan howled with my victory.

She took the heart from my hand, forcing me to release it to her. I leaned over, claiming Bel's shocked lips as he gasped for air, coughing up blood.

"Blessed be, Bel. Thank you for Beltane and the coming summer heat. We ask that you bless our wombs and fill them full. I'm sorry, my womb is taken, but I promise you this," I said, loud enough for Knox to hear. "If my womb isn't filled by next Beltane, I will be back for your son to grow in my womb. Bless us now, and bless us all, for we wish to be fruitful this Beltane night until fall."

"You're a fire, Little Silver. I give you my blessing and pray that your lover is sterile, for I require a rematch next spring. I thought you only pretty. Deadly women are some of the rarest of breeds, for you've kissed with fire and used your claws to rip out the heart of a deity. I am impressed. What *are* you?" he asked, blood dripping from his lips while he searched my face. "You're one of them. You're..." he paused, smiling devilishly as he saw the intrigue burning in my stare.

"One of what, Bel?" I whispered.

He smiled, laughing as his body decomposed to nothing but ashes. I growled, lifting my eyes to Knox, who stood right outside the circle, pacing. Brander and Lore were both at his side, watching me. I raised my hand as the scent hit me. Siobhan dropped the circle, and Knox marched through, jumping fluidly onto the altar without invitation. Siobhan cried out, worry etching her face as Knox grabbed me, yanking me against his body.

"You kissed another man," he hissed.

"I choose you as my King for Beltane," I whispered thickly, watching as he flinched, realizing what he'd just done. He'd violated my circle of protection, in which the queen held all the power. His hands captured mine, still painted in the blood of the last male who had tried to mate with me.

Knox took me down to the altar, hard. His body pressing against mine as black eyes took over the blue. His teeth grew, and his dark gaze slid to my naked shoulder, where Bel had kissed me. Brander rattled, causing the others to rattle their warning that Knox was trespassing where he shouldn't be. His mouth crushed against mine the moment my legs wrapped around him, holding him to me, releasing my hands as my words registered through his jealous haze.

Knox lifted away from my mouth, pulling me up with him, smiling wickedly at me. "I'll be your Beltane King. I'll also be your husband tonight. You're my Queen, Aria."

The crowd erupted into cheers for their King's prowess of passing through the circle to claim his Queen. Knox yanked me closer, kissing me soundlessly, the crowd's cheers echoing through the valley. The fires leaped high into the air, burning greater as the sun came out to bathe our flesh with Bel's approval of our union.

"You seduced a deity right out of his heart, Aria."

"Technically, I ripped it out because the scent I placed on you held me here for you. It wouldn't allow Bel to paint an illusion, rendering me unaware of who he really was. Had you not accepted my gift, I'd be fucking him while you watched. Neither of us could have done anything to prevent it from happening had you declined what I offered. He'd have looked like you and be everything I ever wanted," I swallowed, mentally kicking myself for saying that to him.

His smile blinded me, striking me stupider than I

already was around him. He yanked me into his arms, lifting me and jumping to the ground while he held me. His men watched us closely as he exited the circle and placed me onto my feet.

"Begin preparing my bride to marry me. I'd like to get it over with before she changes her mind again," Knox stated, kissing me softly before his mouth touched my shoulder, slowly sliding to my throat as he growled hungrily. "I want to hear her purring beneath me before the moon rises tonight."

"Wait, Knox," I whispered, turning as the crystals embedded in the valley hummed with power. "Watch," I urged, sucking my lip between my teeth as a smile played on my face. Knox wasn't watching the valley. His attention was on my face and the wonder playing over it as the valley changed and became an ethereal place.

"It's exquisite," he swallowed, never removing his eyes from my face.

The entire valley glowed with Beltane's power, fed with sexual vibes that flowed through the people. Knox whispered his approval by lowering his mouth against my shoulder, kissing it softly with a gentle purr that had mine echoing his.

Fire quartz pulsed while shining rainbow-colored light into the carnelian. The scent of roses filled the air, drifting on a subtle breeze. The air heated, and people cheered as the Beltane Circle came to life. It glowed with power and approval from Bel, fueling the world with fertility and the heat of the coming summer. The bonfires leaped higher, and the orange runes of the stone circles pulsed, glowing as they grew taller to honor the May King and Queen with the raw sexuality of Beltane.

"Blessed Beltane, My King for the night," I uttered, slipping out of his grasp. I allowed the witches to guide me toward the blessing tent where they would dress me to marry the High King of Nine Realms.

Chapter Thirty-Seven

The witches directed me into a large tent that smelled of roses. They filled it with burning candles and crystals that made rainbow prisms on the walls of the tent. Soraya and Siobhan both ushered me into the bath, stripping my body of the outfit I'd worn to lure Bel to his untimely demise. Once inside the bathtub, I released the uneasy breath I'd held.

"You removed Bel's heart!" Siobhan exclaimed excitedly, causing me to jump at her sudden outburst. "You kissed him as his blood sprayed from his mouth. It is unheard of to best him, and you made him look like he was a newly born babe."

Turning toward her, I lifted a brow. Her eyes were filled with excitement and awe. Soraya, on the other hand, noted the way I trembled in the bath. My eyes locked with hers, and she slowly moved toward me, handing me the cloth, covered with the scented rose oil.

"You're not okay with this marriage," Soraya stated, her tone indicating unease. "He's forcing you, isn't he?"

I swallowed, dropping my eyes to my knees before my head slowly nodded once in confirmation. He was, but it wasn't like I could stop it now. Knox held the cards, and I wasn't even certain I had been playing the same game.

Siobhan deflated, her eyes sliding to my face. "If we could get you out of here, we would, Aria. They guard every exit against escape or entry by the dark witches. All magic was nullified until tomorrow morning. We thought the precautions were a little strange."

"Knox would murder you if you helped me escape," I swallowed, slowly washing the sweat from dancing off of my body.

"If he caught us," Soraya snorted, dropping rosemary into the tub.

"You're going to be the first Hecate witch ever to pledge herself to a male for eternity," Siobhan muttered. "You do know that once you've spoken the vows, this cannot be undone, right?"

"I'm aware of the laws and that it is forever."

My heart raced with the words being admitted out loud. Knox knew where my family was hidden, and he'd left them alone because he hadn't needed them to force me. If I refused to marry him, he would use them to tie my hands. It was better this way, for them and me. I lifted my leg, washing it while Soraya and Siobhan sat beside me, frowning.

"You understand that you'll be connected to him

forever, right? Should you follow this path, the king will be able to control your power, your magic, and you can never harm him. If your bond goes deeper, like mates, and you fully merge, your souls will bind together. You get that, correct?"

"I don't have another choice, Siobhan. He knows where my family is hiding. If I don't marry him, he will use them against me until he gets his way. Knox has ensured that I will follow through with what he wants from me. If I don't do this, he will kill everyone I love."

"I get it, I do. Sometimes you have to make hard choices as the queen, and Aria, you're the Queen of Witches, even without your throne. Watch the witches. Watch how they look at you. You already have them following your lead. What you do next matters," Siobhan whispered, but there was an undertone of accusation in her voice that rubbed me the wrong way.

"You've fucked him. Maybe we should trade places," I snapped, glaring at Siobhan while my emotions ping-ponged through me violently.

She snorted, shaking her dark head. "King Karnavious hasn't even turned his eye on another woman or taken one to his bed since he returned from meeting you, Aria. I thought you were this mythical woman, and yet you're rather normal."

"Ew. Never say that again," I shivered. "I try very hard not to be normal."

Siobhan frowned, her forehead creasing in worry. "I just meant that I wasn't expecting someone like you. You care about us. I know that King Karnavious has tied your hands, but there are ways around this being legal. You're a queen, one who is being coerced through threat into a marriage you don't want."

"And who would argue it against King Karnavious, Siobhan? Ilsa? I intend to murder that bitch, and once I have, I will seek to remove the darkness she has unleashed on this land."

"Will you murder the witches upon who she forced her darkness?" Soraya asked, and I swallowed at the pain, lacing her words.

"That depends, Soraya. If they're evil and cannot be saved, then they too shall be put down. Once they've killed another living being, I cannot withdraw the darkness from them. This is my understanding of how Hecate explained the process in our grimoires." She lowered her head, hiding a frown before smoothing out her features. Standing, Soraya moved to grab the drying cloth. "Ilsa has someone important to you, doesn't she?"

Soraya shook her head, exhaling slowly before she turned to face me again. "It doesn't fucking matter, does it? You can't fix anything. You're marrying our enemy, one who intends to magically neuter you before you pose a threat to him or anyone else."

"Ouch, that almost hurt my fucking feelings," I grunted, standing to grab the cloth from her. "I'm sacrificing myself to save others, too. Just so you are aware. He promised to save other witches who hadn't accepted the darkness into them yet."

"You're a fucking savior," Soraya sneered.

"Enough, Soraya. If the king had your family within his grasp, you'd do the same. We're witches, and witches always protect those we love from harm. They're our weakness," Siobhan swallowed. "Aria, if you sit, I will fix your hair. How do you want it?"

"Up, because he prefers it down," I chuckled at the odd way their lips turned up at the act of defiance.

"Don't let the king break you, Aria. Too many depend on you saving us for him to win that fight," Soraya said, not turning toward us while her fingers trailed over the dark onyx, sapphire, and diamond tiara that Knox had sent into the tent with Siobhan.

"Even if I could escape him, he's written his name on my flesh, which allows him to track me down no matter where I hide," I frowned, peering at my reflection while Siobhan smirked, her eyes holding mine like she had a secret.

"You've seen the chest and the picture of his wife?" she asked, holding my stare. "Thought so, which means you know that once he figures out the dark witches planted his wife, your life will be in danger of the rage he'll unleash onto us all for their crimes. Rumor has it, your grandmother played a huge part in the young king's life, and when he wouldn't bend to her will, she forced him to do so without his knowledge. Liliana opened trade between the realms, beseeching her husband to help her own family. Liliana's siblings disagreed, but Knox opened it and allowed trading to happen because he couldn't deny her anything. Hecate achieved her goals through his bride."

"Because what Hecate wants, the goddess gets," Soraya finished for Siobhan, causing my eyes to close.

"So she does," I frowned, standing to slip into the undergarments that had been placed on the small table.

My hair was styled and piled onto my head with flowers poking out around the crown of the Nine Realms. The dress was a work of art, with an open back and swooping neckline that exposed the curve of both breasts. I'd voiced concerns about my girls making an untimely appearance, but Siobhan had scoffed at my worry, reminding me it was Beltane.

I hadn't added jewels or family heirlooms or adorned my body in crystals or other enhancements. Knox was getting me and only me. My stomach clenched, knowing that I was about to marry Knox Karnavious, King of the Nine Realms, and the asshole who enjoyed playing with my emotions.

"Blessed be, Aria Primrose Karnavious, High Queen of the Nine Realms," Siobhan whispered, stepping out of the tent as she opened it to reveal colorful rose petals for my bare feet to pass over. Soraya and Siobhan both held the tent flaps open, bowing low at the waist while I struggled to contain the urge to run away from what was coming.

Squaring my shoulders and calming my heart, I passed through the entrance. The moment I had, witches tossed petals onto my path, covering the earth with them for me to step over. Candles were lit through the pathway, but no magic was used to ignite them. I proceeded until I was at the end of the long, red carpet covered with white rose petals.

My eyes slid over the guests, noting they all stared at me, and yet none stood as was customary. Panic ripped through me, and I stepped back as the witches murmured, mentioning the slight. Siobhan and Soraya stepped up, both blocking my exit. Their hands touched mine in silent comfort, and I turned, slowly taking in the empty side of the ceremony, traditionally reserved for the bride's friends and family. Not a single person had sat there to show support. My heartbeat echoed in my ears as the ravens within me flapped their wings rapidly, feeling as if they would break free.

Knox's eyes turned and locked with mine, and everything fell away around me. A blush filled my cheeks at the look that met and held mine. His mouth curved into a smile that wasn't faked or designed. There was wonder in his eyes as he took in my simple appearance, foregoing the jewels and other things he'd left in the tent from which I could choose.

His gaze slowly traveled down the silver dress I wore. My shoulders were naked of adornments, with no royal house symbol on them to declare my bloodline. No makeup covered my face because I didn't need it to enhance my beauty, just me in my skin. Knox got what he wanted, me with nothing else between us. Well, other than the dress. I'd even chosen to come to the wedding bare-footed, something witches of the lower class within the realms did. It wasn't for him, though. It was a nod to those within the camp he'd saved, showing them I was one of them.

I felt Knox's heat from his intense stare, and mine gradually settled on him in his finery. He was dressed in a white shirt with his cloak hanging over one shoulder. Silver chains held it clasped in place, while a crown of onyx and blue gems, seated in silver, sat on his head, marking him as King. He looked as if they had plucked him from another place and time. He was the perfect image of what a king should be and look like.

Even through his shirt, I could see the strength his body promised and the pleasure only it could give me.

Little girls moved in front of me, slowly tossing flowers into the air while Greer stepped forward, offering me his arm.

"Would you give me the honor of walking you to your husband, Aria?" he asked softly, swallowing hard while taking in my simple appearance. "I know it's reserved for a father or a male relation, but considering your line is all women, I figured you might honor me with the right to take you to Knox."

I slipped my hand into the crook of his arm, leaning over to brush a kiss against his cheek. "I would love that, Greer."

We walked down the aisle between the groom's and bride's sides, which felt like a slap in the face. I didn't begrudge the people for not sitting on the Hecate side of the seating, considering most of them had been harmed by us one way or another. My eyes continually moved to where my sisters would have been, had they been here, feeling their vacant seats to my soul.

At the altar, Greer walked me up the stone stairs and left me to stand in front of Knox, whose eyes searched my face. Sliding to the emptiness of my side, he nodded to the crowd who moved to fill some seats as a show of solidarity. It did little to ease the fact that I was all alone here. Knox continued staring at me as he whispered, "*Wow,*" loudly, shaking his head before the druid stepped forward. Or at least I assumed he was a druid.

"We gather here today to unite two kingdoms into one," the druid announced.

My eyes rose to the skies, watching thousands of ravens flying through the valley, creating a shadow over the sun. They dropped petals from their claws, raining roses down over us from high in the sky. It was beautiful and unexpected, causing tears to burn in my throat.

"They're a bit early," Knox whispered, smirking at me as I continued watching them until they vanished in the distance.

My eyes slid back to him, listening as the druid spoke in Knox's language with somberness. Sliding my attention away from his once more, I turned to the mountain where the sun was setting behind the high peaks, creating dazzling hues of red, orange, and violet where the pass to Norvalla sat. Tears pricked my eyes at the beauty that it held, calling me toward it with something more profound than I understood.

"Aria," Knox whispered, forcing my attention back to him. The tears found a passage to run down my cheeks. He swallowed hard with a worried look in his sea-blue depths. Purring softly, he stepped forward, grabbing my hands before I had a chance to wipe away the tears.

Brander stepped forward with a blade, causing my eyes to widen as he slit a tiny cut into both of Knox's hands before doing the same to mine. The druid continued speaking, but I wasn't supposed to be able to understand his words. They spoke of binding bloodlines, which almost stole a grunt from my lips. They bound our hands together next, with vibrant silks that matched the crowns on our heads.

Knox's eyes slid to the pulse hammering at the base of my throat. The nervous energy within me was coming to the surface, and no matter how much I tried to conceal it, it wouldn't go away. Brander securely tied the knot around our hands. Leaning over, he kissed my cheek before the druid uniting us in marriage spoke in a language I could acknowledge.

"With this knot, I bind these two houses. With this knot, I bind man and woman in soul and magic. I bind their kingdoms into one. I bind a king and his queen for eternity or until death takes one from the other." I flinched at his words, which made Knox's eyes narrow on me. My chest rose and fell, noting the crowd had laughed at the words. "If anyone disagrees with this union, speak now and be heard, or hold your tongue always and forevermore."

"Aria, look at me," Knox instructed, but I couldn't. My lips trembled, and my heart sank to my feet. I yanked on my hands, but he held them, tightening his hold. Purring started from the surrounding men, yet it did little to stop the panic coursing through me. "Breathe, Little Monster. It's okay," Knox whispered. Stepping closer to me, as he leaned his forehead against mine, shielding the tears that flowed from my cheeks to drip from my face.

"I can't," I whispered, knowing I was about to ruin everything. I couldn't get air into my lungs, and everything was happening too fast. Panic consumed my mind with images of him removing my head when he finished with me, replaying on repeat. "I can't breathe," I admitted.

Knox turned me away from the crowd, using our bound hands to force my eyes to meet his. He smiled sadly, noting the never-ending tears that flowed from my eyes. His lips lowered to press against mine even though coughing started behind us.

Drums started on the high cliffside, forcing our attention to where dark witches crowded the edge. Hissing sounded moments before magic slammed into the protective barrier. Large snake-like creatures exploded from their mouths, smashing against the barrier until they were nothing more than bloody pulps of scales. I stepped closer to Knox, watching as he smiled at me, his lips brushing against my forehead softly before he turned us back to where the crowd could see us.

"They cannot reach us, nor break the barrier, Aria," Knox said in a cocky tone, then nodded to the druid. "Continue."

"Under the king's law, and the law of the Nine Realms, I give you the High King and Queen of the Nine Realms. I present King Knox Karnavious and Aria Hecate Karnavious, his wife, and the first of her line to bind her power to a king of any realm."

Knox leaned forward, claiming my lips gently as the oily magic continued to attack the barrier. His forehead leaned against mine, allowing Brander to remove the ties from our hands. The moment they were gone, Knox lifted me and slammed his mouth against mine in a kiss that devastated my senses and took the air from my lungs as the crowd howled their approval.

Coughing sounded, and wine was placed before us. Brander snorted as Knox slowly ended the kiss, staring into my eyes as obsidian took precedence over the blue. I felt warmth from his beast and approval that the laws of the Nine Realms had bound us. Yet Ember didn't react or respond. She watched it all silently as if she didn't care one way or another that we were being bound as man and woman, but then she wasn't of a mind that the wedding mattered.

"Mine," Lennox growled huskily before Knox was back in control. He observed me, taking in my emotionless response to his words. He moved closer, inhaling my scent deeply before a frown played on his mouth, and the tic in his jaw pulsed.

I swallowed before pulling my hands from his, lowering onto the pillows seated before the crowd. Lore handed us a round wafer and asked if we'd defend the realms at the cost of our own lives and happiness. Knox repeated the words with Lore while I waited, searching his face as he spoke in their language. Knox whispered the words, and I dutifully echoed them in the witches' language before Brander gave us wine, speaking in the ancient language.

The assaults on the barrier intensified as the vows neared a conclusion. My lips moved with Brander's, saying everything perfectly until he asked if I willingly offered my power and magic to my husband, giving him the right to leave me barren of it in times of need.

"I do," I stated offhandedly as if it wasn't a big thing. Both men paused, slowly moving their eyes to mine with narrowed worry.

"All of your magic, Aria," Knox clarified, noting the smirk that lifted my lips.

"Only the magic that is mine to give, can I offer you, King Karnavious. I cannot give you what is not rightfully mine."

"Aria," he warned.

"The magic within me comes from the Nine Realms.

I cannot give that to you. It doesn't belong to me. I cannot house it because it is not within me. You may have all the other magic, but that part isn't from me, Knox. It is part of this world, and it is not mine to give you."

His eyes studied my face before he nodded to Brander, who handed us the wine. I slowly lifted the goblet, wincing at the bitterness of the wine before handing it back. Killian removed my tiara, placing a more feminine version of Knox's crown onto my head. Knox stood, holding his hand out to assist me to my feet as Brander stepped forward, addressing the crowd.

"I give you my brother and his bride. Help me in welcoming her to the family," Brander stated, clapping as he stared out over the assembly, all of which turned around, giving me their backs. Brander swallowed, looking to Knox, whose stare narrowed on the crowd, and then shook his head to Brander before looking at me, taking in my reaction.

"Light the largest bonfire, and prepare the ale," Knox stated, turning to gauge my reaction as his people snubbed me. "I wouldn't take it personally. You're a witch, and they loved their queen immensely before she was taken from them by your people."

"I don't blame them for hating me. If you'll excuse me, My *Love*, I have to go sacrifice a goat and drink its blood like the pagan queen I am."

"Aria?" Knox called to my back. I started away, pausing to turn toward him. "You may not partake in your ritual, tonight or any other night. You're no longer a witch. You're my wife and the High Queen of the Nine Realms. You no longer make sacrifices to your grandmother or any other pagan god or goddess," he warned softly as his men studied me.

I swallowed down the urge to argue, knowing the witches were excited over the sacrifice that would bless them for Beltane and the coming summer. I nodded, frowning as Knox held out his hand for mine. Silently, I slipped mine into his as he moved us through the crowd that was still quietly ignoring my existence. The dark witches faded into the shadows, knowing they couldn't break the blessing of the deity that protected us in his sacred circle.

Knox had said nothing about not being able to partake in witchcraft, nor did he understand it if he thought I could just stop. It was a huge part of who I was as a person, and second nature to use it, even if I didn't pull magic the way they did or use the blood that should have reinforced my power, strengthening me.

Chapter Thirty-Eight

Dinner was some kind of meat that had been baked beneath the ground for days. Knox had sent people ahead to prepare for the wedding, instructing them on meats and wine, among other things. The table was made from a large tree cut down and sanded into a smooth surface and spread farther than I could see. I'd spent an hour trying to figure out how they'd managed to get it into the camp without me noticing it all day.

"It's a white oak tree from Norvalla," Knox stated, piling more meat onto my plate. "I figured you would approve since you're aware of their meaning. When the first people roamed the lands, they would use the white oak tree to build their homes and furniture. It's rumored that they would make love to their wives on the tables they made, cherishing her upon the wood with their own wood." His lips twisted into a smirk. I downed more whiskey, forgoing the wine in front of me as I stared at him absently.

"Interesting," I stated, unamused.

I noted the witches were away from the others, dancing beneath the moon, covered in the blood of their sacrifice. Knox noticed the direction I looked, whispering to the guard at his side who moved off toward the witches.

"Eat. You'll need your energy for tonight," Knox grunted, uncaring that the soldiers were pushing the witches away from my view. I could see them enjoying the wedding that I couldn't even pretend to enjoy.

"Doubt it," I countered absently, watching Siobhan turning to frown in my direction. I shrugged at her questioning look as Knox watched.

"You are upset that you can't join them?" he mused, piling more food onto my plate.

"Ember says you're a good hunter. Stop trying to make me fat," I groaned, pushing the plate away.

"You have hardly eaten in three days, wife."

"Removing the heart from someone you trusted after finding out they're a treacherous swine has that effect on a girl's appetite, *husband*."

"Would you like to dance?"

Knox's men sat around us, following the exchange with worried looks as if they thought we'd throw down in the middle of our wedding reception. It was possible with how I currently felt, but I'd been raised better than to beat the shit out of someone at a wedding. Whispers from his people moved down the table about my inability to dance with the king. I rolled my eyes, turning to stare at Knox, deciding if I cared to prove them all wrong.

"Please," I shocked him by agreeing.

Knox pulled me out onto the stone altar reserved for us. My hand lifted to his, and his eyes narrowed, watching the people gather around us to watch.

"Are you sure you wish to do this?" Knox asked carefully.

"Why wouldn't I want to dance with my husband?" I asked, lifting a brow. "Unless, of course, you never learned how to dance?"

"Did you?"

I smirked, moving to the beat the moment the song began. Following Knox's lead, I easily matched his steps as he danced one of the older dances reserved for royalty. His hands brushed against mine, stepping back as I stepped forward and vice versa. Our bodies brushed against one another, here and there, as we moved to the heady notes of the flutes and pipes echoing through the valley. Knox smiled at the way I moved, sure-footed and fluid, with a gracefulness our teachers had beaten into us with their cane's if we missed a single step.

At the end of the first dance, Knox grabbed me and pulled me against him. He lifted my hand, preparing for an ancient dance of the first people. I leaned back, letting him take in the curve of my breasts as his breath fanned against my skin. I moved forward, and he lifted me, turning us around, then set me down. I took a step back, and we bowed to one another, rising to place our hands out in front of us, our palms touching as our fingers pointed to the sky. We took a step close, and I could feel Knox's breath on my neck as his fingers threaded through mine, pulling me closer still, never breaking eye contact. I allowed him to lift me, moving us around in a tight circle, and my body followed while driven by his lead. Once he completed the second circle, I cupped his cheek with my hand. Knox smiled, noting that my crown hadn't moved, secured with the flowers and pins as I'd been taught to do as a child. Knox slowly lowered my feet to the ground before grabbing my hands and raising them over my head as the crowd watched in silence. We moved gracefully, skillfully, in the ancient rite of those who had come before us.

His hand slid down my back, running over my shifting spine as I'd decided to dub it, creating a wealth of pleasure that rushed through me. Knox leaned down, brushing his lips against mine as he purred.

"You're just full of surprises, aren't you, Aria?"

"Yes, but then you don't really know anything about me, do you? You know I enjoy your cock, and I love my family. You know I love history and the written word. But other than that, you know nothing about the monster you married, King Karnavious," I whispered, clasping my teeth against his lip, smiling before pulling away. "If you'll excuse me, I am going to go get drunk without you. Enjoy your wedding and your guests, Knox."

I left him watching my back as I walked away from him, heading toward the dancing couples. Lore danced with several women at once, while Killian danced with one of the camp followers who couldn't dance to save her life. Greer stood beside the fire, laughing at someone who looked at him with doe eyes, gushing over the vampire as he dragged his finger down the male's chest in silent invitation. Brander, on the other hand, stared at Soraya, who was surrounded by men, her eyes narrowing on Brander even though other men were vying for her attention.

I moved deeper into the throngs of people, stepping over couples who were unabashedly having sex out in the open. My senses spiked, and I turned, finding Knox watching me over the top of one of the many bonfires. Sucking my lip between my teeth, I moved further away from him as he followed. Every time I stopped, he would, too, stalking me like I was something he wanted, and he was a predator, hunting me down.

Lore moved into my line of sight, thrusting his hips while women around him laughed. The women began removing their shirts, and my eyebrows hiked to my hairline. Caught between shock and interest, I laughed while Lore shed his tunic, exposing sinewy muscles with a torso peppered in scars and ink that moved over his skin. Walking away from Lore before he was fully naked, I paused, my gaze lingering on Knox over the bonfire as he stared at me with a smile that crinkled his eyes. He lifted his glass of whiskey, and I smirked, drinking from mine and moving away from the dancing altogether before I saw something I didn't need to see unfolding.

Knox followed me, causing butterflies to erupt within my belly. I'd look away, smiling and biting my lip to keep him from seeing my reaction to him, yet when I did, I would be drawn back to his hypnotic stare. Every time I looked across the gathering, Knox was there. Couples lounged about, groping or heavily petting their partner while I moved through the crowd. Turning, I looked at Knox, who was mirroring my movements from the other side of the fires that burned down the middle of the valley.

It was a game of cat and mouse, and I was pretty sure I was the mouse. I paused to step through the cleansing pool, bending over to rinse my feet, knowing he watched me. Standing, I found Knox in front of me, and my heart thundered in my chest.

Knox bent, grabbing my ankle, placing it back into the water as he washed my feet. Laughing at my response, he picked me up, splashing his own feet through the pool before stepping out of it, still holding me. He placed me on the ground, smiling as he bowed low at the waist, holding a hand out for me to place mine into his. He pulled me behind him, moving us toward the maypole. He stopped in front of a bed of coals, lifting me without warning, chuckling at my surprise as I wrapped my arms around his neck.

He didn't speak until he set me on my feet. He grabbed my cup, placing it aside with his own on a table, and turned to me. "Dance with me, wife." He grinned seductively, and I nodded.

Couples cheered Knox on, drunk from the wine they consumed as others observed curiously. In the middle of the dark field was a tall pole with a large flower-covered circle above it. Hanging from the pole were several dozen colorful ribbons.

Witches and warriors prepared to dance and weave in and out of one another's path, braiding the colorful ribbons to the pole. Knox released my hand, holding onto my fingers as I went to stand with the women and him with the men. The flutes and drums began, and we closed the distance between us. Knox extended his elbow, and I accepted it as we started to spin around to the beat, slipping apart to touch hands as we moved the red and white length of cloth in our hands. We parted to move through the people in the wide circle, our eyes never leaving the other.

When we reached one another again, I laughed as Knox wiggled his brows. We twirled through the ribbon and the other dancers as we swayed faster, and the crowd cheered when the music picked up. We moved toward the pole and bowed before we turned. The dancers began moving in the other direction together, and his other hand brushed against mine. We slid between people, crossing the braid as we danced, him moving to me, and me moving to him. Everything within me needed his touch.

The maypole dance was sacred. It signified fertility and was reserved for those who sought to become pregnant. We danced to bless Knox's land, yet my stomach clenched for more than that tonight. We stopped in front of one another, and Knox turned to look behind him as the music stopped, grasping my length of ribbon to his, representing one.

I stared where the silky fabric had tied to our hands while dancing and smiled as Knox slowly untied the knot. Dropping it, the crowd exploded with cheers, and Knox and I bowed to each other. Dark eyes lifted, holding mine, and he held out his hand before someone moved into his path, whispering something against his ear.

"Excuse me for a moment," Knox said as a warrior nodded toward him.

"As you wish," I muttered, uncertain what was happening. I lifted another cup of whiskey to my lips, staring at it before I groaned at lowering my guard to him.

Slipping back into the crowd, I moved through it. I hadn't made it more than a few feet from the maypole before Knox was back on the other side, silently stalking me with a roguish grin on his lips. We walked for a while; him watching me as we moved through the people celebrating, while I pretended not to notice him and failed horribly.

The man knew how to flirt, and he looked amazingly good tonight. I drifted through more people, sliding through them aimlessly, uncertain what to do with myself since no one here cared that it was my wedding night. I spun in a circle in a crowd of people celebrating, but I'd never felt more alone in my entire life. Standing on my tiptoes, I searched for someone I recognized and could engage in conversation.

Giving up my search, I started toward the bridal room again, only for Knox to step in front of me. I gasped and grabbed for my heart, staring at him through sad eyes. His hand slowly lifted, and fingers trailed down my cheek as he leaned forward, brushing his lips against my ear.

"You are so beautiful, Aria," he whispered huskily. "Tonight, you shine brighter than the stars could ever dream of burning. You are the most beautiful creature I have ever seen, or will ever see in my life, Queen Karnavious." Knox swallowed, leaning back as his eyes searched mine.

"Is this where I swoon at your feet, King Karnavious?" I whispered, watching his lips form a devastating smile.

"You're not the type of woman to swoon," he laughed, which was a carefree side of him that disarmed me. His eyes slid to the cabin, frowning before he smirked, holding out his hand. "Come. It's time for you to prepare to receive me before the moon sinks beneath the mountains, wife."

Siobhan and Soraya bowed to Knox, smiling as I moved toward them. Soft rose petals covered the ground in front of the small, stone cabin where I'd be spending the first night as Knox's wife. Nervousness rushed through me, causing my palms to sweat as I took one last glance back at Knox, who watched Siobhan and Soraya drag me into the bridal room with a wicked smile on his generous mouth. His eyes burned with a hunger he wasn't even trying to hide, which sent a storm of emotions coursing through me.

Chapter Thirty-Nine

Inside the cabin, I paused. Candles were lit in sconces on the walls, rose petals covered the floor and bed, and black roses from the Dark Mountains sat on the bedside table. I inhaled their heady scent greedily, turning as the women entered. Smirking, Siobhan, and Soraya prepared the room, pouring drinks as they watched me.

"Would you like us to remove your dress?" Siobhan asked.

"It is a custom," Soraya amended.

"Who's custom?" I asked, knowing Knox was listening outside the door where I'd left him.

"Theirs," Soraya stated, and I smiled.

"Leave it on." They smiled as they bowed, exiting the room silently.

Knox leaned against the door, grinning. He studied me as I walked to the black roses, plucking one from the vase to push against my nose. I closed my eyes, and a moan of pleasure escaped past my lips.

"I'm glad you like them." Knox went to the chest as I spun, following his movements, greedily inhaling the rose's fragrance.

He silently opened the chest before staring down at the picture of his family. Knox's eyes lifted to mine, and I swallowed past the unease I felt knowing where he gazed. I placed the rose back on the small stone stand beside the bed, exhaling slowly. I continued looking away from him, and my heart began thundering in my chest as if it would break free and fly away.

The sound of the chest lid closing forced my hand to move to the back of my neck. Brushing my fingers against the skin, I fought to calm the storm crashing through my insides. I could feel Knox watching me, fighting his emotions for the family he'd lost and the woman he just married. Like his people, he hated me and everything I was, other than the creature that lived within me.

My hands trembled, fighting the thickness swelling in my throat. Tears pricked my eyes as I considered what I'd just done. I'd married a monster that held more power than anyone else living within the Nine Realms. And I'd just signed my soul over to the devil himself, which hadn't been part of my plan.

Swallowing past the uneasiness tightening my chest with apprehension, I frowned, calculating how fucked up tonight was about to go with Knox behind me, watching me fight my internal idiocy by marrying him. I lowered my eyes to the rose, which lay crumpled on the stone bedside table from being touched. I had never felt more connected to anything in my life before.

"Aria?" Knox whispered against my ear, causing me to jump. His hands captured my shoulders, holding me in place as he chuckled huskily. "Come drink with me, wife."

I nodded, turning to find him stripped down to his slacks. My eyes met his, noting the heat burning within them. I walked to the table with Knox, avoiding eye contact. Slowly, I sat in the chair opposite of him, worrying my lip before I reached for the bowl in front of me, his eyes narrowing on it.

"That's the fertility water," he announced when my mouth reached the rim.

"Oh." I set it carefully back on the table, watching his lips curve into a smile.

"Are you're nervous?" Knox noted the way my hands fidgeted in front of me. I searched his eyes before turning away, staring at the candle that flickered across the room. "You promised to let your walls down tonight, Aria."

"And you promised me no ghosts." I placed my hands into my lap, meeting his stare. "You also showed me there's no honor among enemies. You got what you wanted, Knox. Here I am, at your mercy. Do with me what you will."

He snorted before sliding his eyes to the chest, tightening his mouth. His eyes lifted to the ceiling, and he slowly exhaled. He leaned forward abruptly, folding his hands in front of him on the table as he smiled.

"You are at my mercy, *wife*. I got exactly what I

wanted tonight. I got the prettiest little monster I have ever set eyes on as my bride. Did I use malicious means to get you? Yes, and I am not sorry for doing it. Dimitri was a snake in your nest, and he'd have turned on you the first opportunity he got. I needed eyes on your sisters because I couldn't take mine off of you. I get that you're angry. I understand you more than you think I do. I know you, woman."

"You don't know anything about me." I glared at him, lifting the glass before me, inhaling the delicious scent of the whiskey.

"Nothing?" he laughed huskily, a wicked smile curling his lips.

"You know what I allow you to, Knox."

He sat back in his chair, running his thumb over his bottom lip. Leaning forward once more, he tapped the table with his knuckles. "You chew that bottom lip when you're nervous and when your mind is working on a problem you need to solve. You've been hurt too many times by people who were supposed to protect you and love you, so you built walls around yourself because you don't want anyone to get too close to you. You don't even allow your own family to know who you are because you're terrified of the creature within you. You cry when something is beautiful because you're unable to hide your most basic responses. You cry every time I am within you and make you come. You can't hide your emotions because you feel everything so deeply that it hurts. You hold everyone at arm's length because letting them get too close will make you vulnerable."

I chewed my lip, causing him to smile. Knox tilted his head as my mouth opened to speak, but he held up his finger.

"You're selfless to a fault. You'd end your own life if you thought it would save another, and that terrifies me. You married me because I merely threatened your bloodline. If someone else had gotten to them first and made you an offer for their life, you wouldn't have thought twice about doing whatever they'd asked of you. They'd have demanded your life for theirs, and you would have paid that price. I took that choice away from you today when I gave you my name. It may not protect you from being hurt or abused, but no one alive will ever sexually assault you, rape you, or murder you because of my name. I didn't have to marry you. I wanted to because you're right; you've been through hell since entering this world. You're this beautiful, innocent creature who the world would see ruined. I am no better because I want to destroy you. I don't want to hurt you or abuse you, Aria. I want to destroy you in the worst way that ends with you screaming my name and crying those pretty tears you shed while coming undone around me."

I opened my mouth, but he held up his hand again, smirking as I closed it once more. "I know you better than you think I do."

"So maybe you know more than a little bit," I whispered thickly, lifting my drink as he shook his head. "No?"

"I'm not finished, wife."

"I know you hate the sickly sweet bitterness of wine and prefer whiskey. I know you hate me, but more than that, you hate that you can't hate me because there's something between us that is fucking terrifyingly beautiful that neither of us knows how to accept. I know you think if we allow it to happen, everything will change, but nothing will. And it won't matter how much we wish it to be otherwise. You fear letting down your walls because you're the type of woman who will climb them to fix something so fucking broken that it isn't worth fixing. You could spend lifetimes trying to put me back together only to find out that you can't, but you wouldn't admit defeat no matter how hopeless it seemed. I know wanting me is dangerous, but it doesn't change that you do. Accepting that you want me will change everything you've been planning, and if you accept that, everything will have been for nothing.

"I know that this thing between us, whatever it is, frightens you because it's visceral, and it digs deep, twisting everything in which you're fighting. I know I want you, and you want me. I know that right here, right now, what we do won't change anything. In the morning, we will still be enemies. Enemies who are both fighting on the same fucking side but standing opposite of one another. That alone makes you push me away because that is a betrayal that cuts deeper than you know how to handle. Being married to you wasn't something I needed for this war, making me the biggest asshole in existence. I may not love you, Aria Karnavious, but I care enough to put my name on more than just your soul."

I stared at him, knowing half of what he'd said had been about him more than me. He'd admitted things that we both felt, using me as the scapegoat to get them out without realizing they were about him. He'd said I was the type of girl to climb walls, but that wasn't true. I was more like a wrecking ball trying to bring the walls down, which was why we were going at each other so hard. Knox had centuries of mortar up on those walls, and it wasn't something you could just chip away. He built an entire rebellion to go against the witches. Hell, he'd been planning this war for five hundred years. I was challenging him. The fact that he wanted me, coupled with his need to keep me, was hurting him, but that wasn't my fault, and that pissed him off the most.

"I am terrified right now," I admitted sheepishly. Knox stood, narrowing his eyes on my shaking hands, moving to place his own on the table. He thought his words had scared me, but that hadn't scared me at all.

"Because of what I just said?" He cocked his head to the side as if I'd caught him off guard with my words.

"No," I whispered, placing my hands on the table, exhaling. "I'm terrified that you'll find me changed once you enter me," I murmured, fighting the pricking tears in my eyes. "I...we...you and I, we've not had sex since I was taken to the Kingdom of Unwanted Beasts."

Knox exhaled slowly, staring before he moved to crouch in front of me. His hands turned me, and he peered into my eyes. "You don't remember everything that happened to you, do you?"

"No," I swallowed thickly, forcing my eyes anywhere but on him.

"I can assure you that no man or beast raped you. I'd have scented it on you, and I have only ever scented my arousal within you. My beast would know as well, and he has not taken control to mark you, nor gone after another male for placing his scent onto you, and I assure you, he would."

Knox lifted his hands, capturing mine to stop the fidgeting. Exhaling, he lowered his head to hide the anger flashing in his eyes. I shook my head, searching for something to say.

"I should have said I was damaged before you wed me, right?"

He snorted, lifting his eyes to mine. Knox pulled me to my feet and brushed his mouth against my shoulder. His hands still held mine as he brought them up, kissing my knuckles, as tears slid free from the precarious hold I'd held on them.

"You're not damaged, Aria. You were abused and terrorized by monsters. You got back up, and that's the only thing that matters to me. You are stronger than you were, and you didn't let it change who you are inside—here." His finger touched my heart, and he smiled tightly. "They didn't win; you did. You refused to allow them any power over you, and you're not going to give it to them tonight. Not on your wedding night. You only get one, and I intend to make damn sure you enjoy it as much as me." I nodded and smiled tightly. "Your walls are down, wife."

"So they are," I whispered. Knox smiled, pushing my hair away from my face, and I held his eyes without allowing my walls to rise again.

He reached up, removing my crown, setting it on the table next to his. Lifting his hand, he captured my face as he tilted my chin, claiming my lips in a soft kiss before pulling back. Knox moved around me, pushing the wispy strands of hair away from my neck as he kissed my shoulder, undoing the clasp at the back of my neck.

"You're a beautiful bride. You're more than I deserve," he whispered.

The dress slid down my body, and his fingertips trailed over my shoulders and down my arms slowly. Knox's touch sent a shiver racing down my spine as heat pooled in my belly. He turned me around, smirking as he caught the worry dancing in my eyes.

"Can I wash you, Aria? Can I wash away their touch, replace it with mine, and show you how fucking much I want you?"

"You're seducing me. Aren't you?" I asked, noting his eyes sparkled with dark desire, realizing he was showing me up again.

His mouth curved into a sexy grin as he leaned over, whispering against my ear. "Is it working? I think it is." Knox kissed the skin behind my ear, sending a shiver of anticipation rushing through me. "I can smell your body preparing for me. Your spine is arching, getting ready for me to take you hard and fast." His fingers leisurely danced down my spine, grabbing my ass hard, forcing a moan from my parted lips. "Your pupils are fully dilated, and right now, your stomach is tightening with the need for me to spread your legs and fill you full of me. Do you want that, Aria? I want that so fucking bad right now."

"Brander seriously needs to up his game if you're his competition."

Teeth scraped my shoulder, nipping it in silent warning while his fingers drew a bulls-eye on my stomach. At least, that's what I assumed he was drawing on my skin. Knox turned me again, gliding his fingers through my hair as he bared my throat, dragging his heated breath over my racing pulse. His other hand slid between my thighs, pushing against the lace panties I still wore, creating friction.

"I'm going to need your decision. I'm barely able to contain my need to bend you over, part your thighs, and enter you violently, woman. I have reached the end of my ability to wait for the pleasure your body gives me. I really need you to tell me, yes, right now."

"Yes," I swallowed, holding his stare. "I want you, Knox. Unless you intend to edge me again, in which case, you're going to wake up in the middle of the night mounted and ridden by a wild beast who has reached her limit and ability to say no. So yes, I want you right here, right now."

Knox smiled, leaning over to brush his lips against mine, walking me backward, and lifting me onto the table. His eyes lowered to my naked breasts, raising his hands to squeeze them. Assaulted by the sensation, I opened my mouth just as a loud rattle escaped my lips.

"You are the sexiest fucking thing when you make those noises, Aria. Spread your legs, lift your feet onto the table, and hold on. When I am finished washing you, you'll end up on that bed, screaming my name until you're so hoarse that you can't scream anymore."

Chapter Forty

My skin heated under Knox's slow, relaxed perusal of my body. He didn't use a cloth to wash me. Instead, he dipped his fingertips into the water before running them over my shoulders. Once he'd cleaned the skin, his lips followed the trail his fingers had taken. It was frustratingly slow and erotic, and I needed him to move faster. His eyes sparkled with laughter, alerting me he was highly aware of what I needed from him.

Knox lowered his body, forcing me to brace my hands on his broad shoulders. I moaned loudly when he slid his fingers through my apex, tightening with need as he smiled wolfishly. He lifted my ass, stripping me of my panties in a swift, skillful move. He was driving me to the brink of madness, edging me further over the cliff where he'd left me. His lips brushed against the inside of my thighs, forcing me to whimper. My head rolled back, and sweat beaded against the back of my neck.

Every moan created a soft breeze within the cabin

as if a spell was at work, yet if it was, I couldn't feel it or sense one.

"Eyes on me, woman," Knox growled, forcing my attention back to where his heated breath fanned against my sex. "You're dripping wet for me, aren't you?"

"Yes." My voice was laced with desire and lust that made my tongue heavy.

"You need to be fucked hard or soft?"

"Both," I admitted, and he leaned closer, his fingers dipping into the bowl of morning dew, spelled by the witches to make fertility water for Beltane.

Knox brought his fingers to his mouth, dripping the liquid onto his tongue, and then pushed it against my core. I cried out, purring violently. It was a raw, undiluted pleasure he gave me, and my body shuddered as he smiled against my sex. His tongue slid through my arousal, and he watched me tremble against the need rushing through me like a drug in my veins.

He did it several more times, licking his fingers dipped in the morning dew, then pushing them inside my body. His tongue lapped hungrily against my opening until I was whispering his name. I tugged my fingers through his hair, forcing him to stand so I could claim his mouth in a hungry kiss.

Knox rattled his approval, lifting me from the table, his hands cradling my rear, squeezing while holding me against him. He took control of the kiss, dominating it before placing me onto the bed, never breaking the connection. He spread my legs, growling as he leaned back, sliding his starving gaze over my nakedness with a look of sheer ownership.

The heat in Knox's gaze threatened to leave me in nothing more than ashes. I purred huskily, uncertain if I had controlled the noise or if Ember had. Either way, Knox echoed it, and my body flooded with arousal, causing his nostrils to flare.

"Scoot your sexy little ass up on the bed, Aria. Place your hands above your head and don't move them. Do you understand me?" he asked firmly, watching as I nodded. Knox smirked, pushing his hand against my core as two fingers entered me fast and hard.

My body jerked, a cry escaping past my lips. Knox stretched me, forcing me to the edge once more before he withdrew them, slapping my core wickedly.

"I understand," I hissed through curving lips, running my hands down my body. Knox's smoldering gaze followed them to my breasts, unable to look away at the simple motion.

"Good girl, now do what the fuck you were told to do, wife. When I ask you a question, you use your words, even if they come out as a moan. Disobey, and I'll edge you so fucking hard that you can't think straight."

"Maybe I enjoy you torturing me, Knox," I chuckled, and his lips twisted into a sinful smile.

I sat up slowly, making a show of it, rolling over so Knox could see how wet I was as I crawled up the bed. Hearing his teeth grinding together with his need to give me what we both wanted, made me grow bolder. At the top of the bed, I spread my legs further apart, allowing him to see the arousal that Ember had added to my core. A deep growl escaped him, and I yelped as he yanked my legs back and flipped my body over, suddenly there, naked between them.

Knox leaned over my body, staring down at me, before capturing my hands with one of his. He placed his other hand against my mouth and pushed into my body hard. I trembled against the pain and delicious sensations his invasion created. My core clamped down hungrily, ignoring the burning ache from his abrupt entrance into my body. Knox lowered his mouth, kissing his hand against my lips, stilling the scream that would have alerted the men outside.

Knox slowly rocked his hips, staring into my eyes as the orgasm ripped to the forefront of my body. My eyes widened, and he continued to watch as my body started to unravel. It wasn't just a storm building within me. It was the chaos he'd created that was about to be unleashed in the form of pleasure. The more Knox moved, the more it built within me. I started trembling, moaning against his hand before everything within me went crazy. He thrust harder, pushing against the place in my core where he'd written his name, and then it hit me with the force of a hurricane, pounding the shores. It felt as if several natural disasters were all hitting me at once.

The candles flickered as the cabin began trembling. Or maybe that was me. My body pulsed with arousal, pain, and pleasure that ripped me apart violently. Knox slowed his thrusting hips, rocking them in sync with my need as white-hot pleasure tightened my core. He released my hands, lifting my ass to allow himself deeper access to my body. Lights exploded around me, and petals floated in the air from the bed.

Tears slipped from my eyes as the beauty of the pleasure continued to rock through me. Knox smiled, leaning his forehead against mine before he claimed my lips softly, quieting the screams that escaped me unabashedly.

The orgasm was violent and beautiful. It was never-ending, and I knew Knox held me locked in it with every move of his hips, forcing me back over the cliff as I struggled to get over the edge.

He gave no mercy, driving my body at a slow pace that held me prisoner. I realized I was purring loudly. It wasn't a normal purr, either. It was what had shaken the cabin, mixed with the sounds escaping him. Knox lifted his hand, covering my mouth again as he slammed into my body hard, smiling as the orgasm slowly began to abate. His hand left my mouth, capturing my mine with his, holding them above my head. He kissed my throat, scraping his teeth over the soft flesh while slowly moving within me. Knox leaned back, staring at where we were joined while still holding my hands above my head, looming over me.

"Damn, woman! You're fucking perfect. You fuck me like you were built to be mine," he murmured, leaning down to press his forehead against mine.

"Knox, harder," I whispered huskily. I needed him to hurry. The urgency driving me was unraveling. I was fighting against the need to throw him down and take his scent by force.

"Oh, this isn't ending that fast. You teased me and slept beside me naked for months. I intend to savior you all fucking night long."

Knox rolled us, and I stared down at him, lifting my hips to push them against him. I leaned my head over, brushing my lips against his abs. My tongue traveled over muscles that tensed with every rock of my hips while my body clenched against his hungrily. He caressed my naked breasts, and I whimpered the moment his thumbs brushed over my nipples.

Intensity burned in Knox's eyes while he watched me slowly riding his cock. My body moved faster until I dropped my head back, whispering his name repeatedly as I came undone on his thickness. Rolling my head, I smiled down before leaning over to capture his lips. His hands guided my hips, slowly moving me against him until I was trembling with the orgasm that rushed through me without warning. He picked me up, slamming my body down repeatedly, fucking me with the strength he held to control our pleasure, even though I was the one on top.

Rolling us over, Knox slid his teeth across my nipple, pressing his hand against my throat. It wasn't hard or painful, but he watched me react to it as I moaned. He rose above me, pressing one hand against my mouth while the other tightened against my throat. My eyes held his, watching the wicked smile that curled the corners of his lips.

Knox let loose of whatever control he'd held, pounding against my core, and I held my breath while smothering my screams. Light burst behind my eyes, exploding as orgasms rocked through me. Releasing my throat, he pressed his mouth against the hand, holding my screams in as I moaned. I lifted my legs around his waist to take him deeper, needing him deeper than he had already gone. He released my mouth and tipped my ass up, using my body to lift my legs higher until my knees were against my shoulders, thrusting deeper inside me until I felt him pushing against my womb.

"You're so fucking gorgeous," he growled. "Your body is so greedy. You're tightening for me to empty into you, aren't you? You want that, don't you? You need my scent deep against that greedy womb. Tell me you're mine, Aria. Tell me, or you won't get what you want from me."

I lifted my hands, curling them around his cheeks as I brought his mouth to mine. "I'm yours. I am all yours. Mark me, Knox. I need you. I need you so badly right now."

"Good girl," he growled, picking me up until I was sitting up against his chest. The position forced me to take him deeper, and I exploded around him, holding onto his shoulders as my mouth brushed against it.

Knox reached for my hair, pulling my mouth away to crush against his. He kissed me like a starving man, and I was the air he needed. He didn't fuck me hard. It was slow and sensual. His mouth, on the other hand, was ravenous and brutal as he claimed me. His arms cradled me like I was something precious, instead of his enemy.

"Knox," I whispered, and he slammed me down, coming hard as he rattled loudly. Purring escaped my lungs before I could stop it, and everything within me unraveled while I held onto him, knowing he wasn't finished yet. "I'm yours."

"You're damn fucking right you are, Little Monster." Knox laid me down, peering into my eyes as he moved feverishly. He destroyed me with every thrust as he watched me become nothing more than ruins.

My entire body purred loudly for him to continue. My core clenched wantonly, needing all he could give me. My lungs vibrated with the loud purr that filled the space between us. His own added to it as a fire burned in the ocean waves of his gaze. I pushed against him, rocking my body with a violent need that ripped through me. I rattled, and Knox smirked as I opened my mouth, continuing to rattle until he joined me. Sliding his mouth over my shoulder, he sank his teeth into my flesh. I screamed in shock as pleasure turned violent, and his teeth sank deeper into my shoulder. It wasn't like the other marks. This one went further into my skin until teeth marked bones, and then a powerful orgasm followed it. I mewled, whimpered as he held me there, submissive to his dominance as his beast added his mark to my soul.

Knox didn't stop biting my shoulder. He continued until all I could do was lay there as he licked and bit me repeatedly. When everything threatened to turn violent again, he turned me over, spreading my legs and sinking his teeth into the other shoulder while taking me from behind. My ass moved, meeting every thrust, even as I lay there with my head turned, baring my throat to him.

It wasn't until his mouth brushed against my throat that Knox paused, and his lips stalled. He returned his mouth to my shoulder, kissing it where the flesh had already healed from him, tending it gently. He sank his teeth into it again, purring loudly until I answered it, feeling his mouth curve into a smile at the sound.

"You're dangerous, Aria," Knox whispered against my shoulder, tensing behind me as he sent hot spurts of his need into my body. "So fucking dangerous," he groaned, pulling my body against his before he curled me into his arms.

"And why is that?" I asked softly.

Knox didn't reply. Instead, he purred softly, holding me like I mattered. As if he'd forgotten the past and his mission to destroy everyone I loved. It was a glance into what could be if we stopped fighting each other. I wouldn't, though, not until I made him see that not all witches were bad.

Knox had witches here that he trusted enough to place magical tattoos onto his flesh, so why not others? I just had to reach him and make him see the error of his ways. I wasn't the dangerous one here; he was because tonight he'd shown me what it meant to be his, and I craved it even knowing it wouldn't ever work out. Not as I wanted it to, anyway.

At the end of the day, we were enemies, and Knox wouldn't ever let his ghosts find peace to give whatever was happening between us a real chance.

Chapter Forty-One

For days we remained inside the cabin, never leaving other than to bathe or eat. It was as if the world outside no longer existed and only our need for one another mattered. On the fifth day, Knox woke me by entering me before my eyes had even fully opened. He went hard and fast until I was helpless other than to hang on to him, wrapping my legs around him while he took us both to the edge, sending us over it together.

When I woke again, it was to Knox grinning, pushing my hair away from my face. His smile was disarming and left me without shields to protect myself. His soft caresses and gentle kisses kept my walls down.

"You're smiling, husband. I'm not sure if I should be afraid or if I should ride you to keep it there," I whispered huskily, watching his eyes crinkling in the corners as heat ignited within them.

"I think I am going to order our camp to remain here

for a few more days. I've decided I don't want to leave this bed anytime soon, woman."

"Promise?" I leaned over to kiss his mouth, listening to the purring that exploded from him with my touch.

Knox cupped my cheek, slowly rolling me onto my back. Settling between my thighs, he pushed into me gradually as he made love to me. Knox didn't break the kiss, nor did I care if air reached my lungs. He was a drug within my system that ravaged me, destroying healthy cells and replacing them with the addiction. He placed his hands on either side of my head, pushing up from the bed to peer down at me, watching as I fell apart around him.

"You burn so fucking hot for me, Aria Karnavious," he growled, slowing his pace to let his stare slide down my body.

His head lowered to my shoulder, kissing the scar he'd left there. Lifting my legs, he pushed them against my shoulders, thrusting harder and deeper until I was mewling from the orgasm he sent pulsing through me. His dark, husky laughter filled the cabin as our combined scents became smothering. I moved my hands to his hips, lifting my head to place kisses against his heart, and he tensed, gritting his teeth loudly before a moan slipped from his lips.

"I think the sound you make when I am fucking you is my favorite song," he whispered, dropping beside me, gathering me closer, and running his fingers through the valley of my breasts. A knock sounded at the door, causing him to turn and look in that direction. "I want to play it on repeat, woman."

Knox reached for the sheet, sliding it over my body before he exited the bed. He pulled on his discarded sweatpants and answered the door. Killian entered, pausing as he inhaled and turned to give me a look of unease.

"You mind telling me what the fuck you think you're doing in here?" Knox asked, his voice hoarse and strange. His rattle sounded loud, and mine echoed it, causing Killian to step back and divert his eyes from where I sat, pulling the sheet around me tightly.

"There was an attack on a village inside Norvalla," Killian stated, his eyes sliding toward me with a dark look within them.

"Eyes on me, asshole," Knox warned, his tone deadly even though it held command. "Which village, and how badly were they attacked?"

"Kalamet and unknown for right now," Killian admitted. "The rider we sent there this morning to alert them of our arrival is unable to speak. He isn't right in the head anymore, if you know what I mean. We think he was captured and spelled. Siobhan is trying to get more out of him, but it took her most of the morning just to learn Kalamet had been attacked, past whatever magic is holding his tongue silent."

"Kalamet is a stronghold, one of our most fortified ones on the border. Lord Kenly and his wife have held it for over a thousand years without falling to the witches. It has to be a mistake," Knox growled, moving to his chest. "Give the order for camp to be moved. We'll stop in Kalamet before entering the passes, see what happened, and decide if we can help them before moving on. They didn't fall. They couldn't have because I'd have felt it if they had," Knox muttered, sliding his eyes to where I sat on the bed.

"You were preoccupied, Knox. You wouldn't have felt anything past the woman riding you endlessly. From the sounds of things inside this room, it's all you've done for almost an entire week," Killian announced, ignoring the blush that spread over my cheeks.

"So, I was. Have camp ready to move. We'll be out shortly," Knox replied, waiting until Killian nodded and left the room before he sat in a chair, studying me silently. "Come here, woman," he ordered, watching as I left the bed to move toward him.

His gaze slid over my body when the sheet dropped. His hands reached out, pulling me closer before he kissed my belly. Knox pulled me onto his lap, forcing me to straddle him. His mouth kissed the mark he'd left, somehow managing to leave minimal scarring even though he'd bitten me until I'd come undone so many times I'd lost count. He enjoyed that my body found pleasure in his bite and that I climaxed from it alone.

My nose nuzzled his cheek as he lifted me. Chuckling darkly, he set me on my feet and slowly moved me to the table. Turning me to face it, Knox captured my hands, placing them flat against the table before sliding my legs apart with his feet. He held my hands as he pushed into my body, laughing as I moaned loudly, lowering my head to the table as he rocked against me.

"You're so fucking distracting, aren't you?" he asked, bringing my hands back against my spine. "Here I am, unable to stay out of you while places in my kingdom are being attacked," he growled, sliding his hand up my spine to curl his fingers through my hair.

He turned my head, slamming into my body punishingly hard, driving me toward the edge as he pounded into my core, which clasped hungrily against him. "You're the perfect distraction, aren't you, Aria?"

"Knox," I whispered, uncertain if he was pissed or turned on.

"Shut up," he snapped, forcing my head down against the table as he ravaged my core mercilessly.

The table hit my hips, causing me to cry out as pain rocked through me. He fucked me until the orgasm ripped me apart. Knox yanked me back against his mouth, and he bit down through my shoulder. His bite caused the orgasm to keep growing until I could not stand as he continued fucking me. My body clenched his, tightening around him as he growled. Lifting my legs onto the table, Knox spread me further apart, forcing my apex lower. He held me where he needed me, sending pain and pleasure rocking through me.

"Knox," I whispered through the chattering of my teeth. He sent me rushing into the clouds, forcing orgasm after orgasm to crash through me. All I could do was take what he gave me. It wasn't anything like he'd done for the last few days. It was cold, emotionless sex.

I felt him tense behind me, emptying his need into my body, filling me as he withdrew from me. Knox's hand lowered to my core, rubbing his fingers against it to cover my sex with our combined arousal. He moved away from the table, silently standing in front of the chest, which he opened, even though I could still feel his heated stare on my sore flesh.

"Cover yourself, witch."

And there it was.

The slap I'd known was coming.

The distance he craved to remind himself of who he was and what I was. I didn't move because my legs wouldn't hold me, and I knew it. My shoulder ached, alerting me to the fact he hadn't healed it as he'd done since we'd entered this room on our wedding night. My mouth moved toward it, slowly placing my saliva onto the damaged flesh I could reach. I slid from the table, holding myself up, uncaring that he watched.

I grabbed the sheet from the bed, wrapping it around my body before burying my face in the pillows to hide my angry tears. Knox's deep exhale sounded, and I ignored it and him. I hadn't been stupid enough to assume our facade of happiness would last past the sated lust we'd shared. I hadn't imagined that giving him a piece of my unguarded soul would end well for either of us. After all, he was the High King of Bipolar, and his kingdom was filled with miniature versions of him, pretending to like me to help him reach his goal.

Knox ripped the sheet from the bed, capturing me and spreading me out as he stared down into my angry glare. He studied my face, and a dark look filled his eyes.

"Don't pretend you didn't like what we just did, woman."

His head lowered, kissing the wounds on my shoulder, then his tongue jutted out, sealing the injury. Knox turned toward my throat, kissing the jackhammering pulse softly. Inhaling my scent, he furrowed his brow before lifting and searching my face.

"If you or your family had anything to do with Lord

and Lady Kenly being harmed, I'll…"

"I know. You'll take my head and place it on your nightstand, where you can stroke it every night to remind yourself how badass you are. I've heard it all before, Knox."

"I'll do much worse than that, I'm afraid, Aria. I'll chain you to my wall and fuck you every morning and every night. Before I go to war against your people, I'll make sure your pussy drips my come the entire time I am gone. I will never let you escape me, and you'll know what a prisoner of war feels like, viscerally." His fingers slid down my stomach, slowly pausing at my womb.

"You didn't give me your womb, which means you either can't, or you chose not to do so. Are you in heat, or aren't you? Because I'm starting to believe you're not, judging by how you ignored it for so long. Your scent is too perfect. You are too perfect, Little Monster. Everything about you screams to me. I should have known you were too good to be true when you rattled and purred for me. Who made you for me? Did Hecate finally figure out a way to reach me, creating the perfect combination to lure me into her trap? Your pussy is the perfect trap because I can't seem to ignore it no matter how hard I try."

"Fuck you, Knox," I murmured, not moving as he watched me through narrow slits. His fingers pinched and twisted my nipple until I gasped and cried out, arching into his touch, even though I hated him at this moment.

Knox dipped his head, claiming the other nipple with his teeth, and I cried out again. He chuckled darkly, as pain flittered through me, knowing his teeth had just punctured the skin. Blood trailed down the globe of my breast as he laughed, flicking it with his tongue to seal the wound before he chased the blood. He pushed my thighs apart, and I lifted to move away, only for him to grab my arms, slamming them down above my head with one of his large hands.

"I'm not finished with you, wife." Knox's eyes searched my face before he released my arms and pulled me up against him. His hand moved to my throat, holding me against his lips. "Kiss me and fucking mean it." Knox released me, watching as I slowly sat up higher.

I leaned forward, placing my hands around his neck while he laid on his back, staring up at me. My lips brushed his, putting my anger and need into the kiss as he rattled, appeased with the intensity in which I kissed him. He lifted my body, holding himself against my entrance, but he didn't force it, nor did he enter me.

Instead, Knox rubbed against my opening, already hard for more. He was insatiable, with a never-ending hunger. I forced my body down his rigid lengths, crying out as I touched the base and slowly rocked against him. Leaning over, I lifted and lowered my need against his.

He moaned, unable to deny the pace my body took, slowly and sensually unraveling his desire for release. His hands moved to my hips, settling on them as he lifted his head, staring at where we connected. Knox's ocean-colored eyes locked with mine. I lifted, showing him how much he stretched me, his hooded stare lowered again to our connected bodies. I gradually worked him past his breaking point, crying out as he grew larger within me.

"You like that? You like watching your cock stretching my body?" I leaned back, lifting my legs to take him deeper while rolling my hips. He growled, his low soothing rattle filling the room we'd been in for days, making love. "Do I make you come harder than anyone else?" I questioned, slowly moving while his smoldering stare watched my core, greedily tightening around his girth while I rode him.

"You know you do, woman."

"You like fucking me?" I questioned, leaning closer while tightening around him until he gasped. "I'm going to come for you, Knox," I purred, shuddering around his length that created a burning ache within me. My eyes held his as I came apart around him, whimpering while he filled me, tensing as he thrust harder into my core. His fingers bit angrily into my hips, slamming me home on his erection until he groaned, coming apart with me.

"Good girl, Aria. Tonight, you'll take me in my other form if you are responsible for this attack. If you're smart, you'll let your monster out to play with mine. I don't think you are even close to being ready to handle his cock, but I guess we'll figure that out later, won't we?"

"Knox," I whispered, leaning over to brush my lips against his before turning his head to where his family watched us fucking. "Your perfect fucking wife just watched me riding your cock until you emptied your need deep inside of me. Do you think she enjoyed the show? Or do you think she thought about her heartless widower, fucking the same bloodline who murdered her? I'm thinking it's the latter, and she's turning over in her grave knowing my pussy got you off harder than she ever could. And you *do* come so hard in my pussy, don't you?" I sat up, smiling coldly while rocking my hips, glaring at him. I left the bed, grabbing the sheet to cover my body as Knox moved to the chest, slamming it shut. It splintered, and my eyes widened as his lethal gaze slid from the broken chest to me.

My breathing grew labored as his deadly expression turned my blood to ice. I didn't back down as he stalked forward, curling his fingers through my hair before yanking my head back painfully.

"I almost hope your monster fails to show up tonight so I can watch you screaming when Lennox stretches you apart to get to what you've denied him. I tried to do this the easy way, to seduce you into letting me in so that he was sated. You're just too stubborn to allow me to help you. Your sex clenches to mate. Mine expands to ensure nothing escapes when he releases." Knox swept the hair away from my face with this hand, and I shivered from the picture he painted.

"I've fucked your monster. It's time you fucked mine, wouldn't you agree? Do you think I'm fucking feral and carnal in bed? I have nothing on him. Lennox makes me look weak, and gods damn does he want to play with you, Aria. Maybe after you've been fucked by my beast, you'll finally keep my wife and son out of your poisonous mouth. Are you excited or terrified? I can't tell because you're dripping wet from being fucked. Your body is trembling, and your pupils are damn near blown. I can smell sweat beading on your neck and hear your heart thundering against your ribcage. But those perky nipples aren't erect for me to kiss, suck or bite, and when you're aroused, they get fucking rock hard for me. Are you ready to rattle, sweet girl? Because you're about to be whether you want it or not! I'm done protecting you from Lennox. I'm done trying to keep him caged to protect your tender body from the brutality he craves to unleash on it," Knox laughed huskily, moving to the door to open it.

"Brander, bring my bride a dress to befit her new station." Knox left the cabin, nodding for the guards to secure his armor as he followed them out, leaving me alone in the room filled with our scent that had turned ugly.

I didn't move, not even when Brander finally entered the cabin as Knox barged in, fully dressed for war in his armor. Brander walked toward me, staring, and I finally stepped back, grabbing the sheet to cover my body.

"Are you okay?" Brander asked, tossing a wool dress onto the bed.

"She's fine, brother," Knox snapped.

"Aria?"

"I'm fine. You don't have to pretend to like me anymore. You all got what you wanted. Knox has a straight line to the throne and me as his bitch. Get out!" I yell. Everything slammed into me at once as my body trembled violently from the adrenaline wearing off. "Get out!"

Brander turned, leaving the room and closing the door behind him. I dressed, uncaring that the wool itched and burned against my skin. Knox stared at the gray, coarse, wool dress Brander gave me. I ran my fingers through my hair, turning away from Knox as tears streaked down my face.

I wasn't given anything else to wear as the soldiers came in to grab the items inside the cabin. Silently, I waited for Knox's command on where to go and what to do. I felt the eyes of his men outside the door as they took in what was happening. My skin itched with the wool, forcing me to scratch where the arms chaffed.

"Come, witch," Knox snapped, and I followed him out of the cabin. We moved through the line of people that turned and snickered, laughing as I passed them. "Enough," he growled, causing them to stop, but the looks they gave me said more than their laughter ever could.

Knox stopped in front of his horse, hefting me up without giving me time to prepare. I lowered my hands, lifting my sore core off the hard saddle. Men cheered, and my eyes closed, shutting out the world as they praised their king's virility at creating the soreness between my legs. Knox mounted behind me, pushing my body down as he yanked me back against his chest.

We rode out of the valley in silence, my eyes sliding to the proud statue of Bel, who watched us leave his Beltane Circle behind. Knox's fingers brushed over my belly, and I did my best to ignore him. He was aware of the discomfort wool caused, or he wouldn't have asked Brander to secure it for me to wear. Maybe I deserved it for taking a low blow at his family, but he'd turned something beautiful into something cheap. He assumed I was nothing more than a tool Hecate had created to wield against him. The man was so wounded that he grasped at anything or any reason to turn against me.

"Do try to stop your body from making that scent, or I'll turn you around and bury myself into it again. You'd probably enjoy being taken on a horse, wouldn't you? I could turn you toward me, wrap those delicious thighs around my waist and fuck you all the way to Norvalla, and you'd let me, wouldn't you?"

"No," I replied icily.

"No? I think you need to be reminded of what being Queen means, wife," Knox laughed against my throat.

"I'm not a queen. I'm merely a puppet for you to pull my strings. You can use me as you did this morning as a whore, hurting me because you felt something with me. You can abuse me and strike me down because you allowed your walls to drop ever so slightly, but you won't ever touch me, Knox. You will never touch me deeper than I allow." I whispered, knowing they all strained to hear the barely audible words. "You will never touch my soul, and your beast will never get my womb unless I permit it to happen. The only way Lennox will ever get my womb is if he rips it out of me and fucks it without my help. I am not your Queen, and you are not my King. You're nothing to me, as I am to you. Do you know what the scariest creature in the world is, King Karnavious?"

"No, what is it, *wife*?"

"A woman who has nothing left to lose and chooses to build chaos since she is left in only ruins."

Chapter Forty-Two

We approached a settlement, stopping on a rise that overlooked the sprawling stronghold surrounded by a winding village. It was bathed in dark shadows, but the scent of freshly spilled blood wafted on the soothing breeze. Torches burned through the town, alerting us that someone below had lit them to ward off the darkness of night, and yet not a single noise was heard as we waited above the village on a cliff that overlooked the valley.

"Fucking hell," Knox growled, staring at the same thing I saw.

The Hecate flag flew on all four corners of the battlements. The only way for the flag to be erected was for a Hecate witch, directly related to Hecate herself, to fly it. My heart pounded against my ribs as blood coursed through my ears, deafeningly. My hands shook with the reality of what it meant. I was about to be blamed for this regardless of what I did or didn't do. My blood relations, only my sisters, my aunt, and I had enough blood to fly that flag.

Flags directly related to a royal line were magically enhanced and unable to fly without spilling the blood of that line to place them. Since they flew on each of the four corners, I was willing to bet it was about to get more than a little hairy for me with Knox. I shuddered as his heated breath fanned my neck, sending warning bells off inside my head.

"Do you know what those flags mean, Aria?" Knox asked against my ear as Greer waited to accept me onto his horse. "If Lord Carter or his men are harmed or dead, so too, are your family," he growled, tightening his hold on my waist punishingly. "The only ones alive who can fly a Hecate witch flag are you and your family. I know because I murdered all the others."

"I'm aware of the logistics." I stared down the long, winding cobblestone road that led into the stronghold.

A rider moved toward us rapidly, bringing his horse to a stop beside us. His face was tinted green, and his eyes were large and rounded. His mouth opened and closed, his head shaking at whatever he'd seen below.

"You're going to want to see this, King Karnavious," he said before leaning in the opposite direction, throwing up. "It's a fucking slaughter."

"Is anyone left alive down there?" Knox asked, and the man trembled violently before shaking his head slowly, using the back of his arm to wipe the saliva from it. "Take Aria, Greer. Don't let her out of your sight."

A chill snaked down my spine as I exhaled, allowing Greer to take hold of me from Knox's grasp. Greer wrapped his arms around me, and we silently watched the men move toward the stronghold. My heart continued racing as my attention swung to the banners, watching the skull with the mark of Hecate whip in the punishing wind.

Clouds rumbled above us, spooking the horse, throwing Greer and me to the ground without warning. He grabbed me, checking for injury before his eyes slid toward the army that watched us curiously. Once he was satisfied that I wasn't harmed, Greer exhaled.

"Are you okay?" he asked, cupping my chin to look at my face.

"I'm fine," I swallowed. "This looks really bad, though," I whispered, and he gave me a tight-lipped smile that did nothing to dispel my fears.

"That depends, Peasant. If the lord and lady are well, Knox won't be too upset. They're some of Queen Liliana's oldest living friends. They helped Knox through his grief greatly when he struggled for purpose. They've held this stronghold for over one thousand years and are very powerful. I am sure they're fine, all things considered. They probably escaped. They're very resourceful. They have to be to live on the border of Norvalla and Vākya."

"Somehow, with that flag flying, and Lord Carter guarding the gate to Hecate's tomb, I doubt anything is going to be fine." I turned when another rider approached, glaring at me as his nostrils flared with unhidden anger and disgust. "Nothing good comes from that flag, Greer. Nothing," I finished, moving forward as Greer walked with me.

"Bring the witch to the king, Sir Greer," the warrior

said coldly, his eyes narrowing on me with violence.

The walk into the village was torture itself. The closer we got, the stronger the scent of death became. I passed through the large, foreboding gates and stopped. Bodies hung from trees, their heads placed beneath them on a bed of midnight rose petals, causing a sickly sweet scent of decay to slither into my senses.

Animals had begun eating the dead, moving over corpses to scurry away from having their meal interrupted. Canine-type creatures ripped limbs from the dead, baring teeth when we passed as the warriors in our group moved forward, preventing them from reaching us. Rats squealed, and I shivered as I watched one moving into the mouth of a skull that was discarded like trash.

The walls of the stronghold were covered in blood, painted with entrails that were tossed out with purpose. Whoever had done this, they went to great lengths to stage the entire village and keep for maximum shock value. My body trembled as additional torches were lit, exposing more of the dead piled on top of each other, their heads removed before being placed in a neat stack that lined the inner-city wall.

I moved deeper into the street, pausing as more skulls came into view. These held the mark of Hecate, and an X was painted in blood across the mark. Slowly, I slid my stare toward their corpses, finding their stomachs opened with their uteruses placed neatly onto their chest. The babes from their wombs adorned the wall behind them, tiny and lifeless, and no more than a few months in development. Tears pricked my eyes, but I held them in, forcing myself not to react to the senseless murders of hundreds of innocent lives.

Swaying on my feet as my nails dug into my palms, I swung my gaze to where black-eyed witches had converged, waiting on the cliffside where we'd just left, watching us. Soldiers moved with Knox's witches, placing crystals to prevent the dark witches from entering behind us. I inhaled slowly, breathing through the horror of what surrounded me. Someone touched my shoulder, and I yelped in horror, spinning as Lore frowned while he moved up beside me.

"Hold it in, Queen Karnavious. The worst is yet to come," Lore grimaced. "Follow me, and no sudden movements. You're being watched by two factors, which are both hoping you fuck up right now. Let's disappoint them all, okay?"

"Okay," I whispered through trembling lips.

I followed Lore closely, not meeting the stares of anyone else as Greer continued behind us. When we reached the center of town, I fought the bile that pushed against my throat. The trees were strung with heads and entrails across the limbs of giant oaks surrounding a fountain that sprayed crimson blood through the mouths of large cherub statues.

A statue of a mermaid sat in the middle of another fountain, no longer spraying water. Something didn't look right, and the closer we got to the fountain, the more my mind attempted to grasp what I was seeing. It wasn't a statue at all. Blue eyes turned toward me as my brain tried to put it together. The dark witches had staged a woman in the fountain to look like a mermaid, and from her lips, pinkish fluid dripped freely.

"Get Aria out of here, now," Knox demanded, and I shook my head at the horror before me.

Large, round, and familiar eyes blinked at me. I gasped as a scream left my throat. Aine, Luna's twin, sat in the fountain with hemlock running through her. I rushed forward, but Knox grabbed me, yanking me back as he shook his head. I sobbed, unable to get words past my lips as Aine watched me, her skin melting off as the hemlock ran down her body and into the water that shot into the air in an arch, just to refill the fountain. My stomach clenched, and everything within me released as the horror of what I saw bubbled up my throat into a bloodcurdling scream.

"No! *No!* Please, no!" I sobbed, fighting Knox to reach Aine.

Aine sighed, and the light extinguished in her eyes. I dropped to my knees at Knox's feet, my entire body twitching as screams and sobs continued to rip from my lungs.

Arms grabbed me, lifting me as Lore rushed us toward the castle, but power erupted into the area. Lore paused, turning to look up at the dark witches. They opened their mouths, and large, black crows crawled out, shooting hundreds of them into the sky. My screaming stopped, and shock took hold while I stared at the evil playing out in front of me.

I watched through wide eyes as the dark witches' screams echoed through the valley, their mouths wide for the crows to escape through. Their shrill cries were deafening and filled the courtyard as the birds shot toward us, attacking with claws as sharp as razor blades.

Lore dropped me to attack them, fighting the possessed birds off. The moment he freed me, I started crawling beneath the surrounding men's feet, all struggling to get away from the crows. Reaching Aine's body, I slid into the water, trying to remove the poles that held her in place. I ignored the burns of the hemlock, uncaring of the acidic water that sizzled against my flesh.

I yanked Aine forward, sobbing as more of her flesh fell free of her body. I could see bones in places where Aine's beautiful golden skin had once been as I struggled feverously to pull her from the fountain. Arms grabbed and tightened around me, forcing me away from the poisonous water as I was rushed into the castle.

Someone hastily removed my dress as Siobhan and Knox's other witches hurried forward with ointment to cover my sizzling flesh. I cried and screamed as pain and grief held me in their thrall, unwilling to release me as my world crashed down around me. Knox purred softly, but it didn't touch the agony that continued holding me in its icy claws.

Knox studied me, his eyes filled with something I couldn't discern. My attention shifted to the large room as torches were lit, then a scream tore through the room. Only it wasn't my scream, or I didn't think it was. My sobs abated when I took in the utter horror that the light had exposed.

High chandeliers covered in orange, red, and white streamers spun around, carrying children's bodies as if they were dancing the maypole. The adult bodies sat at the tables, stiff and turned in various positions like they were speaking to the man or woman beside them. Although their heads had been removed, the dark witches had pinned them back onto random bodies like ill-fitting puzzle pieces. Blood covered the tables, and the scent of hemlock drifted through the air.

I shivered, turning my attention to the table of honor where the lord and lady sat, their hands bound with both heads resting on a silver platter in front of their bodies. The lady was clothed in a silver dress, her hands wrapped in red and white ribbons. On her head sat a crown of onyx, sapphires, and quartz. A single crow pushed from of her mouth, still alive, struggling to escape.

My body moved closer to Knox's, absently seeking his silent strength while the entire room stood silent. My body continually shook, sobs slowly escaping past my lips as the reason the dark witches had slaughtered everyone in the village and keep was revealed. They had recreated our wedding, using the people here to make their displeasure known.

A commotion behind us forced my attention to a body brought in by Knox's men, and my heart clenched. I fought the tears flooding my eyes, breathing rapidly past the evil of what the dark witches did to those here and my sweet sister.

They'd mutilated Aine. Her flesh was almost completely gone from her bones. My stomach turned over, and I closed my eyes as I swayed on my feet. Hands wrapped around me from behind and purring began before Knox turned and held me tightly. I pushed my nose against his chest, breathing him in to calm the agony I felt. My head swam with images as my body sank into Knox's, knowing he was the only support available at the moment.

"They didn't remove her head, Aria," Knox whispered, barely loud enough for the sound to register. "Aine is immortal, which means with enough time, she'll heal. Come. Let me get you someplace where my witches can treat the damage to your skin before it worsens."

I nodded as a sliver of hope entered my mind. Hemlock was poison to witches, but once you were immortal, it lessened the ability to kill without removing the head. Normally, the dark witches would remove the head once the hemlock had entered the system. So why hadn't they done it to Aine? They had to have known she was immortal since they'd staged Aine in the pool of hemlock for my benefit.

Knox walked me up the stairs as the witches silently followed behind us. Once I was inside a bedroom, he issued orders to the women, placing a soft kiss on my forehead before he slipped out the door.

Siobhan watched me closely, moving to the door before she opened it, peeking into the hallway. A shiver raced down my spine as she spun on her heel, raising her hands into the air, causing several of the other witches to drop to the floor. Soraya handed me a dress, holding her finger to her lips as Siobhan tossed quartz toward the doors and windows, slowly turning to me as I pulled the dress on, preparing to fight them both.

"If you want to live, you need to come with me, Aria. Kinvara is in the dungeon with my sister, Esmerelda. I could not thank you for protecting her because ears are everywhere within the camp. I'm leaving this fight today. Come with us," Siobhan whispered, and the other witches moved to the door, observing me.

"Kinvara is here?" I whispered in shock, moving toward them while Siobhan nodded.

"Yes, the dark witches were merely a convenient ruse to get you out of here," Siobhan confirmed. "They set siege to this castle days ago. Soon, Knox will know the truth of it, and you won't be safe with him. He's secured a spell to open his wife's tomb, and when he does that, everything will change."

"Kinvara cannot be here, Siobhan. He will murder her!" I murmured through chattering teeth.

"He'll murder your ass if you stay here, Aria," Soraya snorted.

"We're leaving with or without you. The high king is about to become unstable when he learns the truth about what lies in his wife's tomb. You need to come with us," Siobhan whispered forcefully.

I shook my head, looking between Siobhan and Soraya, wondering if I trusted them enough to follow them out of the room. It could be a trap, one set up by Ilsa to get her hands on me. I closed my eyes and then snapped them open as images of Aine's body filled them. Aine was here, which meant Kinvara was likely here too.

"Check the hallway," Siobhan ordered. The witches, who weren't littering the floor unconscious, moved to do as they were told.

"Esme is your sister?" I asked Siobhan, swallowing down the unease that moved through me.

"Yes, she is. She hid from Knox and his men when he captured those of us left alive in our village. I have kept the knowledge of her from him since his moods are unpredictable. Us witches always have escape routes."

"And you?" I asked, turning to stare at Soraya. "Who the fuck are you?"

"The High Queen of Witches sent me here to kill

you. She has my sister, and like you, my family is everything to me."

"And yet you've not attempted to kill me?" I narrowed my gaze on her as my creature peered out through my eyes, accessing the threat.

"Julia is filled with darkness. You can remove it without murdering her. I came to kill a Hecate witch who was a nuisance. I found a queen who can save us, even though she doesn't want the crown or throne."

I swallowed and nodded before sliding my attention back to Siobhan. "I'm marked with his blood magic. Knox will follow us."

"No, he won't. You're not marked. That rib you removed? That was where he attached his magic. Bekkah helped with that, but then she wasn't aware of why she needed to rile you. You used what you had on hand and what the world gave you. The king marked you, and we needed to remove it. Men are easily swayed, and so I spelled them to hide what happened from Knox. I have been working on getting you away from him since the moment he captured you. You're something special, Aria Hecate. We all feel it in your presence and your touch. Let us help you escape before it is too late."

"I am here because I need to be here, Siobhan," I swallowed.

"You'll die here. Our people need you. We need our queen, Aria."

I nodded, knowing that if I went with them, everything would have to change. I was where I was supposed to be, but Siobhan was right. The moment Knox figured out that his wife wasn't real, he'd unleash hell on those close enough to be within his grasp.

"Let's go," I agreed, hating the tightening in my chest that squeezed my heart at leaving the unfeeling prick.

When the witches outside the door opened it, we entered the hallway, hurrying in the opposite direction from which Knox had brought me. Our slipper-covered feet barely made a sound as we moved through the keep. I blindly rushed behind Soraya and Siobhan, still not trusting their intentions until we entered the dungeon and Kinvara stepped from the shadows.

"Gods dammit, Kinny," I whispered through the tightening in my throat, hugging her tightly. "You shouldn't be here. You promised to stay safe."

"Things changed, Aria. Dimitri is an enemy, one who works for Knox," she stated, petting my hair while holding me close against her. "He removed Hecate's skull and gave it to Knox. Aine volunteered to be a distraction, hoping that Knox would allow you out of his sight for just a moment." Kinvara's hands touched mine, and the burns vanished as she smirked. "Wolfsbane with a trace of hemlock, burns like hell, isn't lethal to witches. We need to go before Knox meets with Dimitri and figures out we're here to rescue you."

I pulled back, nodding. "I killed Dimitri," I admitted.

"You took his heart," Soraya snorted, her eyes rolling. "He's an alpha king, already crowned and placed on his throne. You didn't remove his head. As an alpha king, you must feed the bastard wolfsbane and then remove his head. Same as us, feed us hemlock and remove our heads, and you end the immortality that holds us alive through time."

I frowned, canting my head as she smirked. "You may come in handy, after all. I guess I won't kill you yet." I slid my eyes to the shadows, where Esme grinned. "You're supposed to be at the sanctuary."

"About that—we moved. Siobhan alerted me to the fact that your lover had men outside the sanctuary, preparing to enter. We're in a new palace that has been recently renovated. Aden arranged it and said you'd be home soon, even if he had to come in and get you himself."

"Good. Don't tell me where it is until we're clear. We need to go now," I stated, turning to feel for Knox but not sensing him.

"Please tell me you didn't really marry him," Kinvara groaned, holding my hand. We rushed toward the other witches, who began opening the portal at the end of the hallway filled with cells. When I just looked at her, she paused and turned to me. "Tell me you didn't marry the High King of the Nine Realms, Aria Primrose Hecate!"

"Just a little bit," I stated, and the others snorted, laughing while continuing down the hallway. A rattle sounded, and I slid my attention to Esme, who smirked.

"Oh, did you think you were the only one?" Esme asked, watching the way my eyes widened. "I know I did until Aden showed up. It turns out we're distant relatives, and just like you, I'm a late bloomer. Come! Aden can explain it all later. He got us in here so we could get you out. You're the one we've all been waiting for, Aria."

Another rattle sounded, and I turned, listening as

the castle shook with Knox's rage. "Run! Now, go!" I shouted, pushing Kinvara toward the portal as I followed behind them.

I watched as they passed through the portal, seconds before I would have followed them through it. I was yanked backward before I crossed the threshold, sent flying back in the direction we'd come. Oceanic eyes held mine as Knox walked toward me, sliding to obsidian while he rattled violently, even though it wasn't loud.

"You thought to escape me, mate?" he laughed cruelly. Knox grabbed me from the floor, pulling me up as he turned us toward the portal. My eyes locked with Kinvara's as teeth touched my throat. Her scream ripped through the hallway as they pushed into my flesh, and my body went compliant. "Mine!"

Brander appeared, moving toward the portal until his eyes swung back to me, lowering on Knox's mouth against my throat. Blood dripped from his lips, his arm holding my chest as my feet hung above the ground. I could feel his body against me, hear his heartbeat becoming one with mine as consciousness threatened to escape me.

Siobhan screamed, yanking Kinvara back through the portal as she struggled to get to me. Brander turned toward them, drawing blades as Siobhan, Soraya, and Esme slammed the portal closed, holding a struggling Kinny in their arms. Esme rattled, which caused the monster to clamp his teeth against my neck to rattle back, and I watched as Esme hit the ground hard. Brander turned, looking at me before his eyes closed, and he shook his head. My blood ran in a steady stream to the floor before Lennox covered it with his mouth once more.

"Knox, stop," Killian growled, causing the beast that held control to turn toward his voice. Killian's eyes met mine with worry in their dark blue depths. "You will kill her if you do not heal her throat. She is not immortal."

"That's not Knox anymore," Brander grunted.

We vanished into the jetstream, and Lennox placed my body onto a large, soft bed. He held his mouth where he'd marked me, moving my hands above my head as he rattled. Lennox backed up, his mouth covered in my blood as he smiled wickedly, reaching down to shred my dress. My entire body shuddered with the reality of what was happening.

I was at the mercy of Knox's creature, and he was going to kill me.

Chapter Forty-Three

Men moved into the room, arguing with Lennox, but I couldn't hear them over the blood pumping through my veins or the creature screaming within me.

"Run, bitch, run!" Ember snapped.

"Does it look like I can run away? Take control. You wanted this. Here's your chance!" I urged.

"Get out," Lennox snarled at Knox's men, and Ember and I both shivered at the warning in his tone, choosing to remain silent as his eyes pierced ours with predatory intent. "So pretty and soft, mate," he chuckled darkly, leaning down to lick my nipple before he slid his mouth to sinking his teeth into the underside of my breast. I whimpered, and Ember purred softly. Lifting my legs, I spread them for him.

"You are mine. You know that, don't you?" Lennox whispered as I rocked my body, my eyes growing hooded and filled with lust.

Fingers slid down my stomach, pushing against the sore flesh that Knox had fucked for days. I moaned, causing Lennox's eyes to narrow. He stood suddenly, removing Knox's armor as Ember and I silently watched. Turning, his cock came into view, and we both blanched from the sheer monstrosity of it. Nope! *Abort!* I didn't so much as breathe as Lennox sat down, smiling at me.

"Bitch, take control!" I shifted my position, and Lennox zeroed in on me. Sitting up, I shed the remainder of my dress, testing to see if I could escape him. *Nope.* That wasn't happening. He'd tensed, fully expecting me to bolt from the bed. I tossed the ripped clothing aside, laying back on the pillows.

"Yeah, sorry, but no. It's not happening," Ember snorted. *"Do you see that thing? It will ache badly."*

"You have a dislocating jaw, hooker. I'm sure you can dislocate our nether region too, right? Right? Please tell me you can do something to fit that thing inside of us!" I pleaded internally.

"Maybe it's why they feed us pineapple? Ask for some fruit."

I slowly blinked as my mouth started to open at the absurdity of her statement but chose to remain silent as Lennox leaned over, exploring my body.

"We're going to die by dick, Ember. Our tombstone will say, 'Here lies that one bitch who died from getting good dick,' *and that's just not going to look great in the afterlife. Do something! Speak, Creature, or maybe I don't know, fight? Can we fight our way out of this?"*

"I think we fuck our way out," Ember admitted, and our gaze slid down to the organ in question before slowly

rising to stare at Lennox in horrified silence. *"Definitely planning on banging you, Aria,"* Ember chuckled, unable to continue looking away from the monstrous cock. *"You should run because that thing is a weapon of mass destruction. Knox said it gets bigger. You are going to need that pineapple, lots of pineapples."*

"Pineapples won't help that thing *get into us! It isn't lubrication. It just enhances the flavor, Ember. Lennox is your mate, remember? Knox was supposed to be mine. I handled him for an entire week while you rode bitch. You get to drive now. You're the freak. Here's your chance for glory."*

"Nope."

"What the hell do you mean, nope?"

"Hard pass, ha-ha, get it?" Ember chuckled, stretching out within me.

"We're breaking up, Ember. Get out of me, now," I snapped.

"Doesn't work like that. I'm not your personal lubrication."

"You're being obtuse!"

"And you're about to be banged by that club between his legs, so which is more fucked? Me or you? You! By that thing.*"*

"I have not given life to another, asshole." Lennox's words caused Ember and I to pause, noting he and Knox were both arguing as well. Lennox snorted, and I wondered what the hell they were fighting over other than the obvious.

Lennox's hand slid to my throat, capturing it while

forcing my eyes to meet and hold his. He purred in a soothing tone that caused something to fall into place as calmness settled over me. His mouth brushed against mine, and I moaned huskily, tasting my blood on his kiss. My hips rocked, and I couldn't turn them off. I felt Ember watching him, enthralled by whatever Lennox was doing.

"Who are you?" I whispered, and I took in a sharp breath, shocked that I had spoken the words, realizing they had come from Ember.

"I am your shelter from the storm. I am your strength when you are weak. I am the fire that burns through your veins and heats you when you are in need. I am the one who will fill your womb and protect the children you give me. I am your light in the darkness and the one who guides your way when you are lost. I am the creature who will destroy worlds to keep you and will never allow you to fall. I am Lennox, beast to the High King of the Nine Realms and King of Norvalla. I am your mate, Aria Karnavious." Leaning closer, locking eyes with mine, Lennox asked, "Who are you?"

Ember pushed forward in my consciousness, and I was both thankful and fearful at the same time. She parted her lips and lifted her hand, cupping her fingers softly around Lennox's cheek, smiling softly as she spoke. "I am your softness when the world becomes too hard. I am the tinder that ignites your flames and feeds your fire. I am your gentle when your hardness becomes too much to bear. I am the one you protect from your enemies. I am the woman who will bear your children and bless you with an heir to strengthen your line. I keep your secrets no matter the cost while treasuring your rough edges that most often cut. I build you up when others reach to tear you down, and I'll take their spines to wear as my crown. I am Ember, Queen—I am your mate, Lennox." The words tumbled from her lips as though on autopilot, and something settled deep into my soul, and he smiled as she pushed me forward, releasing her control.

Lennox moved onto the bed, and I placed my hand over his chest, pushing him back. *"Ember! What just happened? How did you know what to say? Get back here and help me!"* I pleaded while his eyes narrowed in a very angry, very masculine way that screamed he intended for this to happen one way or another. I purred and almost rolled my eyes at Ember's lame version of help. Lennox's eyes slid from black to blue and then black again.

I grabbed his throbbing cock, slowly watching his eyes narrow to slits. I straddled him, knowing that if this was going to happen, which it didn't appear, I could avoid; I needed some control. Slowly, I ran my fingers over his velvety flesh, watching him study me.

"You're going to hurt me, Lennox. It's okay," I whispered, holding his stare. Pushing him against my opening, I begged Ember to help me, even though she'd withdrawn to safety, just to watch me try to force him into my body.

"You're made for me, Aria. Your hips will spread to take me. We will fit. I promise you that."

Swallowing, I felt Ember within me, and my hips spread while arousal flooded my core. I pushed against him, watching where he entered my body. Ember added strength to my resolve, knowing if we didn't do this, Lennox would. There was no way out of it, and I felt it deeper than he intended to penetrate me.

"Holy shit, you're really doing this!" Ember exclaimed.

"One of us is! Pussy!"

"Uh, he's about to destroy your pussy, so maybe we shouldn't speak about that at the moment."

I moaned, my eyes widening at the first taste of pain as Lennox stretched my body. I clenched against him, indicating that not even my body was okay with what was happening. Where the hell was Knox? He'd told me he intended to force this to happen, asshole.

"Yeah, you've pretty much taken just the head. We're so fucked right now," Ember laughed, and I cried out, which made her tense within me.

"You're beautiful," Lennox croaked huskily, continuing to watch as I forced him into my tight body. "Take it, woman, or I'll be compelled to make you."

"Working on it, asshole," I growled, slamming down on him as a scream ripped from my throat, accompanied by Ember's.

"Oh my gods, you took it all! Look at you go!"

"I'm going to die," I whimpered.

"Look at you fucking me, woman. You're the Queen of Beasts. You're my monster, aren't you, pretty girl?"

Lennox chuckled as I rocked slowly against his body. My head dropped back, and another scream ripped from my throat as pain echoed through me. It was a burning ache that left me clenching against him, trying to force him to finish prematurely. Like, seriously prematurely.

Purring started in and out of the room, and I shuddered around him, unable to get past the pain he created while filling me until there was nothing left untouched inside of me.

His eyes shifted, and I saw a glimpse of oceanic-blue as I rolled my hips. His eyes went dark again as he growled, cupping my breasts with clawed hands. I shivered from the sensation of his claws caressing my nipples as I rode him, forcing his entire length into my body. Lennox laid back, watching me work for an orgasm. I grinned as I lifted and slid back down, burying him deep within me. Leaning over, I kissed his chest, forcing him to meet my eyes.

"I'm going to need you to stop being a lazy prick and fuck me like an animal, bastard. My pussy aches, and I need you to man-the-fuck-up right now."

Lennox was up, pushing my legs against my chest, thrusting feverously in and out of my body, edging me closer to orgasm. Releasing my legs, he lowered his mouth and sunk his teeth into my throat. Lennox went hard, and Ember purred, her eyes slowly taking him in as he continued to move. A satisfying moan slipped from us both as I came around him. It was violent and beautiful, sending us both into wave after wave of endless pleasure.

"He's all alpha, Aria. You have him purring. I am so proud of you!"

"Tell that to our vagina, bitch," I groaned inwardly.

Lennox yanked me up against his throat, his hand holding my mouth there as my tongue slipped free, licking where he wanted my mark. He shuddered, filling me with arousal as everything went haywire. Ember growled and moved my hips as I clenched against his release. Pain turned to pleasure, and we both paused before moving harder, faster, rocking against him with our need growing.

"More," I demanded, and Lennox chuckled.

"Greedy Little Monster, aren't you, mate?"

My brain shut down, and everything went off-kilter. I wasn't sure if Ember was in control or if we'd hit our limit, and autopilot had turned on. I felt Lennox growing, but I couldn't stop. My body clamped down around him, sealing him into my opening. He purred, watching me through hypnotic eyes that burned with fiery flecks while he continued rocking, smiling at me with pride.

I moved my arms above my head and lifted my hips, meeting Lennox with every thrust. He lowered his hand between our bodies and began rubbing and flicking my clit, instantaneously sending me over the edge.

Mindlessly, I moved faster and harder, gripping his hips and forcing him deeper inside my body. Ember purred, clamping down around him while Lennox stared her in the eye, emptying himself inside our body as multiple orgasms rocked through me.

"Made for me," Lennox uttered hoarsely. My body moved, knowing every slow-motion I made sent him shifting toward where he wanted to be. He wanted my womb, but fuck them both. They didn't get it. "Do you see her beauty now, Knox? Did your woman ever do this for us? Aria is mine in every way, created by the fires in the Nine Realms to fan our flames and make us burn brighter, hotter. Aria is mine, asshole."

Ember purred at his words, and I forced myself not

to roll my eyes. My body released his, and he withdrew, slowly moving down to stick his nose into my sore vagina as he rubbed his knuckles against me.

My eyes slid closed, relief washing through me that it was over, but Lennox jerked back and clamped his fingers on my chin, forcing my eyes to open. He shook me violently, and I shoved him away. Flipping onto my stomach, I raised my ass in the air and spread my legs, turning my head to show him I was still awake.

Lennox didn't waste any time. He was inside of me, thrusting and destroying me within seconds of me presenting him with my ass. His teeth pushed through the scar on my shoulder, and I exploded. My body hummed with power as I purred loudly, feeling him emptying again within me.

Sometime later, sleep finally grasped me with vicious claws, and I succumbed, ignoring Lennox and Knox while they argued.

"Next time, Lennox is mine. Now you've taken them both and know Knox is stupid because he also fought his beast. You married the man; you also get the beast. Now, what we do next is your choice, Aria. Know this; they're ours. If you want children, you'll open to them. If not, we stay closed like your legs normally do."

"Go to bed, Ember. My vagina is wrecked, asshole. I need to sleep."

Chapter Forty-Four

Knox/Lennox

Taking in the chaos and dead littering the center of the village, I swallowed hard. I'd ridden Aria right into the ugliness of this mess with my anger. She was too soft for this shit, and I hated her being thrown into it at all. I'd watched her face crumple, her mind unable to accept what it was seeing until Aine had turned to look at her. Aria had broken wide open, and my heart cracked with her sobs. I couldn't always protect her because the world wouldn't allow it. But this one, this was on me.

The Nine Realms wasn't the world she'd read about in her books. It wasn't a place you could expose weakness and expect it not to be held against you. Aria was here because I'd brought her into this mess. Lennox wouldn't have allowed me to walk away from her after he'd caught her scent, but I'd at least tried. She didn't deserve to be stuck with me, and yet I'd gone and fucking married her because no matter how much I fought it or argued with it, Aria was mine. I felt it in the very bones of my being.

Aria got close, and I'd pushed her away. She pulled away, and I'd yanked her back. I hated her indifference and the hurt she felt when I struck against her. Aria stood at the end of the aisle in her wedding dress as panic rushed through her, wanting to run from what was happening. She'd looked every inch the queen she was born to become. I'd lied and told her I preferred her hair down when the truth was I loved it up. I loved seeing the soft curve of her throat. I knew sooner or later, I'd lose the fight with Lennox, and our mark would be there for the world to see.

Aria had skipped every tradition on our wedding night, hers and mine. She hadn't worn the jewels I'd left for her or even worn shoes. Aria hadn't worn the Hecate crown, choosing to accept mine in its place. The shoulder chains would have marked her royalty, and yet she'd forgone them to come to me as herself. Her humbleness floored me. She had been a true queen coming to a king, with her body bare of jewels and markings.

The type of woman she was, well, it was what I'd craved since before my cock had ever twitched. She loved everything I did, and we had more in common than anyone else I'd ever met. Aria was this perfect thing that craved me as much as I craved her, and it hurt me deeply to acknowledge it.

She was more than I deserved, and we both knew it. I knew it on a level that I hated, but I set that aside as she'd given herself to me for days without ever wanting more than to be with me. She had been content to spend the time beside me, learning of our world with the mind of a scholar. I'd made love to Aria, something I hadn't done since Liliana was alive, and even then, I couldn't say it was anything like I'd shared with Aria in that stone hut.

Aria, with her walls down, had socked me in the gut harder than I cared to admit. I'd felt her pain and watched tears swimming in her eyes as she brought them down for me. Her voice had cracked when she'd whispered the truth of how she felt. I'd needed to reassure Aria that she wasn't the sum of what she's endured. What those monsters did hadn't defined her or who she would become. I'd told her it wouldn't have mattered if they'd raped her, and it shocked me to know I truly felt that way. I only cared that she'd gotten back up and refused to remain down.

News of the attack on the stronghold had ripped open my wounds, and I'd needed to hurt her. I had been preoccupied, and those days with her in bed had ended in this shit show of a mess. I'd needed her to know that no matter what had happened, nothing had changed between us. I'd slammed her down onto the table, using her as I had countless others. Pulling back, I'd watched her body clenching in both pain and pleasure, leaking our fluids down her legs. I'd hated myself for it, and I'd pulled away because it was how I kept myself in check. It was how I reminded myself that Aria was my enemy.

I'd felt like the world's biggest asshole, but then she'd ridden me slowly, erotically rocking my fucking foundation. I'd never been so turned on in my life as she spoke naughty words, asking me how much I enjoyed her tight pussy. She'd mesmerized me with her slow-moving hips, rolling them while her body clamped down against mine hungrily. Her pretty titties jiggled, and fuck if I hadn't craved to taste the dusky-colored peaks again.

I hadn't seen it coming.

Aria had knocked me to the ground, and placed her tiny foot on my throat, sending her claws into my soul before shredding it without mercy. I'd treated her like a camp follower, and she'd taken it. Or I thought she had. Instead, she'd ridden me before turning my head, forcing me to look at my family as I came beneath the skilled rolls of her tiny hips.

Her words aimed for blood, creating a wound so deep in my soul that I felt her within it, ripping it apart while I emptied into her haven. I'd broken Liliana's gift with the need to prevent them from seeing the monster I'd become. I'd aimed that anger at Aria, and she'd sat before me, telling me how little I'd touched her, even though I'd tried to sink talons into her soul.

"This is a fucking mess," Brander stated, pushing fingers through his hair as a crease formed on his forehead.

"You're telling me," I snorted, closing my eyes before the herbs in the fountain caught my attention.

Staring down at the fountain coated in hemlock, I paused to kneel beside it. Aine's body had been placed for shock value. They'd wanted Aria to see it. Why? Why not remove Aine's head and finish the job? Standing, I brought my fingers to my nose, inhaling the proof of treachery.

"It isn't hemlock—merely a trace mixed into wolfsbane which wouldn't be lethal to witches. Just an irritant against their skin," I growled, looking to the stronghold before rushing toward it. "They're here for

Aria!" I snarled as I ran, knowing my men followed behind me.

We burst into the castle, scaring those within as we sprinted past them. I took the stairs three at a time, pushing against the door that refused to budge. Lifting my foot, I sent the door crashing to the floor, seconds before I entered the room, silently taking in the witches' crumpled forms. I scanned the floor for silver hair, finding Aria wasn't among them. Turning on the men, I lifted my nose in the air, trying to find her scent.

"I don't smell or feel Aria's presence within the keep," I growled, feeling my beast awakening at the news she was gone. "Spread out and find her, now!"

We exited the bedroom, and no sooner had we stepped across the threshold than I felt it. Power unfurled, yet it was subtle. Someone was opening a portal within the stronghold. Lennox roared, sending the warning to Ember that he wouldn't allow her to escape him. I vanished, entering the jetstream before appearing in the shadows to watch as Aria rushed toward the portal with one of her sisters.

Lennox moved, jerking Aria back as his words left our mouth in a hiss. He shoved me into the backseat of my mind, and before I knew his intentions, Lennox sunk his teeth into Aria's throat, claiming her as his mate.

"No! She won't survive it, Lennox! Heal her and give me control."

"We tried it your way. You failed to secure our mate. Aria is mine, and she will survive me. This woman was made for me, and you know it," Lennox snarled, turning as my men surrounded him. He couldn't see or hear

anyone through the red-haze consuming him with the need to claim Aria in the way our kind did.

He grabbed Aria and vanished from the dungeon, appearing in a room. Lennox placed Aria onto the bed, sitting back to look into her eyes as she watched him. Her mouth opened on a whimper, blood gushing from her throat before he leaned down, kissing the wound he'd made. Lennox ripped her dress open, stealing a gasp from her lungs as he dragged his eyes down her body in hunger.

My men burst into the room, and Lennox turned, baring his teeth, and a deadly rattle escaped our lips. I watched them, knowing they sensed I no longer held control. Only one other time in my life had Lennox taken control without my permission, which was to stop the pain I'd felt after Sven's death.

Brander stepped forward, his eyes never falling on Aria because he knew Lennox had claimed her. Her throat carried the mark, proof that he thought she was his other half. Killian entered and paused, finding Aria watching me with panic burning in her eyes.

"Do not hurt her, Lennox. She is soft and breakable," Brander warned, not looking away as Lennox held his stare.

"She is mine," he snapped.

"So she is, but again, if you break her, she won't be. She's not immortal yet because she's refused to meld with Ember. Aria isn't Ember and cannot do that which your mate can," Brander whispered, his voice neutral.

"Get out," Lennox snarled, and I swallowed as he turned back to Aria, who wisely kept silent. "So pretty and soft, mate," he chuckled darkly, leaning down to lick her rose-colored nipple before he slid his mouth to the underside of it, sinking his teeth in as she whimpered, lifting her legs to spread them for him.

"Don't do this to her. Look at her, Lennox. She's human and breakable. Aria isn't Ember and cannot take you in her human form. You'll hurt her too badly."

"You are mine. You know that, don't you?" Lennox whispered, watching as she rocked her body, flooring me while her eyes grew heavily hooded with lust.

Fingers slid down her body, pushing against the sore flesh that I'd fucked for days. Her moan caused his eyes to narrow, and I prepared to fight Lennox to protect her from him.

Lennox stood, shucking my armor from our body while he watched her, ensuring she didn't try to escape him. Aria didn't. She stared down at my cock, enhanced by Lennox's form, and her eyes went wide as she held her breath. After a moment, she shifted on the bed, sitting up to remove the shambles of her dress.

Panic and terror oozed from her pores, betraying the silent strength she showed outside. I prayed inwardly that Ember took control to spare Aria the pain of the mating, yet her eyes never turned electric blue, signaling that Ember was in the driver's seat.

Lennox shed the remainder of my clothes, moving to sit on the bed with Aria as her eyes grew round in fear. He smiled, inhaling her enticing scent that filled the room. He craved her fear, but he zeroed in on the arousal her body created. I groaned, knowing how addicting her smells were. No one had ever drawn me to them with their scent, but hers drove me bug-fuck-crazy with the need to drink it in.

"Give me control, and I will get her to open her womb, Lennox," I pleaded, needing to spare Aria from being ripped apart by his savagery. *"Don't do this, Lennox. If you do this, and she accepts your claim, you will ruin any chance of her ever having a babe."*

"I have not given life to another, asshole."

"We created Sven!" I snapped harshly, listening as he chuckled.

Lennox gripped Aria's throat, forcing her eyes to lock with his as they turned the most beautiful color of blue I'd ever seen before, filling with golden flecks that mirrored flakes of gold in a pan. His mouth brushed against her lips, covered in her blood. He purred against them, closing his eyes as Ember made the feminine version of it against them, moving her ass as if he were already within her tight folds.

"Who are you?" Ember whispered, and my heart stopped cold.

I hesitated, shocked that Ember would know the one question that would begin the mating vows. *"Do not do this, Lennox. Liliana was our mate!"*

I frantically tried to take control, but Lennox pushed me even further to the back of my mind as he recited the ancient declarations that our kind would bestow upon their mate. When he finished, Lennox lowered closer to Aria's face, and I saw that Ember was still in control. Smiling, he asked, "Who are you?"

I frowned from within him as her lips parted, and my

heart hammered. Her hand lifted, fingers curling around my cheek as her features softened, and a smile graced her lips just before she answered Lennox's declaration with her own. I couldn't hear past the blood roaring in my ears as Aria whispered her vows to Lennox. How many times had I whispered the promise vows to Liliana, who had never felt the compulsion to speak them back? Aria shouldn't even know the vow, let alone feel the compulsion to say the words back to us.

Lennox moved onto the bed, but Aria sat up, pushing him away. Fear snaked through me; his anger at her denial to take what he felt was his was dangerous. I didn't have the control to protect her from him, and I felt him shoving me away as he growled angrily.

Aria purred softly, shoving him to the bed before she straddled his hips. My eyes widened as she reached back, stroking the large cock he'd lengthened. It wasn't going to fit into her tight body, and it didn't matter how much arousal Ember added. Lennox wouldn't fit without her hips spreading for him.

He watched her through narrowed eyes, his purr sounding while she worked his cock with her tiny hand, unable to close her fingers around its girth. She straddled Lennox, lowering her lips to kiss his chest and purred softly, soothing the beast while he waited patiently to see if she denied him.

"You're going to hurt me, Lennox. It's okay," she whispered, lifting her eyes to hold his as she pushed him against her opening. I shivered as I felt her tight opening against the throbbing organ that was slowly being slid over her arousal.

"You're made for me, Aria. Your hips spread to take

me. We will fit. I promise you that."

Her glowing eyes smiled as she lifted, giving him a bird's-eye view of her tiny opening. Aria glided the tip against her arousal-slick sex, moaning as he watched her through a heavy-lidded stare. She inched Lennox into her body, moaning as her eyes widened. His attention moved from her face to her pussy, watching as she slowly took more of his length. And my gods did it feel good.

I winced as her scream sounded, and before Lennox could move, Aria pushed down further. Lennox gripped her hips, and she grabbed his hands, using them for balance as she slowly lifted. Her eyes held him with a silent plea, and I purred loudly while he rattled. She didn't try to escape it, or what she knew had to be done to appease him.

Aria was glorious while she slowly moved further down the thickness he wielded. And although the sensation was muted for me, I could still feel the warm caresses of her body as we slid in and out of her arousal-coated core. Her eyes lowered, and a shudder of unease vibrated through her as the walls of her channel clamped down, trying to force us out.

"You're beautiful," Lennox crooned, and yet his eyes weren't on her face. It was on her body that was slowly taking more of us. Fucking pervert was single-minded when his dick came out to play. "Take it, woman, or I'll be compelled to make you."

"Working on it, asshole," she growled, pushing her body down a little further while he smiled with pride. I chuckled until she slammed down, and her entire body shook from the pain.

"Bloody hell, did you see that?" I demanded, hearing him chuckle while he took in how far her body was stretched to take us. *"Help her! She's in pain."*

"Look at you fucking me, woman. You're a Queen of Beasts. You're my monster, aren't you, pretty girl?"

Her head dropped back as another scream tore from her throat. I shuddered, experiencing Lennox's pleasure, watching the tiny woman taking me in beast form. Her pussy was stretched until it was red, and her scream was tortured. Lennox purred, and more purrs sounded, alerting us to the men just outside the room.

He started to pull back, allowing me to surface until she rolled her hips slowly. Lennox slammed me back, and he growled huskily, reaching up to cup her breasts with clawed hands. She didn't recoil from the nails that terrified my enemies. Instead, Aria held his hands to her breasts while she slowly rocked against the inhuman organ she'd forced into her body. Aria lifted, shocking us both as she slowly slid back down, burying us deep within her body. She leaned over and kissed his chest as she peered into our eyes.

"I'm going to need you to stop being a lazy prick and fuck me like an animal, bastard. My pussy aches, and I need you to man-the-fuck-up right now."

Lennox smiled, but it wasn't friendly. He sat up, uncaring that she was seated on his cock. Fingers dug into her thighs, pushing them against her shoulders before slamming home in her pussy. Lennox was thrusting in and out of her body like a well-oiled machine. She moaned then purred loudly, her body bucking while she fucked him back.

Aria floored me, taking Lennox in his form without breaking. She wasn't backing down, and she'd fucking taunted him into going hard. He released her legs, lowering his mouth to sink his teeth into her throat, laughing as her body combusted with an orgasm that made her motions frenzied and unhinged. Her eyes closed, and her body tightened as the orgasm continued to rip through her, causing me to shudder from the sensation. Lennox didn't hold back, slamming against her even though he took up every ounce of space she had. Her body sucked us off, clamping and clenching down as he threw his head back, rattling to bow her back in submission.

Her pupils fully dilated, and golden stars filled them while he continued to rattle, peering down at her belly that still hadn't allowed him access to her womb. He slid his hand behind her head, jerking her mouth against his throat while holding her there.

The tremor rushing through us from her tongue sliding over our pulse at the hollow of our throat caused him to release into her core. Lennox growled, waiting for her to mark us. And yet she didn't. Her body drained ours greedily, sucking us off until he sagged on the bed, releasing her to peer down into her eyes.

Aria didn't stop rocking, didn't stop clenching her body hungrily around the heavy cock still within her. Lennox grew, and she writhed, moving to accommodate him while I watched her in wonder. She was taking him, and she fucking liked it.

"More," she demanded, and he chuckled.

"Greedy Little Monster, aren't you, mate?"

Her arms moved to flatten beside her head, and she

lifted her hips, slamming her already sore apex against the growing organ. Lennox watched her, his smile soft while she took him with eagerness. He'd never done this with anyone else, and yet he held back because he didn't want to hurt her. It was pissing her off, and even though he sensed it, he didn't give her what she needed.

He just watched her fucking us, her curves rolling and moving while she continually adjusted to accommodate us within her body. Lennox moved his fingers between our bodies, slowly rubbing her clit to send her over the edge. Her eyes widened while he watched her, smiling deviously while she moved faster, harder, thrusting, and pumping her ass. A purr exploded from her throat, and he filled her entirely full while she clamped down around him.

"Made for me," Lennox whispered, watching her feverish movements.

She moved hypnotically. It was the most erotic thing I'd ever witness, watching her body do what it was created to do with mine. I felt her tightening against my dick. One he'd allowed to swell within her, sealing her entrance even though she hadn't given him what he craved. She'd locked her body around his, holding him within her while multiple orgasms rocked her.

It should have forced Aria to give Lennox what he craved, and yet she still hadn't opened her womb. I was the key, and she the lock. It should have opened her to him, but she just came on our dick, forcing an orgasm to escape the tight hold he'd held on it.

"Do you see her beauty now, Knox? Did your woman ever do this for us? She is mine in every way, created by the fires in the Nine Realms to fan our flames and make us burn brighter, hotter. Aria is mine, asshole."

She purred as her body released ours, and he allowed it, slowly withdrawing from her to move toward her opening, inhaling it deeply. She smelled mated and claimed, and yet she hadn't given him what he wanted. She hadn't opened her womb for him, nor had she returned his mark. He rubbed his knuckles against her opening, peering up to find her eyes closed.

Panic rushed through us, moving up her body to grip her chin before he shook her violently. She pushed him away, rolling onto her stomach while offering us another view of her arousal covered opening. Lennox chuckled, not waiting for more of an invitation before he pushed into her body, sliding his mouth over her shoulder to bite into the delicate flesh that covered my mark. Aria's whimpered cries exploded, and she rocked in slow, seductive rolling moves that had him needing to give her what she craved. But instead, she purred in a tone I hadn't ever heard before, and we exploded without warning.

"Jesus fuck, what the hell was that?" I demanded.

"Other, not the same," Lennox admitted, shuddering against her opening before withdrawing to look at his dick. *"She's not the same, but it changes nothing."*

"You fuck, it changes everything. She just purred, and we gave her what she needed," I snapped, hearing Aria's even breathing. Lennox looked up, finding her eyes closed again with sleep.

"She's—more. She's rare and ours."

"You just condemned her to be our mate, asshole."

"Aria was already ours. You married her and claimed her. You failed to win her over, and I tried. She didn't finish it, and I need it finished."

"You condemned her to be our mate. Do you have any idea how fucking miserable we are as a mate? We couldn't even keep the last one alive."

"Knox, Liliana wasn't your mate or mine. Smell Aria and touch her. Forget that she is your enemy and feel her against you. She's right and durable. I just proved to you that she wasn't weak as she took us in beast form. We are not the same thing, but we are close enough to mate, asshole. Aria was forged from the fires of the Nine Realms, created in Norvalla, and built to be mine by the legends who ruled before us. Stop pissing her off because she may eventually stop forgiving us, and I enjoy her touch. She is my calm, and I am her chaos. No more harming her. What was it you told her? Spoiler alert, she's mine."

"Liliana was my mate!" I snapped, hating that I'd felt Aria on a deeper level than Liliana.

"It's a miracle Ember hasn't eaten us yet, Knox. Open the tomb as I told you to do. See the bones. See the proof."

"If it is true that the dark witches planned my wife and son, do you honestly think I will keep Aria around? Her grandmother would be the reason for that and the cause of my pain. Could you force our mate to endure that, if it is the truth? I would hate Aria and everything she is."

"At first, she will expect your anger and rage. Aria will forgive you because that is who she is, and she knew

our vows when we said them. She knew them without ever hearing them."

"Why is that, I wonder?"

"When she wakes, get her mark. Seal the bond between mates, and if nothing happens, you will be right, and I will be wrong, Knox. You have nothing to lose by receiving it if what you say is true."

Lennox eased back into my mind and vanished, leaving me with a woman who slumbered, oblivious to what had just happened. He'd given her his mark. Lennox, the King of Beasts, had just claimed his queen and mate, and she'd fucking taken him in all her glory. He'd cursed her to be stuck with me for eternity, which no one woman deserved. It wasn't a blessing at all, but more of a punishment.

Lennox was wrong. I had everything to lose, including Aria, if what they said was true. I'd started a war from grief, waging battles vehemently and without mercy, attacking my enemies. I couldn't stop the war; no one could. It would take an act of mercy, and none of us had any left to give.

Aria was coming into a world that wanted her dead and everyone she loved murdered. This world was going to turn her into a monster, and there was nothing I could do to stop it. Too many factions were in play, with only one possible outcome.

I wanted Aria; that much was a given. Everything she was called to me and that fact bothered me most. I craved her touch, knowing that with every brush of her fingers, my walls thinned and crumbled. If that happened, everything would come out at once. Everything I'd buried behind those walls would be unleashed, and I feared unleashing it on her the most. She was my enemy, but she was also the balm that soothed my battered soul, and that was a fucking problem. It was easier to push her away than allow her to get close to me because it protected her.

I'd made more enemies than friends by becoming the high king, and I'd taken my crown by force. If I allowed the world to figure out I actually liked my wife, they'd make her a target, and that wasn't something I could deal with in the middle of a bloody war.

Aria moaned as I ran my fingers over her naked hipbone. Pushing her over, I peered down at the bite mark on her throat and shoulder. Frowning, I leaned over, licking the wounds, only for her to part her legs, and beckon me to take her. My lips curved into a smile as her eyes opened, peeking through hooded lids to show me she was coherent.

Turning her body, I slowly pushed into her core, carefully draping her leg over my hip. She moaned, turning her needy lips toward me to claim. Swallowing, I narrowed my eyes on her blunt teeth, leaning over to claim her sexy-as-fuck lips to swallow her sweet noises.

I gave her what she needed from me. It was easy to forget what blood burned through her veins when she took me as she did. I felt her body quivering, studying her teeth as she exploded into purring vibrations that hit my balls. She forced me to release into her when I was nowhere close to ready.

"Jesus fuck, woman. What the fuck are you?" I whispered as she rattled her approval. Cuddling up against me, she slumbered, oblivious to the fact she'd just forced me to give her what she needed with her sensual fucking purr that undid me. "More evolved, my ass. You're a unicorn, Aria Karnavious. My unicorn now," I murmured against her ear, pulling her tiny frame against mine, which dwarfed her. She fit me like a glove, perfectly.

Chapter Forty-Five

Knox

A soft knock sounded on the door, and I turned, glaring at it before pulling the sheet up around Aria. Moving to the broken chest that had been brought in, I chuckled. Lennox was sent over the edge, unable to recognize the soldier's scent that entered and was near his freshly washed mate. I pulled on sweatpants and cracked the door open to find the men outside, all standing back at a safe distance.

"Is it safe?" Lore asked, peering into the room through my arm.

I growled without warning, struggling against the change as Lennox sensed someone entering his space. He was territorial over his unconscious, fertile mate who had continued to refuse to mark him or open her womb to him. Lore paused, knowing I'd win the battle with Lennox, having been pounced on by Aria endlessly for days.

"We have a problem that's bigger than your mate not giving you her womb," Brander snapped, entering and walking toward Aria, which caused a rattle to escape. Brander turned, rattling back as his beast answered mine. "Stow it, asshole. Aine's body is gone."

"How is that possible?" I asked, narrowing my eyes on Aria's form that was wrapped in bedsheets she'd insisted on piling over the bed before lying down. She'd even forced me into the damn thing, clamping down on my cock like she owned it. Or worse, she feared I was too stupid to live and was protecting me from Ember.

She irked me.

She drove me insane.

I was perfectly content without ever leaving her heat.

Fuck!

"Yeah, even if it wasn't hemlock within the fountain, Aine would need more time to heal. The problem is that our supposedly loyal witches switched sides, Knox. Siobhan and Soraya are both missing. Bekkah is singing that Aria set it all up," Killian grunted, moving over to Aria and peering down at her neck. "She didn't return the mark?"

"No," I grunted, moving toward the table to sit, before pouring a goblet full of whiskey.

Brander lowered the sheets, which caused a deadly rattle to escape, forcing him to cover Aria's naked form back up. "Is this a nest?" Brander narrowed his gaze on the mess of sheets she had piled on the bed.

"No. It's sheets, asshole," I snapped.

All three men turned toward me, and I glared at each one, pointedly. I scrubbed my hand down my face, sitting back to look at the sheets she'd fashioned into a pile. Frowning, I rose from my seat to loom over her tiny form.

Aria had rearranged the bedding around her body. She had built a nest, but it was a rather crude one at best. It was something the females of old would make or use when trying to conceive offspring. Liliana had never used anything to nest, not even when we'd conceived Sven.

"I told you she was a phoenix," Killian muttered.

"That doesn't mean shit, Killian. Shifters nest, or at least several of them do. Let's get back to the issue. Report what is happening outside." I sat on the bed beside Aria, and she rolled over, presenting her ass to me.

Her hand moved, and I prevented her ass from exposure, rattling to let her know I didn't need her yet. She purred, diving deeper into the sheets while continuing her sweet noises. I frowned as my men started purring with her, each wanting to assure her they were here to protect her. *Fuckers.*

"You assholes planning on purring at Aria all day, or you got something important to discuss?" I glared at them, rubbing Aria's spine as the object beneath her skin shifted.

"Did she feel your need to fuck? Because that's hot! So hot. Daddy really wants one." Lore pushed his knuckles into his mouth, biting them as he continued staring at Aria. "She smells different today…" He inhaled deeply, scrunching up his nose as I smirked.

"I forget how young you are, Lore." I watched the way the others smiled, noting his perturbed look of confusion. "She now carries my mark, which will warn others that she belongs to me. What you smell is the equivalent of me pissing on her leg to mark her as mine."

Lore winced, turning to look at me. "You assholes got to see all the cool things back in the day. I hadn't ever heard a woman purr until Aria did it, and damn did I feel it all the way to my balls, man."

"It's been a very long time since any of us have heard the noises she makes." I hated this fact made Aria a dead ringer for someone planted into my life. "Now, why the fuck has a group meeting unfolded inside my bedroom?"

"Aine's body vanished from the crypt in the last hour. The guard was rendered unconscious after getting his cock sucked outside of the gate by a witch. When Siobhan left, she took most of our powerful witches."

"Aria couldn't have set it up. She's never been out of eyesight, not even as she prepared for the wedding. One of us has always watched her. Greer was with her inside that tent, cloaked beneath the spell Bekkah used on him. He reported nothing, and you know Greer would if he'd thought something was off. I'm guessing her family attempted to take her back, unknowingly choosing a place where the dark witches were. I don't think Aria's family would do this, considering the morbidity displayed. Aine may have allowed herself to be captured. She'd have hung the flags as a way of communicating with the other witches, who we weren't aware she had changed sides. Therefore, letting them know Kinvara was below for Aria. But I scented something else down there when Lennox had control. I smelled someone like Aria, which means there may be more of her kind out there."

"Speaking of witches, the dark witches have yet to leave the cliffs. More have shown up. We're officially stuck in this stronghold unless you and your mate can get us out," Killian admitted, sitting in the chair beside me, staring at me.

"Spit it the fuck out, Killian. I know you're going too, eventually." I stood and poured us both drinks as he frowned.

"Liliana wasn't just nothing, Knox."

Exhaling, I sat across from Killian, folding my hands on top of the table, nodding. "Agreed. Liliana was my wife and the love of my life. Lennox claimed Aria, not me. Sven was my son and my entire world."

"Then why the fuck does that girl have your teeth marks on her throat when you never even attempted to do the same to my sister?" Killian slammed his hands on the table as his jaw ticked.

"I tried to claim her, and she begged me to stop. Liliana was delicate. You want to know the difference between them, Kill? Do you want to know the fucking truth? Aria is bare-bones, fucking raw, and she throws down against me. Liliana couldn't handle me in bed, and I respected that. My bite repulsed Liliana, and she sobbed before my teeth ever touched her flesh. Aria comes undone when I bite her. I changed who I was for your sister. I didn't push her, nor did I force her into anything that would make her feel uncomfortable. Me, the fucking King, didn't sleep with anyone else even though I could have easily. I slept with your sister ten times in two hundred years." Killian's throat bobbed, and I snorted, knowing he wouldn't have done the same.

"I don't know if Aria is my mate or if someone has planted some very powerful bait in front of my nose. I don't trust Aria or anything about her. Hell, I married Aria to claim her for a throne and to be able to access her magic. We still don't know who the hell wanted her alive, or if it's someone who is planning to fucking double-cross us. What I do know is this; she's mine now, married and mated, even if it is one-sided. No one within the Nine Realms can argue it or offer her safe harbor from me. This shit was supposed to be easy. I was supposed to walk into Haven Falls, kill the strongest Hecate witch, return here, and fuck shit up. Instead, she fucking rattled, and I hesitated. Tell me you wouldn't have done the same fucking thing," I demanded, watching as Killian rubbed his eyes.

"I hate that I don't fucking hate the bitch," Killian snapped, downing his drink as Brander and Lore echoed his statement. "She fucking cries when strangers die. She sings to babes that she doesn't even know and has water fights with children. Who the fuck does that? Aria's a Hecate witch. They're supposed to be cunts that are easy to hate."

"You're pissed because you *don't* hate Aria?" I clarified.

"I hate that Aria makes you laugh, which is something you have not done in a very long time. I hate that she's so easily likable. That she can make that cankerous asshole, Greer, into putty while calling him Meat Suit. I hate that she isn't a bitch that I can hate," Killian grumbled, refilling the glasses.

"Killian, you're supposed to be the one asshole in the bunch who wouldn't let us forget who she was. You failed me, my friend. It still doesn't change what happened. During this slaughter, her family was here, and I will not lie to the heads of the rebellion about it, not for a Hecate witch. The Kenley's have fallen, and they were some of our oldest allies. The part of their army that had remained here to defend the stronghold is missing. Siobhan, who knows too fucking much, is in the hands of Aurora Hecate. That in itself is rather worrisome considering I never thought it would be Siobhan who betrayed us."

"Why? Because you fucked her once?" Brander scoffed.

"No. Because her tongue was guarded against lying to me or any of you assholes," I admitted, narrowing my eyes on Brander as he crossed his arms.

"What if Aria wasn't planted or created to be the perfect bait, brother? What if she's just a girl born into a bad bloodline?" he asked, turning to level me with a questioning gaze.

"It doesn't change anything. Aria is a puppet queen, one that I intend to sit on the Throne of Vãkya and rule through. Once Ilsa is out of the way, the dark witches will challenge Aria's right to the throne, and they will fall by our blades, which will be waiting for them. As my wife, I am entitled to her lands, her throne, and her bed. I can defend her by any means necessary."

"And if you create life, Knox? What happens to your children?" Brander countered, sitting beside Aria as he stared at me.

"I can't create life, Brander."

"Forget your ghosts for a moment, brother. It's just us now. Your brothers and your best friend," Brander growled, challenging me. "What happens if you or Lennox can place a babe into Aria's belly? Will your son or daughter rule the Nine Realms, or would you treat them the same as their mother?"

"Aria can't even figure out how to open her damn womb or return the mark, brother. Your point is fucking useless."

"You don't know that she doesn't need to open it, Knox. You don't even know what the fuck she is; none of us do!" Brander stood, moving to the table to lean over it. "That's a fucking nest that she is in right now. Aria has spent over two weeks being fucked by you and you alone. She's breeding. We can all smell it on her. Maybe she can't open her womb because it's already fucking open. Maybe Aria can't return the mark because she isn't like us. Now think about this. Aria is a Hecate witch, and your child will be a Karnavious prince or princess. Hell, you'll probably get two kids out of the deal, considering her bloodline. I doubt you'll get a fucking son, though, since he'd be born dead," Brander hissed, and I lunged, punching him as he hit my back.

"Fuck you!" I snarled, turning as Aria sat up, peering over at us with a raised brow. I had Brander's shirt twisted in my hand with my fist inches from his face. He had his claws into my shoulders, moving to knee me in the nuts. And the moment she rose, everyone in the room paused.

"Morning," she whispered huskily.

"Morning, Aria," everyone said, waiting for her to freak out over her markings or the boxing match in the room. Her fingers slid to her neck, and she smiled, slowly stretching to yawn.

The room went silent as we waited for the hysterics or some indication that she realized the mark's meaning. Instead, she smiled, pulling the sheet up tightly around her body. Her teeth worried her lip as her smile dropped, and her eyes closed.

"Please tell me you didn't bury Aine. She isn't dead." Aria opened her eyes, and I narrowed my gaze on her. Did she know Aine's plan and how her body had suddenly vanished?

"Of course we buried her. In a few years, we will check to see her recovery process," I lied, choosing not to reveal that Aine's body was gone. I slowly moved to the bed to sit beside her as she grimaced. "Aria, it will take your sister some time to heal."

"It wasn't just hemlock in that fountain, and Aine wasn't part of the crap that happened here," she said softly, searching my face. "My sisters were trying to get me out because you're a little unstable and very unpredictable, Knox. And while I'm being honest, you're a huge fucking asshole that bit my throat like a caveman trying to mark his territory. You might as well have peed on my leg." Lore chuckled, causing my attention to swing to him before he went silent.

I turned, finding everyone in the room covering their mouths to hide the humor they found at my expense. Frowning, I looked back to see Aria staring at the bed she'd rearranged every time she prepared to take me. She sniffed it, smiling as she slowly righted the blankets back into order. Looking around the room, I noticed everyone watching intently as she leaned over to sniff the sheets again.

"What are you doing?" I asked, unable to look away from her nesting.

Aria turned, smiling at me before her eyes narrowed, slowly sliding back to the blankets. She backed up without warning, forcing me to catch her before she toppled from the bed. Aria tilted her head at different angles and then slowly exhaled.

"I have no freaking idea what I am doing. It smells—right. It isn't right, though. It's…" Aria leaned over, pushing the sheet further across before tipping her head. "Yup, I'm bat-shit-crazy and obsessing over sheets."

"What's not right about it, Aria?" Brander asked softly.

"It's not filled."

"Filled with what?" Killian asked, and Aria smiled as she faced away from them, staring at the bed.

"Bones. It needs bones and your hearts," she whispered, turning to look at them as they backed up. "I'm totally fucking with you, assholes. I honestly don't know what it's missing." Aria leaned back into my arms, and I swallowed, smiling as the men exhaled in relief.

"If you want, wife," I whispered against her ear, "I can get you some bones. You can add them to your nest, and then we can invite my brothers and Killian over for dinner?"

"Well, I mean, your gifts so far have sucked," she snorted, leaning over to push the blanket again. "I need a bath," she announced, turning to stare at me, her gaze lowering to my neck with heat burning in her eyes.

"See something you want?"

"Nope," she chuckled. "I'm going to pass and take a bath if I can. I smell like you, and it's annoying my senses and making me act strangely and a little crazy. So, can I wash my vagina that you've apparently enjoyed a lot, *husband*?"

"You don't like my scent?" I hated the way she'd said husband while insulting me. I was the High King, yet she acted as if I was just another man. It was unnerving and endearing. I *wanted* her to like my scent.

"I like it, but I'm covered in it, Knox. Like, I'm starting to wonder exactly how I am covered in it, ya know. I barely recall having sex, but I feel like we had a *lot* of it. Like, I'm sore in all the right places." Aria leaned over, which caused Lore to fall out of his chair as her mouth slid against mine hungrily. "I think I need to be sorer, Knox. Like now," she hissed, and I rattled, pressing her down onto her nest as I freed myself, pushing into her body as the men watched.

"Out!" I shouted, moaning as her body clenched around mine. She purred in an erotic tone, finishing me off before they'd even exited the room. I vaguely registered a collective groan, sliding my gaze to where my men stood, staring down at their pants and then at Aria.

"What the fuck did she just do to my dick!" Lore cried, bending over as he placed his hands on his knees. "That's never happened to me before!"

A quick glance at Brander and Killian told me that

whatever Aria had done, it had finished four alphas off from her soft purr without needing to touch them. It tempered my pride, but it raised more questions than it answered.

"She purred, and the entire room came?" Killian asked. "That's not going to help me hate her any."

"Try," I hissed, staring down into turquoise eyes that smiled up at me as golden flecks danced within them once more. "Aria?"

"Yeah?" She rocked her hips as if she were waiting for more.

"Just checking that Ember wasn't here," I lied, staring into her eyes.

"Are you telling me you don't know the difference?" Aria scoffed, pulling the sheet around her as she lifted, nipping my lip. "Don't answer that. I need a bath; a very hot one."

"Have a bathhouse prepared for the queen. I'll be joining her," I called out to the attendants waiting in the hall, watching the fire burn in her eyes, unable to look away as Lennox studied her.

"She's not like us, Knox. She's—so much more."

Chapter Forty-Six

Aria

The bathing room was a large in-ground pool that spread the entire length of the room. The water, heated by coal, also filled the room with steam that eased my aches, of which I had many. Knox sat alone in the corner of the pool. His arms were spread wide in a relaxed pose as he watched me wash my body with a cloth covered in rose-scented soap.

"You know, if you remove all of my scent, I'm going to need to replace it, Little Monster," Knox chuckled, lifting his head to give me a sexy, heated stare that caused my core to clench.

"I don't think there's enough soap in all the Nine Realms to wash you off of me, Knox," I snorted, moving towards him as I placed the soap aside and reached for his.

"Who are you?" he whispered as I reached him.

"I am the calm to your chaos. Who are you?"

"I am the storm to your shelter that keeps me warm," he answered, yanking my body against his, smiling as he brushed his lips against my throat.

"How does that even work? I didn't want to say it, but I couldn't stop the words, as if compelled. I didn't even know what I was going to say until it was said," I admitted, blushing.

Knox's hands drifted down my sides, gripping my hips and pulling me against him. Slowly, he kissed my throat again, dragging his mouth along my collarbone to kiss my shoulder.

"No one knows exactly how it happens. There's a legend that states when a man and a woman are meant to be together, everything would fall into place, including their words to one another," he chuckled as if finding what he'd said amusing.

"Everything would just fall into place?"

"It's a legend, Aria. One that mothers used to tell their sons and daughters." Knox leaned his head back against the marbled edge of the pool, relaxing.

"So, it's a fairytale?" I whispered, lowering my lips to his neck as my fangs slid through my gums.

The moment my lips brushed against his throat, he trembled. His hand lifted, holding my mouth against the pulse that beat rapidly. His cock rubbed against my belly, and I placed a soft kiss against his pulse, licking the flesh to numb it as every instinct I had told me to claim him. Knox hissed as my tongue traced his skin, learning the curve of his neck. My hands leisurely slid around his shoulders, pushing my fingers through his hair, baring his steady pulse to my mouth. I opened my lips, sucking against his vein as he purred loudly. I began to sink my teeth into his throat when feet sounded, forcing me to pull back and swallow as he rattled, watching me.

"Don't stop, Aria," he whispered, barely loud enough to be heard, but we were no longer alone. Others stood at the door, waiting to assist us from the bathing room.

I leaned over, kissing his throat before I left his lap, starting toward the stairs that led out of the pool. Knox grabbed my neck, pulling me back in a fluid motion that brought my lips against his, and he lifted me, kissing me soundly like I was the oxygen that fed his lungs.

He still trembled, causing me to smile as I took what he gave. He pushed into my sex, and I cried his name against his mouth. I purred softly as he set my body on the edge of the pool, driving into it with dark desire rushing through both of us. The only sound within the bathing room was flesh meeting flesh, and the combination of our noises as he drove his cock into me, mercilessly.

Knox pulled back, staring down at me with a longing I couldn't quite grasp, burning in his oceanic depths. He smiled, kissing my throat as he brought my body back into the pool, then walked me toward the stairs, slipping his large hand around mine.

I stared at his firm backside, smiling until the room flooded with feminine scents. Women moved into the room with Knox standing naked, grabbing towels to dry his body. I rattled loudly, my teeth slipped from my gums, and the sound escaping my lips wasn't friendly in the least bit. I watched the women through narrowing slits as they dropped the clothing and drying towels and ran from the room.

Inhaling the air, I scrunched my nose at their offensive odors and turned to find Knox smiling like an idiot. I reached down to the pile of towels, smelling them, unable to stop myself. Once I'd found one that didn't reek of their scent, I moved toward him and frowned.

"I guess I will dry you off, since I was offended by their scent." Knox's smile grew, and he leaned over, kissing my shoulder as his body shook with laughter. "It isn't funny, Knox. I was very rude to them, and I couldn't stop myself."

"It's basic instinct, Aria. You're young, and your instincts drive you during your heat cycle. I was over six hundred years old before I met my mate. I responded the same when any male was near Liliana." I shoved the towel at Knox before grabbing my clothes and towel, stomping off to put distance between us as his stare burned a hole in my spine.

Drying my body, I dressed into the blood-red dress I'd chosen to wear. Slowly brushing my hair, I worked it into a braid, carefully tucking it into a bun to leave my neck bare. Turning, I found Knox standing next to me, silently watching as I did my hair. He didn't apologize, nor did I expect it from him.

He offered me a tight smile before he led us out of the bathing room and back to the bedroom we'd barely left since arriving.

My heart squeezed with the idea that Knox's men had buried Aine and that she was probably very much aware of that fact. I'd brought up the need to see her body as an excuse to get her exhumed from the ground, but Knox had explained that she wouldn't even be aware that they buried her for a few years.

We entered the bedroom to find Bekkah naked and sitting inside the sheets I'd spent all morning arranging. My body trembled, watching as she pushed her curves out, turning to smile shyly at Knox.

"I am here as requested, My King," Bekkah whispered, running her hand down her abdomen as I fought the urge to rip her apart.

Blood pounded through my ears, deafening her words as she continuing speaking. Claws pushed through my fingertips, and my teeth shot through my gums. My body vibrated with anger, causing Knox to turn and stare at me before his eyes moved back to Bekkah.

"Get out," he demanded, moving to the bed to toss her clothing at her.

Bekkah rubbed her body again, touching the bedding before slowly bending over, exposing her apex to Knox's gaze. My nails slid through the flesh of my palms as my vision filled with rage. Bekkah's eyes lifted, holding mine with a victorious smile, as she slipped the dress on and moved to the door.

"I am available whenever you desire, My King," Bekkah said huskily, sliding out of the room before my rattle exploded, and I rushed to the bed.

I ripped the bedding up, sniffing it as tears pricked my eyes. I pulled it from the bed, slicing through every blanket and then the bed itself until feathers exploded into the air. I sobbed at the wrongness of the bed, the contamination of the space I'd created for *us*. Bekkah defiled it with her sickening scent, ruining what I'd built. Voices sounded near me, but I couldn't stop as violence echoed through every fiber of my being. The need to destroy what Bekkah had tarnished and tainted, drove me into a murderous rage.

Once everything was in tatters, and nothing remained of the bed or the sheets, I stepped back, meeting Knox's worried stare through the feathers that still wafted in the air. I inhaled deeply, tilting my head before I wiped away the tears and huffed.

"What did the bed ever do to you?" Lore asked, and I turned, finding all the men standing up against the wall as if they feared getting too close to me.

"It smelled like rotten whore and all the men she'd fucked in the last twenty-four hours. It was supposed to be pure and smell like Knox and me, and no one fucking else!" I shouted, enraged that Bekkah had destroyed it.

The bed creaked and broke in the middle as the wood gave way. Knox's eyes slid from the demolished bed to lock with mine. His expression was worried, as if he wasn't sure how to respond to my reaction. I chewed my trembling lip, and tears burned my eyes, pricking them with heat as my failure bubbled up, tightening my chest.

"Aria?" Knox whispered, moving his attention to the others inside the room as if they could offer help to my reaction.

"I failed," I whispered thickly.

"Failed what?" he asked carefully.

"I don't know. I just know I failed to protect it from

Bekkah and her scent," I returned. "It's insane. Right? It's not even fucking logical."

"We can move to a new room," Knox stated while offering me a reassuring smile.

"What do you need, Aria?" Brander asked, forcing my attention to him.

"Sheets, pillows, and Knox," I muttered, watching as Knox's lips curled into a disarming grin. He moved around the bed, picking feathers out of my hair before leaning over and kissing the top of my head. "I'm losing my sanity, aren't I?"

"No, you're not losing your sanity. You're nesting, which is normal for most female creatures in heat. When we fail to produce a child, this need will no longer be present."

"And if we make a baby?" I countered, watching the tic that started in his jaw.

"You'd worsen," he answered, watching me as I nodded.

"Because I'd make a nest for us, and our child—like I'm a freaking bird?" I noted the anger in his gaze, and clamped my mouth closed before it ended in an argument or worse, violence considering my short fuse. "Okay, thank you for answering even though you didn't want to, Knox. It's a lot easier to cope when I understand that my actions aren't actually me losing my mind and going insane."

His features softened as he nodded slowly. "Greer, you can stop hiding behind the door now. Aria needs help securing the items she will need to make us a new—bed.

Have the guards remove this one, or what is left of it, and the witches can remove the mess," Knox instructed until I rattled, shaking my head. "No?"

"I'll clean it and get rid of the wreckage. I'd rather not have anyone else's scent inside our space if it's okay? It sounds crazy, but it's important."

Knox exhaled, smiling tightly. "Brander, Killian, Lore, a little help here."

The men started purring together, and Knox rattled, raking his fingers through his hair as he threw them an angry glare. I lifted on my tiptoes, pulling out the feather in Knox's hair, which caused him to purr along with his men. Knox settled his hands on my hips as he leaned his forehead against mine, brushing his lips softly against my mouth.

"I meant help with the bed, assholes. For now, Aria is rather easy to handle when all she wants to do is..." I kissed him hard, cutting his words off, feeling his lips curling into a smile against my mouth. His hand rose, cupping my cheek as he rattled low and sexy from his chest.

Knox and his men moved the pieces of the bed out of the room before they vanished. Greer and I made quick work of the bedroom, filling it with freshly laundered sheets and blankets. I spent hours rearranging the bedding until something shook the castle, causing my hackles to rise. The sounds of heavy footfalls filled the hallway, making Greer and I turn, tilting our heads as what sounded like explosions filled the night air.

The door slammed open, and I jumped, baring my teeth until I realized it was Knox. He glared at me, and my stomach flip-flopped. He didn't enter the room. Instead, he stood in the doorway, his eyes cold and filled with murderous rage. My heart dropped as he shook his head slowly.

"I found your sister Luna, which I'm guessing is who took Aine from the crypt where I placed her days ago. Luna is attacking us, and she is standing beside Ilsa, who has this castle surrounded by her army. Dimitri said that your family was working with the high queen, but I chose not to believe they would be capable of the atrocities that Ilsa left in her wake. Yet, your sister is standing beside her, Aria. You kept me distracted as they surrounded us, and now you'll watch them die. Give me your hands," he snapped, and when I didn't move fast enough, Knox grabbed me, yanking me out of the stupor his words had caused. I watched him placing a second pair of cuffs onto my wrists, clanging against the spelled ones I already wore. "You almost fooled me, wife. Too bad they fucked up and made you too good to be true."

Knox yanked me with him, dragging me down the hallway, past the guards who glared at me in loathing. He marched me through the empty great hall and into the chilled night air as he forced me up the stairs, onto the battlements. Once I was standing in the middle of the stone walkway, he secured the cuffs to a large chain attached to the stone wall.

"I hope you enjoy the show, *wife*," he snorted, turning to leave me standing there, alone.

My eyes slid out over the large force that covered the cliffside and spread deeper into the forest around the fortress. Upon a great warhorse sat Luna, and beside her on another warhorse was a black-haired witch who stared out over the troops surrounding the castle, preparing to defend it with their lives. Nausea swirled through me as Luna lifted her eyes, smirking coldly, when she found me watching her. Her dark head tilted, and she slowly lifted her fingers to her lips, blowing me a kiss before her attention returned to the army with her.

I swallowed past bile that pushed at my throat, my body trembling with fear. Ilsa was here, and so was Luna. Worse than that, mixed into the high queen's forces were unwanted beasts, which meant Gerald's army had a new leader, Garrett.

I searched the sea of monsters, finding Garrett's larger form standing back, hidden in the shadows, staring up at me as if he'd known where I would be. Ice rushed through me, and I shivered violently as unwelcomed memories ran through me. I closed the emotions off, dismissing them, shoving them back into the box where the bad things I didn't have time to deal with went.

Why was Luna with Ilsa? Didn't she see the black teeth or the poisonous magic Ilsa used? Not that it mattered. Knox was about to destroy them, and I would be forced to watch it all unfold from my perch on the battlements. On the outer wall, below me, sat archers, dipping arrows into liquid hemlock, which they angled toward the sky before lowering them, aiming for the army of witches.

I slid my eyes to the warriors in the courtyard, finding Knox looking up at me through cold eyes that sent a tremor of unease rushing down my spine. I pulled on my wrists, but the chains only tightened. The humming sensation of magic slithered over me, forcing my attention to the east side of the keep.

Beside the castle, far enough out of sight from the ground, sat a power grid compiled of dead bodies covered in dirt. I frowned, noting that most of the deceased were missing their skulls and had stomach wounds. Then I noticed scores of unwanted beasts pulling wagons containing massive crystal formations around the stronghold's perimeter.

I could feel the vibrations radiating from the quartz, realizing they were using the crystals to ensure that witches would be the only ones able to cast magic. My attention whipped back to Ilsa, who smiled at me coldly. She was going to kill us all because she was using the grids to fuel her dark power, amplifying the magic beyond what any witch should be capable of wielding. And with the crystals, Knox wouldn't be able to use his magic to fight her.

Ilsa was going to kill Knox, and I was helpless but to watch it unfold. I looked down at my hands, frowning as the realization hit me. Closing my eyes, I whispered to the monster within, knowing the only way to end this was to inflict pain by removing the head of the snake before she removed the head of my mate.

"Ember, I need you right now. I need you to help me save Knox from himself," I whispered, feeling her stretching within me. "Ilsa will kill them all. We can't allow that. I need him to live. If he dies, our plan fails."

"And it would be a waste of a good dick."

"That too," I agreed.

"You need me to do what exactly?" Ember asked, staring out over the armies marching toward one another.

"I need you to remove my thumbs so that I can free

my hands."

"I'm not that *hungry, Aria,"* she snorted, looking at my hands through our shared vision. *"This is going to hurt you."*

"It will hurt a lot less than losing Knox, Ember. We need him for our plan to work, remember? You and I made a plan, and if we fail, this world will fall to the dark witches. Evil will rule, and no one will be safe from what rises from the ashes. If the high king falls in battle, the goddess will rise from her tomb. Hecate cannot rise because she wouldn't rest until every Hecate witch in the line is lying cold and dead in her tomb. She would use us as her grid to refuel and remake the Nine Realms into the barren wasteland she intended it to be when we put her down five hundred years ago without the world knowing it was us."

Battle drums sounded as a horn blared. The armies began moving toward one another faster, rushing into battle as their forces collided, and the tang of blood filled the air. I watched Knox, following him as he swung his blade through the men rushing toward him. He was ruthless, dispatching enemies as he fought to get to Ilsa, who dismounted from the horse on which she sat. Luna followed beside her, rushing toward Knox as they moved their fingers in sync, working together to ignite the power grid that began glowing.

"Now, Ember," I demanded. "They're going to kill our mate!"

Chapter Forty-Seven

Pain ripped through me as I removed my thumb with my teeth. One thumb and I was on my knees, screaming in pain. Ember purred as if she could comfort herself over my screaming. She moved toward the other one, ripping it off, which added to the blinding pain causing nausea to roll through my stomach. I pulled on my hands, forcing them through the cuffs Knox placed onto my wrists, knowing I was without magic, but I wasn't without my monster.

"We have to reach the grid, Ember. We have to disturb the power source. If we don't, Ilsa will unleash the power it is feeding her, and we will lose Knox forever."

"Give me control!" Ember demanded. Standing, I stared down at the blood dripping from where my thumbs had been. *"We will heal eventually."*

"Don't let them hurt Knox. He is stupid and broken, but he is our stupid, broken male."

"On it," Ember said, shoving me into the backseat as we zipped into the jetstream.

Ember moved into the shadows, watching the dark witches standing around the grid, protecting it. Ember didn't mess around, using her speed to move through the clearing like lightning, snatching one witch away from the others without making a single sound.

The moment Ember was within the forest's protection, she snapped her head from her neck, tossing it over her shoulder. Turning, she stared out at the other witches, watching them look around as they realized one was missing. They slowly stepped away from the circle, and when they began separating from one another, Ember took out another, and then another until only one witch remained.

Ember slammed into her, using eight claws to cut through flesh and bone to remove her head. I winced inwardly as she spun, staring at the mutilated bodies. Ember grabbed a foot from a body on the grid, pulling it away from the pattern. Nothing happened. The grid continued to pulse with power, even though Ember had disturbed the connection and pattern. She canted her head, assessing the problem and computing it on the fly. Taking control of the corpses, they mimicked her movements, pausing when she got to the magic source in the center of the grid.

Aine sat in the middle of the grid. Only she wasn't a corpse. In fact, her flesh was completely healed, along with her beautiful face. Ember dropped beside my sister, slapping her cheeks, but nothing happened. She picked Aine up, snapping her neck, and I gasped the moment she tossed Aine to the ground like she was just another body instead of my beloved sister.

"She is powerful, feeding the one who wishes to murder our dicker. Now, she cannot feed them her magic."

"I don't think that's all they intended to use her for, Ember." I noted Aine's naked body no longer held the protection runes to prevent Hecate from rising. *"They're trying to raise Hecate. Why would anyone want her alive?"* I whispered more to myself but still got an answer.

"They are stupid, obviously," Ember replied, shrugging nonchalantly like it was a dumb question that got a silly answer.

The sound of swords crashing together filled the air, and Ember zipped toward it. Stopping in the middle of the fray, she looked left and right, settling on the largest male who had just removed the head from the body of a witch.

Slowly, Ember stalked toward Knox as he continued slicing witches into two parts. Swords swung at us, and she ducked, sliding beneath them, laughing like it was a game. Luna came into sight, wielding her magic toward Knox, forcing him to deflect it. Shocked, I watched him try to pull magic from the Nine Realms, but what he got was weak and limited. His realm magic wasn't like mine since I could draw and use endless power, tapping into its source like a lifeline.

The crystals were doing their job since only the witches were casting. Then I noticed Knox wiggle his fingers, and the marks on his witches ignited, called upon by his power, giving him the strength to aid him in this battle. My heart thundered in my chest, and I swallowed past the shock of him drawing magic from them. He wasn't a witch, though. He was something—*else*. But it wouldn't be enough against Ilsa and Luna.

Knox's deflection of magic was precise, displaying learned, skillful movements that sparked the power, amplifying it. He was reaching for the magic of the dark witches now, taking it by force. I realized he was going to use their power against them. Knox was a conduit that captured and reflected their power, which explained why he hadn't just ended the war the moment he'd started it. It also explained why he didn't seem concerned about the crystals, since he could still wield a witch's magic without actually being a witch. Knox only needed to get close enough to gain some of their powerful magic to use against his enemies; hence why he'd wanted me.

Sure, all immortals could pull some power from the Nine Realms that was readily available. They couldn't, however, use it as we did. It was a Catch 22. They had access, but not the strength or ability to use it past the basics.

Ilsa and Luna were edging Knox away from his men, sending in monsters to separate them. I dodged a sword, sliding through one corpse before I landed on another, pausing when I realized Ember wasn't in control anymore. My stare slid to the edges of the field where witches formed a barrier, holding large crystals that pulsed with magic.

They were forcing the men to fight as humans! *Shit!* I lifted my gaze, staring at Ilsa, who smiled, revealing black teeth and gums. Her hands were missing fingers from the rot of being dark for too long, literally wasting away to nothing. All I had to do was reach Ilsa before she got to Knox. Pushing from the ground, I moved silently to where she stood as she withdrew a sword from a scabbard that pulsed with magic, spelled not to miss its mark.

Power slithered through the clearing in front of the stronghold, and I moved into action as Ilsa lifted the sword, fueling it with more magic. Ember's power was dormant, held hostage by the crystals that were forcing us to remain human, and the bracelets Knox had placed on me to protect his people had weakened my magic.

Exhaling, I slowed my heart as weapons clanged near me. Swords swung, forcing me to move as the air displaced beside me. A warrior lunged, his mangled face grotesque, mirroring a combination of warthog and man. I danced out of his reach, sliding toward one of Knox's warriors who swung at me, his eyes cold and dripping hatred as he moved to strike again, even as the unwanted beast warrior did the same.

I ducked as one swung his blade cutting through the air. Dropping to my back, I rolled through blood and gore to escape them. They followed me as other swords swung toward them, rendering them both headless as they fought. I stood slowly, staring at where Ilsa crept toward Knox, who was holding Luna's magic at bay, forcing her backward, leaving him exposed to the blade Ilsa was about to swing toward him.

I rushed forward without magic or the strength of my beast. The only sound that entered my ears was the blood pumping through my veins as I ran blindly toward Knox. Men fought around me as heads rolled across the ground, forcing me to jump over them or chance tripping.

No one sensed me because I held nothing that could hurt them. Ilsa stepped behind Knox, lifting the blade to swing, and I screamed, rushing the last step to jump onto her back. I felt Ember adding what strength she could manage. My nails lengthened, and I wrenched Ilsa's head from her shoulders. Knox spun around, staring at me until he realized who stood in front of him.

He lunged, sliding his sword through Ilsa's chest as I fell backward. My gaze slid to Luna, who glared at me, then moved her attention to the group of sightless witches, who dropped the crystals that had forced the men to remain human. Luna tossed a crystal on the ground, and a portal exploded in front of her. She smiled coldly at me, lifting her fingers to her lips before she stepped through, vanishing.

Knox's attention moved from Luna to me and then to where his men were dispatching the last of the beasts. The dark witches left behind shimmered and then slowly turned to ash, proving they were tied to Ilsa. Knox lifted his blade, moving toward me, and I closed my eyes, preparing for him to take my head. I whispered the prayer that would see me reborn and then peered up at him as the blade swung over my head, showering me with blood as something thumped against the ground.

Knox stared down at me, then lowered to his haunches and grabbed my hands. He held one up to inspect as his men formed a circle around us. I exhaled in relief, dropping my head back as he wiped the blood away from my cheek.

"You removed your fucking thumbs?" Knox's voice was tense and filled with rage.

"There was a power grid in the clearing. If Ilsa had

accessed it, she'd have been unbeatable. I build you up when others reach to tear you down, and I'll take their spines to wear as my fucking crown." I sagged onto the ground, holding my wounded hands closer to my body. "I am your mate."

"Check and verify that there are bodies placed onto a grid," Knox snapped.

"They're—well, Ember sorta threw them everywhere to break the grid down. Aine is there, Knox. Her body was used to feed the grid. They removed her runes, which means she can become a host for Hecate. They were here for you, not me. I believe they're attempting to raise the Goddess of Magic."

"Find that body, now," Knox growled, pulling me up from the ground as a shriek sounded, forcing him to spin with me in his arms.

A hooded witch moved into the clearing, screeching until my ears threatened to bleed. She pushed her hood back, and the noise ended. Her black eyes opened and leveled on me.

"You have not displaced the High Queen of Vākya," she hissed, her eyes oozing black liquid.

"You are mistaken. Aria is the new High Queen of Vākya. She defeated Ilsa." Knox's tone was firm, holding all the authority of the high king.

"Aria didn't defeat the high queen. She merely fought a puppet which is what you intended to make your wife, King Karnavious. A Hecate witch sits upon her rightful place as High Queen of Vākya as we speak."

Knox's fingers bit into my skin as he glared down at

me in anger. His eyes lifted and narrowed on the witch who watched us, smiling coldly at his response.

"Aurora Hecate isn't strong enough to hold that throne, witch," Knox sneered.

"Agreed, but it is not her of whom I speak."

"The others are not stronger than Aria either. She is a blood-born Hecate witch, and she is the most powerful one within the Nine Realms. Aria is heir to that throne."

"Aria isn't stronger than the Hecate witch who sits upon the throne, sweet king."

"She is the daughter of Freya Hecate. She is a third generation of the bloodline. We will take that throne from whoever sits upon it."

"The high queen disagrees with you and found your whore unworthy of the name she carries. She thanks you for removing it from her," the witch laughed as Knox let me down.

"There are no other Hecate witches alive inside the Nine Realms," I whispered, staring at the witch.

"Ask your husband how many heads sit upon his throne, Aria. He murdered your mother and her sister, yet you spread your legs for him, oh so willingly. He abused you, has treated you like the trash you are, and you still allowed him to claim you as his bride, giving him your power to wield against your people? You belong with him, but you will never sit on the throne of Vākya. We will never allow it, choosing to leave you to your fate. King Karnavious has told you of your brilliance, but you're not even smart enough to see the truth staring you right in the face. He intended to murder you for the magic that runs through your veins. He only had to claim you as his mate to do so. He took you as his wife as an easy way to get the throne and to make the witches bend their knee to you. Your days are numbered, traitor. When Hecate rises, she'll come for your head first; you, who betrayed the line, and your husband, who declared war upon her daughters," she laughed soundlessly. "I'd bless you, but you're fucked." The witch threw down a crystal, and her body burned. I turned away, closing my eyes from the carnage of the incineration spell as it claimed a life.

A soldier approached the burning witch behind me, reflecting in his eyes. He swallowed the bile at the sight of burning flesh that singed, smothering the air with the putrid scent.

"There are no bodies of any witches in the woods, My King," he announced.

Knox turned, staring at him before he looked at me with something worrisome burning in his stare.

"The forgotten witch," I whispered. "Kamara vanished and was forgotten."

"Indeed, it would seem she's the only Hecate witch missing," he growled. "Brander, my wife seems to have harmed herself in battle. See that her hands are wrapped and treated. We wouldn't want her getting an infection, now would we?" he asked, stepping back as Brander moved into his place. Staring at my hands, Brander turned, watching Knox walk away from us.

"How did this happen?" he asked as Lore and Killian moved in closer.

"I removed one thumb with my teeth and ripped the other away to protect Knox from Ilsa," I admitted, watching Killian flinching before he turned to follow Knox. "I couldn't let her kill him. I couldn't stand there and watch him die, even knowing he intends to murder me."

"He doesn't intend to murder you, Aria. He intends to keep you as his pet. There's a difference. Besides, I know you watched him fight and did the math on his true nature."

"A conduit for magic," I swallowed, turning to see that Knox stopped, staring back at me as Brander held my bloodied hands. "He doesn't intend to wield me as a weapon. He needs me to fuel the weapon that he is by being able to direct an attack where he wants it, without having to place his people in danger."

"Let's get inside, away from the dead." Brander pulled me with him, and I locked eyes with the warrior who had knowingly tried to kill me.

Knox may not have intended to kill me, but his people did. According to the witches I'd met in camp, his people had suffered similar fates as Knox, beneath the witches' rule. All the Nine Realms hated us, which meant everyone wanted us dead.

Knox didn't avert his gaze, and I glared at him while walking past. I didn't even pretend to care that I pissed him off. I was used to it, so numb to the way he treated me that it didn't bother me anymore. I knew half of it was to protect himself, and the other half was because his enemies had eyes everywhere. The witch had given that away since Knox had never spoken about me being smart outside of when we were in private.

The more I studied him, the more I figured out most

of what he did was to guard himself and others being used against him. Witches utilized rodents and anything small to watch him through cracks in stone structures. I knew Knox fought what was happening between us, but how much of what he had done was to protect me? And how much pain had he meant to inflict?

Knox was the picture of broken. He had so many cracks it was hard to get through to him. But what if I had, and he was afraid to admit it? His enemies would use anything they could get their hands on against him.

I knew that because I was here to find his weaknesses, yet had I discovered any, I wouldn't have told a soul. I felt myself growing attached, and I knew I had no future with him. However, he'd bitten me, and I had felt that mating mark on my throat to the very center of my being. He felt it too, and that meant that if the rumors and shit going around were true about Liliana, I was his true mate.

I paused, causing Brander to stumble and turn to look at me. I slowly started forward, peeking back at Knox, who walked behind me. If Knox hadn't been true mates with Liliana, that meant we could create life. However, it probably wasn't the smartest thing to do during a time of war. He kept telling me to open my womb, but my womb didn't have some magic door. Ember had said we could only allow it to happen if we chose him as our mate. I wasn't even certain she knew what the hell she was talking about since we were the blind leading the even blinder. Unless Lennox had told Ember something she didn't want me to hear, in which case, I probably should figure out what it meant so I didn't do something stupid on accident.

Entering the castle, Brander walked me to where the

wounded were treated. He sat me down, tending to my hands as Knox appeared, leaning against the castle wall, observing until they were wrapped, leaving my fingers exposed.

"I need to know what you know about Kamara, wife."

"Nothing," I admitted. "There's nothing significant about Kamara in any books or anything the Hecate line has documented. She was said to be sweet and timid, and then she lost a set of twin boys, and no one has heard from her since. They assumed she went mad and found someone to end her suffering. I do know that out of all the sisters, Kamara was the most powerful."

"I was really hoping you wouldn't say that. Guess you're not the high queen, after all."

"No. It would seem I'm not on either throne," I snorted. "If you're finished, I'd like to rest. I'm sure you intend to move the army at first light, and I am rather exhausted from fighting in a weak human form to save your life."

I stared at Knox as he narrowed his eyes on me, dropping them to my wrists, which still held the nulling cuffs. He creased his brow, turning to look at Brander.

"Place the new cuff on her when you're finished tending to her wounds. See that Aria isn't disturbed and has what she needs to nest."

"I don't need a nest anymore," I whispered, moving past Knox. He turned, burning my spine with his gaze as I left him, wondering why I was upset.

Lennox was right to worry about me eating Knox.

Even if the things he did were for show, they hurt me. His actions proved to his people I was disposable, and they'd tried to make me as such today as I fought to protect their king and my husband from their enemy.

They could all get bent. I wasn't the evil in their midst, and I'd never given them a reason to hate me. This entire place needed a huge wake-up call if they thought the sins of the ancestors damned the line.

My sisters and I had killed no one out of spite. We hadn't harmed anyone inside the Nine Realms that wasn't dark. We hadn't even been born when the shit had happened, yet we were found guilty. It wasn't right. Not when we were fighting with Knox and his people, standing beside them—even if it was to the far right of them, or maybe the left.

Wherever we stood, I'd be fine as long as it was away from Knox Karnavious, at least until the war ended.

Chapter Forty-Eight

Knox gave me a necklace that did the same thing his magic nullifying bracelets had done. It was a simple chain holding a raven charm with a red jewel for the eye. We hadn't spent the night at the stronghold, forcing me to sit with him on his warhorse for grueling hours as we traveled through the perilous passes between one realm and another. As far as I'd been told, we were finally heading toward Dorcha.

Knox hadn't included me in his plans, and we'd been moving nonstop until some horses showed signs of exhaustion. I was beyond that point. The days it had taken to get through the passes had felt endless. I'd finally been allowed to ride a horse of my own with Knox and guards close by, but no one spoke to me since leaving the stronghold, not even Greer. I felt alone again, even though people surrounded me.

In the silence, I'd found more chaos than peace. I wanted to scream. I needed to shout. It felt as if everything was wrong. I was the enemy, so they treated me like I was just another witch in their army. Fear had spiked several times as guards cast curious gazes toward me, but Knox didn't rattle the warning he normally used to scare them off.

Worse than that, something was happening to me. My body had felt as if it were covered in pins and needles. Ember was silent, her mewling noises and grunts the only sign she was still within me. Today I felt like there was a fever burning inside me, itching to be set free. I would slide my eyes to Knox, and I'd watch him move on his large warhorse, hunger burning in my stare.

By the time we'd stopped to set up camp, I was pacing aimlessly while the men observed. I talked to my creature, asking her what the hell was happening, but she only groaned or moaned within me. I paused, stretching my back as the thing on my spine twitched, itching against my flesh.

There was violence within me that needed out in the worst way. I felt as if I was burning from within and filled with rage. My chest rose and fell, my breathing ragged and labored. I was about to explode, and I wasn't sure how to stop it from happening.

Lifting my nose, the scent of male filled my senses, and I growled, but it wasn't right. I was hungry but didn't want food. I wanted something more. I clasped my hands against my ears as my heartbeat echoed through my head, a steady drumbeat that forced me to look around for the source of the sound.

My attention moved around camp, settling on Knox, who grinned. *Bastard.* I purred low and huskily. My nails slid free, and I peered down at my blackened hands, rolling my eyes as my skin came alive. Knox rattled, and my gaze snapped up and zeroed in on him. I tilted my head to the side, and I smiled coldly. Knox reached down, lifting his shirt over the rows of sinewy muscles that drew my attention.

His scent made my feet move, but I stopped, forcing my body to remain in place. Knox lifted his hand, pushing it through his hair while I studied his slow movements. He lifted his nose to the air, and I mimicked it, unable to stop myself. His thumb trailed over his lips before I licked mine, watching the heat bank in his tranquil stare.

Knox dismissed me, walking toward the largest tent. My feet moved, inching me closer to him while his men followed. I wasn't stupid. They were there to stop me from going anywhere but where Knox wanted me to be. I entered the tent, finding him sitting in a chair, leaning forward.

He nodded toward a drink, watching me with something dark in his gaze. I moved closer, growling as his lips spread into a smirk.

"Drink. You're going to need it," he stated, nodding at the glass again.

"I don't like you," I pointed out, my hands fisted at my sides while I studied every curve of his body.

The smirk that jerked the corners of his mouth into a sexy curve pissed me off. Knox smelled like a man, primal, exotic masculinity that made something within me need to bury my nose against the rows of delicious muscle, inhaling him until I was drunk from it.

Knox studied me like I was an animal, which I felt to the very center of my being. My sex was soaked, clenching with hunger. I wanted to rip him apart while riding him. Something was happening, something animalistic that actually scared me. Sweat beaded on the back of my neck, and I felt it slowly rolling down my spine. My thighs clenched, causing Knox's pretty eyes to lower as his nostrils flared.

I sat in the chair, leaning back, shuddering from the heat burning through me. Knox turned, spreading his legs out in front of him while he studied my face. His thumb ran down the glass, rubbing over the moisture outside of it. My eyes followed his thumb, tracking the movement while his attention remained on my face.

Knox didn't speak more than that. He didn't argue with me when I'd told him I hated him. It was strange and unsettling. Warning flags were being erected, and they were bright red. I grabbed the glass, downing the drink in a hurried motion that made me gasp. Knox grabbed the bottle, refilling my cup without a word as his eyes roamed over my face.

Why wasn't he talking or threatening me? Why wasn't he doing *anything* other than pouring me a whiskey? Why did I feel like my skin was crawling, and everything was coming unhinged? I lifted my hand, pushing the stray hairs away from my sweat covered face, his eyes following them as I grabbed the whiskey, downing it.

Knox leaned forward, his scent assaulting me until I squirmed in the chair. My tongue jutted out of my mouth, licking my lips as his pupils dilated. Nostrils flared, and I stifled a moan that threatened to rip from my throat. He could smell my need as surely as I scented his.

Basic Animal Mating 101.

Predators tracked their prey, marking them and hunting them down by scent. My nipples hardened, and those sinfully blue eyes lowered to where they pressed against my restraining top. Unhurriedly, they settled back on my face, and I purred huskily, causing his smile to turn predatory.

"We're about to get pounced, Aria."

"Now you talk? I am going insane!" I snarled inwardly.

"Not insane. It's here—the last stage. Knox is aware and is just waiting for you to reach your breaking point. I must warn you. I feel—violent. *I think he knows what is coming and is allowing nature to take its course. I can barely contain the need to take control, and yet I feel trapped within you. I have never felt trapped. I feel— scared."*

"What? *Ember, you're never scared. Why would you be scared? What is happening? I feel like I'm about to combust and rip everything to pieces inside this place!"*

"Look at Knox," Ember instructed, and I did, peering at him with hunger burning in my eyes. Worse, he looked—*excited.* His tongue escaped his mouth, trailing over his lips before he sat forward, and both Ember and I flushed with need.

My back arched, and my body moved forward while inhaling his earthy masculine scent of sandalwood and citrus. His lips curved into a sinful smile that held my eyes stuck on their fullness. Lifting his glass, Knox licked the rim, and I swallowed past the tightening of need that swelled in my throat.

A droplet fell from the glass, landing on his stomach,

and I followed it down his chest. I tracked it until it met his pants, becoming absorbed into the material. My eyes didn't leave the V-line that sat exposed until I gradually brought my eyes back to his, glaring at him. I hated that he was perfection, with tattooed ink and hard, sinewy lines I wanted to bite and listen as he gasped.

I snatched my cup from the table, shaking as my body released a scent that made me wince. Knox's body released one of the same, and I moaned loudly, causing his eyes to grow heavily hooded. Where my scent was delicate, his was raw sex dripping with lust that made my eyes flutter. My womb clenched, begging to be bred like some cow on the farm. Okay, so not so much like a cow as per se a wolf who wanted the alpha to give her some pups. I felt like I was a monster, staring down her dinner, and he was about to be devoured.

"I don't like you," I repeated in a breathy tone.

"You don't have to like me to fuck me, Aria." I shivered before reaching up and tearing the dress from my body. Knox lowered his eyes to my naked breasts, and his jaw clenched before he slid them away.

I wanted to rip his eyes out for looking away from me. He'd spent days without me, forcing me to feel like nothing. I wanted to hurt him. I needed to rip him apart, shredding his skin until he fucking bled for me. Cracking my neck, he smirked, pissing me off even more. He lifted his fingers, trailing them over his throat, and my teeth pushed through my gums. Heat scorched me from his stare, and I forced my teeth back.

"Whatever happens next, Ember, we do not mark this prick. Shred him, rip him apart, fucking destroy him, but we don't put our teeth into him. Understand? If he

wants my fucking mark, he can earn it."

"Agreed."

"This is going to be bloody and violent, isn't it?" I asked in a hushed tone, as if I feared he would hear me.

"On your scale from one to ten, it's off the chart. Mating isn't sexy. It's a violent instinct, and I feel the need to rip Knox apart and take my mate out of him. I'm guessing we're about to fight him, and you're going to enjoy every moment of it, Aria. Go for his balls, please. For me. You owe me."

"I owe you? I got monster dick because you were too much of a sissy to take on Lennox, who, by the way, fucks like a ravaging monster and literally made me get stuck on his dick, simply because he could. Where were you again? Oh, yeah, hiding from that big ole dick like a little sissy while I rode it like a cowgirl showing off at a rodeo! I even walked like it afterward, and you never even tag-teamed in to give me a break!"

"I told you to run. Maybe listen next time. When a dick gives me pause, Aria, the answer is never to get up on that thing and ride it!"

"No, your answer was mother-fucking pineapple! Pineapple is never the answer to anything!"

Knox stood, walking toward his wooden chest, and my body moved without warning, standing silently behind him. He turned and then spun around, his eyes sliding from me to the chair in which I'd been sitting. His throat bobbed as he swallowed, and my eyes zeroed in on it. I'd left the dress in a heap on the ground with my movement. Knox opened his mouth, and I pushed him, watching him falling over the chest that pissed me off even more.

Knox rose, his eyes slipping to obsidian and then back to oceanic blue. His lips twisted, and his claws extended to match mine. I stepped back, studying the way his body filled out more. He strode forward, tracking me. My mouth opened, and he mimicked me, rattling thickly.

"It's about fucking time, woman," he snapped.

"I'm about to fuck your world up."

"Something's about to get fucked," he countered, and I lunged, but he caught me, slamming me down on the bed.

I remained there, watching Knox prowl around me while his eyes slowly slid down my body. He lowered his hands, and my eyes followed to where his thumb flicked the button on his pants, sliding them down to reveal the state of his arousal. He turned, blowing out the candle, enveloping us in darkness.

My eyes followed him easily, turning predatory while his glowed with the fire from within him. He leaped onto the bed, but I rolled and then slammed my elbow into his stomach the moment he turned to grab me. Springing to my feet, I crept closer while he lowered his head, rattling softly, causing my spine to arch with heat tightening in my belly.

"You want it rough?" he asked, and I laughed, but it wasn't friendly.

"I want your screams, asshole."

"One of us will be screaming, woman. You're about to find out who is alpha and who isn't."

The sound escaping my lips was hollow and empty.

Knox followed me, forcing me to maneuver around the chest and onto the bed. I needed extra room to move, but outside the tent were more of us, itching to join the fight we danced. He moved faster than I could track. Capturing my body, he slammed me against the bed and parted my legs. I lifted my nails, raking them down his chest as he howled in pain.

Knox captured my nails as my mouth lifted, sucking the blood from his chest. His entire body shuddered with the need for my teeth to sink into his flesh. He waited, and when the bite didn't come, he flipped me onto my belly, holding my hands behind my back. He pushed my legs apart and entered me hard and fast.

His mouth lowered, kissing over my shoulder before his tongue slid against it. His bite sent my body into a downward spiral as his serrated teeth sank into my shoulder. I bucked against him, forcing him to release my hands while he held me in place. I pushed my hands beneath me, and he growled huskily, releasing my arm to chuckle.

"Good girl. You play with that pussy for me, *fucking* bitch!" Knox snarled as my nails pushed into his thigh, nicking his balls. His hands gripped my arms, yanking them against my back as he unleashed hell against my body. "That was my fucking balls!" he snapped.

"They don't work!" I roared back, meeting his thrust with a violent need that shot through me.

One of his hands grabbed my wrists, forcing them higher up my back until it ached. His other hand grabbed my hair, yanking my head back, lifting me into the air. I was rag-dolled as he took what he wanted.

"You like that, don't you? Naughty little bitch," he snapped harshly, thrusting against me as I howled. My orgasm exploded, sending aftershocks echoing through me while he continued relentlessly slamming into my body. "Fucking take that dick, Aria," he demanded.

"Stop fucking me like a little bitch that just discovered a beat with his hips, and fuck me, asshole!" I screamed, freeing my hands from his to pierce my claws into his thighs as he howled in pain.

Knox yanked me up, shoving my legs against my shoulders. One hand grabbed mine, capturing them above my head as his other slammed sharply against my ass. I jerked from the pain, snarling and spitting with rage as he laughed while I struggled to get out of his hold. My leg got free, slamming into his nose, shattering it, sending blood across my body.

Knox roared with anger, grabbing me before I escaped the bed, pushing me down, and entering me painfully. I shuddered, rocking against him as he crashed into my body. The only sounds within the tent were his moans mingling with mine. Knox lifted my hips, moving deeper into my body until the orgasm started to crescendo out of control. Instead of giving me what I needed, he pulled out. I spun, hissing as I sliced my hands down his chest. My foot slammed into his chest, sending him flying across the tent.

I laughed, falling onto my back, watching him rise to his feet. My fingers trailed through his blood as he slowly paced in front of the bed. My laugh enraged him, dying down as I lifted, taking in the state of his body that was dripping blood from my claws.

"That's funny?" The dead calm in his voice forced

Ember to peek out with worry. I swallowed as Knox paused in front of me, tilting his head. The smile that spread over his mouth made my heart thunder in my chest, roaring in my ears. He lunged, flipping me onto my stomach before he forced my legs open and entered my ass.

I screamed in burning pain. It was violent and wrong. My entire body shuddered as the screaming turned into rage over the wrongness of it. I came hard, unraveling from my toes to my fingertips as he laughed darkly.

"Dirty—*fucking*—girl!" Knox roared, slamming into my body, and it clamped down, trying to force him out as I howled and cried until the sensation changed. "You come so fucking hard when I tear this ass up, don't you? Fucking scream, bitch," he snapped.

"Knox!" I shouted, whimpering, and trembling violently.

I exploded into a violent orgasm that ripped through me. My body sang with it, and Knox chuckled as I matched every thrust with renewed need. It was an out-of-body orgasm that forced lights to blink in and out of my vision until I roared, fucking him just as hard as he was taking me.

Knox ran his hands through my hair, forcing my head to the side before sliding his teeth through my throat. He sucked, licking the wound as I continued unraveling around him. My body clenched and unclenched, forcing him to groan.

"Gods damn, woman. You come so hard when I wreck your ass," he snapped.

"Mother-fucking-son-of-a-fucking-beast! Get out!"

I snarled. He just laughed darkly, flipping us until I was on top, staring down at him as my body took control.

"That's it, ride me, wife," he demanded, lifting his head to flick my nipple with his tongue before sinking his teeth into the globe of my breast, sending both of us over the edge. My body tightened again, milking him until he tensed and howled right along with me.

We spent days attacking one another for what we needed and wanted. Other times, we'd spend the day looking at each other in worried silence. I wasn't sure we'd live through whatever the fuck was happening with us. Our monsters were silent, refusing to be a part of it. Ember sat against the wall of my mind, telling me this shit wasn't normal. Knox spoke to Lennox, calling him a pussy, grunting when I'd snarl in warning. It was violent. It was beautiful. It was fucking everything wrong, yet nothing had ever felt more right.

We hadn't left the tent because the moment one of us rose to do so, the other would call them back with a simple rattle or purr. There were a lot of worried gazes, side-eyes, and *what-the-fucks* displayed on our faces.

On the fourth day, I dressed and slipped from beneath the broken tent we'd toppled this morning. Lore's eyes held mine as I almost escaped, only for a rattle to sound behind me. Knox grabbed my ankle, and I smiled coldly as my teeth elongated, and my nails pushed through my fingers.

Knox howled, and Lore screamed. "Fuck that shit. Daddy doesn't want that!"

We screamed and ripped each other apart until we'd torn one another down to our genetic make-up, which wasn't even close to being human. Knox escaped from the tent next, and I followed him.

The men slid their gazes over the wounds they could see. Brander bent, picking up his med-kit while Knox snarled at him, and I echoed the warning with a rattle. Brander dropped it, and all three men stepped back at once, fear and worry flooding their gazes.

Knox was torn up, and he'd covered me in bruises from where he'd held me down to prevent injury. Knox issued orders, and Brander nodded to something. I slid my attention to the other tent, and Knox turned to smirk at me. I lifted a finger since my voice was hoarse and barely able even to speak. Knox rolled his eyes, and I rattled. He turned, hefting me up over his shoulder before entering the new tent. Hours later, we emerged a little more beat up and missing more flesh.

"You two aren't right," Killian whispered, so softly that I wasn't certain he'd meant for us to hear it. Our heads snapped in his direction, and he straightened, preparing to run.

"So, listen, guys." Brander flinched as we turned our battered faces toward him, giving him our attention. "People are afraid," he announced. We stepped closer, and rocks crunched beneath my bare feet. I glanced down, noting the mixed crystals as if they'd tried everything and had given up their attempts to dispel our anger management sessions unfolding in the tent.

"Who the fuck is afraid?" Knox asked harshly.

"Everyone," Brander stated.

Our eyes rose to the camp that had moved, barely visible from where our tent sat in a heap of singed, charred piles of leather. I laughed, turning to look at Knox, who stared at me with a smoldering look in his eyes.

"No," I groaned, but Knox rattled, and I followed, jumping onto him as he walked forward. I shredded his shirt, sinking my claws into his shoulders, and he destroyed me the moment we were out of sight. We emerged again, and the men all groaned, staring up at the sky while we marched past them, heading toward the water.

"This isn't normal," Knox snapped.

"You're not normal!" I returned.

"Who keeps attacking whom?" he shot back.

I paused, looking at his back that held a multitude of claw marks. I smiled, stretching my arms, continuing to follow him. Shedding the dress the moment we entered the water, I dove into it. I came to the surface, shivering at the iciness of the water as Knox watched me, smiling while the water healed our wounds. Opening my mouth, I grinned at him as something grabbed my ankle, and I peered down before being pulled beneath the water.

Chapter Forty-Nine

I was pulled deeper in the water and slammed onto the river bottom. Fighting against whatever held me, I thrashed my arms and legs until pain tore through my leg. Spinning in the water, I took in the huge leviathan that held my ankle between his teeth, not breaking the skin. Bubbles exploded from my lungs as I reached down and sunk my nails into the leviathan's mouth.

It was like a creature from a science fiction movie. Blue fins covered its back and all along its long, slender, snake-like body. Its sightless eyes were sunk far into the back of its head, blinking at me in surprise. Blood filled the water from the leviathan. I kept slicing against the beast until blackness threatened to take control of my mind as my air ran out. Its tail wrapped around me, pulling me deeper into the murky depths, slamming me back against the sandy bottom, and encasing me in an enormous bubble as air rushed into my lungs.

Flat on my back, I peered up at the dome, gulping

in large amounts of air to my deprived lungs. Knox was pounding against the clear enclosure, his eyes no longer sea-blue, but fiery obsidian, angry that he could not reach me. Knox retreated to the surface as I sat up, staring at the beast that flopped around, hissing and spitting before it started convulsing.

Slowly rising to my feet, I backed up against the dome, snarling when it sent a warning jolt of energy rushing through me. My entire body shuddered while the beast gradually shifted to the form of a man. He turned electric blue eyes on me as he stood, revealing masses of muscle and everything else.

"You," he hissed, his voice coming out in layers.

"Me?" I asked, wishing I had some clothes to put on.

The male smiled, letting his gaze take in my body before his hand moved, and water covered my nakedness. Okay, not the strangest shit to happen to me lately. He started forward, but nails slid over the outside of the dome, and we looked up as four angry alphas attacked the bubble.

"I am Karter, King of the Nymphs."

"I am wondering why you just tried to drown my ass," I returned, observing him. My eyes slid back to Killian and Brander as they fought with Knox to break the bubble.

"You freed Taren from Hecate's curse."

I stared at Karter for a moment, then looked around the dome before focusing my attention back on him. Sucking my lip between my teeth, I frowned while considering my move.

"I almost died in the process," I pointed out.

"I am not as powerful as Taren. You're stronger now, too. You can hold the power that I have, witch," he chided. "You need it to accomplish what you intend to create."

"What do you know about what I intend to create?"

"The Tenth Realm for the witches. You're a part of this land, and when you speak, the elementals hear from your soul, which is now attached to the realms. Let me show you," Karter urged, holding out his hand.

Knox and his men continued to bang on the barrier, shaking their heads, urging me not to accept Karter's hand. Swallowing, I looked away from Knox and considered Karter's offer. I stepped forward, holding my hand out before he yanked me closer to him. His hands clapped over my head, and my body jerked. Pain echoed through me as I felt water filling my lungs.

When my eyes opened, we were in a different place. I looked to the castle behind me, noting the giant firebirds filling the air while dragons flew around them. Men and women moved about, laughing, celebrating something. Large dragons and phoenixes shot blue and red flames from their mouths as smaller creatures flew around them, sailing through the air. Looking around, I noticed a familiar male leaning against a wall, staring down at the celebration with a soft smirk on his lips.

"Aden," I whispered.

"Wow," I whispered thickly. "This is Norvalla?" Karter silenced me by nodding toward a dark figure that moved from the shadows.

"This is what happens if you don't claim your rightful place and power. Watch," Karter said from behind me.

A petite blonde woman went to stand beside Knox. Both proudly wore their crowns as the King and Queen of Norvalla. Knox turned, smiling at the woman as they lifted their gazes to the monsters flying above. Huge dragons landed on the battlements, wailing as they flapped leathery wings. The crowd exploded in cheers as several phoenixes perched beside their king and queen.

The queen turned, her smile curving her lips as she and Knox hailed the crowd. They celebrated a body that hung upon the wall, causing my blood to turn to ice in my veins. The crowd cheered louder for the murder of the Hecate witch whose headless body swung in the breeze. My eyes scanned those on the battlements, not recognizing anyone. Lowering my stare, I searched the crowd until I found silver hair that hung down around slender hips, the face the only stoic, unsmiling one in the group.

Familiar turquoise eyes turned to the crowd as a smile twisted on the woman's lips. No, not some random woman. They were my lips, and the crowd continued to cheer me. Knox and his queen bow, and my twin followed suit. The dragons snarled, pushing up and off the battlements, sailing into the air as the future me called upon her fire. All at once, the dragons turned on the crowd, sending flames scorching through them.

I screamed as bedlam ensued, bodies melted to ashes that drifted over the crowd. People were on fire and ran all around us, but the dragon's flames spread far and wide. The king and queen watched, their eyes slowly taking in the damage as the men beside them held true, never flinching or recoiling from the massacre unfolding in front of them.

"Why aren't Knox and the queen stopping the dragons?" I demanded, watching a child run from a dragon. It flew at her, ceasing its flames to capture her, throwing her into the air as another dragon shot flames toward her.

"Because as the High Queen of the Nine Realms, you ordered it," Karter whispered, his eyes filling with tears. "You do this because the power you hold is unstable, and your grief fuels your rage. Norvalla took a sister from you, so you unleashed hell to ensure no other tried to do the same. They made you into a monster, and without the ability to stabilize the power and magic within you, this is what happens."

"No," I snorted. "The dark witches are trying to make me into a monster. They're mistaken. They'll stop once they realize I already have a monster within me. This is a slaughter with no justification."

"They murder one of your sisters in front of you, ripping her limbs and head from her body. Tell me you wouldn't crave revenge, Aria Hecate."

"Not like this," I stated, watching the dragons return to ash, raining onto the flames still sizzling on the ground.

The future version of me turned, her eyes sliding through the chaos. Blades shot forward from her hands as she smiled at the Knox and his queen, severing their heads from their necks. Bile rushed through me, and I shook my head at their deaths.

"I would never do that," I whispered vehemently.

"But you do," Karter exhaled. "Now that you've seen one path, let us see what your other future could be."

"All the little peeks into the future, provided by an elemental, are random and never make sense."

"Says the woman who just tore the fuck out of the largest alpha the Nine Realms ever created while getting her body's needs fulfilled, many times, I might add."

"There are some things you all could skip eavesdropping," I grunted, placing my hand into his before the world spun out of control around us.

I stared at the Palace of Vãkya, watching another version of me holding my swollen belly before turning at the sound of laughter. My sisters moved around me, slowly dancing as music played from flutes and other instruments. My eyes filled with tears, slipping to my rounded belly as Aden stepped forward, kissing it. Rising, his pretty eyes held mine as he leaned forward to place a soft kiss onto my forehead.

All around us, people celebrated, yet my heart ached at watching Aden with me. I stepped closer, listening as he assured me I was beautiful in my last stage of pregnancy, even though I was larger than the palace. My eyes scanned the crowd, praying to see Knox within the people who celebrated.

"He isn't here," Karter stated, knowing who I was hoping to find. "In this version, neither of you chooses the other."

"But I am having a child," I swallowed, turning to look at Karter. "I never get what I want in these fucking things, do I?"

"You choose the realms, as it was what they created you to do."

"What about me? What about what I want?" I asked and blinked as I realized I wanted a child with Knox. I wanted a life with him. It slammed into me, and my eyes grew large and round.

"You can't have it all, Aria. No one can. You either become the evil you saw and wage war on the Nine Realms or choose to live. Knox cannot heal unless he has help, and you can't do that while healing the damage this world has endured."

"What if I fight the war with him?" I asked, noting that Karter flinched.

"Then, you both die, and he finds his eternal sleep to meet his previous wife."

My eyes narrowed at Karter's words, sliding to the scene unfolding before me. I appeared happy, yet my eyes didn't reflect it. I looked—settled. My heart squeezed, and I nodded. Fuck that and fuck their reality. I'd make my own.

We reappeared in the dome, and Karter smiled while watching me. His head tilted, and he nodded.

"I believe you would try, but only those with the ability to forgive can create the world they want. Can you forgive Knox for what he intends to do?"

I looked at Knox outside the dome, still trying to gain access. He paused, and his obsidian eyes met mine, tilting his head in question. I looked away and didn't answer Karter. Instead, I shot one back at him. "Why did Hecate place you as the Keeper of Water?"

"My wife asked her to do so because I refused to allow Hecate to rule my lands. Neven wanted power, craving it for herself. A queen cannot overrule a king, and so she got rid of me. I intend to take back my throne and deal with my errant wife once I have returned."

"Taren tried to kill me."

"So he did, but Taren hated your lover. I respect your husband. He tried to prevent this from happening to me. He warned me that my wife intended to remove me from power, but he was so young. A king does not listen to a prince's words. Had I done so, I wouldn't be here. You will survive this, Aria. Your lifeline is long and winding. You are the unknown, the promised one with the power to heal our lands. You are pure of heart and untainted by grief or pain. Your father is watching you, and he is so proud of the little monster he created."

"If he is so proud, why isn't he here? Why hasn't he come for me?" I hissed, watching Karter carefully.

"Because you're not ready, Little Queen. His people have assisted you along the way, and he knows your intentions. You allowed the King of Norvalla to capture you for a reason, and if he thought for one moment you were in danger, your father would rain down hell, unlike this world has ever seen to prevent it. You're not alone, Aria. You've never been alone, not even when you were outside the Nine Realms."

I stared at the honesty shining from within Karter's eyes. I exhaled before nodding, "Let's give it a go. What could go wrong?" He opened his mouth as if intending to answer the question, but I lifted my hand. "That was rhetorical."

Karter pressed his lips against my ear, whispering, "If you want Knox, you must fight to keep him. Love is not easily obtained. Fight for him and break through the barrier to touch his heart. Remind him he still has one."

Karter smirked, and his hands touched mine, grounding me as I called to his power, taking it within me. My body trembled as the dome exploded. Knox and his men flew out of the river and onto the banks. The water in the river transformed into droplets that hovered in the air. Pain echoed through me, but Karter added his power to mine while Ember added her strength into the equation.

The droplets continued climbing into the air, then crashed down over me all at once. My eyes widened when the water slammed into us, sending my body to the ground as pain echoed through me. The taste of pure, unfiltered magic assaulted me. My ears popped, and my lungs filled with water as everything crushed within me. I felt consciousness slipping, and then hands grabbed me, yanking me toward the surface.

Knox pulled me from the water, watching as I sputtered, coughing it from my lungs. His eyes were blue, and his teeth bared as his body shook with rage. I turned over, staring up at him as I rose from the ground, gasping while the water elemental's power sizzled inside of me. Once I was on my feet, Knox rattled his rage, and I whimpered.

His eyes slid to obsidian as anger filled the air between us. "What the fuck was that?" he demanded.

"The King of Nymphs," I admitted, struggling to remain upright.

"You think I'm stupid? That was the Keeper of Water, Aria. You fucking played me to get inside my realm!" Knox snarled.

"I did not! I had no plans of being sucked into the damn river!" I shouted back as lightning struck, and it rained. The rain intensified as Knox peered up, slowly sliding his gaze back toward me through the torrential downpour unfolding.

Knox moved without warning, grabbing me and crushing his mouth against mine. He kissed me like a starving man that hadn't tasted a woman in centuries and never would again. His fingers pushed through my hair, holding me against him. He kissed me as he lifted me, continuing to kiss me even though the rain was threatening to drown us.

It hadn't been rage he'd felt. It was fear. He kissed me like I meant something, like I belonged to him. Knox held me against him, and it wasn't a kiss of ownership. It was deeper, as if he'd feared I would die. When he finally pulled away, his hands clasped against my cheeks, holding my forehead against his.

"I thought I lost you." He swallowed thickly, removing his cloak to place it over my shoulders. "Never do that again," Knox warned. "I need to be inside you, Aria." The rain dissipated, and rainbows covered the skies. Knox stared up, smirking as the men exhaled around us.

"What are you waiting on—an invitation written in crayons?" I grinned as his eyes dance with amusement. "Now," I demanded when he hadn't done what he'd warned he would do. Knox smirked and yanked me to the tent, and this time, he wasn't hard, and I didn't attack. It was slow and erotic and beautiful.

Chapter Fifty

Knox had pulled away again the moment we moved camp, not that I hadn't needed distance. He'd gone to war on my body, and I'd met him full force. We'd gone hard, violent, and brutal on one another, and I'd loved every second of it. From the glances he slid my way, I was willing to bet he'd loved it too.

In that tent, we'd gone bare-bones against one another. We'd met full throttle with a need that had shocked and left us both horrified and breathless. Knox had imprinted himself onto my soul, and I'd done the same to him. Neither of us held back, and we hadn't wanted the other to do so either. We'd terrified the others, and we couldn't be bothered to care.

Hell, we'd even scared our creatures with the violence we had unleashed on one another. Ember had taken to snickering and reminding me that I'd matched her need. There were times when Lennox and Ember peeked out from within us as we'd gone slower.

Knox made love to me, slowly showing me an entirely new side to him. I'd allowed it, letting him push me over the edge while he'd taken my hands prisoner. He'd held me afterward, his fingers playing with my hair while he spoke of his home. It was an unguarded glimpse into the man who had married me.

The camp had moved, though, and with it, Knox vanished back behind his walls. He'd erected them the moment we'd stepped out of the tent, after the rain had washed the world clean. Maybe Knox thought I wouldn't survive Karter's magic entering me, recalling I wasn't immortal yet. Perhaps he'd realized that I could be lost to him and had woken up to the reality that I wasn't whole yet?

The closer we got to Norvalla, the more unsettled I became. The men, on the other hand, grew excited. Their banter changed, and the mood within the army became lighthearted and good-natured. They turned from warriors capable of mass destruction to people returning home to embrace their loved ones. It created an ache deep within my chest that caused a pang of regret, knowing I'd never feel at home again.

We crested a peak, and my breath got stuck in my lungs. A bustling city built above sea-level spread out before my eyes. Large birds flew around a tower, and I smiled at their loud shrieking noises. High mountains surrounded the city, with splashes of color so perfectly placed that tears filled my eyes, burning them as Knox beamed with pride.

Dorcha was the capital of Norvalla. Brander told me it was the home Knox had shared with Liliana and their son. He was going to open that tomb, and when he did, everything would change. His world was about to fall apart, and no matter what I did, I couldn't stop it from happening, nor would I. My bloodline had dealt Knox a shitty hand. No one could argue that fact, not even me.

The war party stopped on a towering cliff, staring down at the beautiful palace that spread out as far as the eye could see. The towers stretched high into the clouds, concealing their spiraling tips from sight. To the east of the castle stood elaborate statues of women with wings, facing the crystalline-blue water, filled with actual ships that looked as if they'd stepped out of a historical romance and into the present day. Large sails billowed with the breeze, moving the boats out to sea or into port.

Several bridges sat over large bodies of water, forcing anyone who sought entrance to the palace to cross over them. Each bridge held a warrior statue in a defensive pose, their shield's held above the entrance. Below the land on which the palace sat, a bustling city went about their day as they worked.

Creatures filled the skies. Large birds of every color crested the bridges, carrying packages between them, diving toward the city, and screeching their presence as they descended. My throat bobbed, and my heart pounded deafeningly against my ears as tears threatened to escape, taking in the beauty of Dorcha and its sprawling palace. Knox tightened his hold on me, smiling against my shoulder before he kissed it softly.

"Welcome to my home, wife," he whispered, rubbing his thumbs over my belly.

"It's beautiful," I admitted, feeling something within me settling into place, which bothered me.

"You have seen nothing yet," Knox continued, sniffing my hair. He'd spent over twenty minutes pretending to wash it before he'd replaced both his marks with fresh ones. "Maybe you'll find a place in our room for a nest."

I shivered as he chuckled, knowing that I was still sensitive to the need to mate. Worse, there was something primal about the way my body reacted to his. The desire to take from him was becoming dominant again. I was losing the fight against the need to mark him as he'd marked me.

In our tent, I'd fought the urge to nest, which had been the hardest thing to do. Well, other than the attraction to the asshole that marked me and kissed me like I was more than something he needed for his war.

We started moving again as horns blared from the palace, and flags were raised on the battlements to signal the king's return. Ignoring the men's excitement, I watched the people rushing toward the tunnel beneath the palace, vanishing from sight. The closer we got to the palace, the more vivid the details became.

The castle itself was built from smoky quartz, giving it a darker appearance from further away. Runes were etched on the palace walls, written in the ancient language of the first people. Water rushed beneath us as our warhorse trotted toward the gate where I could see people gathering with excitement that the king had returned.

Men laughed or told others beside them how they couldn't wait to visit the town and see the women who freely offered their bodies to the bravest knights. Others talked about their wives and their hopes of being fertile from the Beltane ceremony. They spoke of families, siblings, and parents, which caused a tightening in my chest that settled into emptiness.

Men and women cheered, shouting as we entered the palace's inner courtyard, filled with greenery that popped against the high walls. What I had thought was part of the palace was actually a shield that stood tall and imposing, surrounding and protecting the castle.

Inside the shield, the palace stood just as tall, if not taller. It reached for the heavens through the clouds, and large birds flew around the spiraling towers. Below the suspended courtyard sat the people who hadn't crawled up the walkway surrounding the city we'd entered.

Knox or his parents had built a city that could be protected from witches, and they'd done it in layers. The cries for the king's return sounded from beneath and all around us, while Knox took us deeper into the city. Kicking his horse into a slow, easy gait, he maneuvered us through the crowd and toward another wall surrounding the palace.

The wall was an elaborate work of art that depicted men at war, defending a palace that mirrored this one in appearance. Once we'd moved through the large, opened gates, guards rushed forward. People waited on the stairs, lifting on tiptoes to look through the men returning. Knox slid off the horse as a stable boy ran forward, taking the reins as I moved to dismount behind him. Knox didn't offer help as he turned, staring at something behind us.

Once I dismounted, I turned to look at what had captured his attention. An imposing statue of a familiar woman stood in a garden, adorned in beautiful budding flowers. Standing beside her, his hand in hers, was

Sven's much smaller statue. My heart plummeted as Knox turned, staring at me while I studied his reaction to the memorial he'd had made to honor his family.

Sliding my gaze toward a feminine voice, I saw a slim woman rushing toward Knox, jumping into his arms. She embraced him, smiling at him before she leaned forward to kiss him on his lips. As if she'd surprised even herself with the action, she pulled back laughing as she spoke loudly.

"Welcome home, My King." She smiled shyly before stepping back to bow. "I am pleased you've returned to us whole," she said demurely.

Knox leaned forward, kissing her forehead before cupping her cheek while grinning. "It is good to see you too, Celia. I do hope you didn't give the staff too much hell with the welcome feast." he teased, and I swallowed past the knot in my stomach caused by the tenderness in his voice.

"I would never do something like that, would I?" she asked, and Killian snorted behind her. "Killian!" she announced, moving forward to kiss his cheek chastely before turning her eyes back toward Knox, flirting openly with him. Blinking, I took in her face and instantly recognized this petite, blonde woman as the queen standing next to Knox in one of the possible futures that Karter had shown me.

"You so would," Lore joined in, smiling. She leaned over kissing his cheek, then dismissed them to stare at Knox again with doe eyes.

"I heard you caught that murderous bitch you went off to chase. I do hope you removed her head and hung her body where the world could see it rotting." Well, I must admit that I didn't hate the part of that future where I removed her head.

I exhaled slowly, narrowing my eyes on her. Knox's gaze slid toward me at her words. He smiled tightly, shaking his head as Celia moved closer to him, pushing her hand through the crook of his arm as she sidled up next to Knox.

"Not quite," he admitted, and she patted his arm to ease the annoyance of his words.

"You're the strongest, most primal man in the Nine Realms, My King. She'll be handled accordingly soon enough, I'm certain of it." Celia patted his arm, reassuring his male ego that he'd captured me.

"I got her, Celia. I just didn't take her head. I found a much better option for her than death."

"She's a Hecate witch. The only thing to do with them is murder them and place them where the world can see that you're King, and they're nothing but garbage. What other use could they possibly serve?" Realizing her mistake at arguing with the king, she placed her hand against his unarmored chest. "I am sorry. My hatred for them is as deep as yours. I miss my sister every day, and your son, my nephew, very much. I still feel their absence deeply."

"I know you meant nothing by it, Celia. Aria is the strongest Hecate witch in her line, and there are many ways in which I can use her. I believe she will be the key to evening the playing field against the witches," Knox explained softly, uncaring that I was standing alone, listening to them.

"They must die for what they have done to Norvalla and us. If you say you have a plan for this vile whore, I am sure you know what you are doing, Love," she leaned forward, kissing his cheek while his eyes met and locked with mine.

"I do, sweet girl. Meet my wife, Aria Primrose Hecate Karnavious, Queen of Nothing as she likes to call herself." Her shocked, silverish-blue eyes slide to mine, hatred burning bright within them.

"You married her instead of just handfasting?" she snapped, stepping back to peer up at him questioningly.

"I did, therefore, claiming Hecate bloodline magic that I may use at will," he stated, watching me.

"You put a Hecate witch on my *sister's* throne?" Celia asked through feigned tears, lifting her hands to push her knuckles into them, forcing them out.

Knox smiled tightly, dismissing me. He pulled Celia against his body, rubbing her back while placing a kiss on the top of her head. "No, Aria will never sit upon a throne, nor hold power over anything in this realm. I would never do that to the memory of Liliana. Aria is mine now to do whatever I want. She will never rule this kingdom or any other. Once the Hecate witch sitting on her throne is out of the way, Aria will ascend as the High Queen of Vãkya. She will be nothing more than a puppet I use to rule their kingdom and the witches we allow to live. Aria's very powerful, and now that I've married her, they can't question my right to keep her. Aria can never unleash her magic or power on our people or threaten them because I have control over her."

I swallowed past the anger his words ignited. Silently,

I observed as Celia cried loudly and dramatically into Knox's chest, holding him to her. He tightened his arms around her, whispering against her ear while holding my stare. I didn't rattle a warning, nor did I care if he bent the whiney bitch over and gave her what she wanted in front of everyone.

She pulled back, bowing her head, pretending outrage while crying actual tears. Celia moved toward me, her eyes narrowing to slits as she stopped before me. "You're nothing, and you'll never be anything but the trash that this world intends to destroy, whore."

"So I've been told, many times before," I stated, holding her eyes that found me lacking.

"I hate that you're forced to endure this *ugly* woman. Her hair is all colors of silver and dull. Her skin is ghostly, and she's so—ugly. You must have found your wedding night tediously horrid."

"Nights," I corrected, watching her eyes grow wide with outrage at my words.

Her teeth ground together loudly while she glared at me. "You will find no welcome here, in my sister's home, witch."

"I didn't expect a warm welcome here, or anywhere else for that matter. I'd be on my way out the door, but according to Knox, he never intends to let me go," I taunted, and she lifted her hand and slapped me. I knew I couldn't defend myself without others reacting to me as the aggressor. Instead, I took it soundlessly, without reaction.

I didn't budge or wince as Celia held her hand against her chest, cradling it. I could feel the heat burning in my cheek while pain throbbed from the assault. I stared at her unwavering, not giving her the reaction she desired, which caused her hand to rise once more. Knox stepped between us, staring at my cheek before he turned, cupping hers softly.

"You cannot harm Aria, Celia. She must appear to be here willingly and remain unmarked. Do you understand?"

"My emotions are raw at knowing you were forced in this direction because of her and her murderous bloodline. This war has not been easy on me, either. I have waited day after day for your return, My King."

Knox's eyes softened for her. He nodded, smiling while he folded into her palm. He pulled her close, hugging her tightly. "I have returned, and all is as it should be."

"Are you finished with the dramatics yet? Some of us want to welcome our brother home," a deep, soothing voice interrupted the pathetic bitch trying to garner attention from Knox in any way she could. A tall man with dark hair and smiling, silver eyes clapped Knox on the back before pulling him into a bear hug. "Good to see you made it back in one piece, brother. Welcome home."

"Gideon, I am glad to be home, and I see you have not starved in my absence," Knox laughed, patting the large man on his back while his brother took me in with narrowing eyes.

"The rumors are true, then? Our King took their Queen?" Gideon asked, letting his gaze slide down my blue dress and low hanging waistline, exposing my curves and the raven necklace.

"I did, but then I'm certain your spies have been reporting everything that's happened back to you. You think we didn't discover them as we searched for enemies throughout our camp?" Knox snorted, lifting one brow as he stared at his brother pointedly.

"If you hadn't, I'd have thought you were growing lazy, brother. Had they not reported back, I'd have found them unworthy to send to our enemy's camp," Gideon stated, watching me. "She's easy on the eyes, brother. At least she's not grotesque or deformed. I imagine your wedding night wasn't hard on you at all. Nor the five days after that either of you hardly left the bed you shared."

"Enough of politics," another male snorted, moving up to the other side of Knox. He clapped him on the back hard enough that had it been anyone else, they would have crashed into me. "It's about time you assholes returned."

"Faderin, you miserable prick. I've missed your cankerous ass," Knox snorted.

I studied the large male with darker blonde hair and stunning blue eyes. He slowly let his startling electric stare lock with mine. Silently, I took in the long scar that ran down his cheek. Even scarred, he was beautifully masculine and made the wound look sexy. Faderin smirked, noting how I studied his bare chest and scars that covered his sides and chest.

"I see you've seized the day and their Queen," Faderin snorted, slowly lowering his gaze to the raven charm that dangled from my neck.

"I did indeed. Aria is very powerful and is going to turn the tables in this war, hopefully ending it faster than we'd anticipated," Knox smirked, watching my reaction. "What do you say, wife?" His eyes narrowed as if he expected me to scream or make some sexual statement about how much he'd seized of me.

"I think you should fuck off and get bent, *husband*." I smiled tightly. Knox's eyes narrowed further yet, slowly dropping to my lips before rising once more. "But, as for seizing me. You seized the wrong queen. Anything else you wish to ask, bastard?" Fuck him and fuck them. I was right here, and I wasn't some prized beast he'd captured to show off to his people. The anger burning in his stare caused my throat to tighten with the pain he was fully aware he was causing me.

"Does she bite as loud as she barks?" Faderin snickered. He reached forward to touch me, and my rattle sounded in warning, causing his eyes to widen while he lowered his hand to his side.

"Unfortunately, no, Fade," Knox snorted, dropping his eyes to my lips. "She doesn't bite at all."

I glared at the men staring at me, oblivious to the others who openly gawked. They studied my face before sliding their attention to Knox. They rattled low as their attention moved back toward me, settling on my face as my rattle answered the call of theirs. The moment it stopped, they paused, waiting for more.

"Do it again," Gideon whispered, stepping closer as he stared at my chest. "Make that noise again, woman." I glared at him, then Fade's hand lifted, brushing his knuckles down my cheek, and Ember purred as if she enjoyed the attention.

"That is amazing," Fade uttered, continuing to touch

me. Knox watched without intervening. "She does both, which means she can be bred, brother."

"If I can punch you in the throat without having to move my feet, then you're in my personal space," I warned, stepping back, only to inhale Greer's scent.

"Are you sure she doesn't bite, brother?" Fade asked, his eyes searching mine while ignoring my words. "How is this even possible?"

"She can speak for herself, asshole," I growled.

"Can she now?" an unknown voice asked, entering the reunion. "She purrs, and she rattles, but she does not bite? Depressing if you asked me," the newcomer growled. He moved in front of me as sapphire eyes, close to the color of Brander's, clashed with mine. He was as tall as Knox, with heavily tattooed forearms, which he folded over his chest, glaring at me. "If she can't bite, how is she to hold a throne? Or hold her tongue in the presence of her King? Maybe she needs to be muted. That way, she may learn her place and where she belongs within it, brother?"

"I have no intention of silencing her lips, Mateo. Aria is a force to be reckoned with on her own. She knows it, and soon, the world shall hear her rattling for me. I do not wish to change or control her mouth. I am mature enough to understand that with her outspoken brazenness comes the challenge to those around her. She has fire and a spark that could ignite the world if she knew how to wield it against her enemies. Aria's mind was built for warfare, and my enemies will become hers, which benefits me and our kingdom. A queen reflects on her king and shows his strength to his enemies. The stronger the queen, the more strength the king who tamed her has," Knox stated softly, staring at me with heat burning in his eyes.

"When waging war, you choose the strongest weapon to wield against your enemies, and I have done that. I wouldn't have chosen a weak Hecate witch for the throne, nor my wife. Weak men choose weak women so they may become alpha to her by default. This little monster hiding within her pretty flesh knows who is her alpha, don't you, Aria?"

"What, from the bottom of my heart, do you want me to say to that shit?" I snapped, rattling loudly as he rattled back, smiling with victory. He stepped forward to brush his lips softly against my forehead, and my spine arched for his beast.

"Greer, take the queen to her bedroom and lock her in for the night. She's rather moody in her time of need. Be sure to give her anything she needs for our nest. Aria's losing her battle against the compulsive need to build one in which to fuck me. I have a welcome home party to attend, Little Lamb. You're not welcome to join us, considering your current disposition and state of need that is drawing every male's attention in Dorcha by your scent. Not to mention, they're even less thrilled with whom I married than I am."

"Oh, that actually hurt my feelings..." I grabbed my chest and narrowed my gaze. "Oh, no, my bad," I laughed soundlessly. "I have no more fucks or feelings to give you, Knox. I don't want to nest with you, nor does Ember wish to nest for Lennox. You're not worthy of us, or did you miss the memo when we passed on the opportunity to mark you?"

"Is that so? Who are you?" Knox whispered, and I

closed my eyes.

"I am the flames that will build your fire. I am the heat that will fuel and feed your unquenchable cravings while igniting your darkest desires," I whispered breathlessly, swallowing as my eyes narrowed angrily. "Who are you?"

"I am the strength when you are weak. I am the chaos within you that unleashes your unbridled lust. You are the storm within me, and I intend to feel it unleashed upon my skin." Turning smugly to Fade, Gideon, and Mateo, Knox grinned, "And that, my brothers, is how you cage a wild animal and tame her shrew tongue. Don't let her pretty eyes fool you, for the most beautiful skin hides the most rabid beasts. Aria is one of us but born with Hecate blood pulsing through her veins. She wields her sarcasm well, though, doesn't she, brothers?"

"You know, Knox. I'll stop being a sarcastic bitch when you stop being an asshole," I hissed, turning to Greer as he frowned. "Knox has freed me for the night. Care to escort me to my newest cage? My husband is rather—*disappointing,* as per usual. Maybe you can find me someone that has enough stamina to sate my growing hunger. I'm rather ravenous tonight, and my mate forgot to feed me, yet again," I stated loudly, moving with Greer as the courtyard stood in silence. "Turns out, Ember was right. He's just not mate material and too stupid to live after all."

"You do not speak to the king in such a manner!" Celia snarled, but Knox quieted her, stopping her before she could reach me. "She cannot get away with that!"

"She won't, but how I choose to punish Aria is my business and mine alone, my sweet Celia." Knox's tone sent my teeth pushing through my gums, and I turned, lifting a brow as Greer continued moving us through the courtyard.

"I'll secure you some food, Peasant. Remember, I am rotten meat and don't taste good," Greer snorted, patting my hand. I felt the courtyard watching us as we departed; their hatred ran deep and bore into my soul, crushing it. Once we were inside an empty hallway, Greer paused, turning to look at me through sad eyes. "You could make this easier on yourself if you just tried to get along with him."

"He just allowed his dead wife's sister to slap me in front of the entire courtyard. His brothers treated me as if I were some rare pet they could stroke and prod. He is making me into a monster, and he knows it, Greer. Yet when I act as they assume I am, he gets angry. I am trying to show them I am not a monster, or at least not the one they believe me to be."

"You will always be a monster, Aria. You cannot escape what you are. You can only choose what type of monster you are to become. That choice is entirely yours to make." Greer scowled while scratching the back of his head. "His heart is filled with ice. Returning to this palace with a new bride cannot be easy for him. The people loved Liliana greatly. They will see you as a necessary evil, but still evil. You want Knox to change? Light the fire within him again and melt the ice that encases his heart. You are better than this, Peasant. Consider this before you reach your talons into his heart, seeking to give him pain. You can learn nothing, not until you realize that even monsters have nightmares. Come, I have a feeling the king won't remain at his welcome party for long, not with the scent you're creating right now. There's also the fact you brought up his masculinity and said it was rather lacking and flawed in front of his brothers."

"I'm losing control, and he knows all he has to do is wait for it to happen."

"So stop fighting it, Peasant. Let go of that monster within you. It isn't a weakness to give in to the urges you are feeling. Stop looking for the light and learn to accept what comes to you willingly in the dark. For without that darkness, the world would have never discovered the beauty of the stars. We can only see some of the most beautiful things through the darkness of the night. No one understands that within the darkness, monsters can hide in plain sight, not having to pretend to be anything other than what they truly are."

"You're very smart for being a meat suit, Greer."

"You're very stupid for being brilliant, but I wasn't going to point that out since you've dealt with enough today. I think once you open your eyes to the world around you, you will discover so much more is happening. He can't look away from you, Aria. Knox looks at you like you're the most beautiful thing he has ever seen. You can't see it yet, but you will. Neither of you understands what is truly happening here, but those who are watching, we see it."

"I know he looks at me and finds me pleasing, Greer. Not in the way you think, though, obviously. He looks at me the way people look at a forest fire burning out of control. It's beautiful, but you know it is deadly. You know it will destroy you and leave everything that once stood, in nothing more than ruins. He knows I am not the monster he wanted. I am the one he made."

Chapter Fifty-One

Greer directed me to an empty bedroom containing only sheets and blankets. Frowning, I moved away from the obvious attempt at a joke as I sat in the window seat. I hadn't expected to be welcomed to Dorcha. I'd known the entire way here that it would be hard for Knox to bring me to the home he'd once shared with his wife. Wrapping my arms around my knees, I stared out the window at people dancing and celebrating in the courtyard below.

His people planned his return with a party that showed how much they loved him in Norvalla's capital. Knox was the hero in their story while I was their villain. I didn't even pretend to find humor in it, considering it was laughable. I wasn't villain material, caring about the weak that needed protecting, well, it made for a weak monster. I fought for those who couldn't fight for themselves, for the assholes outside dancing who deserved to live free in the world without fear of being slaughtered. Yet they treated me like shit, like a monster.

Maybe I needed to stop fighting what they thought and just embrace it, as Greer had said. I was fighting a battle when they were waging war. I was trying to keep myself the same as I'd always been, but the cost was me, and maybe I had to change to be what they needed. I continued to bend, and if I kept doing that, I'd eventually break. I'd let Knox in. I'd fucking let him in to see me, and he'd completely destroyed me in the process.

Luna was working with dark witches, and Aine was missing. I'd come here for a reason, to get close to Knox, to make him see we weren't all evil, but he wasn't willing to see me yet. He looked, he judged, and he'd found me guilty without a trial or proof that I held ill will toward anyone. Knox wasn't ready to free the ghosts that haunted him or face the reality that we went deeper than the whisper of flesh or the marks he'd placed upon my skin.

This was a different time.

A different world!

But it was the same graveyard.

I couldn't turn back time or raise the dead. I couldn't plant flowers over their graves and think it would ease the grief and pain of those who were wronged. Knox wanted me to bow to him, and I couldn't. I couldn't bow to a king who wore a crown studded in jewels representing the lives he had taken from my people. He constructed his throne from the skulls of my bloodline, and he intended to force me to stand beside him as he sat upon it.

Knox tortured me with pleasure, undoing me with his stolen kisses and disarming me with the rare, blinding smiles. I got closer. He pulled away. He got closer. I pulled away. It was a game of tug-of-war that neither of us was even ready to play. Maybe once he'd buried his dead and could see past the shadows of grief that clung to him, we could finally try for something more.

I couldn't keep dancing with the devil and wonder why I was still in hell. It didn't work like that. I was standing in his fire and pondering why the flames burned me, and I'd enjoyed the feel of their fiery kisses upon my body. Knox wouldn't tell me how he really felt. How he acted and treated me left me confused, giving him a tremendous advantage on the gameboard he was stacking against me.

A knock sounded at the door a moment before it opened. Brander slid his gaze from the window to the folded sheets that sat on the floor, untouched. He glanced around the empty room, exhaling as he entered, leaving the door open.

"You're being summoned to dinner so your mate can feed you." He studied how I sat with my head against the window, witnessing the festivities below.

"I'm not hungry anymore," I swallowed, sensing him moving closer. Brander leaned against the windowsill, staring out at the party with me. His scent created a warning that rushed through me, forcing my body to react to it strangely.

Brander lifted his hand, skimming his fingers over the scar on my shoulder before moving to my neck. His touch sent heat rushing through me, the gentleness of it a change from Knox's intensity. He didn't speak, nor did I, silently watching his reflection in the windowpane. Brander leaned over, inhaling the smell of my hair before he smiled, dropping his mouth to kiss my shoulder. I didn't move, uncertain what was happening as he watched me silently studying him.

"You're so beautiful, Aria Karnavious. Our name on you sounds right and fits you perfectly."

I smiled darkly, turning to look up at him as he backed away from me. Slipping from the window, I stalked him, noting the fire burning in his eyes. He inhaled my scent deeply, drinking it in like a salve to his soul that he couldn't rub in deep enough.

"Sometimes, I want to go back in time and punch myself in the face for not throwing you down on that basement floor and claiming you first."

"Is that so, Brander?" I asked huskily, gasping in shock as he turned the tables on me. He pushed me against the wall, his arms caging me there, his hands beside my head, preventing escape. My chest rose and fell as Brander lowered his mouth, barely brushing his lips over mine, gauging my response. His heated kiss moved to my collarbone, slowly sliding up to kiss the pulse in my throat.

Brander slipped his foot between mine, parting my thighs as he captured my hands, pinning them against the wall, smirking wickedly when I didn't fight what was happening. "I'd have spread you apart and rocked your fucking world, Little One." He drug his nose to my marked shoulder, purring softly. "I'd have kissed you so fucking hard and deep that no other name would have felt right on your tongue after I'd finished showing you belonged to me."

I swallowed past the need rushing through me.

Inhaling Brander's scent deeply, causing Ember to frown as she woke and noted it wasn't Knox. Brander's free hand lowered, pushing against my breast as he watched me carefully.

"Can I steal a kiss from the most beautiful woman I have ever met?" He lowered his mouth, kissing my throat, pinching my nipple in sync with his soft bite. "I can smell your need soaking your pussy, Sweet One. I have never wanted to taste anything more than I do you right now."

"You know what, Brander? Sometimes I wish my life had background music so I could mentally prepare myself for whatever fucked up game you and Knox are playing with me," I whispered, studying his smirk and the naked desire burning in his jeweled sapphire eyes. He released my nipple, slowly sliding his fingers up to brush over the mark on my throat while he surveyed me.

"Who says I am playing a game?"

"I do. There's also the fact that Knox is standing outside the door. So too, are all of your brothers," I laughed soundlessly. "I can smell them as they listen to the sound of my voice, my tone becoming huskier as you taunt me with the lust your words created. I can hear their hearts beating at a rapid pace as they anticipated the noises I would make for you."

I lowered my hand, stroking over the very large, very hard cock I'd known I'd find. Brander's scent became stronger, more primal, and I tightened my grip until he swallowed a growl of pain. "I can sense my mate fighting against the shell that houses him, needing to rip into my flesh to remind me I am owned and marked. I can smell the pre-come of the other males who are turned on by my scent, itching to throw me down and take what they want. I know six men within five feet of me desire to fuck me. Maybe since you think I'm such a *whore*, we should invite them all to take a turn on me? Do you share your women with them? I mean, I only have three holes, so of course, you'd all have to take turns fucking me. But hell, why not, right? I am just here for your amusement, after all. I am nothing, nor worth more than the orifices you and your brothers wish to fill. Right, Brander?" I whispered through emotion that tightened my throat. "If you were to have theme music playing right now, it would be Billy Squier's *The Stroke*. In fact, it would be the theme music for all fucking six of you drunken assholes tonight. Now, if you'll excuse me, I do believe my *mate*, and I use that term so very loosely right now, intends to feed me," I snorted, pushing Brander away from me, and he frowned, bowing his head.

"Aria," Brander whispered, and his throat bobbed while guilt burned in his eyes.

"Shove it up your ass, Brander. I can smell the alcohol on all of you. I'm not your fucking pet you get to tease and play with for your entertainment. I'm not a whore who can be touched or taken when you want to play your petty fucking games. I am Aria Primrose Hecate, Princess of the Hecate line. Nothing you or Knox does to me can change that. No matter what cage you throw me in, or what you do to me, you can't change what and who I am."

I stepped into the hallway, finding Knox leaning against the wall with a sober look in his eyes. The others shuffled on their feet as I gave them a scathing look of annoyance. Knox exhaled, shaking his head. He pushed off the wall, holding out a hand while pushing the other through his hair. Brander exited the room, watching me move toward Knox's extended hand.

"Let's get you something to eat, Little Monster," Knox muttered, looking like a child who'd been caught in his own twisted game. "It was all done in fun, Aria. It wasn't done through malice or to hurt you."

"I'm sure you would have done the same with any woman you didn't respect," I swallowed, feeling his hand tightening against mine. "I'm just your enemy, and I should learn not to expect common decency from my husband and mate. It was my mistake to think you had a shred of honor where I was concerned. I'm just a game you enjoy playing."

"That's not true."

"Then make it so, because I fucking hate you," I swallowed past the pain and tears burning in my eyes. I placed my hand into his, and his brothers fell into step behind us.

In the great hall sat tables that were placed and seated according to station. Smaller tables were set around the wall, leaving the floor open in the middle. Knox walked me through the opening, and everyone hushed, whispering behind their hands. I followed Knox to the platform where a large table sat overlooking the others. He pulled out my chair, staring at me as I settled into it, thanking him.

Knox clapped his hands, and servers moved forward. Leaning back, he looked out over the people who all stared at me. They expected a monster, and I didn't intend to give them one. Instead, I thanked those serving me, smiling as they poured whiskey into a silver cup and piled meat onto my plate.

Reaching for the silverware, I unfolded the napkin, placing it onto my lap before I grabbed the knife and fork and cut into the steak. I used every etiquette technique taught at the finishing school they'd sent us off to during summer. Once I cut the meat, I folded my hands in my lap, staring toward Knox, waiting for him to approve of the meal.

"You may eat, Aria," Knox announced, grabbing the meat with his fingers and biting into a large piece before he placed it back on his plate. I watched him licking his fingers clean as heat entered my core, clenching with the need I'd felt for hours while he'd gotten drunk.

The steak melted in my mouth, cooked to perfection, and my stomach rumbled with approval. Fireworks exploded on my taste buds as I slowly ate, ignoring the eyes that continued watching me like I was a viper in their den. Drinking deeply of the familiar whiskey, I scanned the people's faces that continued to study every move I made. I'd just set my goblet of whiskey down as Celia entered the room with entertainers behind her, clapping her hands.

When she reached the king's table, she paused, bowing low at her waist before smiling eyes landed on me. My stomach clenched, threatening to return the food I'd just swallowed back onto the table at the gleam in her eye. Celia had changed into a gown, revealing so much cleavage that her breasts flowed over the corset she'd worn. Her arms were covered with silver bracelets, clanging as she righted her body. Jewels sparkled on her throat, hanging just high enough on her chest to draw the eye to her assets.

"To celebrate your victories and your return home, I've put together a show for you, My King. We didn't have much warning of your return to prepare your entertainment, so we hope you enjoy this small reenactment of your many victories in which we have just learned. I am certain had my sweet sister been here upon your return, she would have welcomed you home properly. The kingdom feels her loss greatly tonight, as you return with her murderer's granddaughter as your bride," Celia whispered, wiping away feigned tears as the audience nodded, agreeing with her every word.

"I'm sure we will enjoy whatever you've planned for us tonight, Lady Celia," Knox reassured her.

Celia beamed under his compliment, blushing as she moved toward the table with a quick nod to the entertainers. I swallowed, noting some actors were camp followers who had been with us as we'd marched into Dorcha. A silver-haired woman caught my eye as I noted she wore a similar dress to the one I was wearing. Celia sat on Knox's other side, slipping her hand onto his lap and squeezed his thigh.

"I am so glad you have returned. I am available to help you with anything you may need, Knox," she whispered, barely loud enough for me to make out the words.

His hand lowered to hers, squeezing it as the people moved into place, arranging items as I forced my hands into my lap. I swallowed, praying that I didn't make a fool of myself as my heart hammered against my ribs. I schooled my features as the blonde who wore a silver wig stepped next to the male dressed in raven armor and a crown similar to Knox's.

A man stepped on the stage, carrying a script. He nodded to the actors and began to read. "I come to you tonight with a tale of might, of a king so brave and virile, that he tamed a shrew hag, threatening heads in a bag, for her sister's and aunt's survival," the man recited, and the audience clapped as the two entertainers behind him stepped forward. "He promised us victory and fought with might, and brought home a queen of evil delight," the narrator continued as the actors danced awkwardly. "Our King took a whore of Freya's womb. He chased her, then fucked her on Hecate's tomb. Training this beast was a burden indeed, but he beat down that bitch until we all heard her scream."

I winced as a backdrop unfolded behind the actors depicting a gravestone while the male pretended to slap the woman. She dropped onto all fours, facing the audience. She pulled up the back of her dress, spread her legs, arched her spine, and stuck her ass in the air. The male circled her, rubbing the crotch of his pants as he winked at the audience. She whined and tried to purr as he sunk to his knees behind her, bucking his hips against hers. She threw her head back, screaming in mock passion, and something black spread across the floor beneath her as if every thrust sent evil poison flowing from her body onto the ground.

"Though he loathed his place behind her rear, he plowed that evil cunt while we stood by and cheered." The male grabbed the female by the hair, continuing to grind into her while other actors entered the stage to cheer him. Releasing the woman's breasts from her dress, he grabbed one with his other hand and began pinching her nipple.

"Her body tired and beaten just right. Our king fucked his whore until she gave up her fight." The man pulled the woman's head back by her hair and pretended to slap her. She fell to the ground, whimpering. I turned to look at Knox, who stared forward with no emotion showing on his features, seemingly enjoying the show.

A new backdrop appeared of a forest with a campfire as the narrator spoke, "She tried to make friends with the witches in camp, but they knew when they saw her, she was a Hecate tramp. She was chained and cuffed to deplete all her magic. And a witch without her powers? Well, there's nothing more tragic." The woman thrashed around, crying and whaling, begging to fuck the males on stage who pretended to be Knox's men in exchange for setting her free. It turned my stomach, and a slow rage began building within me.

The storyteller cleared his throat, and the actress went silent. "As fortune would have it, the witch did escape, then she got into trouble and cried out, '*rape.*' Our king's men lay bleeding except for one brother, and the two found her fucking one traitor then another. Betraying the king, his men slaughtered them all for a taste of that pussy was Andres's fall." More men entered the stage, acting out the events as the woman laid back and spread her legs. She begged the men to fuck her as they battled, who I assumed was Lord Andres and his men. Finally, the actor playing Knox shoved a wooden sword into the man, and he fell, pretending to be dead as the curtains closed.

My nails had extended and were now pushing through the skin as I gritted my teeth. And still, Knox did not show any emotion. The curtains opened once more, and the backdrop had changed. This time it was a crude painting of the Beltane ritual location.

"Our King, he was smart, and he bargained her heart; to give her family a home. For he promised her lies as he parted her thighs, and it only cost her the throne." The male and female appeared on stage in wedding clothes, dancing around a maypole, batting their eyes at one another. "He married that witch, and he did not flinch when their hands were bound together. He took one for the team, all part of his scheme to keep the Hecate line tethered." The couple on stage had ribbons binding one of their hands. The mock king slipped a rope around the female's neck, leading her around the stage like an animal. My nails pushed through my palms, and the napkin on my lap soaked with blood.

"She couldn't wait to be fucked, to be licked, and be sucked, so she pulled him along by his penis. Then she licked, and she sucked, and was thoroughly fucked by the king we would all call a genius." The woman on stage sat the mock king in a chair and pretended to suck his cock. Then she lifted her skirt to straddle him as he freed her breasts from her dress. He sucked one into his mouth as she ground her body against his, whining and purring while the male pretended to rattle.

The narrator grinned as the crowd cheered, and he continued, his voice rising an octave. "For he took what he wanted and would never commit, so the things that she wanted, she'd never get. Love and affection won't come for this heathen. The longer he keeps her, the more she will weaken. If it's children she wants, to further her line, the king would spit on her grave before birthing her swine." At that moment, the woman leaned back in a fake orgasm as a herd of piglets ran squealing from under her skirt, running around the stage. The males playing Knox's men ran around the stage trying to catch them.

Rage began to pulse through me, and I could see from the corner of my eye that Knox was gauging my reaction. I would not let these pathetic people know how much they were getting under my skin. I would not rise from my chair and rip the face off of Celia, who, no doubt, was enjoying herself immensely at my expense.

Once the piglets were caught, and the excitement of the crowd had quieted, the storyteller continued, "Straight to battle they went; her body filled with his scent, just to learn that it wasn't her throne. Disappointment would follow, but he pumped, and she'd swallowed, then he abused her cunt all the way home. Now, this dumb bitch is here, and it's perfectly clear she will never replace our fair queen. For she was beauty and light, and everything right, that this witch could not possibly dream." The woman impersonating me went to sit on a throne and was pushed to the floor by the faux king and used as a footstool. "When the war has been won, and her uses are none, a place for her head, there will be. Then the king can remarry a proper bride that can carry the memory and crown of our Queen." The man playing Knox swung his wooden sword, and the woman bowed her head low, concealing it under her arm as she tossed out a melon adorned with a silver wig, a crown, and lipstick. As the woman sunk to the floor, the male removed the crown from the melon and carried it over to Celia. She laughed and clapped as she accepted the offering.

"Welcome to Dorcha, Aria Hecate. We do hope you

enjoyed your tale," the narrator stated, bowing as the crowd clapped and cheered.

"I think they may have missed the mark a little regarding what I had requested them to do tonight, Knox. I do hope you didn't mind it too much, Aria?" Celia asked, and I smiled at her, hiding the emotion that was flooding through me.

"No, it was actually rather truthfully honest. I'm sure the people enjoyed it immensely as they seemed to have found great humor in the show," I stated barely above a whisper, feeling the blood that oozed from my hands, soaking into my dress.

"If you ever do anything like this again, Celia, I will send you home to tend to your house. Do you understand me?" Knox asked through clenched teeth, and when she didn't respond, he hissed. "I am not speaking to you as your brother-in-law, but as your King. I expect an answer."

"I understand," Celia whispered, sliding her eyes between Knox and me. "I shouldn't have allowed others to see to the preparations. I merely allowed the camp followers to assist with the tale of how you'd captured your bride and treated her during your time away. I wasn't privy to what happened. I will see that the actors are punished for the atrocity that played out tonight," Celia lied, frowning as she lowered her eyes demurely, placing her hands into her lap. "The people seemed to have enjoyed the tale that was told tonight, though."

"Indeed, they did. For the record, I enjoy my wife's body and what it offers me when I am within her. She is an amazing lover and matched me completely in need. Your place here is because you are the sister of Liliana and Killian. I can easily replace you as stewardess if you insist on pulling shit like you did tonight."

"The people are upset with the presence of this witch in Liliana's home. I thought to make light of it so it would put them at ease. I didn't mean it as an insult to Aria, or expect them to make a mockery of your intentions with her. I do think it offered them a little laughter to lighten the fact that a Hecate princess is here in my sister's home. They loved Liliana and Prince Sven greatly. Every day we are all reminded that they're no longer here with us."

I peered at the men at the table who all watched me with twitching lips, other than Knox's brothers and Killian, who looked mortified at my expense. Knox pushed his chair back abruptly, pulling mine out as he grabbed for my hand, lowering his eyes to where I held the napkin with a death grip. I stood, slipping my hand into his before he yanked me closer, brushing his lips against mine softly for show.

"Come, wife. It is late, and there is much I must do before I find sleep tonight." Knox slipped his arm through my elbow, and his people went silent as he walked me out of the great hall.

Chapter Fifty-Two

Knox didn't speak until we stopped in front of large double doors at the end of the hallway. "That shouldn't have happened, Aria."

I didn't answer him, choosing to stare at his feet. His fingers lifted my chin, and his stare narrowed on the tears swimming in my eyes.

"Aria." He leaned forward, but I stepped back, putting distance between us. "I've behaved badly in my excitement to be home among my people. I allowed alcohol to lead me into a bet that Brander could seduce you and steal a kiss. Thank you for not kissing him. He owes me one hundred hours of training the soldiers for failing." Knox opened the doors to reveal the library.

"Next time, leave me out of your bets," I whispered, dropping my eyes from his. I entered the library, not wanting him to see the light he'd extinguished tonight. I may have been alive, but he'd broken something within me by bringing me to his home, where his wife's ghost haunted the hallways.

Knox stopped me by grabbing my hands and pulling me back as he searched my eyes. "What just happened? What changed?"

"I let you get too close to me, and you decided to destroy me. I thought you saw the fire in my eyes and wanted to play with the flames. In reality, you just wanted to watch me burn. I was wrong to think you could see me; silly me. I thought maybe you actually liked me, when in reality, I have been a pawn all along, on both sides. Leave me alone, Knox." I pushed through the doors to enter the library.

The game we played had begun to feel like an algebra test when I had yet to learn addition. Knox was breaking down my walls faster than I could replace them, and he wasn't even trying to get them down. Greer was wrong. Knox's heart wasn't encased in ice; it was ashes that had no way of ever becoming whole again. You couldn't take ash from a fireplace and turn it back into a piece of wood.

I moved deeper into the library while Knox followed, noting the smell of defeat that wafted off of me. Knox captured my hand, pulling me back to face him. His eyes searched mine, finding them empty. Stepping closer, he cupped my cheeks and lowered his mouth to brush it against mine. I didn't respond. I couldn't.

I'd seen myself through the eyes of his people tonight. I was their enemy, and they had enjoyed watching everything he had put me through and what he had planned for my future. To them, the play depicted exactly what I was and how the events had unfolded. They'd taken something beautifully visceral and showed me their version of it, and it was ugly.

"Aria," Knox whispered, his thumbs pushing away my tears. "Don't let them break you or extinguish your fire," he murmured, but it wasn't in English. "Let me help you to bed, woman," he said, switching to a language I could understand.

"I can put myself to bed. I'm sure you have matters to attend to tonight after being away for so long." I moved away from him, standing before the fire as I rubbed my arms, staring into the dancing flames.

"I'll be back in a few hours." His stare burned into my back as I nodded, dismissing him. I listened to his feet padding on the floor as he exited the room, closing the doors before a key sounded in the lock.

Turning, I looked around the library. "I know you're alive," I whispered, feeling the subtle stirring of magic. "I'm here for the knowledge owed to me. Seal the walls and close the doors. Show me the vault that holds all lost souls and the tomes of those who lived before the Hecate bloodline ruled the Nine Realms."

I spun slowly, watching as the walls rearranged to block off the entrance into the room I now stood inside. Smiling softly, I wiped away the tears that rolled down my cheeks. Knox thought this place belonged to him and him alone. It didn't. It was mine too, and I'd felt it calling to me with every question I'd asked during my time away from it in the Nine Realms. Now, I intended to show Knox that not everything here was subdued by him, including me.

The library pulsed with magic as it came alive before my eyes. Large spheres of every color glowed brightly around the edges of the room as I stood in amazement. Large, ancient tomes and grimoires lay open on pedestals, untouched by time or dust. The spells on their parchments sent soft plumes of magic into the air, appearing like flowery fireworks.

I drifted toward one book, noting the spell to create the House of Magic sat opened, glowing with what looked like embers of glitter coming up from the page. My fingers slid over it before a glowing door caught my eye.

Silently, I approached the door that pulsed with power. My hand slid over the onyx center that didn't change with my touch. I swallowed hard, lifting my head to the glowing blue ancient scrawl that covered the edges of the door, flowing down toward the floor, pulsing with immense power.

"How do I open it?" I asked the library and cried out as the room moved me to a window. I stared into the darkening shadows of a flower-filled courtyard, watching a familiar form standing before a mausoleum, head bowed with one arm against the door.

Knox turned, peering up toward the window from which I stood. Moving into the shadows out of sight, I continued to watch him fight his demons. Knox placed his hand back on the door, bowing his head as his shoulders dropped and shook. My eyes slid to the statues on either side of the embellished grave. Liliana and Sven's likeness stared back at me, taunting me, while I worried my lip. He was fighting his need to know the truth without having to disturb their eternal rest. Knox dropped to his knees, his head still bowed as rain drizzled onto him.

"I asked you how I open the vault. I didn't ask to trespass against Knox and his ghosts," I growled, feeling as if I was intruding on his privacy.

The room changed again to reveal a wall with ancient pictures drawn on it. There were human-like creatures with talons protruding from their fingertips. One was a man and one a woman. Moving toward it, I ran my fingertips over the glowing images, sending magic rushing through them as the couple moved. I swallowed, gasping as the woman hunted the male, prowling on all fours as he walked obliviously through a forest. She'd lunge, and he'd danced away from her as if they played a game. My teeth slid from my gums, and my head turned as the sound of my neck crunched, my spine tingling while I watched the scene play out.

The woman caught the man, and he lifted her, pushing her against a tree as his body rocked against hers. I swallowed at the fact that I was standing in a magical library, basically watching stick figure porn come to life. The scene changed, and the man and woman became Knox and me as a chair slammed beneath my legs, forcing me to sit. I peered around me, leaning back to watch Knox slam into my body as my eyes held mine. It was erotic watching us together without actually participating.

"Damn, now all I need is popcorn. You're pretty handy, aren't you?" I whispered and then frowned as popcorn began raining from the ceiling. "And apparently, you're rather touchy too." I lifted popcorn from my lap and popped a buttery, fluffy piece into my mouth. My eyes narrowed to slits as my teeth grew on the wall, pushing into Knox's throat. He trembled, and blue lines slid through his body and mine. The sex became primal, his beast taking control as my own released. "Bloody hell," I groaned loudly, shoving more popcorn into my mouth. "I have to finish it, don't I? I have to finish the claim he began?"

"Yes," I whispered to myself.

The image of Knox vanished, and the library spoke, "Daughter of the Nine Realms, you must claim your king to discover your truth. Your father awaits you, Aria. Your enemies are many, but your heart is pure. Come, take your place among those who lived before you. You were born for greatness, with power unimagined running through your veins. Finish claiming your mate so that your mind is unhindered, and your fate sealed with his."

"He wants to destroy me, in case you didn't get that memo," I whispered, standing up to move back to the window, finding Knox missing from the mausoleum. "If I mate with him, then he will own me."

"You're meant to be his and his alone. You were both forged in the same fire. Knox is your mate, and you are his. He will not be easy on you because you stand for everything he hates. Only you can change his mind, Aria. You're everything he wants, yet he hates himself for betraying the memory of those he lost. You already know the truth surrounding the identity of his first wife. You've considered it a thousand times but never voiced it out loud for fear it would waft into the air and reach the ears of others who would use it to harm him."

"If it is true, then he will hate me even more. He will crave my death and every witch who ever lived. If Knox discovers who lies in that grave, we're all doomed."

"Replace what he has lost and give him new purpose. You're his mate, Aria Primrose. You alone can give him what magic made him assume was real. Open yourself to him and then escape. Make him see that you're everything he needs. The heart often never realizes what it needs until it is gone. He will uphold his end of your agreement. Let him. Welcome what you are, and what you can create together."

"We're going to war against one another. You understand that, right?" I challenged with tears burning in my eyes. "He wants to destroy everyone I love, and he won't ever change his mind."

"You were built for war, but even in times of turmoil, there is peace. You are chaos in motion, and he is the ruins that you will rebuild. In war, there will be casualties, and when that happens, you will both break apart. But inside that havoc, you will reach for one another, for you are his, and he is yours. Two flames that will become one and burn brighter than this world has ever witnessed." I looked at the wall, smiling as Knox's figure reappeared, brushing his hands against my belly, which grew large as he held it protectively. "When the time is right, you will both know it and seek solace in one another. If you want access to the vault for the knowledge within it, then you must claim your king," the wall shimmered and then returned to what it had been. I was lifted and dropped onto the bed, and blankets were tucked around me as Knox entered the room.

The door creaked opened, and I closed my eyes, curling onto my side, breathing in Knox's scent, mixed with the earth he'd sat on, talking to his family. The sound of clothes being removed filled the space, and then the bed sank with his weight as he crawled to where I lay. He yanked the blankets off of my head, pulling me against his warmth, holding me. He exhaled, trembling with whatever emotion rushed through him.

"I should have stopped Celia tonight, but everyone was watching us. Like my grief, they've not learned how to ignore theirs. You made me proud tonight by choosing not to react to the shit-show they played for your benefit."

"My entire life is a shit-show, Knox. Celia showed them the truth of us. At the end of the day, that is what we've done to get to where we are. It may have been a joke to you and them, but that is exactly how our tale has played out for me. I am Aria Primrose Hecate. The Hecate princess that you have taken as your wife. I am the evil being that has replaced your sweet wife, whom they adored and loved. You, yourself, told me that I am nothing. When you treat me like I am nothing, you cannot expect your people to treat me differently. I am okay with being the villain because sometimes it's okay to be the bad guy."

"Bad guys don't sing pretty songs to babies, wife. They don't crave a child of their own or save those who are weaker and unable to save themselves. You'd make a horrible villain, Aria Karnavious. You'd be a very sexy one, but you'd suck at making the hard choices real monsters have to make."

I didn't reply, choosing to just bask in the heat his body offered. His arm wrapped around me as he kissed my forehead, remaining silent. I searched his eyes, wondering if he was right or if one of the visions Taren and Karter had shown me would become my reality. Leaning forward, I gently claimed his lips before pulling away even though he chased my kiss.

"I can't hide from the monsters anymore, Knox. I have to face the fact that I am one and that I like what I am becoming. Good night, husband."

He'd stood in front of his family's crypt, which meant he was fighting for the strength to enter it and had failed tonight. Knox was the strongest being within the Nine Realms. Eventually, he'd stop failing. I couldn't be here when that happened. It was time to leave.

I had to finish what I'd come to do, get what I needed, and escape before Knox opened that damn tomb and discovered who lay within his wife's grave. I'd done the math, figured out the equation, and I didn't intend to be around to be the one he went after when he learned the ugly truth.

Chapter Fifty-Three

I woke to women staring down at me with unease burning in their eyes. Lifting from the bed, I stared up at them in curiosity. One stepped forward, or more to the point, the others opted for her by moving backward. The scent of roses caught me off guard as I turned, finding a large bath placed in the middle of the room.

"Uh—I..." she paused, trembling. "I don't know how to address you properly." The girl couldn't have been any older than sixteen. Her wide green eyes rounded in horror as if she thought I'd smote her down or some shit.

"Aria. My name is Aria."

"Queen Aria, we're here to bathe you," she whispered while watching me stretch out, still wearing the dress I'd fallen asleep in last night that was covered in blood droplets.

"Just Aria is fine," I muttered, slowly standing to strip out of the dress. "You can leave. I can bathe myself,"

I announced.

"They cannot leave," Celia snorted, stepping from the shadows to glare at me with a coldness that sent a chill racing down my spine. "King Karnavious instructed them to bathe his whore queen. They will assist you, or the guards can come in and do it for them. Your choice, Aria Hecate," she spat out, like my name on her tongue was vile, and hurt her to say it.

"It's actually Aria Karnavious now," I informed coolly. I dropped the dress, revealing the mating mark he'd placed on my shoulder and throat as she glared at me.

Settling into the water, I leaned back while my attendants poured water over my hair, preparing to use the soap Knox had created for me. Celia gradually moved around the tub until she was in front of me. Today, she had pinned her blonde hair back, and jewels adorned her head to appear as if she wore a crown. Her corset pushed too small breasts forward, making them seem a lot larger than they really were. Her blue eyes that matched Killian's would have been pretty if they weren't filled with hatred.

"The king will never love you. You will never be more than a body he takes at night to ease his needs. He hates everything that you are and will ever be. You will never hold more power than I do in this kingdom. Once the war is over, Knox will end your life, and I will sit on my sister's throne, at his side." Just like I'd seen in one of the potential futures that Karter had shown me, with the exception that it was I who would end their lives.

"Well, that explains your bitterness at him coming home with a bride. Although, to be honest, he doesn't return your feelings," I smirked, tilting my head as the girls washed my hair. "That must upset you greatly, him not returning the lust you feel for him. He's a very generous lover."

"I'm aware of Knox's virility and his stamina, Aria. I have been with the king more than once to ease his grief. I am who he comes to when he misses Liliana. I alone remind him she lived. Do you think you're the only one that carries his mark?" Celia asked, pushing her dress aside to reveal a similar pattern on her shoulder. "You're nothing more than a whore who warms his bed, for now. You are what the people call you, the Queen of Nothing, and he hates you. Knox pretends otherwise, but I see it when he looks at you. He hates everything you are, right down the very center of your poisonous being. Has he told you how beautiful you are yet? Or how he enjoys the fire burning in your eyes? How he craves you and can't stop his need to be within you?" Celia continued, causing my stomach to somersault as she repeated what he had told me. "Or how you're a storm raging within him? He's very adept at seduction. I should know. I taught him what to use on you before he ever left for Haven Falls. I told him what to say and how to get underneath your skin to lower your guard and become susceptible to his kisses and stolen glances. I even told him to handfast with you on Beltane, inside the circle."

"You're lying," I snorted, watching as her smile didn't waver.

Celia produced a sheet of paper from the skirt of her dress, handing it to one girl, who passed it off to me. I stared at the writing, frowning as my eyes scanned the words.

My Dearest King,

> *Marry the evil bitch on Beltane. In the eyes of the law, hers included, she will be yours for one year. Tell her she's gorgeous and that you crave her more than you want to admit; that she is a storm within you that rages unhinged and without end. Hold her at night, make her feel as if you could want more from her. She's young, My Love. Use it against her, for the wishes of a young woman can easily be wielded against her. You know how I enjoy you washing me after a night together? Do the same with her, making her feel desired. You only need to keep her blinded to the possibilities until after Beltane. Once you've returned, we will be united, and she will be caged. I know you loathe touching her and that it makes your skin crawl to be near her, but do what is needed. I cannot wait to feel your teeth against my flesh, claiming me.*

Forever yours, Celia.

"I can't speak your language, Celia," I swallowed, whispering gutturally, crumpling up the letter as she watched me. "And no matter what it says, it's your handwriting. There's no proof it was ever delivered."

"No? Ask him who came up with the plan to handfast with you, Aria. There are so many plots and plans we've made together as a *family.* You are just one among many. The king may enjoy your body because of the beast you house, but you're still his enemy, and that won't ever change."

"I know that everyone is planning shit," I snorted, sitting up to stand, accepting the towel, before moving toward the bed. "Where is Knox?"

"He's at a meeting with the other heads of the rebellion, letting them know that he secured your hand in marriage," Celia said, and I turned, watching as the girls stepped closer to her. "Tell her who Knox spends his evenings with when he is here. Tell this stupid little bitch who will be queen."

"He's been with our lady several times and even marked her as his mate," one girl said, her words sounding rehearsed as Celia smiled coldly.

"See, everyone here is aware of who runs this palace and who will become the next real High Queen of the Nine Realms," Celia whispered, nodding to the girl who smirked, her red lips twisting into a sinister smile as she brushed her blood-red nails on her black dress. "You will die here, Aria. I will ensure it. You're going to be a good little bitch for me and stop fucking the man I intend to claim as my King."

"Tell him that, since he is the one who keeps insisting I come for him," I countered, dropping the towel and smiling as Celia took in the marks Knox had left on my pussy during our rutting fest. He'd freaking bitten me there, placing a claim on my sex that any male would see if I was with them.

"I'm going to enjoy watching him destroy you. Every night he will stand in front of my sister's grave, mourning her and reminding himself why he's forced to endure the use of your vile body. I imagine that every night he returns, he will fight the need to remove that pretty head from your neck. Instead, he holds you close because I told him to do so. Remember that tonight when he pulls you close and kisses your forehead." Celia snorted, smiling demurely as she fixed her hair and righted her dress before heading out of the room. At the door, she clapped her hands, which sent the young girls racing toward her with fear marring their eyes. "I hope you enjoy this shitty little room he's placed you into, unwilling to allow you into his actual bedroom that sits beside mine."

"This is the library, which happens to be my favorite thing in the world."

Celia's eyes looked around the room, and the girls mirrored her curious stare. She frowned before throwing her head back, laughing like she found it amusing.

"You're insane too? Brilliant! You're the perfect mindless queen we needed you to be. I couldn't have chosen you better myself to be the one whose magic we steal and place on a throne we intend to rule together. You're going to be the downfall of witches everywhere, puppet. All we had to do was find your weakness and exploit it. You know, Amara was an easy target for me to wield against you. I gave that simple-minded girl a tonic, and she fell in love with a monster so easily. Amara kept returning again and again, and I would meet her each time, assuring her I was a witch and her guide. It was easy to steer her in the direction I wanted because she hated not being the center of attention. You stole all the attention, making it simple for me to win her over by giving her mine, undivided, ultimately claiming her trust. Amara was starving to feel as if she mattered, bathing in the glow of being someone important for once. It took very little to manipulate her by feeding her potions that turned her against you.

"Garrett, well, he did love her, because what beauty falls in love with a monster like that? I took great pleasure in knowing that you removed her head, unknowing that she was innocent of the crimes she committed. I watched you do it and knew that once you found out she was being controlled, you'd hate yourself for killing your twin sister. You shouldn't have touched what belongs to me, little bitch. Once was expected because the king's magic carries a heavy toll on him and on those he uses it on. You couldn't stay off his dick, though. Could you? No, because you're nothing more than a worthless whore. So I took steps to end your life, and since I no longer needed Amara to get you and your sisters back into the Nine Realms, she was expendable. Knox interrupted it unknowingly and brought you to his castle before Garrett's father could remove that nasty head of yours. You should have died in the Kingdom of Unwanted Beasts, Aria. It would have been much kinder than what we intend to do to you," Celia laughed, watching the tears swimming in my eyes as I swallowed.

"Didn't know that, did you? Amara wasn't a monster. In fact, she was sweet and begged me to spare you even while under the influence of magic. Her love for you was that strong. It took three times the amount of magic to force her to persuade Garret and his father to get you into that throne room, where you dangled like a piece of rotten meat that doesn't even know it's rancid yet. Watch your back, witch. Your days are numbered. Keep fucking the man I intend to marry and see which one of us wins that fight," Celia laughed coldly, turning on her heel as she left the room, sealing it before the lock clicked into place.

I covered my trembling lips with my hands as rage rushed through me. Had Knox known about Amara? No, he couldn't have. He'd come to save me. Brander had told me as much, and his anger at finding me like that had been real. Did he have any idea of the psychopath he'd created by sleeping with his dead wife's sister? Probably not. He wasn't bright about that sort of thing. Did I believe that she'd given him hints on how to seduce me? Maybe, but he'd chosen different words and had done other things with me she hadn't mentioned.

The thing about crazy bitches was this; you couldn't trust what they said or take it as truth without digging up the dirt. She was obviously obsessed with Knox, and while I didn't blame her, she'd just signed her death certificate in my sister's blood. I'd smelled the magic around Amara, but I'd trusted my eyes with the proof of her guilt. I needed to know how much of her death rested on Knox, if any. If he'd helped drive her into that kingdom of horrors, I'd never forgive him.

Knox may not have known about Amara or what Celia had done, but he was guilty of creating that monster the same as he was creating me. I'd spent enough time trying to reach him and learned that he wasn't ready for me yet. I couldn't force him to change his mind. And the moment Knox opened that tomb, all hell would break loose. It was time to initiate my exit plan, which I'd already begun.

Chapter Fifty-Four

Greer walked me around the palace, taking me deep into the family rooms. We silently made our way through the halls, him watching me as I took in painted pictures of Knox and his family. In every painting were his bride and him. I paused in front of one, studying the amulet Liliana wore that I suspected held the tonic that masked her scent.

Sliding my gaze to an image with Sven, my stomach tightened, noting his familiar features, complimented by dark wavy hair and striking blue eyes that looked up at his father as if Knox was his hero.

"Master Sven loved his father very much," Greer said beside me, exhaling. "His mother, though, she wasn't much for the rearing of her child. I think had Sven been born female. She may have taken a liking to him more."

"You knew," I stated, turning to look into Greer's soft gray eyes.

"Know what, Aria?" he asked, his gaze sliding over my face.

"Nothing," I swallowed, spinning toward the library as people stopped to watch us walking through the hallways.

The entire palace was a memorial to Knox's family. Every hallway carried pictures or statues of what he'd loved and lost. On each one sat a hex bag, causing memories to spring to the front of people's minds. It was like forcing someone to relieve Liliana's and Sven's deaths on repeat. People stood in front of the statues, sobbing over individuals who had been gone for five hundred years.

"You know, if you remove those bags that carry the hex to remember, people might eventually move on," I stated beneath my breath, watching Greer pause to grab one.

I stopped, turning to see him toss the bag in his hand before slowly shaking his head. "I thought Celia added the bags to the statues to preserve them for a millennium. I had no idea that she was forcing everyone to relive the memories of the past. No wonder no one has moved on from the loss. That woman is a fierce hunter and refuses to allow Liliana to find some resemblance of peace in her death."

"She says she has slept with Knox," I pointed out, hearing Greer exhale, which was proof enough of Celia telling the truth. "That's low, even for him."

"Consider her hex bags as proof of her magic skills, Peasant. Celia is very adept at getting what she wants, and she very much wants your husband."

"She can have him, with my blessing," I returned, pausing in front of the library. "Where are the gargoyles?" I questioned.

"They're around, but sometimes they need more sleep than usual. Like all creatures, they go through times where they need to create new life. When that happens, they choose to slumber to prevent creating life with another race."

"Are they against creating mixed offspring?" I asked curiously.

Greer smiled, slowly shaking his head. "They turn to stone when they—release into their mate, returning to their hardening form. If they did so with another, they would die. They can only create new life with certain races in the Nine Realms. Witches are one of those, if that is what you're asking."

I snorted, rolling my eyes. "No, far from it," I laughed as Greer's eyebrows shot up, and his head canted to the side. "Thank you for showing me around the palace."

"You mean the memorial?" he chuckled, watching my face fall. "Knox is worth saving, Aria. Some love is worth fighting to get and keep. I know you think he's broken and that you won't be able to reach him, but if anyone can, it is you."

"You think I'm a miracle worker, Meat Suit. I'm afraid that after last night and this morning, I don't care if he is saved or not anymore," I smiled sadly, moving into the library as Greer studied me with a worried look.

Inside the library, I closed the door before whispering the words to bar the entrance. My eyes slid around the room, moving toward the shelves that were revealed without me needing to ask. Wiggling my nose, a cart appeared, and I smiled.

"Thanks," I said into the air, knowing the library was a living, breathing thing that only showed itself to those worthy of the knowledge it held.

I pulled books from shelves, piling them onto the cart before taking them to the far section of the library. I passed an opening to my left and peered down a dimly lit hallway, lined with shelves on each side, stacked from floor to ceiling with books and other objects. The hallway seemed to be never-ending, and although I felt the need to explore, my inner voice told me that now was not the time. Pushing the cart forward, I headed toward a large door that opened to my touch, revealing a substantial room decorated in masculine colors.

Inside the room, a substantial four-posture bed sat in the middle. On the walls were pictures of Sven and Liliana, all at different ages. I went to the dresser and pulled out a shirt, inhaling it to breathe in Knox's scent. Placing it back into the dresser, I crawled onto the bed, staring up at the picture that covered the top of the canopy. Lying down, I studied a picture of me standing naked in the creek outside of the House of Magic, in the human realm.

Floating in the creek around me was the red dress I'd worn to the gathering where I'd emasculated Fallon. Claws were pushed through my nail beds, and my hands were in my hair, holding it away from my face as tears slid from my eyes. How the hell had he captured the image? I looked vulnerable and beautiful. My walls were down, broken from hearing the alpha wolves murdering Fallon after I'd brought him down for them. Sitting up,

I frowned, then moved from the bed, smoothing the blankets before heading deeper into his room.

A bust of my face sat on a marble stand, and my hand slid over it, smiling. If Knox hated being around me so much, why had he captured images of me in my most vulnerable moments? I infatuated Knox when I was at my weakest? Why?

Inspecting the room, I noticed large spikes of ice that filled one long wall at the back. Stepping closer, I lowered my body, squinting to see inside them. The longer I looked, the clearer the ice became until it exposed the silhouettes of people. Moving closer still, I realized I was looking inside Hecate's tomb, and my heart sped up, hammering, as my sisters appeared, pacing through the narrow space that was recording their images.

Standing, I scanned the room filled with images of people through the ice. Exhaling, I bristled, understanding how Knox had so easily found me even when I'd figured out how to null the effects of his tattoo for a few moments. Heading to the adjoining room, I paused as huge bones came into view, positioned around giant eggs that looked like they were created from skulls.

My hand trembled as I lifted my fingers, brushing them over the porous surface. My image shimmered in front of me, and I yelped, jumping out of my skin.

"Dragon eggs, My Queen."

"It's creepy that you appear with my face," I grunted, glaring at my image as I spoke to the library.

My image shimmered, turning into Knox. I snorted, shaking my head. "Is this better?" The library asked in Knox's thick and husky voice. I nodded, relieved that I wasn't being forced to speak to myself anymore. "Long ago, the dragons flew within the skies of Norvalla. They were giant creatures that had wingspans of over one-hundred feet." Knox's image waved its hand before an enormous dragon landed in front of me, its wings wide and its mouth open as it screeched in front of me, shooting my hair into the air.

I laughed, lifting my hand to touch it, but my hand slid through its body as if made from mist. Looking at the library version of Knox, I frowned, noting it watched me with a cheeky smile on its lips. Huge arms crossed over his chest, and then we moved without warning.

I gasped, staring around as we stood in an extensive field full of phoenixes and dragons. They were together, moving around with one another as smaller ones flapped their wings wildly, shrieking as the larger ones watched them play.

"They're beautiful," I swallowed.

"They were when they lived freely within the Nine Realms," he agreed, lifting his hand, and a small, fiery phoenix landed in his palm. "Do you know what we call it when they mate together?"

"No, I never even knew they existed," I admitted, not afraid to be truthful with the library. "I was never taught about them because we were told they didn't exist."

"They were real," he stated, pulling me toward him, handing me the phoenix.

I cradled it in my arms, watching it as it slowly rubbed its head against my chest. Red eyes watched me, slowly blinking golden lashes. Something else flew toward me, and I held my hand out, and a baby dragon with shimmering green scales mixed with red crawled up my arm. My heart thundered with excitement, seeing the creatures of myth that moved over my arm and chest. I laughed softly, the first carefree emotion that felt real in a long time.

Knox's image laughed, moving to wrap his arms around me, holding me. It didn't feel like the library; it felt like Knox, causing a storm of sensations that rushed through me.

"Stop overthinking it," he whispered against my ear.

He held his hands out, and both creatures leaped onto them. They turned toward one another, opening their mouths, sending red and blue flames into the air. Their fire connected, and sparks of gold ignited. I leaned back, watching the fire that blazed brightly.

"Imagine if they made a child together, one that could create both flames in one soul," he swallowed tightly.

A noise sounded behind us, and the sensation of falling took hold of me. I landed on a couch seconds before a book slammed into my stomach. I yelped, sitting up in the tiny little nightgown the library had placed onto me. I held up the book, peering over the top to see Knox marching through the doorway. His eyes slowly landed on me before they slid down my body.

His mouth curved into a smile, and he spun on his heel, stripping out of the armor he wore. My eyes feasted on his body, drinking in the sight of his sinewy muscles. A fire crackled to life beside me as the lights dimmed. My eyes narrowed, slipping around the library with an accusatory glare.

Knox turned, grinning as his eyes took the same slow look around the library that I had just given it. He removed his shirt and changed into a pair of sweatpants. Holding up his hand, a book dropped from the sky, forcing my eyes to lift as he settled on the couch, stretching out beside me.

"I trust your day was uneventful, wife?" Knox asked, looking at me over the top of the Alpha Male's Guide to Kama Sutra. "Interesting choice of books," he said into the air, directed at the library as he dropped his eyes to the pages.

The book I was reading was The Art of War. I smiled, licking my finger to change the page. I lifted my eyes to him, and his head tilted while I studied his unguarded face. His eyes rose, and mine dropped, slowly sliding over the pages while seeing nothing. I brought my finger to my mouth and chewed the tip of the nail, peeking beneath my hooded lashes to hold his heated gaze that leisurely slid over my naked legs.

Swallowing hard, I shifted my legs, parting them slightly while lowering my eyes to the pages. I could feel Knox's gaze on my naked sex. The hunger burning in his eyes floored me. I could feel the heat pulsing from the way he looked at it, slowly making me tighten with the need to feel him pulsing within me. I lifted my eyes to find him watching me.

"How was your day?" I asked, unable to keep the lust from filling my tone.

"Eventful, unfortunately," he stated, lowering his book to sit up. "It helps," he grabbed my book, turning it right side up before handing it back to me, "to have the book the right way when reading, wife," he whispered, grinning.

A blush heated my cheeks as he lay back, lifting his knee, resting his left arm over the back of the couch. He held the book with one large hand and licked his finger, letting his tongue slide over it before he smirked, hearing the groan that filled my throat.

"You're wet and dripping onto my couch," he rumbled.

"I could be dripping on your tongue, but you're a dick." I sat up, slowly curling my legs beneath me. I brought the book up to prevent him from seeing the smile cresting my lips. I could hear the pages crinkling, turning. His scent unleashed without warning, and I closed my eyes, shuddering.

"Doing okay, Aria? You seem to be trembling," he teased.

My smile dropped with the book, sending my scent rushing toward him, and his expression faltered as his hooded stare captured mine. I looked pointedly at him, watching his chest rise and fall while he struggled against the scent my body was creating, one that Ember assured me would bring Knox to his knees.

Knox sat up, slowly placing his book aside, looking at me. I set mine down, closing my eyes against the scent that he intensified. I lunged, landing on him as everything unleashed within us. My body touched his, and I exploded. He grunted, groaning as our eyes met and held. My arms glowed, and his lit up as well. Trembling, I whimpered as Knox yanked me onto his lap, freeing himself to enter me hard and fast.

"I wasn't even reading," I admitted, hearing him chuckle.

"I was staring at your naked pussy the entire time, beneath the pages," he grunted, devouring my mouth. I rocked against him, pushing my hands through his hair, fighting him for control of the kiss. Knox pushed me back onto the couch, thrusting slowly into my body even though we'd already finished before ever starting. The room darkened, and I pulled away, staring around the room while he smirked. "You feel so fucking good, Aria," he growled, forcing my attention back to him.

I watched his eyes, holding them until I was screaming his name. I came undone around him until his body tensed, and he growled, lowering his mouth to my shoulder, kissing it as he pressed his throat to my lips. My tongue slid over his flesh, feeling him trembling against me. I felt his need for me to finish it, to claim him, yet I couldn't. It had to be the right way. I knew when and where I would claim him, and he wouldn't see me coming.

"Aria, please," he growled, and yet I shook my head. Pushing him away, I stood to clean myself off before I moved to the fire, cradling my body.

I had to claim him, and if what Celia said was true, he'd helped force me to murder Amara. The thought made me nauseated. I shivered, even though the Ifrit's flame blazed within the fire. Arms wrapped around me, and before I could figure out what he intended to do, his teeth sank into my shoulder. Then everything went dark around me.

Chapter Fifty-Five

Knox

Moving into the war room, I paused, sliding my gaze over Celia's desperate outfit. Today, she squished her breasts against the top she wore, and her skirt was slit to her waist, exposing both thighs. Exhaling irritation, I stepped into the room, scanning my brother's faces before Celia entered, taking her seat beside me.

Her hand immediately slid onto my thigh, skimming against my cock as if done on accident. My hand grabbed hers, placing it on the table as I gave her a withering look. It wasn't a secret we'd been together once, which had been years after my wife's death, with grief fueling a drunken rage in which she'd taken advantage. Not that I'd been innocent.

Celia had pretended to enjoy it, but I'd seen the fear and pain lingering in her eyes as I'd gone hard on her, unleashing the monster that needed an outlet. She'd bled, and I'd woken up with her still in my fucking bed, disgusted with myself. I'd tasted the magic within the air, knowing she'd used it on me to gain entrance into my bed and onto my cock. The bitch hadn't been back to it after the first time.

"I told you to handfast the whore, not marry her," she hissed.

"I'd be very fucking careful, woman," I growled, sitting back to stare at Killian, who slid his attention to his sister, knowing what she craved and would never have. "You'd do well to remember who you are speaking to inside this room."

"My apologies," she rushed out, her hand immediately moving to my dick again.

I caught it before she could accidentally grab me again. I wasn't stupid. I knew she wanted Aria to scent her on my dick. It wasn't fucking happening. Aria had almost claimed me last night. I'd felt her need, the compulsion to finish what she'd started, and yet she'd stopped short. I had a feeling Celia's visit to my room had something to do with that.

"You shouldn't have married her, Knox. You know nothing about her," Celia continued, and I turned, taking in her face.

Celia was beautiful, but she didn't hold a candle to Aria. Where she was cold, Aria had a fire that burned within me, raging out of control. Celia hadn't even moved me when she'd pretended to enjoy my bed. Aria unleased hell against me, meeting me in passion and then some.

"I married, and it's done. I know that girl better than I know you. I studied her, watched her, and charted a course that took us to an altar, making her my wife. I cannot undo it. I won't allow it to be undone. Fucking deal with it and keep away from her. Any more stunts like you pulled in front of the court, and you will go home. Do you hear me? I won't give you another warning."

"She isn't Liliana!" Celia snapped.

"And neither are you! I fucking know who and what that girl *isn't!* You will watch your fucking tone inside this room. Do you fucking understand me? I'm not your fucking brother-in-law right now. I am the King of the Nine Realms, woman. Answer me," I shouted, slamming my hand onto the table, sending drinks into the air as she gasped, shooting her chair back onto the ground to escape my wrath.

"I understand!"

"Good! Now, report."

Killian glared at his sister as she righted her chair and smoothed out her dress before sitting. "We have asked the heads of the rebellion, and not a single one requested that Aria Hecate be kept alive. We went through the higher-ups as well, and nothing."

I turned it over in my head and looked to Brander, who frowned. "That doesn't make sense. We all heard the order. Who could hold enough power to fuck with our heads?"

"Witches," Celia snorted, her hands shaking as she reached for her drink. "Ilsa could have wanted her alive to add to a grid, or maybe she wanted the murderous little bitch at her side."

"It's possible, but we're covered in runes and spells that prevent her from reaching us with her magic. There's also the fact that her magic wouldn't work on me," Knox admitted.

"You can nullify Aria. You did it inside Haven Falls. You're her fucking kryptonite, and she's aware of it. That will make her desperate to escape once we bring in her family. You plan to manage it, brother?" Lore asked, his fingers drumming on the table.

"If we knew where the fuck they were, I could. The thing is, Lord Carter's body was returned in pieces by his army. They are all madly in love with a witch named Reign, who spelled them all. Carter broke the orders I gave him, which means I need to get back to what fucking matters, which is being seen in the army and running the fucking thing."

"Aria's family drew blood, which means you're no longer bound to the oath you gave her on your wedding bargain. Is that going to be a problem?" Killian asked.

"Aria will end up murdering Aurora once she learns the truth about who she really is," I scoffed, pulling the drink to my lips as I considered the pain she would endure when she discovered the truth.

"All the digging you had me do, and you don't intend to use it against her?" Celia asked, her tone snide and filled with loathing.

"No, and neither are you." I placed the drink back onto the table, sitting forward. "The silver-haired men following her are too close in their similar appearance for it to be a coincidence. Minus Aden, the one who wants to breed her. I think they're family."

"I'm surprised Aden didn't chase her through our gates with the little show you gave him in the cave," Killian snorted. "I know I wanted to."

"You wish, Killian. Aria would chew you up and spit you out," Lore goaded.

"Would she? Because I'm pretty sure she'd ride me through the gates of hell, and I'd let her," Killian teased.

"Can you guys stop thinking with your cocks for five minutes? She's a problem. You have a Hecate witch as your bride. It doesn't matter what your other half is. If you die in battle, Knox, she's the fucking heir to your throne," Celia sneered

I smiled, turning to look at her before narrowing my eyes on Brander. "You want to tell her?" I asked, watching Brander snort before running his hands over his mouth.

"In the event Knox is unable to lead, I will take his place. I am his heir since I am the second-born son."

"And the High King?" she asked, sliding her eyes toward Killian.

"Aria, because they won't follow a witch," I admitted, watching her anger spike. "If she kills me, they will crown her, and as they place the crown, they would remove her head and the threat she would impose without me here to handle her."

"You've got it all figured out, don't you?"

I smiled, standing as the others joined me. "I'm King, Celia. It's my job to be ten steps ahead of everyone else. Gentlemen, care to accompany me to the library for some research?" Everyone rushed toward the door, drawn by the need to be close to the one woman they felt most.

Aria wasn't just my wife. She was a beacon of hope that more like her were out there. After encountering Eva, and the woman who ran from us as Aria had tried to escape, we knew there were more out there. We just had to figure out how to get to them and show them we weren't their fucking enemies.

It brought hope for new life and little monsters within the kingdom again. The thought of finding a mate was exhilarating to my men because I had subjected them to the beauty of Aria. Smiling, I left the cankerous bitch behind as I made my way toward the door.

"Knox? What about us?" Celia called to my back, and I turned, staring at her.

"Considering you are the sister of my deceased wife, I suggest you forget that there was a slip on my part that would lead you to believe there was an '*us.*' You're here because Killian asked me to allow it. I couldn't care less where you go or who you fuck. I only care that you stay the fuck away from my wife. She may be my enemy, Celia, but make no mistake, she's mine and under my protection. Break the law I granted, and I'll snap your fucking head off."

Chapter Fifty-Six

Aria

The room was dark when Knox entered, laughing at something one of his men said in the hallway behind him. He stopped dead in his tracks, and I studied him as he slowly lifted his nose, inhaling the mating scent I'd released for hours. Oceanic-eyes narrowed as he moved further into the room, followed by his men, drawn in by my scent.

"Why does your bedroom smell like heaven, Knox?" Lore asked, lifting his nose, rattling, and I echoed the sound.

All sets of eyes swung to where I would have been if I'd remained there. I was the hunter, and they were the prey. No noise escaped me as I silently watched Knox stepping further into the room. He rattled softly, and mine echoed it, forcing his eyes to where I sat on all fours, perched on a shelf, dressed in only the sheer material of the white see-through gown.

"What is she doing all the way up there?" Brander asked, his eyes studying me. I locked gazes with Knox, marking him as my target, lowering my head with him in my sights.

"Fuck if I know," Knox admitted, narrowing his eyes on me.

I rattled a challenge, and Knox's mouth curved into a sinful smile. He echoed it, and I let loose a soothing purr that caused his men to moan. His eyes slanted, and his attention moved to his brothers, who fought the urge to answer my call.

"You guys should go," Knox warned, moving deeper into the library. Vanishing, I entered the jetstream to lose him while recalling my scent so he couldn't trace me.

I watched him appear where I'd been standing, only to find me gone. Stepping back into the shadows, I studied the gracefulness of his form as he slowly turned, exploring the darkened space for me. His men didn't move. They remained in the doorway, watching as Knox searched for me.

"She's fucking hunting you, isn't she?" Killian asked, his tone filled with awe.

"Indeed. And she's controlling her scent. I can't feel Aria or sense her within the room at all," Knox admitted.

I lowered my form, zeroing in on him before I kicked him from the shelf on which he stood. He dropped to the floor, landing gracefully on his feet before he spun, staring up at me as I rattled huskily.

I was more creature than myself, and yet *I was in control*. I'd stared at my eyes for twenty minutes, watching the gold flecks dancing within the darker turquoise depths. Knox answered me loudly, but his rattle wasn't one I intended to acknowledge, knowing I held all the control in the mating hunt.

I was the huntress, and he was the one who would answer me with the right call or not at all. I purred, crouching before hissing, expelling a low rattle in a sultry song that rustled through me as his eyes grew hooded and begun smoldering with heat.

"Felt that one in the balls," Lore snorted. My eyes slid to his, echoing the sound as Lore dropped to his knees. "Consider this my surrender, Aria. Mount daddy. Daddy needs you, baby girl. Come on. I'm right here." I hissed, and his eyes narrowed. "She just rejected my dick flat out, didn't she?"

"Indeed, she did," Brander growled, rattling to gain my attention. I glared at him, watching as he exhaled. "I think she's still peeved that I tried to kiss her on a bet."

"Look at her eyes, she's—stunning," Fade stated, his rattle low and soothing as he gazed at me.

I rattled loudly, threatening them all, causing Gideon to step back, pressing his back against the wall. His chest rose and fell in fear that smelled enticing, drawing the predator within me to him for the easy meal. I felt Knox before he moved. Jumping into the air, I flipped backward, landing on the other side of the library, hidden within the shadows.

Knox turned, staring into the shadows, searching for me with anticipation echoing through him. His scent was primal and heady to the monster I'd released. I wanted him in the worst way imaginable. I could feel his need matching mine, pulsing hungrily through the room. The need to capture and conquer fueled him as it lit every cell of my being with the need to do the same.

"What the hell *is* she?" Mateo asked. When it came, his rattle made my spine arch, releasing my scent, and Knox turned, zeroing in on my location.

I moved with speed, slamming into Knox, taking him with me to the floor. I flipped midair, using my legs to send him sailing through it until he landed on his feet. He slid to a stop, fluidly standing from his crouched position, facing me.

I prowled toward him as my teeth retracted, and my claws slid into my nails. He lowered his head, and his mouth slanted into a sinful grin. Knox's eyes changed to onyx with golden sparks burning within them, mirroring mine as he merged with his beast, becoming both while holding his human form.

"Who are you?" Knox asked, and I rattled loudly.

My mouth opened, and the ancient language slipped free, rattling and purring until he swallowed, closing his eyes as his hands tightened into fists at his side. The other men within the room exhaled a sultry purr, floored with the language and sounds I made.

Knox's smile darkened with desire, slowly cocking his head to the side. He'd heard it, creature and woman speaking to him in a language only we could understand. Knox stepped forward, rattling. I laughed huskily at his attempt to bring me to my knees with his mere scent and rattle alone. I vanished before his eyes, appearing in front of him, ripping his shirt off to reveal the muscles beneath.

"You want me. Come and get me," I taunted before vanishing into the jetstream as Knox turned toward where I stood on the opposite side of the room. He rattled loudly, and my body ached, curving my hips as he slowly walked to me. Knox released his scent, sending it straight to my core that tightened with the need to bow to him and surrender beneath the dominance he promised.

"What the fuck are you doing?" Knox asked, turning his head to discover the large nest to which I was luring him. He halted, noting that I'd filled it with shredded pieces of stuffing from his bed, or what was left of it. Sheets covered the material, creating a soothing, soft place for us to mate. "You made us a nest, Little Monster," he whispered huskily, a cocky grin playing on his generous mouth. His brothers all inched forward to see my creation, sending fear rushing through me with their combined scents, getting too close to the nest I'd made to mate.

I rattled loudly in warning, and Knox peeked over his shoulder as the men moved closer, taking in what I'd done. He rattled low in his chest, matching my warning before his attention slid back to me, finding me gone.

I studied him from my perch, noticing his eyes had turned to match mine this time. Instead of the fiery sparks that had burned within them, golden-hued flecks were dancing in their endless depths. He'd freed himself to be both beast and man, to handle what I'd done, intending to claim him fully.

"Gods damn. That's a nest," Fade stated.

"No shit? Isn't that what Knox just said?" Mateo snorted.

Gideon lowered himself to touch it, but paused before he could. His eyes lifted, hearing me zipping around the room, getting closer to him. I placed my scent all about them, and Gideon's eyes lifted, finding me directly above him on a shelf. I crouched forward, purring in warning, preparing to defend my territory.

"Get the hell away from her nest, now," Brander hissed in a low warning. "The last time someone other than Knox touched it, she went psycho. It was cute, but she didn't seem to think so. The only thing going into that nest is her and Knox."

"That's amazing," Gideon said, purring up at me while I watched him through narrowed slits. I crouched even lower, fully intending to protect it with my life. He stood, slowly backing away as Mateo and Brander stepped between Gideon and me, realizing that I would rip Gideon apart before I let him touch my nest.

Knox used my need to defend our nest against me, slamming into me as he chuckled darkly. His fingers pushed through my hair, preparing to claim my throat, but I slammed my hand into his mouth. I forced Knox back as he went over the edge of the bookcase, landing on his feet once more. He growled angrily, staring up at me as I smiled down at him.

"You want it rough, Little One?" Knox's eyes burned with a fire that threatened to consume me. "Last time, it took a week for you to sit without wincing."

I purred throatily, the sound vibrating through the room as I called to him. Knox swallowed hard, running his hands over his mouth. He rattled his need back, telling me he would fight me to breed me. My mouth opened, and the sound that escaped was both rattle and purr, which gave him pause. It was bare-bones escaping my throat. It was both me and my creature, promising him dark desires that he would meet one way or another tonight.

"Battle of the sexes up in this bitch!" Lore chuckled, staring up at me before he lunged forward. He landed on the shelf, creeping toward me before I dove, sending him back to the floor in a heap of limbs, hissing at him in warning. "Ouch! That wasn't nice, Aria!"

"She's not fucking playing, Lore. You need to stop being stupid before she actually hurts you. Aria intends to claim her mate, and that's a battle you aren't ready to wage," Brander growled, pushing Lore behind him as he bared his teeth, rattling.

My spine itched, and I let the rattle build until it boomed out of me as I rose. It was a carnal sound, dropping the men to their knees while Knox watched with fire blistering in his eyes. He opened his mouth to rattle, and I slammed into his body, wrapping my legs around him, claiming his mouth hungrily. He moaned, mirroring my rattle, shredding the dress I wore, before turning my body to slam me up against the wall.

Knox's hands captured mine, pinning them above my head, pulling back as I purred against him. My legs wrapped tighter around him as my full scent escaped, and his eyes grew hooded. I felt his erection and purred louder, inhaling his mating pheromones until it sent me into a frenzy.

Knox barely got his pants off before I freed my hands and hit the floor, forcing him up against the wall. I used his shock against him, dropping to my knees, ripping his pants down the rest of the way, enjoying the sound of the clothing being destroyed. I took him in my mouth and up to the base as he cried out, shielding us from the others, before dropping his head back against the wall while I moaned around him.

"Extending jaw time!" Lore's tone was filled with interest and awe. The others shuffled closer, but Knox turned, glaring at them, using his hands to prevent them from seeing what I was doing to his dick.

"Get the fuck out!" Knox screamed, and his voice was layered and guttural, which sent all the men tripping over their feet as I smiled up at him. He reached down, pulling me up, taking me to our nest, and carefully lying me down. He grabbed my legs, parting my sex as he dropped his mouth to it insatiably, tasting me and making indecent sounds as he ravaged me hungrily.

I yanked on his hair, beyond the point of caring about anything else but getting him into my body. I rolled him, pushing my body above his, aiming him where I needed, and he observed through eyes that looked as if he'd collected stars, burning within them.

"Who are you?" I whispered huskily.

"I am the man who protects you in your need and who soothes your aches while you wish to breed. I am the mate who heeds your call. I am the one who will give you it all. I am Knox, High King of the Nine Realms," he returned. "Who are you?"

"I am Aria Karnavious. I am your mate, Knox," I murmured, sliding down onto him, and I lowered my mouth as my teeth broke free.

His hand threaded through my hair, holding me against his throat as my teeth pushed through his flesh, creating the mark that caused his entire body to shake violently. I opened myself to him. He groaned as I licked the mark, moving my mouth to his shoulder, kissing it before I moaned while biting into him, sensing the need as I slammed my body onto his. I licked his shoulder and cried out as he rolled me, staring down at me. Something within us changed.

"Do you feel that?" he whispered in wonder, his mouth kissing the curve of my throat. Wrapping my legs around him, I lifted my hips to take him further into me.

"I feel you, Knox. I feel all of you," I admitted, crying out as he claimed my throat softly, sending my body over the cliff. He increased his speed, and I continued to open for him until there was nothing between us.

"I feel you opening your womb for me, woman," he growled gravely, his movements fevered as he continued thrusting until he lifted his head back, rattling as the room shook around us.

He lifted me, wrapping his arms around my back, peering into my eyes. Knox unguarded without clothes was worse than Knox unguarded *with* them. I rocked with him, wrapping my arms around his neck as he kissed me fervently until everything else melted away. I whispered his name before purring exploded from both of our lungs. Our creatures fell apart with us as the orgasm that held me lost within it released. Worse, I was lost in the sensation of him as he continued pounding into my body, unwilling to let the mating end.

Knox gently laid me onto the nest, smiling down at the hooded look I gave him as he started the act anew. He moved slower, gentler as he took me to heaven and sent me soaring into the stars. His forehead brushed against mine as my fingers touched the mark I'd made on his throat. He smiled roguishly, pushing forward harder, causing a moan to slip past my kiss-swollen lips.

"You built a nest for us, and then you opened your womb to me. Aria, you claimed me, and I have never felt anything like it. I've never felt anything like you. You're truly a unicorn, woman. You took me to heaven tonight and showed me what it truly meant to feel claimed. Thank you," he whispered, pushing my legs up as he moved into my body.

I purred, and he answered it, rattling as he rolled his hips, finding the perfect place within my body that held his name upon it. He didn't rush it or make it go faster than it should. Knox made love to me in a nest I'd created for him to fuck me. He hadn't questioned the insanity of the need for it to happen here. He hadn't made it into something ugly or turned it against me. He'd realized what little control I had during the mating hunt, and even though he could have fought me and dominated me, he'd chosen to see where I would take him.

Knox purred his pleasure, echoing mine. He increased his speed, grabbing my hands to hold them beside my head as he pumped into my body. Opening my mouth, I cried out his name as the orgasm washed through me, sending me floating on the waves, now coloring his eyes. The intensity burning within them sent me rocking upon the white caps. He tightened his hold, increasing his speed while growling my name, claiming my mouth hungrily, and filling my body with arousal.

He didn't move away from me, staring into my eyes. I trembled and came undone as the mating finished, and his scent forced my body to shiver and shake violently.

Knox lowered his mouth, pulling on my lip as he smiled against me.

"You are mine, Little Monster. Now until forever. I claim you as my mate, Aria Primrose Karnavious," he whispered so softly that I almost missed it. It also wasn't in English, which meant I had to pretend I hadn't understood.

"Again," I whispered as he smiled.

"You're not too sore?" he asked, lifting as he released my hands.

I cupped his cheek, smiling seductively up at him before speaking softly. "Stars, hide your fires. Let not light see my black and deep desires."

"Are you quoting Shakespeare to me now, woman?" Knox's smile was blinding as he searched my eyes.

"We're fucking in the library, so it seemed fitting," I laughed as he lowered his eyes to my mouth.

"Fate gave its light tonight, and all the pretty stars then did align. And yet she shined brighter than any star ever could burn, with an inner fire that burned me hotter than even Ifrit's fire. She burned me with her darkest pleasurable desires and lit up my night as she became my brightest light," he swallowed, watching me.

"Knox Karnavious, my husband and mate," I whispered, tears filling my eyes as he kissed them away.

"There's something I must do tonight, Aria. Do not leave this nest. Do you understand me? I enjoy seeing you naked within it, knowing that it is only ours. I intend to return and find solace within your heat."

"You don't think it's a little weird that I make a nest

where we could get busy? I really hope I'm not one of those three-headed bird-like beasts that tried to eat us when we were going down the waterfall."

Knox laughed, kissing my lips as he lifted to stand. I watched him walk away, his hands forming fists at his sides. Turning, he stared back at me with indecision playing in them. My heart thundered at the idea of him leaving to do what I knew he intended, tonight. Pain pierced through my heart as it clenched tightly, choking my words.

"Those aren't shifters. They're birds with no human form." Knox bent to retrieve his pants before holding them up to smirk as he took in their shredded legs. "You were amazing tonight, Aria. I didn't expect you to give me this. I know I have not earned it, nor am I deserving of you."

I lifted into a sitting position, smiling at him sadly while my heart cracked, knowing I was losing him again. "Kiss me, Knox. One time without your walls up. Just once," I whispered. Standing, I waited to see if he would fulfill my request.

"Every time I kiss you, my walls are down, Aria. You're the second women I have ever kissed in my life. Kissing insinuates feelings. I haven't kissed other women because I don't care about how they feel, which makes me an asshole, but I am okay with that. Yet you, I crave your lips and the sweet nectar of them against mine." He closed the distance between us, cupping my cheek as he lifted me, claiming my mouth in a kiss filled with longing and something else. *Something deeper.*

Knox went to war against my lips, and by the time he finished, he was inside of me again, and I was holding on for dear life. He unleashed his control, taking us both over the edge until we slid down the wall together. He cradled me as if I was precious, and I gasped for air, whispering his name since that was the only thing that would escape my lips.

"That's how you kiss a woman until the only thing she can whisper is your name, for the record," he growled against my ear, pulling back. I smiled at him, still trying to get my brain to work enough to figure out what words even were after that kiss.

Knox placed me inside the nest before he dressed, moving toward the door with a cocky grin on his lips. When he reached the door, he paused to look back at me as I smiled. He shook his head, leaning against it as if he was trying to decide what he wanted more, me, or answers to why our mating felt real. I swallowed the moment he chose his path, slipping out the door which he locked, telling me that even if we were mates, he still didn't trust me. I'd seen the worry flashing in his eyes and knew where he was going.

I stood, grabbing the clothes I'd placed aside before creating the nest today. Silently, I walked to the window, gazing down at Knox standing before the statues of his family, and then touched the door between them, opening it with magic.

My head leaned against the cold window, listening for what seemed like an eternity until, finally, his rattle exploded. My back arched, and everything within me demanded I go down to my knees.

"This is where you get me out of here because the moment Knox reaches me, I will be the target for that betrayal and rage," I whispered to the library, feeling the pause before the need to kneel for the more dominant beast abated. "He's going to kill me this time."

I turned, watching as the vault appeared. I placed my freshly mated hand against it, and the door slid open, and I entered. I was leaving Knox to deal with the turmoil of emotions he was forced to face. I couldn't be his whipping post this time. The pain he'd need to release was too high. He was about to wage war against the witches on an entirely new level, and I had to protect the people I could from his wrath.

Chapter Fifty-Seven

Knox

My hand pushed against the stone door, opening the one place I haven't entered since the day I'd buried my wife beside our son. Inside, candles leaped to life, feeling my presence. The door sealed behind me. Silently, I moved toward Sven's tomb that held his image on the top. My hand slid through the dust and silt that had built over his tiny grave.

"Sven, it's daddy," I whispered, fighting the prickling of tears. Fresh pain ripped through me, raw and unchecked without warning. I swallowed through the tightening in my throat. My gaze slid to Liliana's tomb, and I made a fist over Sven's. "I miss you, Little Man. I miss you every day. You're my first thought each morning, and my last before sleep takes me where the pain of your loss doesn't hurt so much."

I moved toward Liliana's figure, touching the crown that matched the one I'd placed on Aria. It hadn't been the real crown as I'd been unable to put it on Aria's head, knowing her bloodline had killed my mate. She'd known. I'd seen it shining in her eyes as I'd handed it off to Siobhan, yet she'd not said a word about it. Aria had worn a fake crown because I'd been hell-bent on her not being Queen or wearing the one my mother had worn to wed my father. I'd been blind to what was right in front of my face the entire time.

Tonight Aria had opened to me, and I'd never felt pleasure quite like it before. I'd felt her womb accepting me, welcoming me inside. I'd felt the connection that mates shared, settling into place. The way Aria's tiny teeth had pushed through my throat had blown me away, sealing our connection deeper than any other I'd ever felt. I'd fought against the orgasm rushing through me, forcing my body to wait for hers to join mine over the edge.

Aria was this force of nature that ripped through me without warning, wreaking havoc in her wake as she sent me barreling into uncharted territory with her. I'd never felt or met anything like Aria before, and it felt right when she was with me.

I'd watched the horror show Celia planned to force Aria over the edge, to make her into a monster in front of our people. Instead, Aria had simply folded her hands into her lap and pretended she wasn't affected. But I'd felt her pain, and it ached. Worse, she'd felt as if she'd deserved it because of me. I was the biggest asshole to put her through hell, but I knew if I let my guard down in front of my enemies, and so much as fucking smiled at Aria, they'd move to reach her. I couldn't watch another person I cared for die.

They wouldn't just hurt Aria. They'd torture her and ship her back to me in pieces. Or even worse, they'd keep her alive and slowly destroy her until she was nothing more than a shell. Not even Ember was strong enough to stand against the enemies I'd made by declaring war against the Nine Realms, removing the high king they'd chosen through deception and betrayal.

No, it was better to pretend I hated Aria, and sometimes it was a close line that I felt for her. She dug deep, ripping my heart out with those sexy talons, and I swung back. I enjoyed the fire that lit in her eyes as her anger ignited and aimed that rage at me.

"Lili, I'm here. I think you'd have liked Aria. Her mouth would have floored you, but you'd have smiled that sexy little smirk you got when you liked someone's forwardness. You'd have welcomed her into our world. You'd have liked her," I swallowed, running my fingers over the stone slab image of Liliana. "I'm so sorry for what I said to you before I left. I didn't mean it, baby. I didn't mean any of it. Pain fueled my rage, and I couldn't turn it off. I missed our son, and the images inside my head wouldn't stop. Every single death, each gasp of air that left his lungs as death finally found him; it strangled me," I whispered. "It felt like I was drowning, and you weren't there for me. I'm sorry, Lili. I am. I love you, and I'll always love you. Aria, though, she's real. I feel her inside of me. I feel her so fucking deep that my entire world started turning tonight when she let me inside. I'm sorry for what I am about to do, but I can't do this without knowing the truth. I have to let you go so I can give Aria what she wants from me. I have to give her myself without the ghosts."

My hand slid over the picture of Liliana, and I waited for the pain to come. I waited for the sucker punch to the gut from my guilt. I'd told her I wished she'd died instead of our son, only for her to be taken from me right after. I pushed her tomb open as I closed my eyes. I inhaled, slowly peering down as I exhaled.

Inside the tomb were her remains, but on her forehead was the mark of the Hecate bloodline. I lowered my hand, touching the amulet Liliana had never taken off as I ripped it up, inhaling deeply of the scent, and then holding it away from my nose as I covered it with my arm. My heart clutched as my gaze slid to my son's tomb. Pain wrapped around my chest, clenching, and I swallowed the scream that threatened to come out as rage filled my soul.

Moving to Sven's tomb, I paused, touching the picture before I pushed it open and peered inside, finding the mark upon his skull as well. My gaze lowered to the raven toy his mother had made for him, lifting it as I inhaled, repeating the action.

I turned, staring at my wife's grave. I moved toward it, ripping the skull away from the body to hold it up, starring at it in anger. Spinning around, I started slowly toward the door before moving toward it with purpose.

If Liliana was a plant, then so, too, was Aria fucking Hecate. I rattled until the windows shook with my anger, imagining her on the floor, pumping her hips in submission. I was about to chain Aria to the wall and leave her there until she was nothing more than a mindless slave for her part in this deception. Witches had manipulated and driven my entire fucking life, and now they would all pay.

Chapter Fifty-Eight

Aria

Knox kicked the door to the library opened violently, marching into the room, followed by his brothers, who flanked him. All eyes were on me where I stood, staring at him dressed in a black, flowing maxi dress that held the symbol of magic on the bodice.

"Did you fucking know?" Knox demanded, staring at me through a murderous glare as he continued to advance on me. I smiled sadly, dropping my gaze to the skull he held along with the amulet.

"Not at first, no," I admitted. "On the chest that Liliana made for you was a picture of her, and she was wearing an amulet. Amulets are very hard to spell, and it takes a very adept and powerful witch to create one strong enough to trick anyone with a heightened sense of smell. It would require someone to refill it often. Lore said she visited a witch once a month, confirming my suspicions."

"So, you did know! I should take your fucking head right now, Aria," Knox snarled and lunged for me, but before his feet could leave the floor, he and his brothers were frozen in place by the library. I laughed sadly as I lifted my hand to the scar on my throat. "That won't save you, and neither will the library once it sets me free."

"You would remove my head for a crime I didn't commit? You're angry right now, and I understand that rage. I didn't play any part in the deception done to you. I won't allow you to punish me for that, or anything else anymore, Knox. I wasn't even born yet!"

"I don't fucking care," he growled. Knox lowered his head to the skull he held, glaring at it. "I've killed all the Hecate bloodline witches except Kamara, who we believe to be the High Queen of Witches, Aurora, your sisters, and Hecate. We know your aunt and sisters are alive, which means Hecate was my wife, and I never even knew it was her pretending to be Liliana."

"I wasn't aware of the truth, nor was my family. You should know that. Dimitri brought you the skull we intended to use to create a new House of Magic. I figured out that Hecate wasn't in her tomb. I didn't tell anyone that our entire plan hinged on getting Hecate's skull when we left Haven Falls to return here, when *you* forced us to return. Do you have any idea what went through my head when I figured out that she wasn't in her tomb? I thought all hope was lost to create a new House of Magic. Then I thought, who else would know to take Hecate's skull to prevent us from being protected by the magic it held?"

"Me," he snapped harshly.

"You," I agreed before sucking my lip between my

teeth, watching his anger.

"Knox," Brander interrupted. Knox turned, leveling with him with a murderous look. "It's important."

"What the fuck could be more important than figuring out that Hecate was my fucking wife?"

"There are pregnant women from Beltane in the infirmary. A lot of them, and most are mistresses, and there are very unhappy wives present as well." Brander's eyes slid to mine as Knox's returned to me.

"Am I supposed to believe you are responsible for that too?" Knox demanded.

"No. I told you, Knox. I'm your villain. No matter what I do or how many wrongs I right, I will never be anything more than your enemy. I told you that you would regret marrying me. I let you catch me because the only other place in the Nine Realms where that skull could be was here. I had no knowledge of a Hecate witch being your wife. It is decidedly a little awkward considering you, and I just fully mated."

"You think I care that you're my mate? Your death ends that, Aria." Knox growled, struggling to break free of the library's hold.

"I know, which is why I'm about to take your fucking library and leave you here to stew in that anger that is brewing within you." I stepped back into the protection of the barrier erected by the library. "Marriage is 50/50 after all. Right? You can keep your thrones and your kingdoms. I just wanted your fucking library and my grandmother's skull back. I wish she hadn't done this to you, but I can't change the past. I can only focus on the future. You wanted me to become a monster, Knox.

Well, here I am, probably not the monster you thought I would become. I probably won't make a decent bad guy or the ideology of what the world thinks one should be. But in your story, I am what you made me. Not by choice or because I became it. I am your villain because you want it to be so. I am your wife and your mate."

"You think this skull will save you? Take it," he snapped, throwing it at me.

I caught it, frowning as I lifted my attention to him, then dropping it back to the skull. There was no rush of magic or power that echoed through me. I stared at the symbol of the Hecate bloodline, shaking my head.

"Is this what was inside the tomb?" I whispered through the closing of my throat.

"Your murderous whore of a grandmother's skull? Yes, that is what was inside my wife's tomb!" Knox hissed murderously.

"This isn't Hecate, Knox," I swallowed, tossing it back to him as my mind rushed through the scenario. "It's not Hecate. Is there any chance you lost your wife's corpse?" I asked, watching the hatred burn until it liquefied. Probably not the best thing to ask him, all things considered.

"No, I didn't lose her fucking corpse, Aria!" Knox shouted, holding up the skull as he glared at me. "It's the mark of the first witch! The same fucking mark that is on your skull and was on my son's," he growled.

"Not your son, Knox. Sven wasn't yours. Hecate doesn't carry the mark the rest of us have. She carries the mark for the Goddess of Magick, *the* first witch. Liliana was timid, like—Kamara. It was right fucking there the entire time," I whispered, dropping my head back. Exhaling slowly, I leveled my gaze on Knox, who watched me, frowning as he did the math.

"Hecate wouldn't have been timid, ever. She'd have taken that dick and rode it home. No one ever entered her tomb once she went to her eternal slumber. It wasn't allowed, not even for us." Of course, her daughters had been the one to lock her into that tomb. They'd tried to prevent her need for power and greed from ruining their home.

"Aurora couldn't access Hecate's tomb. I had to break into it with my magic to find out she wasn't there anymore. Kamara being used as a substitute for your wife actually makes perfect sense. She'd have trusted her mother blindly, doing what she was told. They'd have replaced Liliana before you wed her, which means she's probably the woman in Hecate's tomb. They'd have studied the way Liliana acted, the way she moved and spoke. They would have replicated her scent, and Kamara would have easily held enough power to hold the image of Liliana's appearance. The amulet was for you, so you would smell her scent and find her pure and untainted, mimicking the essence of a true mate." I swallowed, chewing my lip as tears pricked my eyes while I watched Knox shut down right in front of me.

"Hecate was enraged because Norvalla failed to do as she bid, so she sent you her daughter to change your mind. I'm guessing Kamara either got too close or had served her purpose here and could better serve her mother as a power source. I can't explain Sven, or who he really was, other than they needed him to hurt you."

"Liliana was pregnant for seven months. She gave

birth to my son! Even if she wasn't Liliana, Sven was mine."

"No, he wasn't. It wasn't possible for Kamara to have more children. Aurora told us that after Kamara lost her boys, she destroyed her womb because she couldn't live through another loss like that again. You thought Sven was yours because the magic told you so. Hecate's magic is absolute, Knox. It can glamor a pregnancy and make you see what she wanted you to see. Did your son ever rattle or purr? How did you bypass the curse of your people to breed? Hecate cursed you and your people never to breed again the day you stood against the petty, vain goddess who had never been told no. You weren't wrong about that. It is in our books and our library. Did you think Hecate would just forget your slight against her? That she wouldn't reach out to tear you apart any way she could? Hecate is evil in the *purest* form. She is the darkness because the other gods cursed her, removing her from their presence for reaching for what wasn't hers. I removed that curse against your people, and I'm working to remove every other curse she ever placed onto the Nine Realms so everyone can be free of her and her dark magic."

"Kamara is the High Queen, Aria," Knox snorted, raising his eyes to stare at me.

"I thought so too, Knox, but we were wrong. Hecate is the High Queen of Witches. Her daughters and her descendants carry her mark. She carries the star of power, and we are the circle that surrounds her as protection, with her mark in the center. That is why we carry her star, and the surrounding circle, Knox. Kamara would have been an easier choice. Kamara was powerful, but she wasn't strong of will. Hecate had forbidden all of her daughters from reaching for the throne. I'm going to take a guess and say she's always been the High Queen of Witches and chose a face to appear before the Nine Realms. She came here to rule, and so she has. We think we're five steps ahead, but she's twenty steps further than us."

"You're saying I am not going to war against one Hecate witch, I'm going to war against them all, and a goddess?" he asked carefully, eyes glaring at me to make certain I knew that I was on that list too.

"Pretty much, unless you can make myth and legend into fact," I swallowed, holding his stare.

"Which one? Because there's many surrounding your family, Aria," he countered, studying my face.

"Do you know why Hecate forbid us from birthing male children?" I asked, feeling my stomach flip-flopping as he glared at me with loathing and a coldness that rebuilt every barrier we'd just broken through. His mortar was gone, but in its place was ice.

"No, but I'm sure some lie will spew from those pretty lips of yours."

"Hecate was given a prediction, a fortune if you will," I exhaled, dropping my volume to barely a whispered breath. Moving closer to the barrier, I stared through it. "When the son of the first people finds life through a Hecate witch's womb, the world will turn to chaos, and the goddess will be in ruins. When the son rises and reaches for his rightful birthright, the battle will settle upon us, and the world shall rattle with might. For when the beast is unleashed, and the son discovers his truth, he will aim his fire at the goddess and send her back to her tomb."

"Did they teach you that in preschool, Aria? Hecate witches don't birth sons, so the entire fucking point of your little tale is unlikely."

"It wasn't always like that, Knox. We did birth sons at one time. It was Hecate that later cursed her line to birth only girls."

"Assuming that's true, do you think I'd want to place my son into that poisonous womb of yours and chance him being born to something like you?"

"You're not of the firstborn people who dwelled here before Hecate unleashed hell upon the Nine Realms. I, on the other hand, am a Hecate witch, with a working womb. You don't mind if I go find someone else to fill it, do you?" I snorted, watching the obsidian fill his gaze as Lennox fought for control.

"If I find out you were created to make me think you are my mate, I will end your life, Aria. I won't fucking hesitate."

"I know, but then unlike you, I also know what we felt tonight was real. No magic could make you feel what you felt with me. You sensed me in your soul as I sensed you in mine, Knox. That went deeper than any magic ever could, and you know it even if you're afraid to look at it right now. You're hurting, and my family did that to you. I am so sorry that this happened. I wish there was a spell I could cast that could undo what Hecate did, but there isn't. I need something from you before I leave. I need to know the truth because that will determine who I am coming for first."

"And what the fuck is that?" he snapped harshly, struggling against the library's hold to get to me.

"Did you help Celia use magic on Amara? Did you make my sister into a monster? Did you willingly allow me to murder my sister, who Celia had spelled to do what Amara did to me at the Unwanted Beast Kingdom? Celia wanted me dead because you'd been with me more than once, and that wasn't the deal that you guys made, apparently. It wasn't the sweet words she told you to whisper to me as you seduced me. It wasn't the simple comforts she told you to offer me. I became a threat to her place beside you when you took me to bed more than once. So she set up a plan, using Amara to gift me to Gerald to rape and murder me," I whispered, taking in the confusion in his eyes. He shook his head, and relief washed through me. "I have my answer, but you have vipers within your nest, King Karnavious."

I turned, moving toward the vault that opened as I stopped in front of it, pausing. My hands touched the necklace, and I turned, smiling at Knox, before yanking it off and tossing it at him. His eyes narrowed, noting that it hadn't taken much effort to remove.

"Siobhan helped you make it, Knox. The thing about witches is this; light witches stick together because we're sisters, no matter what blood rushes through our veins. I didn't come here to hurt you or to give you pain. I came here to see if what I felt was right, and it is, but it isn't the right time for us. I'll find you when I go into heat, and if at that time, you decide to take my head, well, that's on you."

"You think you get to just walk away?" Knox snarled, breaking free and rushing the barrier as magic tore through the library. "You're not going anywhere, *mate*."

"Come and stop me, Knox," I challenged, watching while he approached the barrier, pausing as he realized its power. "Every witch's soul you took in the past five hundred years fueled this barrier. There were thousands of souls you failed to send to Hecate to be reborn. I had Esmerelda take me to the mass graves before you caught me. I siphoned the unclaimed souls before ever leaving to go to Asil's castle. I didn't put up that barrier that held you outside because I'd planned to run from you and escape. While I wasn't ready for you to catch me, I knew it was probable that you would. I depleted my magic while draining my blood into the cauldron to use as an enhancer. It was our best chance for undoing most of the curses Hecate had placed on the people of the Nine Realms."

"You expect me to believe that after what I just found? My son has the same symbol you have on your fucking head, bitch."

"Someday, you'll feel the truth. You will hold your *own* son in your arms, and the pain of Sven will fall away. We've already discussed the many reasons he couldn't have been yours. Liliana wasn't your mate. I am," I swallowed, and pain lit in Knox's eye as the truth hit him. "I do know that what happened between us wasn't magic. It was real. I am real, Knox, and I am not alone. There are other females like me out there, and you know that to be true since you've met a few. There are more of us, and I intend to find them and join them. Aden wanted to breed with me, and I will ask him to do what you cannot if you decide you can't stomach to be with me anymore. Again, I'm sorry that it happened like this."

I spun on my heels, but Knox rattled, forcing me to the ground. Knox and his brothers watched me struggle beneath his dominance. My hands dropped to the floor as my legs spread, preparing for him to mate with me.

"I'll be seeing you soon, *wife*. I intend to burn down your kingdom and paint the Nine Realms red with your blood."

"I know you do," I whispered, feeling my womb clenching with need. "That's why I'm on this side of the barrier, and you're not."

"That won't save you, woman."

"I know because you rattle, and I purr. You'll be the death of me or the reason I turn and become the real monster this world needs. But you won't catch me before I create a place where young witches can hide from your rage. I am *not* Hecate, and I *will* defend them, Knox."

I pushed off the floor, moving into the vault and closing it, leaning my head against the door. I turned, finding Esme, Siobhan, Kinvara, Sabine, and Aurora watching me.

"You have some serious fucking explaining to do," I hissed at them.

"Luna is with Kamara," Aurora whispered. "I can reach my sister and make her see how wrong this is. Kamara is reasonable."

"No, you can't because Kamara is dead. Hecate is the High Queen of Witches. And I'm going to rip her fucking head off for what she did to my mate and our people. She's murdering babes, and Ilsa was her puppet,

Aurora. She is the one running the Kingdom of Vākya, torturing innocent people! You," I stated, turning to glare at Esme, who sniffed me, wincing at my scent. "Spill it! Who is your father?" I noted Aurora jerk as she turned to look at Esme.

"That's the thing, Aria. I've met him, but I couldn't tell you who he is or what he looks like. I remember parts of our meeting and him telling me to find the others and gather them. I can't tell you the color of his eyes or hair. I can't tell you what you are because I don't know what I am either. I'm guessing I was spelled to forget the details."

"Okay, so besides the episode of *Who's Your Daddy*, we have shit to get done," Sabine interrupted, hugging me. "I have missed you so much!"

"I missed you too," I whispered, pulling back from her as Ember watched from within me. "Let's build a new realm, shall we?" I suggested, lifting my eyes to them. "Who says women can't rule the world?" Knox's rattle sounded, and I smiled sadly, wanting to wrap my arms around him and send his pain below.

"You're mated," Siobhan whispered. "That's a problem."

"I couldn't get the library without completing our mating bond, and I couldn't be there when Knox figured out what role Hecate had played with his dead wife," I snapped, turning angry eyes on Aurora, who frowned. "Glad you weren't part of it."

"How do you intend to build a new realm?" Esme asked.

"I have half of the library that holds the knowledge to

create worlds. I moved books and items into this section that we would need to create landmasses. I needed to be mated to gain access to the vault. And this place? The library is a world of its own that isn't connected to anything else. The problem is, Knox can get inside here once the barrier drops. We have one year to figure it out because this is our home until that clock runs out."

I turned as Knox's pained sounds echoed through the outside section I'd taken from the Library of Knowledge. Knox should have been happy I'd left him his portion, but since we were mated, and I wasn't certain I wouldn't go right back into heat, I wasn't willing to lock him out completely.

The women moved deeper into our portion of the library, talking with excitement about the possibilities we would have as I leaned against the door. I felt my stomach clench while his pain whispered through me. I'd just turned a beast into an enraged monster, and the only way to face a monster was to become its equal in strength.

I'd reach Knox, not today, not tomorrow, but eventually. I'd break down the walls and make him understand that I wasn't his enemy, or I'd die trying. And in the meantime, if I faced off with Hecate for her crown to end the unjust treatment of the people of the Nine Realms, I'd probably die trying to end her reign of terror, anyway.

THE END FOR NOW

Crown of Chaos Coming 2021

Nine Realms' Compendium

Key Players in the Series

Knox Karnavious – King of Norvalla

Brander – Brother of Knox, full-blooded

Loren (Lore) – Brother of Knox, full-blooded

Faderin (Fade) – Brother to Knox, full-blooded

Gideon – Brother of Knox, full blooded

Mateo – Brother of Knox, full-blooded

Celia – Younger sister of Killian and Liliana, full blooded

Killian – Liliana and Celia's brother and Knox's best friend

Liliana – Deceased wife of Knox and sister to Killian and Celia

Greer – Friend, teacher, and butler to Knox, vampire

Hecate Bloodline Introduced So Far

Aria Primrose Hecate – Daughter of Frey

Freya – Daughter of Hecate and Aria's mother, deceased

Aurora – Daughter of Hecate, sister to Freya who raised her kids.

Hysteria – Daughter of Hecate, deceased

Kamara – Daughter of Hecate, deceased

Hecate – Goddess of the House of Magic, in deep slumber

Amara – Daughter of Freya and Aria's twin, deceased

Kinvara / Valeria – Daughters of Freya and succubi twins

Aine / Luna – Daughters of Freya and alpha werewolf twins

Sabine / Callista – Daughters of Freya and nymph twin

Reign / Rhaghana – Daughters of Freya, species unknown

Tieghan / Tamryn – Daughters of Freya and witches twins

Alpha Pack

Dimitri – King of the Wolves, pure-born alpha werewolf

Jasper – Pure-born werewolf, Fallon's son, and Prince of the Alpha wolves, deceased

Fallon – Pure-born alpha wolf, King of the Wolves, deceased

Minotaurs

Gerald – King of the Kingdom of Unwanted Beasts, deceased

Garrett – Son of Gerald and newly crowned King of the Kingdom of Unwanted Beasts

Other People

Neven – The Queen of Nymphs

Karter – The King of the Nymphs

Ilsa – The High Queen of Witches

Esmeralda – Unmarked witch friend to Aria Hecate

Asil – Witch holding a stronghold against Knox for Ilsa

Tristan – Slumlord

Taren Oleander – The King of Gargoyle's

Soraya – Witch that works for the High Queen of Witches and Julia's sister

Julia – Witch controlled by Ilsa and Soraya's sister

Siobhan – Marked witch under Knox's rule

Bekkah – Marked witch under Knox's rule

Aden – Unknown – Silver-haired male

Eva – Unknown – Silver-haired female

Lord Carter – One of Knox's Lords

Lord Andres – One of Knox's Lords

Items and More

Grimoire – A book of ancient spells

Scrying – The ability to search a map with magic to find a location.

White Oak Trees – Grown only in Norvalla in the Arcadian Forest of Knowledge

Frost fire – Ice from the Dark Mountains, appears as regular ice until it swallows up anything, or anyone it can touch. Unbreakable by anything other than witches fire, a spell that only rare witches can use. It was used to protect Norvalla from the Kingdom of Unwanted Beasts.

Midnight Blooming black roses – Grown in the darkest passes in the Dark Mountains. A rare type of rose that blossom's in the icy snow caps of the mountain, holding a unique essence that witches covet.

Tonics – medicinal potions for healing

Gargoyles – Protectors of the Library of Knowledge

The visited lands within the Nine Realms to date

Dorcha –The Darkest Realm, realm in which Norvalla sits as capital

Norvalla – Knox's Homeland

Kingdom of Unwanted Beasts – Realm that borders Norvalla

Kingdom of Vãkya – Aria's homeland, where Ilsa currently resides within the Palace of Magic

Valley of the Dead – Land that borders between Vãkya and Dorcha

House of Magic – Formerly known as Kerrigan Keep, now Aria's sanctuary below the ruins of a castle she claimed.

The Dark Mountains – The Mountain range bordering The Kingdom of Unwanted Beast and Norvalla's high passes.

Library of Knowledge – An ever-changing room that only reveals its treasures to those it finds worthy of the knowledge it holds.

Beltane Circle – Bel's temple, and circle where Beltane is celebrated to welcome new life.

About the Author

Amelia Hutchins is the number one national bestselling author of the Monsters, The Fae Chronicles, and Nine Realm series. She is an admitted coffee addict, who drinks magical potions of caffeine and turns them into magical worlds. She writes alpha-hole males and the alpha women who knock them on their arses, hard. She doesn't write romance. She writes fast-paced books that go hard against traditional standards. Sometimes a story isn't about the romance; it's about rising to a challenge, breaking through them like wrecking balls, and shaking up entire worlds to discover who they really are. If you'd like to check out more of her work, or just hang out in an amazing tribe of people who enjoy rough men, and sharp women, join her at Author Amelia Hutchins Group on Facebook.

Stalker Links

Facebook group: https://www.facebook.com/groups/1240287822683404/

Facebook Author Page: https://www.facebook.com/authorameliahutchins/

Instagram: https://www.instagram.com/author.amelia.hutchins/

CPSIA information can be obtained
at www.ICGtesting.com
Printed in the USA
LVHW050717271021
701668LV00010B/554

9 781952 712081